THE EDGE OF DOMINANCE

THE *Edge*
OF DOMINANCE

DOMS OF HER LIFE:
RAINE FALLING (BOOK 4)

by
Shayla Black,
Jenna Jacob,
and Isabella LaPearl

THE EDGE OF DOMINANCE
Doms of Her Life: Raine Falling (Book 4)
Written by Shayla Black, Jenna Jacob, and Isabella LaPearl

This book is an original publication by Shayla Black, Jenna Jacob, and Isabella LaPearl

Edited by: Shayla Black and Amy Knupp of Blue Otter

Excerpt from *Falling in Deeper* © 2016 by Shelley Bradley LLC
Excerpt from *Bound to Surrender* © 2016 by Dream Words LLC

ISBN: 978-0-9911796-1-9

ACKNOWLEDGEMENTS

Special thanks from us all to Rachel Connolly, Shayla Fereshetian, Shannon Hunt, and Bria Joslin for their very snappy beta reading and helpful input. We appreciate you especially for putting so much on hold to give us feedback and not murdering us over the tight timelines. Extra thanks to Hari Singh for his invaluable, expert help and insight. Thanks, too, to Julie Kenner for helping us focus an idea or two in the right direction. Last—but never least—our heartfelt thanks to our fans for your patience and support.

Shayla Black

To my husband and daughter, as always, for keeping me happy, sane, grounded, and alive during this long, emotional process. Thanks also to Rachel Connolly for all her incredibly hard work that most readers don't see but I'd be lost without her. To Jenna and Isabella for making me laugh, making me see things in a completely different light, and for all your friendship. We make a great team!

Jenna Jacob

To Shayla and Isabella. Along this amazing journey, a unique and trusted friendship was born. You both are forever etched in my heart. Thank you for all the laughter and tears, but most importantly, for your unconditional love.

Isabella LaPearl

My love and thanks to my family. My grateful thanks to Shayla Black and Jenna Jacob. My love, respect, and hugs to you both always. I love our precious creative writing time together. You rock! We make magic happen. How wonderful is that?

CHAPTER ONE

Friday, February 8

SHADOWS WAS HAUNTED.

Macen "Hammer" Hammerman stood with his back to the wall in the dungeon of his BDSM club, watching scenes play out around him. The scent of leather filled his head. A whip cracked. A sub he barely knew let out a feminine moan. Bodies entwined. The constant erotic ebb and flow of pleasure that played out around him night after night made him hunger for the only woman he'd ever craved.

Raine Kendall.

In the corner, a Dom spanked his sub. Hammer clenched his fist. It had been too long since he'd felt the burn of his palm on Raine's taut, lush backside, heard her cry in his ears.

But after the trauma she'd suffered last December, his Dominant urges raged too hot for her. If he unleashed them, he'd break her. Much better for Raine if he stayed away.

In his pocket, his phone buzzed. He pulled out the device and glanced at the screen. His best friend and the man he shared her with, Liam O'Neill, had texted him a video.

When he clicked on the clip, Raine parted her bare thighs. He'd know her body anywhere. Petal-pink silk clung to her hips, framing transparent black lace that kissed her pussy…where Liam had conveniently focused the lens. She dragged her fingers over the damp, clinging fabric, pausing to rub her clit with an audible pant. "Please…" she cried. "Macen!"

Instantly, his cock jolted to life.

Liam's accompanying message read: Don't you wish you were here?

Yes. Balls deep. Every fucking night.

Yet you're always working while Liam is at home, getting his fill of

Raine.

Because his best friend was better at balancing his Dominant needs with his sexual ones.

Goddamn it, every time Hammer closed his eyes, the memory of Raine on her knees, looking up at him with blue eyes full of yearning, taunted him. The phantom grip of her pussy squeezed him. Hell, he could almost taste her on his tongue right now.

More blood surged downward. He went from merely hard to steely enough to pound nails.

Hammer shoved the phone in his pocket with a growl. The nagging in his cock wasn't going away on its own. It never did.

He'd learned that the hard way.

Biting off a curse, he headed to his fucking office. Again.

As he whirled around, he nearly ran into Pike, one of his dungeon monitors. "Carl is coming to bitch at you. Same shit. Just a warning."

"I don't have time. Deal with it."

"He's insisting on talking to you."

"Then throw him the fuck out," Hammer called over his shoulder.

"For the night?"

"Or for-fucking-ever. I don't give a shit."

Macen just wanted five damn minutes alone.

He'd barely finished the thought when Carl—an egomaniac of a Dom—approached with an angry scowl.

"I'm getting tired of Knotty Master not cleaning the equipment after—"

"Either tell the man to clean it up or have your sub do it. Do I look like your maid? Your mother?"

Carl narrowed his eyes. "You can't talk to me that way."

Hammer clenched his fist, fighting the urge to punch the prick. "I just did."

Without waiting for Carl's reply, Hammer stormed across the dungeon, glowering at anyone who dared to make eye contact. The crowd took a collective step back.

Except Beck, Shadows' resident sadist. He wore a disapproving smirk.

"What?" Macen glared, never breaking his stride.

"Just admiring your people skills…"

"Fuck you."

Beck shook his head.

This night just kept getting better and better. Hammer's cock throbbed. Raine's luscious video burned a hole in his pocket. Why wouldn't everyone go the hell away so he could enjoy it in peace?

Lewis, his new security geek, approached with a question on his face.

Hammer preempted him. "Is it death, blood, or a lawsuit?"

"Huh? Oh, no. I'm just not sure how to—"

"Save it for later."

Macen finally prowled the last steps through his office and into his bedroom. He plucked his phone free as he slammed the door behind him. With one hand, he jerked off his tie. With the other, he tapped his thumb on the cell phone's screen. The video launched. He lay on the bed, yanked down his fly, and lost himself between Raine's legs.

His dick was already desperate and leaking when he wrapped himself in a tight fist. He jerked on his shaft as Raine's breathy plea echoed in his ears. The insatiable lust he'd always felt for her flared in his belly. His hold turned brutal at the sight of her slender fingers teasing the nubbin he loved to suckle. Fuck, what he wouldn't give to plunge his tongue beneath that veil of lace, lap at her sweet-tart cream, and fuck her with his mouth until she screamed his name.

Batting his thumb over the play button again and again, Hammer watched Raine's self-induced suffering in an endless loop. Memories of the first time she'd drowned him in the wicked heat of her mouth—in this very bed—assailed him. He'd broken his own rule and sunk his fat crest into her narrow slit right here, too. The devastating friction had unraveled every one of his good intentions. He'd fucked her hard.

His cock grew thicker, his skin stretching impossibly tighter, as he quickened his fist and pawed himself with unrelenting strokes. A familiar tingle edged down his spine.

"Fuck, yes."

Hammer slammed his fist down to his hilt, aching to feel Raine shatter. When she came, her snug cunt clamped down as if she sought to force him out. But he always shoved his way back in, taking her again, driving through her spasming flesh until she clawed him and screamed.

He stroked harder. His balls drew up tight. His pulse thundered in his ears.

With a yell, he erupted into his hand, his seed spilling, his body humming.

As he lay staring at the ceiling, panting and sweating, he dimmed his phone.

This shit would be so much better if Raine were really with him. In cuffs. Begging. And Liam loomed behind her, squeezing into her tight ass while Hammer stuffed her cunt full and—

"Fuck." He rolled off the bed and kicked his pants away. If he didn't stop thinking about Raine and sex in the same sentence, he wouldn't make it out of his office for the rest of the night. He should know. He'd been jacking off in here for weeks.

Each night, he went home so fucking desperate to claim her. To make her strip. To tie her to their bed. To crawl inside her head and, together with Liam, command her body.

But two months ago, Hammer had found her car door gaping open in his empty parking lot at four thirty a.m., the contents of her purse on the ground, and Raine nowhere in sight. He'd been shaken to the soul. He and Liam had searched frantically to stop her attacker before the bastard raped and murdered the only woman who completed them. Miraculously, they'd found her in a dingy warehouse nearby. She'd been clutching a slick knife in her delicate fist, naked and freezing, rocking despondently in a pool of blood near the father she'd been forced to kill.

She hadn't been the same since. None of them had. So when he forced himself to go home in the wee hours of the morning and saw Raine sleeping, guilt and contrition inevitably strangled him. His cock battled his conscience.

His needs almost always lost.

Why should Raine have to fulfill his sexual demands when he hadn't even provided her the basic safety she deserved?

Shoving his question aside, Hammer rose from the bed and made his way to the shower. He scrubbed his body as if he could wash away his failures. It went against his grain to sulk like a bloody weeping vagina, as Liam would say.

That manipulative son of a bitch. He'd sent the video of Raine to torture him.

It had fucking worked.

With a heavy sigh, Hammer shut off the water and snatched a towel off the nearby hook. Wrapping it around his waist, he stepped from the shower stall.

"Did you give yourself the best thirty seconds of your life again?" Beck leaned against his bathroom wall with a smirk.

"Don't tell me your sad personal stories, man."

"You're not funny. Didn't your momma ever warn you that if you keep pulling on your peter, you'll go blind?"

"Is that why you wear glasses when you work?" Hammer drawled and stepped toward the fogged mirror. "What the fuck are you doing here?"

Beck held up his phone. Not even three days of dark stubble could disguise the sneer on his face. "Why is your BFF texting me to ask if everything's all right?"

"No idea."

"Want to tell me why you're biting off everyone's heads?"

Fuck. Beck was here to be "helpful." The last thing Hammer wanted to do was talk. It wouldn't change a damn thing. "Because people like you won't leave me alone."

"Oh, you're hurting my little feewings." Beck chuckled. "Seriously, all this pouting is going to ruin your big, bad Dom reputation."

"But you think a sadist acting like a nagging wife will improve yours?"

"I haven't even started nagging at your sorry ass." Beck reached behind him and shoved a bottle of tequila at Hammer. "Drink up. I'll drive you home later."

"What is this for? You think I'll be your cheap, easy lay for the night? Pass."

"Your witty one-liners are sounding a lot like someone avoiding his problems. I've been telling you for weeks to vent whatever's bothering you, but—surprise, surprise—you're not listening. Since the only time you ever purge your shit is when you're drunker than fuck, I bought a bottle of your favorite. Go for it."

"Blow me."

"No, thanks. You're not my type."

Hammer glared. "I don't have a goddamn thing to purge."

"Really? Then why have you become the poster child for self-induced happy endings?" Beck scoffed. "Raine is smarter than you. She knew she needed a therapist to process everything that's happened. But you, dumb fuck? Still refusing to talk to anyone. Do you really think you can fix yourself? Or are you just afraid they'll shrink the wrong head? I promise, when they're done, you'll still have your little toy to play with."

Hammer didn't even want to look at him. "Go whip a sub."

"Nah. I'm having far more fun with a masochist right now."

Beck meant him, and Hammer wanted to punch the asshole. But he'd probably psychoanalyze that need, too. "I'm not in the mood for this."

"But you're in the mood to masturbate?" Beck sent him a sly glance. "Are you beating your meat so hard because it owes you money?"

"Are you giving up the medical field so you can take this act to The Improv?"

"Raine would give it to you for free, you know."

Macen nearly lost his temper. "Get your thoughts out of my sub's pussy."

"Believe it or not, I'm worried about you. When was the last time you took a night off?"

Hammer didn't need Beck dabbling in his life right now, even if his old pal was right.

"Most every Sunday. But it's a busy Friday night, and I have a club to run. Thanks for stopping by." Macen gestured him to the door.

"It's so busy you have time for self-love. Got it." The stare Beck shot him said to get real. "Go home. You've got a competent staff. The place practically runs itself. I'll watch over everyone and call if there's a problem."

Why should he go home and torture himself with what he shouldn't have?

Goddamn it. The soothing serenity he'd felt when Raine had first come into his life was long gone. Of course, back then, he'd done a pretty good job of protecting her. But once Liam had come from New York and forced him to see her as a woman, Hammer's long-tested restraint had torn off its leash. He and his best friend had fought like snarling dogs to claim her...before they'd realized they should put her between them. Together, they had turned her life upside down.

They had gotten her pregnant.

And they had unwittingly roused the monster who had nearly taken her life. When Raine had needed him most, Hammer hadn't been there to save her. He would never forgive himself for that.

"I can't," he finally admitted.

"Liam's text says you can. Go. Sandwich the princess between you two."

He didn't take orders from Beck—or anyone. Still, the video of Raine's legs spread open in invitation for him to drown inside her was burned deep in his psyche. Hammer didn't want his hand. He wanted her.

"Fine." He sighed. "I'll cut out early. You have a key to lock up?"

Beck patted his pants pocket. "Right here."

"Thanks."

With a sly smile, the sadist bumped his shoulder. "Don't do anything I wouldn't do."

"So basically, anything goes. Got it." Macen sighed. "And thanks."

"I'm sure you'll be happy to kick my ass if I ever need it." With a wave, Beck headed for the door, closing it softly behind him.

After tossing on some clothes and combing out his hair, Macen pushed his way out the building and jogged for his Audi, jingling his keys in his pocket. He was going to go home, hold Raine, and talk to the two people he loved most. Somehow, he was going to fix whatever was wrong between them because he was tired of fighting the ghosts lingering in the dungeon, haunting his life.

Halfway across the parking lot, he glanced over his shoulder to make sure the door had shut behind him. His gaze snagged on the camera in the alcove—the one that had captured Bill Kendall's snarling face when he'd tased Raine and dragged her away to her near death.

Just like that, the ghosts swarmed Hammer again.

He jerked his car door open and revved the engine. He tried to picture Raine waiting for him at home, wearing those panties...and nothing else. He strained to imagine him and Liam enveloping their woman together for the first time in months and blowing her precious mind.

Tires screeching, Hammer tore out of the lot. One of the last times he'd squealed away from Shadows, he'd been frantically searching for Raine after he'd realized she was in her father's clutches. A memory of the fucker's maniacal grin stabbed its way through his brain. The array of implements he'd spread out in order to torture Raine in that fucking warehouse hit next, obliterating every thought except murdering a man who was already dead.

Hammer's heart thudded. With one fist, he gripped the steering wheel. With the other, he punched the dashboard. When would he be able to chase these ghosts away?

Maybe never.

That thought terrified him.

Fuck, he couldn't go home to Raine and Liam half-hinged. He'd be a liability, a loose cannon. He had to get his shit wired tight.

Because if he didn't, Hammer already knew his ghosts would follow him home.

Saturday, February 9

LIAM ROLLED OVER and spooned Raine in the big bed they shared to calm her restless dozing. He stared at the clock. Two thirty-four a.m. The other familiar body who should be surrounding Raine—and taking more than his third of the mattress—was disturbingly absent. Again.

What the hell had kept Hammer out late this time?

The door between the garage and the kitchen banged shut, rending the silence.

So Macen had finally come home.

Liam eased away from Raine, leaving her with a soft kiss on the forehead. Then he pulled on his boxers, squared his shoulders, and left.

Would Hammer care if the bedroom smelled like the sex he hadn't come home to share?

A few months ago, nothing and no one had been more important to the man than their girl. After denying how he'd felt about her for six years, Macen seemed ready to make up for over half a decade of denial and misery.

Everything had changed the terrible morning Bill had taken her.

As Liam marched down the stairs, the kitchen light flipped on. A cabinet door slammed shut. Hammer hissed a curse.

Ready to remind Macen of everything they stood to lose if he didn't stop wallowing in the past and start focusing on their future, Liam trekked into the room. The sight that greeted him stopped him short. His friend wasn't dragging in, tugging off his tie in exhaustion, full of excuses about how crowded Shadows was on a Friday night. No. Hammer was slumped against the cabinet wearing only gym shorts, athletic shoes, and head-to-toe sweat. He chugged from a fresh bottle of tequila in his fist.

"Your disapproving-parent face says you're itching to give me a lecture. Don't." Hammer lifted the bottle.

"You've left me no choice. I haven't said a word until now, and we've got problems."

He jerked the tequila to his side. "Raine? The baby?"

"Both fine, but—"

"Good." Relief filled Hammer's face. "Then let's talk later. I need a shower. I'll see you next to Raine."

Liam blocked his path, snatching the bottle away. "This won't wait any longer."

"I'm not done drinking."

"You are now." Liam shoved the booze onto the counter behind him. Reasoning with a sober Hammer was much easier. "You're absent every night, Macen. I don't like it."

"I'm working. You could cut me some slack, you know."

"When you cut us some, I will." Liam rummaged Hammer's phone from his gym bag and shoved Raine's sexy video in the man's face. "I know you saw this. Raine was waiting for your reply. Your silence crushed her."

"I meant to come home when I got it and surprise her. But…shit got in the way."

"You let it, more like." Liam slapped the mobile on the counter. "What's going on with you?"

"Nothing. I'm just swamped."

"Stop with the excuses."

"Seriously. When we moved to the house, it was Christmas. I didn't realize how many things I did for the club after hours that I couldn't walk into the next room to finish or ask Raine to handle. The renovation to the private rooms still isn't done. I'm short a couple of DMs." Hammer sighed. "I'm being pulled in twenty directions, but I'm hoping to find some fucking normalcy soon."

"You mean if the stars align, pixies fly out of your ass, and karma plays nice?" Liam snapped. "Why don't you let me help?"

Hammer shook his head. "I want you here with Raine, just in case."

"In case of what? Her pregnancy is going well. She's young and strong, and she doesn't need a babysitter. She's busy remodeling the house, setting up the nursery, and shopping for furniture. Hell, I'd be happy for a break from comparing paint swatches."

"I don't want her alone in the house with a bunch of strange men."

"Raine spent six years in a club full of men dedicated to kink. I think she can handle herself with a plumber. Why don't you spend a few days with her? I'll take care of Shadows."

"No."

Liam raised a brow. "Because…?"

"Because there's a lot going on and I should handle it myself."

More bloody excuses. "Are you even in this relationship anymore?"

"What kind of question is that?" Hammer gaped. "I'm in. I've been in since we claimed her together. Jesus, a few late nights doesn't change that."

He wasn't only lying to Liam but to himself.

"A few?" Liam scoffed. "That's a bloody understatement. Is it the baby?"

"No, I'm happy she's pregnant. Thrilled!"

"You should be. When you thought she'd gotten her period on Thanksgiving Day, you cried like a bleating nancy. But you've missed the first three months."

"Bullshit. I'm with Raine every day. We eat lunch. We talk."

"Is that what you call it? You prop her feet up, shove prenatal vitamins in her mouth, then tell her to nap as you're walking out the door." Liam grasped for his patience—and failed. "She needs a man, not a nanny. What the hell is wrong?"

"Fuck you. I'm not dealing with this now. I'm exhausted."

"I want answers." Liam gritted his teeth. "Raine deserves them, and we're both tired of living with a ghost."

Hammer blanched. "I'm not—"

"Yes, you are. Are you bothered that we've no idea which of us fathered the child? It's probably yours…"

"I took her bareback once. You had her in your bed for weeks. Condoms fail." Hammer shrugged. "Yours. Mine. I don't give a shit either way. The baby is ours, like Raine is."

"Exactly. So let's work this out. Did you know she's worried you don't love her anymore?"

"What?" He scowled. "If I had any way of falling out of love with Raine, I would have done it years ago."

"Then reassure her. How else do you expect her to feel like the precious you call her?"

Hammer snatched up the bottle and guzzled another third of the booze. "Why hasn't she said a word about this to me?"

"You're never here, so how is she supposed to pour her heart out to you?" Liam rolled his eyes. "Instead, she blames herself for driving you away. And she cries herself to sleep at night. Why don't you man the fuck up?"

Hammer looked stricken, as if Liam had punched him in the gut.

"Did I finally say enough to pull your head out of your ass?"

He hung his head. "Yeah."

"Then listen to me. Raine is reeling now. Counseling has helped her cope, and her nightmares have eased, but she's still struggling to accept that Bill killed her mother and sister. For years, she thought they'd abandoned her, and it almost destroyed her. Now you've all but left her, too."

He grimaced in guilt. "Hasn't finding their bodies brought her any closure?"

"Some. She still has no idea if her brother is dead or he simply walked out on her, so that's eating at her."

Hammer raked a hand through damp hair. "I was hoping Seth would have found River by now. It's been months."

"He was a Green Beret, trained for unconventional warfare. He can vanish with the wind."

"I know," Hammer growled. "But his disappearance makes me want to hit something."

"How do you think Raine feels? She's processing all this while she's hormonal. I've done my best to keep her happy but…"

"Oh, giving her all those orgasms must be a real hardship for you."

"Not in the least. You're clearly bitter you've been missing out, but you've done nothing to change that."

Hammer slammed the bottle on the counter, jaw clenched. He said nothing…but remorse tightened his face.

Liam lowered his voice. "When was the last time you made love to Raine?"

"I don't know. I didn't file it in my day planner."

"It was more than two weeks ago."

"You're keeping track?" Hammer raised a brow.

"We sleep in the same bed, so I know when you climb on top of her and fuck her like you haven't had her in decades."

"I want her and I'm a Dominant. Have you looked in the mirror lately? You're as perverted as I am."

"But I don't roll away from her two seconds after my orgasm and flee as if my ass is on fire." Liam sneered at Macen. "You're bloody using her as impersonally as your hand."

"I'm done with this little chat. Really. Fuck you." Hammer turned away.

Liam grabbed his arm and pulled him back. "You haven't made love properly to Raine since *that* morning, which was also the last time you slowed down enough so we could take her together."

Hammer shook off his grip. "What the hell do you want from me?"

"For you to park your ass and tell me what's troubling you." He sat at the kitchen table. "I'm your best friend. You can tell me anything." Hammer hesitated, and Liam lost his temper. "We haven't been through months of hell for you to fuck this up. Sit and talk. Or I can't guarantee she'll stay."

Sucking in an incredulous breath, Hammer sank into the nearest chair. "Are you serious? You think she'd leave?" He blinked. "Holy shit. Why would she run away without talking to me? She has to know I love her more than anything. More than my own life."

"How do you expect her to know that?" Liam challenged. "By

reading your mind? We sent you that picture over three hours ago. She tried to tell you she was thinking of you. She wanted to please you. But you couldn't fucking be bothered." He shook his head. "I fear it was the last straw."

Hammer hung his head in his hands. "I'm just...out of sorts. I needed some time at the gym to work off stress."

"So you took your frustration out on a Stairmaster? She would have been more than happy to let you ease some of that between her thighs. And you could have given her some orgasms, too."

Hunger flared in Hammer's eyes before he doused it. "I would have been too rough on her."

Is that what he thought? "You're bloody clueless about pregnant women and their hormones. She's so insatiable now she might even scare you a bit."

Macen looked somewhere between stunned and confused. "Really?"

"Absolutely." Liam paused. "She's fourteen weeks pregnant, so her body is changing. She's worried you've noticed and you don't find her attractive anymore."

He scoffed. "I've *never* not found her attractive. Ever."

"Then tell me what's on your bloody mind."

"Nothing." Hammer didn't meet his gaze.

"Stop lying to me."

Macen stood. "I'm done here."

"Not unless you're done with the three of us."

"Don't threaten me. Me stepping back is best for Raine. You're better at helping her through emotional upheaval. I suck at touchy-feely shit."

"No, you suck at dealing with your problems. Snap out of it and stop beating yourself up for not saving her."

Hammer halted, glared.

Ah, so now they were getting to the problem.

"I can't, all right?" Hammer shook his head, anguish all over his face. "Raine and our baby nearly died. That fact eats at me every fucking day, spools through my brain every fucking night. I can't wipe all that blood out of my head."

"But she's all right. Be strong for her." Liam urged him back into his chair. "She needs us both."

"I'm worried she pictures Bill when I touch her. And trust me, her hormones are nothing next to every dirty, Dominant thing I ache to do to her. But some nights, I come home and look at her, and I can't stay the fuck away for another minute, so I use her hard. I don't mean to. I want her so bad and she doesn't say no and…I lose my head for a minute. Then I feel so shitty afterward. Guilty. Jesus…" He sighed. "So yeah, I'm all over her about rest and vitamins and crap so that I can tell myself I'm doing the right thing by her. That sounds fucked up. Obviously, you're dealing with this much better, as always. Happy?"

"I'm happy you're finally talking to me."

Hammer's mental anguish didn't surprise Liam but it concerned him. Worse, now that he had Macen talking, he needed to forge ahead, make him purge all the pain. Liam knew he'd start another war with his next words, but the man would never heal if he didn't resolve the issues that haunted him most.

"I know your avoidance isn't merely about Raine. So let's cut to the heart of it. When will you forgive yourself for Juliet's death? Or does your shit go back even further than that?"

Macen leapt to his feet and leveled Liam with a murderous glare. "Shut. The. Fuck. Up."

CHAPTER TWO

*T*HE MINISTER STOOD *before the group of mourners, speaking words Macen never wanted to hear again. His throat constricted. Déjà vu tightened around his neck like a barbed-wire tie.*

Before him, the lid of a bronze casket lay open, lined in ivory velvet. He'd given Juliet the best in death because he had failed her in life. His wife had been pregnant and distraught and…he hadn't known until it was too late. He couldn't look at her now. Hell, he didn't deserve to.

Beside him, Liam stood, hands clasped in front of him, looking stoic and red-eyed and damn close to falling apart.

Hammer frowned. Liam hadn't loved Juliet. He hadn't even been present for her funeral.

What was going on?

Dread churned Hammer's guts as he leaned in and peeked over the edge of the casket. He didn't see his blond bride in everlasting repose. Instead, Raine lay there, porcelain, lifeless, her blue eyes forever shuttered.

Stunned, Hammer couldn't look away. He couldn't stop staring at her beloved face or the round swell of her pregnant belly. She was gone? When? How? Why?

God, he hadn't been able to save her.

He turned to Liam, gaping and empty. His friend didn't seem shocked, just utterly heartbroken. Grief had felled him into silence.

Hammer dove for her, braced his hands beneath her prone body, and lifted, desperate to hold the woman he loved again, hear her laugh, and promise that none of his nightmare was real. Instead, Raine dissolved into fine grains of sand and slipped through his fingers. Agony besieged him. He crumbled to his knees and scrambled to gather her against him. But the wind surged, blowing away every trace of her.

Leaving him with nothing except his eviscerated soul.

Filled with rage and grief, Hammer threw back his head. A cry stuck in his throat. He'd never felt more alone or desolate. But wasn't he simply getting what he deserved?

With his hand pressed to his chest, Hammer woke with a start. Tense and covered in cold sweat, he dragged in a breath. Terror sludged toxic through his blood. Desolation followed.

Exhausted, Macen slammed his eyes shut. He was losing his mind.

He wouldn't be able to find it again until he knew Raine was all right.

Hammer cracked one eye open to look around. Instantly, his head protested. He was feeling last night's Patrón. The muted gray light straining through the curtains gouged his eyeballs.

Now he remembered why he was rarely awake at the ass crack of dawn.

As his vision cleared, he spied Liam sitting on the far edge of the bed, his broad, bare shoulders working. With a few words last night, the damn Irishman had exhumed Juliet. Hammer didn't need his old friend rubbing his nose in his mistakes. He already couldn't forget their stench. Thankfully, the hint of cocoa lingering in the air gave him something else to focus on.

So did the sight of Raine.

She stood between Liam's legs, her filmy white robe a beacon as it flowed away from her shoulders. Shadow outlined her bare breasts. Liam caressed her with familiarity and possession. Hammer's body tightened. His primal directive to protect her mixed with his restless need to fuck her in every way known to man.

He'd made her doubt his love. Would she even welcome him now?

Propping himself on one elbow, he watched through the shrouded light as Raine relaxed every muscle for Liam and let out a purr. The ache in Macen's head no longer registered because the throbbing between his legs had taken over.

God, she looked beautiful.

Mouth dry, he reached absently for the water on his nightstand and sipped, never taking his eyes from her.

"We'll be needing more lotion soon," Liam whispered as his hands glided over their woman's breasts.

"Mmm. I'll pick some up later today."

"Good thinking. There's bugger all left."

"We can't run out," Raine moaned. "I look forward to this every morning."

Hammer's brows furrowed. He'd never partaken in this ritual, never even seen it. Their unmistakable closeness pinpricked him with jealousy.

Despite the months he'd been Raine's lover, they had never shared this level of quiet intimacy.

That realization flattened him.

We're both tired of living with a ghost...

For years, Macen's idea of utopia had been him and Liam sharing the submissive of their dreams, working in tandem to watch her bloom. Raine was that woman. The life he'd always wanted was in his grasp. But if he didn't get his head together, they might well leave him behind.

"Morning." His scratchy voice disrupted the quiet in the room.

"I didn't hear you come in last night." Raine focused her wary gaze on him as she drew her robe shut and belted it at her waist.

Closing herself off to him.

Worry grabbed Hammer's throat. "Sorry I didn't respond to your text last night."

"You're busy. I know."

He vaulted from the bed and scrambled toward her. God, he needed to hold her. Warily, she stepped back. She didn't want him touching her, either?

Macen's chest cleaved in two. "Talk to me, precious."

She shrugged. "About what?"

He grasped for a topic that wouldn't upset her. "What cream is Liam rubbing on you?"

"It's just cocoa butter."

Liam slipped a hand under her robe and stroked her thigh, glancing at Hammer. "I cover her breasts and belly with it each morning to keep her skin soft and help prevent stretch marks."

Picking up the container on the mattress beside his friend, Hammer sniffed it, looking for any excuse to touch her. "I could help."

She looked to Liam. The insecurity lurking in her face was a guilt-ridden punch in Macen's gut.

"If you want to."

"Of course I want to." He gripped his hard shaft in hand, willing Raine to see his hunger. "Does this look like I don't want you?"

She looked away. "Is the fact you're hard supposed to make me feel special?"

Wrong approach. Hammer sat on the mattress beside Liam and covered his lap with the sheet. "Precious, I'm sorry I've been absent. I never meant to make you doubt my commitment."

Other than her chin trembling, she remained still and silent, telling him without words he'd done precisely that.

He couldn't stop himself from grabbing her hand and laying her palm over his beating heart. "Say it, Raine. Tell me I've been a bastard and that I've hurt you. Get it out."

She wrenched away. "For the last two months, I've felt like I did the first six years I lived with you at Shadows. Invisible. Unworthy." She shook her head. "I can't do it anymore."

Hammer's heart stopped. "Raine, baby, you could never be either of those things. I've been preoccupied. I know. But I swear, nothing could ever make me stop loving you. *Nothing.*"

"I want to believe you...but I know you. Your appetites." She crossed her arms over her chest as if to ward him off. "You've never been a man who goes without for long."

She thought he had someone on the side?

"I haven't touched another woman since you." He lunged to his feet and gripped her face, willing her to believe him. "You've ruined me for anyone else."

"Don't tell me what you think I want to hear." She tried to pull away.

This time, he refused to let her go. "You know me. I'd never bother to spoon-feed you bullshit to spare your feelings. I don't like going without. You're right about that. So my fist is getting a hell of a workout."

Liam groaned. "Wrong thing to say, mate. I should just hand you a shit shovel."

"Your fist?" Raine's eyes narrowed. "I've been waiting and ready and worried you've lost interest. And you would rather get off with your own hand?"

"Fuck, no. I'd always rather be with you."

"Then why did you ignore my video? Why aren't you here anymore? And when you are, it feels like I could be any woman. I'll bet you gave Marlie more attention when you screwed her."

Macen released her, ducked his head. How could he refute her when she was right? After Bill's attack, he'd been so mired in his worries about Raine's emotional fragility that he'd given her too much time and space. He'd actually hampered her recovery because he'd failed to simply love and reassure her.

"Precious, I'm so sorry I've made you feel that way. When I come home every night, you're sleeping. I won't wake a pregnant woman to service me. It's goddamn selfish. But I swear neither my cock nor my flogger has touched another sub."

"I see you every afternoon. We spend most every Sunday together. You haven't once asked me to kneel."

"I'm worried you're not ready. I'd go the rest of my life without tasting your surrender again if that's what you need. But don't give up on us. You, Liam, and our baby are my whole world. I love you."

"Do you?" Naked yearning filled her face. "Or did you only decide you wanted me because Liam did?"

He cradled her cheeks again. "I've always loved you. You know I'm fucking lousy at showing it."

"Fix it. Communicate with me! You were so insistent I tell you *everything* I wanted, thought, felt… I've done my best to be open. I've turned myself inside out in freaking therapy because I want this to work. And you…" She sniffed back tears and clenched her fists. "I have no idea what's in your head or why you pulled away or—"

"I didn't save you from Bill, and I struggle to accept that failure every single day."

"Do you think I blame you for what happened?" She looked stunned. "You didn't provoke him."

"I stopped paying the bastard. I knew he was violent. I didn't think he'd dare to come after you." Hammer looked away, regret choking him. "I was wrong."

"Macen…" Her body softened as she pressed against him.

"I could have saved you all that terror for a measly two grand a month—and I didn't. I can't tell you how fucking sorry I am."

"He blindsided me, too. What he did to my sister…" She pressed an earnest hand to her chest. "You kept him away from me for years so I didn't wind up like Rowan. Please stop beating yourself up. He's already taken so much from me. If he comes between us again, he wins."

He curled his hands in her hair and tried impossibly to bring her closer. "I know. You're right."

"I wish you had told me how you felt sooner. I would have been here for you." She curled her fingers around his shoulders. "I love you. I want to comfort you. I can't when I don't understand what's wrong."

"I used to be your rock but lately I've been fucking crumbling. Don't ever think it's because I don't want you. Or don't care. I find you wildly beautiful. I love everything about you."

Tears fell. As she wiped them away, she cried fresh ones for him. "I thought you couldn't feel that way anymore after everything Bill nearly did to me. I've tortured myself, worrying the whole truth would push you further away."

"There was more to Bill's attack than the police report stated?" The twisted shit compiled in that document already made Hammer's blood run cold. And there was more?

Raine nodded, composing herself, like she sought to slip away somewhere safe in her head.

Hammer tensed. The depraved son of a bitch had been capable of raping and killing his wife and older daughter. Hearing that he had done more to Raine than either of them knew opened up a gaping black hole of dread. And she hadn't told him because she'd been afraid? More guilt piled on.

Liam rose to his feet, appearing equally bowled over. "You're not responsible for anything that sick fuck did, love. I've been by your side all this time. Why didn't you confess your troubles to me?"

"I needed to tell you two together. And I won't lie. There was so much shame." She closed her eyes and pulled back. "I agreed to do dirty, terrible things to stay alive. I felt like I'd sold my soul."

Jesus. Hammer grabbed her face again. "Listen to me. Whatever you had to do or say to survive won't change how we feel."

"We'll always love you," Liam vowed. "Tell us."

She wrapped her arms around her middle, as if shielding herself from judgment. "When Bill had me trapped in the warehouse, I didn't care about dying with dignity. So when he couldn't get hard enough to rape me…h-he demanded a blow job. I told myself to give him what he wanted and not to throw up. Finally, he untied my hands so I could touch him. I grabbed the knife and…" Raine pressed a hand to her mouth, unwilling to finish that sentence. "You know the rest. Since then, I've been trying to live with the fact that I would have given him parts of myself I hold sacred for you two."

While Hammer had been trying so hard to keep his shit together, he had left Raine swimming in guilt that she'd done what she'd had to. "I wouldn't care if you'd given him a hundred blow jobs. You survived."

Liam tipped her chin his way and fused their gazes together. "Precisely. If you hadn't used your head, you and the baby would have been lost to us."

"But you saw the way I killed Bill," she choked out. "I gutted him, carved him up—in less than a minute."

"I'm proud of your strength and courage." Liam tucked a strand of her hair behind her ear.

Hammer nodded. "If I could kill him all over again, I would happily slaughter the bastard."

"I didn't just kill him because I had to. I *enjoyed* ending him. What kind of monster does that make me?" Her voice cracked. "Does it ever cross your mind that you're having a baby with a killer?"

Hammer cradled her close. "We're having a baby with a survivor."

"And a defender," Liam added. "You'll protect our child until your dying breath."

"If you were a cold-blooded killer, Raine, none of this would worry you," Hammer pointed out. "He deserved everything you gave him for the years of pain and abuse he heaped on you and your family. So don't think for one second that I'm at the club working late because I don't want you or I'm horrified by what you did or regretting that we're starting a family. Nothing could be further from the truth."

"Do you understand?" Liam prodded.

She exhaled a shaky breath. "I needed to hear that."

Hammer pressed a soft kiss on her forehead. "How long have you been holding that in?"

"Since Christmas." She dropped her gaze, looking contrite. "I tried saying something around New Year's but…I didn't. I've been working on this with my therapist. She kept pointing out that if I didn't tell you, I'd always wonder and feel insecure."

Hammer stared. While he'd been wallowing, Raine had made miles of progress. "The way you just communicated… I'm so proud of you." He tried to lighten the mood. "It worked a whole lot better than throwing dildos, right?"

She choked out a laugh between her tears. "Yeah. But you have to admit, when I tossed half the toys across the dungeon, that got your attention."

"It also got you a red ass." He squeezed her hip and shot a glance at Liam. His best friend had both supported him and forced him to see their train had been inches from jumping the track. "Thanks for everything, man."

"You're welcome." He looked relieved. "And can I say that I've never met two more stubborn people in my life?"

With a watery laugh, Raine threw an arm around them both. Her hot tears spilled down Hammer's neck. "I've been so worried. And I've missed you. Will you stay this morning? Make the bad memories go away?"

Liam's raised brow told Hammer they'd both interpreted her words the same way. She wanted them inside her.

Hammer's blood pumped. "I'd love nothing more but are you sure you're ready?"

"Very." A little smile floated across her lips. "And I wouldn't mind a red ass, too."

"Is that all you want, minx?" Liam skimmed his fingers along the hem of her robe.

"No. I want to feel you two deep. Touch me." She released a shuddering breath. "Please."

Hammer ached to put his hands on her, command her. It would silence the chaos inside him.

He anchored his hands behind his back. "I've missed you, too, precious. Kneel."

Beside him, Liam squared up and stood tall, shoulder to shoulder, in a silent show of unity.

Raine dropped to her knees in a graceful slide before them.

The Dom inside Hammer roared and stretched. Pride rose. His cock burned with need as he breathed her in. He was relieved to see her submissive side still responsive.

Beside him, Liam caressed her hair. "You sure you're ready for more than the spankings I've been giving you?"

"Do I have to beg?" Desperation rang in her voice.

"Probably. Liam and I will spread this lotion on you. Then…" He leveled a hungry stare at her.

Hammer sat on the mattress and urged her up so he could tug her short robe back, then he dipped his fingers into the jar of cream. He smoothed the lotion over the flare of one hip. The feel of her warm, velvety skin made him groan.

As Liam dropped his hands to Raine's stomach, Hammer caressed his way up until he cupped her lush breast. Was his imagination playing tricks or did it feel heavier than before?

He brushed the pad of his thumb over her pebbled nipple. Raine sucked in a sharp breath, filling him with primal delight. His mouth watered for a taste of her candy-hard buds. And as she melted into his and Liam's touch, Hammer's desire surged again.

As he teased her breast, she let out a blissful, shuddering sigh. A knowing smile slid across Hammer's mouth. If this went as planned, he and Liam would soon be drowning in her silken heat to a soundtrack of her mindless pleas and spine-bending screams.

Liam plucked at the satin bow tethering Raine's robe closed. Together, they brushed the fabric from her shoulders, letting the garment slide down her arms until it puddled at her feet.

When she stood naked before them, Hammer leaned in and captured her nipple between his lips, laving it with his tongue and scraping his teeth over her drawn-up peak. He sucked deeper, pulling more of her flesh inside his mouth to lick and nibble. Raine whimpered and rocked her hips. A glance told Hammer that Liam had settled his fingers on the sensitive pearl between her legs. The scent of her tart musk rising above the cocoa only heightened the demand thundering through his veins.

"You're wet," Liam murmured in approval, kissing his way across her belly.

"You two make me wet," she whispered breathlessly.

Hammer's cock jerked.

As the air pulsed and surged, Raine gripped their shoulders. Hammer felt her nails biting into him as she let out a cry. Her muscles grew taut. Her back bowed. She sank her fingers into Liam's hair in an urgent grab.

As if scenting desire, the beast Hammer kept on a short leash reared its head. If he didn't get Raine between him and Liam soon, he feared the thing would gnaw through all restraint.

Skimming his palm down to grip the curve of her waist, Hammer plucked her off the floor and tumbled her onto the mattress. She sucked in a startled yelp. The sound morphed into a moan when his hand went straight to her pussy.

"We need to fuck our girl."

"We do," Liam agreed, rolling to Raine's other side.

Hammer stared at their precious one splayed out on the bed. Naked. Inviting. Willing.

The beast within him roared again. Restless. Pacing. Impatient to lay claim to her.

Take.

Bind.

Possess.

Macen tried to temper his lust. But the more he struggled to rein it back, the more fiercely it fought the chain.

Before he could blink, Hammer found himself on top of Raine, taking her mouth like a starved man. With urgent fingers, he clutched the soft curve of her hip, branding her with his palms. She met him, opening her mouth and legs, squirming beneath him with kitten-like mewls that fed his rabid need.

God, he craved her. She made him feel alive again, eased his burdens, his failures, his regrets. She soothed his savage beast.

As he moved his lips across her jaw, down the graceful curve of her neck, Liam swooped in, taking her mouth with a passionate kiss. Hammer slid his hand down again, teasing her clit. She spread wider, arched more. Then he drove his digits into her wet, silken pussy.

She let out a cry. Liam swallowed it. Hammer couldn't hold back his groan of delight as her smooth, slick walls clutched him. He barely resisted the urge to slam himself inside her.

"Yes…" Raine murmured as Liam nipped her ear and plucked at her nipple. "I've missed you both."

"We're here with you now, love," Liam whispered. "Let us take care of you."

Yes, Raine deserved to be made love to. But try as Hammer might, he couldn't slow down, couldn't wait to have all of her again.

Sinking his teeth into her other dark berry nipple, he gave it a tug. Raine cried out and arched. Still, it wasn't enough. His inner beast demanded more.

Withdrawing his fingers from her pussy, he licked her tart cream. Instantly, Liam scooted between her legs and covered her pretty pink folds with his mouth. In the spill of soft light, Raine flushed and closed her eyes, squirming against his busy tongue.

Hammer watched. The erotic sight had him shuddering. He knelt near her head, fisting his cock as he saw the pleasure ripple over her face. Christ, he loved seeing her so lush and uninhibited. So theirs.

"His tongue feels good, doesn't it, precious?"

"Yes," she whimpered, lifting her heavy lids. "More. I'll give you and Liam anything you want."

"Anything?" Hammer taunted.

She nodded frantically, eyes pleading for the ecstasy they could choose to grant…or deny.

"Open your mouth for me, Raine."

With a hungry stare, he watched the tempting bow of her lips part. He braced his palm against the headboard, feeding her every thick, hard inch. The feel of her sinful mouth made his balls draw up and shot tingles of pleasure up his spine.

"Yeah. That's it. Suck me deep. Hard."

She worked his shaft with her eager little tongue. Basking in the bone-melting sensations, Hammer closed his eyes and gripped the corner of the headboard, craving something he hadn't had the chance to do to her in months…

Yanking open the drawer of the nightstand, he jerked a bundle of silk rope free, then dragged himself from her mouth. Instantly, he missed her sweet worship but vowed he'd be buried inside the snug clasp of her pussy in a handful of seconds.

"I need you under me, bound. Immobile," he muttered roughly as he gathered her hands above her head, winding the length of rope around her wrists with an urgent tug. "At my mercy."

As he tightened the restraints and began securing her to the bed frame, Raine froze. Her eyes flew wide, pupils dilating at lightning pace.

"No! Stop." She thrashed like a wild thing, shoving against his restraints, kicking, tossing her head, wailing. "Stop. God, stop! Paris!"

She'd safeworded out. Hammer's inner beast heeled instantly. Stunned, he unwound the ropes. His guts liquefied.

Between her legs, Liam sat back on his heels. They shared a glance. His Irish friend looked as stricken as he did. Two months ago, Raine had loved rope and cuffs—anything that put her under their command. Back then, the moment restraints touched her skin, she'd melted.

Now, she seemed terrified almost beyond solace.

Hammer tossed the silk rope away, out of sight. She still looked pale and shaken and afraid.

"It's all right, love." Liam crouched over her. "No one will hurt you."

"Take a deep breath." Hammer's command was a quiet lash above their harsh breaths. "The restraints are gone. No more. Focus on us."

She blanched, tore away from him, and curled onto her side.

Hammer felt as if he'd been kicked in the balls. He should have fucking learned all the things *not* to do after his late wife, like getting drunk on power and giving in to his impulsive needs. Why did he seem so hell bent on repeating the past?

Fuck.

Fuck.

Fuck.

As one, he and Liam moved to surround her, holding her close, giving her their body heat and reassurance.

From the moment she'd entered his life, Hammer had made it his mission to know everything about Raine. Her menstrual cycle. The brand of her favorite citrusy shampoo. Her loathing of pickles. The movies that made her cry. Her every dirty fantasy and "secret" crush. Every achievement. Every regret. Every expression that accompanied every one of her moods. He'd missed nothing…until now.

He'd been feeling unworthy since he put Juliet in the ground eight years ago. In some ways, this failure hurt just as fucking bad.

"Raine," Liam murmured. "Sweetheart, talk to us."

She didn't respond to his words. Her body merely bucked with a silent sob.

That didn't deter Liam, and Hammer kept his mouth shut. Right now, Raine didn't need him commanding her to open up. She needed Liam's compassion. When their girl crawled into her head, he turned into the Raine whisperer.

Hammer stilled to watch.

"You're safe with us. At home. Can you hear me, love?" Liam spoke the words so gently. "Follow the sound of my voice. Do it now."

She stilled, hiccupped, blinked up at Liam.

"Good girl. Now tell us how you feel."

"Mortified." She sucked in a wrenching breath. "I kicked you. Oh, god. I'm sorry."

Liam shook his head. "Don't be. We understand."

"I don't. What happened? One minute I was melting between you. The next, I needed to fight."

Hammer's guts tightened. "Did you see Bill in your head?"

"No." She sat up, backed away, bringing her knees to her chest. "But I felt that fear again. It screamed that if I let myself be restrained, I would die." Apology softened her eyes. "I thought I was ready for anything but…"

"You're not, and I'm the one who's sorry," Hammer insisted. "I bound you and dredged up your fear. Jesus, if I'd known…"

"You can't blame yourself," Liam said. "That's why it's called a hidden trigger."

Who else could he blame? "I would never intentionally push you past your limits, precious."

She stared down at her kneecaps. "Being restrained is one of the things I'll work on with my therapist, but what just happened is no reflection of my need to submit or my feelings for you."

Hammer worried she wanted that to be true more than it actually was. The one bright ray was that she had communicated her fear and its reason—something Juliet had never done. Something Raine had never been good at in the past. She'd made amazing progress.

"There now, love," Liam reassured as he drew Raine into his arms. "We don't need to tie you up to give you pleasure…or let you make us feel good."

"I don't know when I'll be able to handle restraints again, but I'll keep trying." She clung, her voice shaky but resolved. "It hurts me because I know it disappoints you both."

After what she'd been through, she was worried about disappointing them? Fuck, he was the bastard here.

"You haven't disappointed us at all," Liam crooned.

She tried to smile but looked as if her perceived shortcomings were ripping her in two. "I'm sorry I killed the mood."

Hammer brushed his fingers through her inky mane and muzzled the howling beast inside him. "You were scared. Don't apologize."

"Can I fix you a nice breakfast? Apple spice muffins and date scones? I know it's not sex, but maybe we could snuggle."

Yes. Raine's love of baking had always been her go-to escape when the pressures of life overwhelmed. She spoiled them both with her sweet delights.

"I'd appreciate you sending me off to the club with my favorite muffins and your affection," Hammer assured.

"Why don't you go downstairs and get started?" Liam suggested. "I'd like to clean up a bit before I join you."

That was Liam's code for *let's talk.*

"Same here." Hammer sent Raine a reassuring smile and kissed the top of her head. "We'll just be a few."

"I'll get some coffee brewing."

"That will bring us down sooner." Hammer managed to wink.

After Raine left the room, he escaped to the shower to clear his head. Despite the hot spray loosening the muscles of his neck and shoulders, his hangover reasserted itself. Unfulfilled need still churned in his cock. Yeah, it was going to be another shitty day.

By the time he stepped out of the bathroom and tossed on some clothes, Hammer found Liam waiting just outside the door expectantly in a pair of sweat pants, wearing a frown.

"Any idea what the hell happened there?" He thumbed in the direction of the bed.

Liam shook his head. "I'm a bit shocked, too. She's done well with spanking. I've held her down here and there. But I confess, I've avoided bondage because I worried about her reaction."

Hammer wished he'd been thinking with his logic, not his lust. "Everything was perfect until I brought out the fucking ropes. I should have been more cautious since Bill tied her down and damn near raped her. I'm sorry, man."

"Don't blame yourself. Neither of us knew for certain she'd react that way."

"I wanted to get her under me so badly I just didn't fucking think. I've taken ten steps back with her." Hammer paced restlessly. "She doesn't trust me anymore."

"That's not true."

Sure it was. "Raine has never once shut me down. If she trusted me, she'd never worry I'd hurt her the way her fucking psychopath father did."

"You're being too hard on yourself."

Hammer tried not to scoff as he grabbed his keys and shoved them in his pocket. "I need to get my head on straight. I'm going to the club. Tell Raine I'm sorry I missed breakfast."

Anger flared across Liam's face. "If you leave now, you might as well tell her you blame her for this morning and she's not worth your effort."

"What? I need time to figure out how to make this right." But deep down, Hammer feared if he looked across the breakfast table and saw the accusation in Raine's eyes, it would tear out his heart.

"To her, you'll just be absent when she needs you again. But because you haven't worked through your past, you'd rather flee like a coward."

Hammer froze. "You're full of shit."

"I'm right. No one knows you better than I do. So I know you're blaming yourself now. Just like I know you'll stay half the night at Shadows to avoid facing your problems. I also know you'll miss Raine like mad." Liam poked a finger in his chest. "You'll try to cure your blue balls by jacking off. We both know it won't work because your hand is no substitute for our woman. But while you're polishing your knob, think about the fact that I'm sinking deep inside Raine, drinking in all her pleasure. You could be joining us and feeling her love for you—if you'd grow a pair."

Macen clenched his jaw and headed for the door. He hated Liam for being right.

"Yeah? Good for you. Just make sure when you're done fucking Raine, you have enough energy left to go fuck yourself."

CHAPTER THREE

RAINE STEPPED OUT of the pantry holding a bag of flour and a tub of shortening, hoping some home-cooked goodness would put a smile on Hammer's face. Hearing that he felt responsible for anything her violent excuse of a father had done made her ache to soothe him.

So did her reaction to his restraints. They all connected when she submitted to the heady Dominance he and Liam gave her. After fractured months apart, they needed to cement their bond again. God knew she missed their touch, craved their pleasure and tender pain. But this morning's fear of rope had been real and instantaneous. Not something she could have controlled.

So where did that leave them?

Before she could ponder the question, rapid footsteps pounded across the kitchen floor. The door to the garage slammed shut. Moments later, the engine of a car revved. Dread slashed through her. She peeked out and saw Liam standing in the middle of the room, looking both frustrated and madder than hell.

When the sound of the car grew fainter until it disappeared, her heart sank. "He left, didn't he?"

Liam turned to her, his dark eyes softening. His expression said he wished like hell he didn't have to answer her. "Sorry. I tried to talk to him. I probably said some things I shouldn't have."

"It's my fault." She pressed her lips together, feeling her dreams of a happy life with the two men she loved slipping away. "I didn't mean to freak out."

"His behavior has nothing to do with that."

Of course it did. This morning, she had allowed herself to hope they could talk out their problems and finally be happy. Being surrounded and touched by them had felt almost like their idyllic days at the lodge—until she'd halted everything. "I'll call the therapist when the office opens and find out if she can see me today."

Liam took the ingredients from her arms and set them on the nearby counter, then grasped her hands. "Raine, I just said he's not upset about the ropes. And it's not you. He loves you."

For years, Hammer had taken care of her, protected her. He'd wanted her like hell once. Sometimes he still did. But it seemed as if everything had changed after… "I'm worried he's going to leave us for good."

Liam led her to the table. "I need to tell you something. I wish Hammer would have 'fessed up himself. I thought he might when we were last at the lodge. But the way he's acting, I'm not sure he's faced it yet so he can."

"About his past? I asked him—"

"He told you the bare bones. If you'll listen, I'll tell you the bit you really need to know. Not his whole life story, mind you. Hammer told me that once when he was shitfaced while we lived in New York. But what I have to say affects all of us."

With her heart in her throat, she glanced at the beginnings of the breakfast she'd planned. Did it even matter now? Liam wouldn't mind simpler fare, and she had lost her appetite. "All right."

He sank down beside her, turning her chair to his. "He's drowning in guilt, and not simply because he failed to rescue you."

"Then why else? Because he may have gotten me pregnant? We don't know for sure who fathered the baby, and I don't care."

"We don't, either. That's nothing to do with it." Liam sat back. "I have to go back a decade. Can you bear with me? It's still hard."

Raine knew where this was going. As much as she didn't want to hear it, she needed to. "I'm listening."

"Some of this you may know…" He paused, seeming to gather his thoughts. "Hammer and I met ten years ago at Graffiti, a BDSM club in New York. I was new to the lifestyle and learning all I could. One night, he approached me about topping Juliet while he watched. I agreed. Things went well, so he invited me to join them in the bedroom. We shared her for a year and a half."

"That long?" Raine always imagined the flame had burned fast and hot before being snuffed out tragically.

"Well, I stayed on more than I might have because Hammer is the brother I never had and I didn't want to lose that. But our relationship with Juliet was nothing like the one we share with you. I deferred to Macen because she was his wife. I never agreed to be exclusive with them."

"Did you want to be?"

He shook his head. "I cared for Juliet. I didn't love her."

That was a guilty relief, but Hammer was still hung up on his wife. His feelings for her must run so deep even now. Raine bit back a cry. How was she supposed to compete with a ghost?

"When Juliet committed suicide, I was in Miami on business. Before it happened, I'd decided to stay an extra week because the weather was warm and the club scene was fantastic. For years afterward, I wondered if my absence had anything to do with her decision to end her life. Or if not having my heart hurt her too much. I never knew. But Hammer told me this past Thanksgiving."

She remembered that awful day—the stilted dinner, the migraine, the misunderstanding. The argument between him and Macen. The blame. And the two of them yelling at one another, surrounded by a sea of broken dishes. At the time, Raine had assumed their disagreement was about her.

"So you fought that night in the kitchen about Juliet?" That shouldn't hurt...but it did.

He nodded. "I waited to tell you this because I hoped Hammer would do it himself. But he won't. Hell, he'll barely talk to me. And you need to know."

Though the suspense was eating at her, Raine wondered if she was ready for the truth. "What?"

Liam dragged in a breath. "Juliet was eight weeks pregnant. Neither of us had a clue."

Raine's heart stopped. "Did she?"

"She left a note saying she couldn't handle the shame of not knowing who had knocked her up."

Then Juliet had swallowed a bottle of pills.

A million feelings raced through Raine. Shock. Horror. Sadness. Empathy. Both men had assured her they were looking forward to watching her belly swell and filling their house with children. After Liam's admission, she wondered if Hammer's excitement was less pure.

"So he's using me and our baby to heal his wounds?"

"No." Liam squeezed her hands. "That's not what I'm saying, love. Neither of us wanted you pregnant simply to fix the past or repeat a pattern. We're certainly not playing a game. Just because the babe you carry isn't the first between us doesn't mean he or she will be any less special in our eyes."

Liam was right, and she had to stop letting insecurity run away with her. Knee-jerking with her emotions and not thinking before she reacted was an old pattern and always complicated the situation.

"Sorry. That was an unfair question."

"But an understandable one." He caressed her face. "Raine, you're so special to us. There's no comparison, so don't think otherwise."

"I'll try." Raine knew she'd have to work hard at that.

"I know you will."

She tried to absorb Liam's story, but there was one thing she simply couldn't understand. "What kind of woman could end her child by ending her own life? I don't mean to pass judgment but…"

"Juliet had problems. I doubt she even thought about the babe when she made her choice."

Raine placed a protective hand over her belly. "I would never do that. Hammer should know. Tell him. I couldn't—"

Liam nudged her palm aside. "That's not what has him turned inside out, love. He had no idea she was unhappy, much less in despair. Neither of us did."

Because Juliet didn't communicate. Raine remembered Seth saying that.

"It's one reason he's so different with you," Liam went on.

Pieces of the Hammer puzzle slid into place. "That explains why he always watched me so closely, why he kept track of my cycles…" She gasped. "Why he kept my medication. Why he was desperate to know the second my period was late. And I fought you both."

Raine closed her eyes. They'd all gone through hell. If she had known Hammer's feelings, she would have been more compassionate, more honest. But she had to focus on here and now. Regrets were a waste of time.

"I'm sorry I shut you two out and failed to communicate." Raine slid her hands down her face, surprised to find her cheeks wet.

"Hammer prides himself on having control of every situation and taking care of those around him. Juliet's suicide must have made him question everything about himself as a man and a Dom."

"Precisely. The pain and guilt crippled him. He pulled stakes out of New York almost the moment Juliet's funeral ended. He came here and started over."

"Then he walled himself off and became the big, bad Dom of Shadows, plowing through one pretty sub after another. He ignored me because I loved him."

That still hurt.

"More so because he loved you," Liam countered softly. "Fiercely. I saw that the day I arrived. None of the other women mattered to Macen. In his head, if he didn't touch you, he couldn't harm you. It was his way of protecting you—and himself. He's afraid to give anyone the power to truly hurt him again."

"But his aloofness only hurt us more. It still does now."

"I know it feels as if he's slipping away from us. I don't mind saying that scares me, love. I've tried to reach him, but he shuts me out." Liam frowned. "He's stalled. Stuck. Now that he finally has the life he's wanted, he's scared shitless of losing it. He loves you far more than he ever did Juliet. If something happened and he no longer had you and the baby in his life, it would end him for good."

"I'm fine. I'm careful. I'm—"

"Human and vulnerable. Bill nearly made his worst nightmare a reality. It messed with Macen's head."

Raine knew that morning had taken a toll on everyone. "Bill is gone, and nothing that bastard did could drive me over the edge."

"I know. But Hammer has only cared about two women, and he's shared them both with me. The first time didn't end well. When she died, neither of us knew she was pregnant. You almost died, and we had no notion you were expecting, either. In both cases, he was powerless to stop the worst from happening. The parallels disturb him."

"He doesn't want to lose me but he's pulling away?"

Liam gave a sad laugh. "It sounds mad, but fear isn't logical, love. As you well know."

Raine couldn't disagree.

After her abduction, she'd known she would have to deal with her trauma, but it had seemed possible because she'd believed Liam and Hammer would be beside her, every moment, every step, every day for the rest of their lives. But soon Macen had begun drifting away. She'd been so confused and angry and hurt. Hammer had begun acting more like her bodyguard and caregiver than her Dom and lover.

Now it made sense.

Ignoring her screaming insecurities wasn't easy, but her therapist had coached her about stepping outside of her emotions and looking at things logically. Hammer was quick to help others…and slower than molasses to ask for anything in return. When he screwed up, he barely apologized. For years, she'd assumed he simply had too much pride. But she knew now he tried to deal with his issues alone because he didn't want to affect others. After Liam's revelation this morning, she could see that Hammer had shut down because he hadn't forgiven himself for failing to rescue her from Bill. He'd closed himself off years ago after not saving his pregnant wife.

The implications weighed a thousand pounds on her heart.

"You're right." Raine tried to hold herself together. She was stronger than all this crying, damn it. But the thought of losing half her soul tore at her. "My heart hurts for him, and I wish I could heal his pain."

"If I had a magic wand, I'd do it myself. It took him eight years to confide in me, and I was the bloke sharing Juliet. Only he can decide to let go of the past. I'm thinking you may be the only one who can help him."

"Me?"

"He'd do anything not to lose you. I'm not saying opening his eyes will be easy, but I think you can do it."

"I can't even make that stubborn man stay for breakfast. How am I supposed to make him let go of years of guilt?"

"You're looking at me with those beautiful eyes and the body that drives me to distraction, and you're telling me that you don't know how to get his attention? You may not believe it after this morning, but you turn Hammer's head. Give him a smile and a come-hither glance. The man will fall over himself to be with you. Then you shower him with your love. And you talk to him." He cupped her cheek. "I'll be there with you. We'll convince him to let go of the past."

"What if that doesn't work? Liam..." Raine understood that he'd run out of options, but failure terrified her. "What if he's not ready to move on? This is our family. Our future. We don't have years to make him see the light." She pointed at her belly. "We have six months."

Raine hated to sound negative. Of course she would give it her all, not only to keep their unconventional family intact but because Hammer deserved happiness. Deep down, he wanted the paradise dangling just in front of him. Maybe she needed to remind him of all they had.

"You can do it. We've weathered worse, love. We can survive this, too."

Liam had a point. Marlie and Gwyneth. All the jealousy, insecurity, and fighting. The breakup, the tough reunion, the difficulty confronting their pasts. Bill, the kidnapping, the violence, the bombshells, the awful aftermath. Seth often remarked that their lives resembled a soap opera. He was right.

"Thank you for telling me. I know he would probably be angry, but I needed to hear the truth. I'll do whatever it takes until we help him understand that Juliet's choice wasn't his and no one blames him."

"Unfortunately, Juliet's family does, and they were never shy about expressing their opinion. That hasn't helped Hammer, either."

Raine had never met those people, but she wanted to punch them. "That's ridiculous!"

"They were looking for someone to blame."

"Assholes."

"Language..." Liam raised a brow. "You wench."

She did her best to look contrite—but she stood by her opinion. "Do you want breakfast now? I can—"

The ringing of her cell phone broke into their conversation. She looked at the display and frowned.

Liam approached. "Is it Hammer?"

"No. That partner who works with Macen's lawyer, the one who's representing me in Bill's probate." She pressed the button to accept the call and turned on the speaker. "Hello?"

"Ms. Kendall? It's Silas Hoffman from Barnes, Hoffman, and Laughlin. How are you today?"

"Fine. Do you have news that could resolve my father's probate?"

Not that she wanted anything from Bill's estate except to throw a can of gasoline and a match at it. But this might be her only chance to locate River. "Has anyone found my brother?"

"That's why I'm calling. I just received word from an army representative who informed me they've advised him to call me about your father's estate."

Raine's knees buckled. She nearly dropped the phone. "Really? River is alive?"

In the last few months, she had often wondered during the sleepless hours of the darkest nights whether Bill had lied and somehow done away with her brother, too. Knowing that her father hadn't was a relief. And a confusion.

Where had River been for the last dozen years? She knew he'd joined the army when he turned eighteen…but that was a long time ago. Had he been in the service since? Overseas? Or maybe when he'd left home, he had written off his family and not given a shit about his younger sisters.

"Apparently, yes," the attorney said without offering anything else.

Raine tried to stifle her frustration. "Do you know how I can reach him?"

"I'm afraid not. The army won't release his personal information. I only know he's no longer active duty."

Seth had managed to find that out weeks ago.

She sighed. "So you don't know if he's even in Southern California?"

Hoffman murmured a sound of regret. "I'm sorry, no. The good news is, since you've already filed the federal and state taxes on your father's behalf and completed the inventory of claims versus assets, once River contacts me, we can resolve your father's estate quickly, probably six months or less. As soon as I've spoken to your brother and notified him of the impending probate, I'll let you know."

Until then, she could only hope—wonder—if her last remaining family wanted anything to do with her. "See if he'll give you his contact information to pass on to me. Please."

"Of course." Then, with a polite goodbye, the attorney hung up.

Liam cupped her shoulders. "You look shocked, love. Tell me what you're feeling."

"So many things." She blinked at him, grateful to have his beloved, comforting presence to anchor her. "He moved out when I was nine. I know almost nothing about him or his life. The last memories I have of River are him and Bill screaming about his teenage hell-raising and their ugly, parting fight. But I don't know *him*."

"He's your brother. He's family. Don't you want to talk to him?"

"I think so." She sighed, trying to sort through the barrage of her emotions. "But maybe there's a reason it's been so long since we've spoken."

Liam frowned. "I can't imagine what. If I hadn't seen one of my sisters in years, I'd be elated to clap eyes on her again."

"If you had one, I can see that."

"Actually, love…" He gave her a sheepish grin. "I've got six of them."

At that, Raine stiffened. Her fingers went numb, and she dropped her phone. As it clattered to the floor, her eyes bulged. "Six? You never told me."

"Well, they live in Ireland. My parents are Catholic, love. So we're a prolific bunch. I assumed you'd know I have siblings." He shrugged. "Honestly, the subject never came up."

"Never. Came. Up?" Raine swore her head was going to explode. Her temper shot up with her blood pressure. She couldn't take much more. She might be over a foot shorter than her men, but her temper could tower over them both. "So I'm the only one who has to cough up all the nitty-gritty details of my life? While you two hide all kinds of shit? And don't talk to me about language, Liam O'Neill." She wagged a finger at him. "First, it's Hammer and his suicidal, pregnant wife. That might have been important for me to know. And now you have all these sisters I've never heard a word about?"

"Raine, I suggest you take it down a notch."

When monkeys flew. "Tell me their names. Are they married? Do they have kids?"

"A passel of them. I'm the youngest of the family, mind you. So they all have children."

She put a hand over her belly. "Our baby will have cousins. And I didn't need to know that?"

"Don't be angry. I didn't intentionally try to deceive you."

She narrowed her eyes at him, bouncing between hurt and fury. "You once said that I needed to tell you everything, including what I wanted for breakfast. You threatened me with a jar of pickles. So you not telling me about major branches of your family tree is a fucking problem for me." She stomped her foot. "Maybe you didn't tell me because you never intended to introduce me to them. Or our child."

"That was *never* my intention. Don't think you haven't met them because I'm not proud of you, love. We'll go to Ireland, if you like." He rubbed at the back of his neck. "The truth is, they're a bit overwhelming."

"So you were sparing me, is that it?" Raine wanted to believe him...but at barely ten a.m., she had already reached her drama quotient for the day.

"A wee bit, yes. You'll see what I mean someday. Ask Hammer. He'll tell you."

"He's met them?"

"They came to New York for Christmas one year. I think one or two had a crush on him, but he was married at the time," Liam explained, then sent her a hopeful smile. "You look adorable when you're mad, love."

"Don't you dare try to sweet-talk your way out of this. Cough up the details. What else don't I know?"

"Well..." Liam hesitated, as if realizing that he might not be able to charm his way out of this mess. "Caitlyn is the oldest. She's a bossy, wee thing. Meg will always be in your business. Full of questions, that one. Shauna and Rosaleen are twins. They're two peas in a pod, finishing each other's sentences. Funny thing is, they married brothers."

"Twins?" Was he kidding? She looked down at her stomach. "Twins run in your family?"

"Don't worry. Multiple births depend on the female. It's to do with the number of eggs and..." He grimaced. "The next sister is Aisling. She's the quiet one...mostly. But she'll talk your ear off if she's a mind to. And Maeve is a bloody handful. I almost feel sorry for her husband."

Raine was glad she was sitting or she might have fallen down. "Wow. So many."

"They're more overwhelming than I can even explain. Be grateful they're not here. But we were talking about River. Now that he's reared his head, do you want to find him?"

Raine knew the bait and switch when she heard it. Damn it, Liam was lucky she wasn't hungry or she'd eat his balls for breakfast. "I don't know. I need to think about it. I'll be working on the nursery."

"Good idea, love. I'll just…um, nip out to the club so I can retrieve that picture of Hammer and me that you wanted framed. How about that?" He looked relieved that he'd thought of a plausible escape, and it would be funny if she weren't completely pissed off. And worried.

Six sisters? And her brother was god knew where.

"While you're out, you rack that conniving Irish brain of yours for any other secrets you might be hiding from me. I want them all."

THE SOUND OF workmen hammering away and a saw whining down the hall greeted Liam as he entered Shadows and made his way to Macen's office. How the man managed to get any work done with all the racket was beyond Liam, yet there Hammer sat behind his desk, signing checks, seemingly oblivious—until he looked up and spied Liam.

"If you're here to dissect me, I'm not in the mood."

"Bugger that. I've got news." Liam sank into the chair opposite with a sigh. "River surfaced."

"What do you mean…surfaced? Where is he? At the house?" Hammer leaned in, scowling. "You didn't leave Raine alone with him, did you? We can't until we know whether he's a sick, violent bastard like their old man."

"Don't be daft. I wouldn't be here if he'd knocked on our door. The probate lawyer rang this morning and spoke to Raine." Liam filled him in on the details. "She still doesn't know where or how to find him."

"But she knows her long-lost brother is alive and that he hasn't contacted her. I'm sure that upset her."

"Yes. He's the last of her family, so I thought she'd welcome him with open arms. But she wasn't dancing a jig. I think she's wary." He cocked his head. "I have this feeling it won't be long before we see him."

"So we may have another Kendall male on our hands." Hammer rose and rounded the desk, perching on the corner in front of Liam. He pinched the bridge of his nose. "This day just keeps swirling down the drain like a well-flushed toilet… I don't like it. We don't know much about River, except that he hasn't seen Raine for over half her life. I hope he doesn't think he can just show up and turn her world upside down."

"From what Raine said, he hated Bill. Maybe that's a good sign."

"You don't look as if you actually believe that."

Liam didn't, and he hated to say so. Something about the man niggled at him… "I don't know what to believe."

"He's probably just a selfish bastard who wants half of Bill's crap and won't bother crossing paths with Raine. But it might be smart to ring Seth and see if he's learned anything new about her brother."

"I'll take care of it."

"Is Raine home alone now?"

"She is, but I set the alarm before I left. It'll be a bit before the contractors arrive." Liam shifted uncomfortably in his seat. "But I had to leave before she lost any more of her temper."

Hammer grimaced. "Is she still pissed that I left? I didn't mean to upset her, just think."

"She has every right to be angry, but no. After she got the call about River, we talked. I wish you'd been there to lend me that shit shovel I gave you earlier because I really put my foot in my gob."

"You did?" A smile played at Hammer's lips. "How did that taste?"

"I'll bet Raine likes pickles more. I swallowed my toes down so far I think they're lodged in my gut. Oh, but you should have seen her, Macen. She was the Raine we fell in love with, all full of vinegar and sass. Magnificent. I probably shouldn't have told her that while she was upset."

"Yeah, never tell a woman she's cute when she's pissed off. What did you do that riled her up in the first place?"

"We were talking about River…and I might have spilled the news that I have six sisters."

Macen's eyes grew wide. "She didn't know?"

"No, I didn't want to bloody scare her."

"That's valid," Hammer conceded. "Stupid but valid. How long did you think you could keep them a secret?"

Liam wanted to be annoyed, but now that Raine wasn't breathing fury at him, he saw the humor.

"Honestly, I didn't think about it at all. I certainly didn't think she'd lose the plot when she found out. But I mentioned the nieces and nephews and that two of my sisters are twins…and her head spun like a top. I should have shut up then, but I got a case of verbal diarrhea and confessed that more than one had taken a fancy to you years ago. After she turned three shades of red, I thought I'd give her some time to cool off, so I told her I'd find that picture of the two of us. You know, the one she took the first night I arrived in LA. She wants it framed."

"So you escaped here?" Hammer chortled. "Jesus. I would have paid money to see you run."

"Stop laughing, you wanker. It's not that funny."

"You're right. It's fucking hilarious."

"To you, maybe. But I've grown rather attached to my balls, and I'd like to keep them. I think you should stay home with Raine tonight and put her in a good mood. I'll mind the club."

Hammer sent him a rueful smile. "Are you afraid of our girl?"

"When she's this feisty, I might be. She stomped her foot at me."

"Oh, that's when you know she's good and mad. I'm a little afraid of her then, too," he confided. "She'll forgive you…eventually. Don't worry. Once she has, you can sneak into her purse and retrieve your penis."

"Bite me, you bastard." Liam flipped him off for good measure. "This is a serious problem. She wants to meet the family."

Hammer's smile froze in place. "Oh, shit."

"Precisely. I know I should have said something sooner, but I wanted the three of us to be more settled before I called the family."

"The *whole* family?"

Had he gone mad? "I don't think she's ready for that."

But Liam knew he'd have to say something soon.

"If she finds out before you cough all the details up, you'll need a backhoe to shovel yourself off her shit list. How long do you think you're going to hold them off?"

Liam winced. "It's not as if I have a choice now."

"Nope. I'm not surprised Raine wants to meet them. Unless River turns up and proves he's not butt-fuck crazy, she doesn't have any family."

"God, I must love that woman. All right. I'll ease her into the family." Liam gave a long-suffering sigh. "You're enjoying my problem, aren't you?"

"Yep." Macen gave him an unrepentant grin. "What's your next step?"

"I have to give our little hellcat time to calm down. Whatever I say now will only overwhelm her."

"Especially after everything that happened this morning." Hammer sighed. "It didn't go well."

"No. We can't go on this way, Macen."

Hammer wasn't laughing now. "I know. And I need to handle my shit. I just don't know how to do it any faster."

As frustrating as waiting was, Macen's admission gave Liam hope. It was a step forward. Hopefully, he and Raine could break through the stubborn man's walls.

"I'll help you any way I can."

"Thanks. If you and Raine weren't everything to me, I wouldn't bother."

He wouldn't. As much as Liam had wanted to throttle the man earlier, he finally had hope that Macen was trying to resolve his issues, maybe for the first time ever.

"Just don't give up. We need you."

Somewhere between grim and resigned, Hammer nodded. "How about we find that photo? I can think of a few others stashed in her old room she might want around the house. Maybe that will make her smile."

"I'm thinking it would, along with some of those chocolate donuts she's been craving."

"You're bribing her. And you called me a coward?"

Liam shrugged and grinned wryly. "I have to make peace with her somehow."

"Good point." Hammer stood. "I'll help you look through the pictures. We'll call Seth together, then you can pick up your sugary offering."

Behind him, Liam scraped out of his chair and followed. "Good thinking. But let's not make it too quick, mind."

Macen withdrew the club's keys from his pocket as they headed toward Raine's old room. But when they reached the door that should have been locked, it stood ajar.

Worry danced up Liam's spine. "Are you remodeling her room, as well?"

Hammer shook his head and frowned.

They both went on alert, shoulders squared, jaws set. If someone uninvited was poking around Raine's space, they would make it clear the place was off-limits.

Macen flung the door open, hurtling it against the wall. Together, they rushed through the doorway. Senses heightened, Liam scanned the room.

A tall man in a construction vest had invaded Raine's private space, glaring as he clutched a handful of photos. He zipped around to meet them.

The man looked familiar—about thirty years old, brown hair, blue eyes, firm jaw. He wore an expression filled with hate.

"Who the hell are you? What are you doing here?" Hammer demanded.

"I'm here for Raine." He sneered. "I assume you're Master Pervert, her pimp..." Then he growled at Liam. "That would make you her john and her baby daddy, right?"

CHAPTER FOUR

H AMMER HAD SEEN this guy before but he couldn't recall where. The tall, square-faced menace had broad shoulders and wore a glare that pelted him with fury. He'd used the same slur Bill Kendall always had. And Macen definitely knew those eyes.

They mirrored Raine's.

Son of a bitch. This must be River.

And Hammer remembered now where he'd seen this scum sucker before. The morning Raine had been attacked, he'd been the guy in the emergency room hiding behind a damn magazine, watching him and Liam so closely.

"I am not her pimp any more than you're a construction worker."

"Nor am I her john," Liam growled. "River Kendall, I presume?"

"Yeah. Where the fuck is my sister? Do you degenerates have her chained up on her knees somewhere?"

Hammer lunged into Kendall's face, barely managing not to pulverize the prick—and only because Raine would be pissed. Besides, if River pressed charges, he'd leave her short one protector. "Not today."

"But you admit you have?" Kendall grabbed a picture from the dresser and slapped it into Hammer's chest. "I'm not surprised. The news called her a sex worker. I know you've been fucking her since she was a minor."

"Your daddy tell you that? Sounds like you listened to every line of shit he fed you."

"Don't lie to me. You been pimping her out all this time? Yeah, especially to your buddy O'Neill."

"He hasn't," Liam insisted. "Hold on. There's been a misunder—"

"I'm not misunderstanding anything. This picture proves he's a disgusting pedophile." River turned back to Hammer, his voice full of contempt. "How old was my sister here? Fifteen? Maybe sixteen?"

Macen snatched the picture from the front of his shirt and studied it. Raine's eighteenth birthday. The two of them standing in the dungeon, her wearing the sexy red dress that had knocked him on his ass and made him realize she was all woman. He stood close, arm curled around her possessively, while Raine sent him a sideways glance full of hunger.

Beside him, Liam studied the photo, then swore.

"She was eighteen, you cocksucker," Macen bit out. "You have no clue what you're talking about."

"Oh, I do. I've spent two months researching you pricks. I know everything, including the fact that she's lived with you in this cesspool of sex offenders since she was a minor. I bet you popped her cherry the first night, too. But then, I knew what a quality guy you were when I found out you'd driven your wife to suicide."

A white-hot rage roared through Hammer's veins, shutting down his ability to speak. The urge to snap River in half thundered through him. He lunged at the son of a bitch, fists raised.

Liam all but tackled him, managing to pull him back. "Stop!"

"You don't want to end this fucker now?" Hammer snapped.

"Oh, I do. But Raine will never forgive us if we kill him. I think we can break the maggot a bit, though."

"Give it your best shot," River challenged.

Hammer clenched a fist. "He goddamn deserves to die."

"I know. The feckin' gobshite is as thick as a plank." Cold fury rolled off Liam. "I was ready to reserve judgment, but now… I've made up my mind."

When his friend's inner Irish came out, Hammer knew the gloves were off. It reassured him. He and Liam might had their differences, but they were always on the same page when it came to protecting Raine.

"Good. She hasn't really missed her brother all these years," Hammer assured. "Let's end him. And make it hurt."

"You can die trying," River shot back.

"This is mental. You've no mind to hear the truth, only run off at the mouth and point fingers," Liam barked. "You should be grateful to this man, you fuckwit. Be kissing his bloody feet! He's watched over and protected your sister for years, especially from that pitiful excuse you called a father. Where the hell were you when he tried to rape and murder her, the way he did your mother and Rowan?"

"Yeah, you're a little late to Raine's rescue party," Hammer sneered.

Contempt glowed in River's eyes. "Fuck you. I was dodging bullets and defending freedom so perverts like you could stick your worthless dicks in my sister and get her pregnant. You let your buddy here watch? You proud of your big accomplishment?"

Liam scoffed. "You've got all the answers, don't you?"

"I do. I know your society whore of an ex-wife fucked every other man while you were married. You must be a real Casanova in bed. Maybe that's why you like to force my little sister. Hold her down and crawl all over her like a disease. That make you feel like a real man?"

"Christ, you're a festering lunatic like your father," Liam growled.

River glared. "Don't you fucking com—"

"We don't force Raine to do anything," Hammer cut in, his stare icy. "She begs and moans for it."

His words struck a nerve in River. The soldier sucked in an angry breath, chest puffing out. "You're going to be sorry when I'm through with you. Where's Raine? I want to see my sister right now."

Hammer seethed. No way would he even hint that Raine no longer lived at Shadows. It would only motivate River to search for her somewhere else.

But if he had to look at this asswipe for another minute, Hammer would rip his head off. "Liam, it's time to take out the trash."

"Couldn't agree more. But I'd be even happier to see him hauled out in cuffs. He is trespassing, after all."

River raised a brow. "You want to call the cops? Please do. I'll even hold the phone for you. I'm sure they'd love to hear how your pal here repeatedly violated my sister. I have proof of the terrible shit you've done to her. So here's the deal: If you give Raine back to me and disappear from her life, I won't tell the cops everything I know. I'll take care of her from now on."

Hammer got up in his face, pressing nose to nose. "Over my dead body."

"Mine, too," Liam snarled. "Go fuck yourself."

River shook his head and backed away. "Stupid bastards. I'll make you sorry."

"Get the hell out of my club and forget Raine ever existed. She's finally happy, and no one—especially not some dickless pus-bubble like you—is going to screw that up for her." Hammer unleashed all the menace churning inside him. "You've got ten seconds to disappear. If I see you again, I'll kill you."

"I am not leaving without Raine." River planted himself in the middle of the room, daring Hammer and Liam to forcibly remove him.

Since he and Liam were both volcanically angry, Hammer was pretty sure he'd enjoy that.

"You're sure as hell not leaving with her, either," Liam vowed.

Together, they seized the jackass. Raine's brother resisted, fists flying, arms flailing. He braced against doorjambs and walls—anything to remain inside Shadows.

Damn, the fucker was strong—but outnumbered. Hammer and Liam hauled a cursing River out of Raine's room, down the hall, past startled construction workers and the wide-eyed club members who'd spent the night.

With a chorus of grunts, a vicious struggle, and more than a few insults, he and Liam shoved River out the back and into the alley.

As the door slammed behind the bastard, Hammer turned and glared at the foreman, who stood gaping in shock. "River Kendall might work for you, but if that piece of shit ever shows up at my club with your crew again, you're all out the fucking door."

"I've never seen the guy in my life," the foreman assured. "One of my employees called in sick today. Maybe that guy took his vest and—"

Hammer didn't stay and listen to the rest.

Turning on his heel, he followed Liam back to Raine's room. Her photos lay scattered over the dresser, smudged with the man's huge fingerprints. Macen's fury bubbled at River's violation of his property and her privacy.

"You know he's no intention of giving up, right?" Lines of worry bracketed Liam's face.

"He's just getting started. Seth needs to give us some usable info on that sack of shit now."

"And the bastard's been gathering information on us. He's got a two-month head start."

Hammer whirled, paced, cursed. "If he's been poking into our lives for that long, how can he be so wrong?"

"Because he's a spanner."

"What the hell is that?"

"A gowl. A gimp." When Macen still didn't understand, Liam sighed impatiently. "A fucking idiot."

"Yeah." Hammer couldn't agree more.

Problem was, River wasn't just an idiot. He was a potentially dangerous one.

Suddenly, Liam stiffened. "Fuck me. We've got to go. I put the house in Raine's name. If River looks into property records—"

"It won't be long before he finds her." Hammer's blood turned to ice. "Let's go."

As they zipped around to leave, Liam snatched the photo he'd come for, then they both raced toward the parking lot. As they cut through the dungeon, Beck strutted out of the kitchen, coffee cup in hand.

"What the hell was all that shouting about? You two fighting over a box of tampons?"

"No time to explain," Hammer barked. "If we don't get back here tonight, keep an eye on the club or find someone who can."

"Sure," Beck called, his brows furrowed in concern. "I'm off today."

"Thanks," he shouted over his shoulder. "And if a man with Raine's eyes shows up, don't let him in."

"Actually, skin the bastard," Liam growled.

Beck smiled. "Sounds like fun! I'll go sharpen my knives."

Once outside, they raced to Hammer's sedan. A scan of the parking lot proved Raine's brother had gone—for now. He made a mental note to see if his tech, Lewis, could pull footage and come up with a license plate to trace.

Liam piled into Macen's car, leaving his SUV at the club. With a screech of tires and a burst of gas through the first yellow light, they wove through traffic. Hammer honked and cursed, swerving past slower cars. Desperation to get home and lay eyes on Raine gnawed at him. Beside him, Liam looked equally tense. If River figured out where

THE EDGE OF DOMINANCE

they lived and tried to take her, medical examiners would be hauling his corpse to the morgue. In fact, Bill's death would look downright pleasant by comparison.

Hammer tried not to think that he might already be too late. He could not fail her again.

"Call her!" He gestured to Liam with an impatient hand. "Tell her we're on our way home and to make sure the doors are locked. Fuck!" He laid on the horn at the slow-moving car in front of him, then bypassed the vehicle and stomped on the gas. "Get off the road, asshole!"

Liam jerked and gripped the armrest. "Slow down, will you? Christ. We won't be able to protect our girl if we're belly up in a heap of twisted metal."

"Just call her," he bit out, not bothering to ease off the accelerator.

Liam dug into his pocket and dialed Raine, looking decidedly nervous. "It's ringing. Since River thinks she's just a sex worker, maybe he won't check property records."

Maybe. But Hammer refused to leave anything to chance. Fear had him by the balls. Guilt for all the ways he'd been failing her and Liam squeezed his throat.

"She's not answering." Liam clutched the phone in a white-knuckled grip. "Her voice mail picked up. I'm worried."

"Try again."

Liam was already on it, intently focused on the device in his hand. With another tap, he raised it to his ear, his expression turning bleaker with every second.

Ahead, the light turned red. Hammer swore. Urgency pounded through his veins. "C'mon. C'mon!" He turned to Liam. "Anything?"

"Voice mail again. Macen… Fuck, I'm bloody shaking."

Fear ate at his composure, too. "Damn it. Keep trying. She's got to pick up. Maybe she's in the shower. Or has her head in a recipe. Or she's with the contractor."

Liam redialed again. "Let's be logical. River thinks he's protecting his sister. I don't think he's planning to hurt her."

"I don't fucking trust that son of a bitch. What if he's Bill reincarnated? Hell, River may actually be worse."

Besides being younger, stronger, and clearly capable, Raine's brother hadn't bothered to discuss, negotiate, or placate. He hadn't listened at all. He'd come with terms and demands and a whole lot of fuck you. "Not knowing his next move scares the hell out of me. We can't let him hurt—"

"I know. Don't go there. As long as we reach Raine in time, we'll protect her. He can't get past us both," Liam assured. "But I'm gut sick with worry that he'll twist the truth and somehow convince her she's better off with him."

"She loves us," Hammer argued.

"Yes, but that hasn't come without its difficulties."

Hammer knew all too well that a woman with a problem could be unpredictable. Maybe Raine might decide she valued peace more than this angst-filled, difficult, all-consuming love they tried to keep together.

And if she left, who could he blame but himself?

Liam looked ready to crawl out of his seat. "Bloody hell, we have to keep Raine away from him."

"How do you propose we do that? The minute we forbid her to see that shithead, she'll insist on meeting him. And if the law somehow gets involved, River has more legal rights to her than we do. That fucking chafes. We should have demanded she marry one of us. We still should."

"She doesn't want to choose. How can we push her before she's ready?" Liam frowned, ending one call to Raine and starting another. His hand trembled. "River could have come forward at the hospital that morning and blocked us from seeing Raine. Why didn't he?"

"Who knows? Maybe the TV news calling her a sex worker shocked him, so he came to investigate. He must have overheard us celebrating her pregnancy. I'll bet he decided then who and what we were."

"And used the last two months to dig up dirt on us." Liam frowned. "If I'd been in River's position, I bloody well would have talked to my sister and heard her side of things before I made up my mind."

"Well, you're reasonable." Hammer grimaced as he sped toward their neighborhood. "In River's crazy-ass head, we've abused and deceived Raine. Now he thinks he has plenty of material to persuade her we're first-class deviants who are ruining her life."

"He means to confront her. Despite all his fact checking, River hasn't managed to unearth the truth." Liam sighed. "I can't believe I was ready to give that prick the benefit of the doubt. And now we have to tell Raine we tossed her brother out of Shadows and that he might be dangerous. And before you say she doesn't need to know, think."

As much as Hammer wished he could shelter her from this, he couldn't disagree. "I've learned my lesson."

"Good. We have to explain everything and keep that cocktrough away from our girl," Liam growled.

"And make her marry one of us."

"You're really not good with touchy-feely shit. Good luck keeping your balls if you present marriage to her like that." Liam rolled his eyes, then dialed her again.

"I won't be that big of an asshole. I'll bring her flowers and shit. That's romantic."

"That's transparent," Liam shot back. "We'll have to do better if we're going to overcome her reluctance and convince her to legally marry one of us."

Hammer hated to remember the day they'd proposed. He and Liam had both dropped to their knees and professed their love. Raine's eyes had filled with tears of joy. But she'd quickly wiped them away and reminded them that only a handful of days ago they'd been at each other's throats.

You've both said you never wanted to marry again, and now that I'm pregnant you've changed your minds? Before anything else, I need to know that your friendship and our relationship is strong enough. Besides, I promised you at the lodge that I'd never choose one over the other. I won't break that promise.

"So we will," Hammer shot back. "But she needs to be Mrs. One-Of-Us ASAP. Where is Raine's head at these days? You've spent more time with her lately than I have."

"She's growing more secure every day, but...our circumstances haven't changed. Legally, she can't marry us both, so she would still be forced to choose. And I'm worried River will rattle her all over again."

Hammer nodded somberly at the phone in Liam's grip. "Still no answer?"

"Nothing."

Trying to ignore the biting fear, Hammer sailed through the subdivision, careened up the driveway, then slammed on the brakes. Both men were out of the car in seconds.

After shoving their key in the lock, they ran into the house, calling for Raine at the top of their lungs. She wasn't in the living room. Only workmen occupied the kitchen.

When she didn't answer either of them, Hammer broke out in a cold sweat.

He pulled one of the carpenters aside. "Have you seen our..." Damn it, she wasn't their wife. "Raine. Have you seen her?"

The older man in jeans shrugged. "Maybe an hour ago. I think she went upstairs."

Hammer didn't bother asking if anyone had come to the door. River had already proven he had a nasty habit of breaking and entering.

Whirling out of the room, he followed Liam across the house, taking the stairs two at a time. At the top, they hurried to the bedroom and burst through the door, panting, frantic, scared.

Raine lay curled up on the mattress, sound asleep.

Relief slammed through Macen like a gale-force wind. He slumped against the wall and swallowed the panic that had lumped in his throat. Thank fucking god.

Liam exhaled audibly, obviously grateful as well, as he climbed onto the bed next to Raine. On the other side, Hammer kicked off his shoes and sank down, too, never taking his gaze from her delicate face. God, he hated to wake her and rip away her serenity. But they couldn't wait to warn her about River. He already had a bad feeling they should be braced for a shitload of trouble.

RAINE LAY ON a silken cloud of comfort, enveloped by her two men. They both lavished her with tender caresses and velvety kisses. The low, husky murmurs aroused her. Individually, their virile scents were heady, but together they made her swoon. With a little moan, she writhed softly, aching to feel their hands stroking her, their mouths consuming her, and their hard bodies driving her to paradise.

As she reached for Liam and Hammer with open arms and an open heart, they faded away.

Consciousness crept in. It had just been a dream.

Raine crawled up through layers of sleep. She cracked one lid open. A beam of afternoon light danced on the bedroom ceiling. Her men weren't home…yet their distinct musk lingered. So did their problems. Hammer couldn't seem to resolve his past, and Liam had chosen not to tell her he belonged to a big, boisterous family who might—or might not—welcome her and their baby.

Closing her eyes, she hoped sleep would take her and give her escape again, even if just for another hour or two. Because the reality was, she had no idea how to fix her life, and it was killing her.

Warm fingers suddenly caressed her cheek. Raine gasped and jerked toward the touch. Hammer lay beside her, hazel eyes unusually tender and concerned. What was Macen doing home this time of day?

Body heat behind her beckoned. She flipped her gaze over her shoulder. Liam lounged on her left, head propped on his hand, watching her with a darkly gentle expression.

Their scents swirled, combined in the air. If she'd been standing, her knees would have turned weak.

Then Raine remembered she was supposed to be angry. Did they think she'd let them out of the doghouse so soon?

When Liam captured her naked hip in his heated palm and stroked his way up to her bare breast, Raine's breath caught. Clearly, he did…

How easy it would be to close her eyes and let ecstasy sweep her away. But they couldn't rely on sex to patch over their deep, very real issues. Her therapist had taught her that, too.

Pushing her way up between them, Raine grabbed the sheet and sat against the headboard. Now that she really looked, they both appeared surprisingly anxious.

"I wasn't expecting you for at least twelve hours, Macen." *If even then.* When his expression suddenly turned somewhere between angry and grim, Raine's pulse quickened. "What's going on?"

"It's your brother. River conned his way inside Shadows. He broke into your room."

Raine gaped. Nothing Hammer said could have shocked her more.

River had returned after twelve years of silence?

"Did you talk to him?" She pushed out of bed and plucked up her undergarments, wriggling into them. "Is he downstairs, waiting for me? I want to see him."

She reached for the yoga pants and T-shirt she'd draped on a nearby chair, butterflies swarming her belly. She hadn't seen her brother since he'd been a gangly teenager. Puberty hadn't even set in for Raine yet. His last night in the Kendall household had been loud and ugly, punctuated by accusing curses and angry fists. Then River had slammed into his room, grabbed all his things, ruffled her hair on his way to the door…and left for good.

She understood full well wanting to escape Bill. All the Kendall children had chosen to, in their time and way. But she'd never understood why he hadn't once checked on his younger sisters instead of simply leaving them to the dubious mercy of a violent man. Maybe, after he'd gone, River had made a conscious choice not to give a damn about his family. Or maybe something else had kept him away. The brother she'd known had always wanted to be a hero.

Thunder rolled across Liam's face. "There's no way in hell we'll be letting that bastard anywhere near you."

"Absolutely not. We threw him out of the club." Hammer's face hardened. "If he knows what's good for him, he won't come back."

Menace rolled off her men. Naturally, they wouldn't be thrilled River had wormed his way past club security, but their fury zipped way past irritation.

Dread dumped into the gaping pit of her stomach. "What happened?"

Liam's eyes narrowed. "You should have heard the accusations he hurled at us."

"Like?"

"Well, I'm the pedophile who's been debauching and pimping you out since I brought you to Shadows as a minor, and Liam is the john who raped you repeatedly while I watched until he got you pregnant— simply for our sick amusement, of course."

Her clothes fell out of her numb fingers. Yeah, the pedophile accusation wasn't new. Bill had been fond of it, too. But the fact that River agreed with any of that creep's opinions made her wary.

"You set him straight, right?"

A jerk of Liam's head conveyed more anger. "He gave us no chance."

River had always been a hothead and more than a bit impulsive. The two of them had that in common. Maybe if she explained…

But when she glanced at Hammer's forbidding expression, he clearly was not in the mood to listen.

"No chance at all."

Raine winced. The whole confrontation must have been wretched. "Damn it."

Liam loosened his tie, looking hot under the collar. "The fuckwit seems hell-bent on 'rescuing' you from us."

"Fuckwit is putting it nicely. River is batshit crazy." Hammer glowered.

Raine's head buzzed with shock. Her only brother thought she was a pregnant hooker being taken advantage of by two perverts. It made her sad—for her, for River. For Liam and Hammer, who had tried to love and protect her.

Then again, what would she have thought if she'd found one of her siblings in the same shoes?

"Okay…he jumped to terrible conclusions. But think about how it must look on the surface. Liam, if one of your sisters, as a minor, had been living with a man more than a decade older than her, who owned a club like Shadows, what would your first thought be?"

"That I'd kill him and get her the hell out of there," Liam admitted. "But I'd have bloody talked to her first, asked what was going on. River had already made up his mind. Nothing we said was going to change it."

"In his position, I'd probably assume whatever you two had to say was crap, too."

"He spent two months digging through our lives, so he should have rubbed a couple of brain cells together and come up with a better conclusion. He seemed to know about everything else, especially Gwyneth." Hammer gnashed his teeth. "And Juliet."

Raine winced. "I can see where he might think you two have a…colorful track record with women and assume the worst."

"Colorful, is it?" Liam quirked a brow.

Hammer jerked his coat off. "He can go fuck himself."

"River twisted half-truths and lies into damning accusations. It was all we could do not to strangle the bastard."

"So the conversation didn't go well. He doesn't understand the situation, guys. But I'll make him see. Tell me." She reached for her clothes again. "Where can I find him?"

"You're not going after him," Hammer insisted. "Not in this lifetime."

"I have to. Be reasonable, Macen."

"I am. The fucker is still alive."

Liam scowled. "Which wasn't my first choice."

Raine rolled her eyes. "My brother just needs to see that I'm finally happy. Don't look at me like I'm crazy. I'm not asking to spend time alone with him." In fact, it was better if she didn't right away. Yes, River might have misunderstood the turns of her life since he'd gone, but for all she knew, he'd inherited Bill's delusional streak. "You'll be with me every moment."

"I don't care if you have a whole SWAT team with you, you will not see, talk to, or be within fifty miles of that prick," Hammer roared.

"Exactly." Liam's dark eyes blazed with insistence. "We mean it, Raine. Don't test us."

Clearly, after Bill and the horrific end she'd almost suffered, it was too soon to ask them to be calm or reasonable. "It's a misunder—"

"We don't give a shit," Hammer said. "You won't be seeing River, even if I have to chain you to the fucking bed. That's final."

Liam nodded. "It's obvious that the nut hasn't fallen far from the tree."

"It's an apple," Hammer hissed.

Liam scowled. "What?"

"The saying, dumb ass. It's an apple."

"Whatever. In this case, nut pretty well sums River up, I'm thinking."

She crossed her arms over her chest. "I'm not a little girl who needs her two daddies' permission. He's my brother, the only family I have left. I have to resolve this."

Hammer yanked her against his body. Disapproval rumbled across his face. "Oh, but you do need our permission. You're our submissive to protect. And we want you safe."

The terror Bill had subjected her to had affected them all, Hammer especially. She knew that now. She understood. But their stubbornness pissed her off.

"I can't live in a cage, be your perfect little sub, and say, 'Yes, Sir. Thank you, Sir,'" Raine shot back. "I know my brother upset you. But I'm not giving up. When you've cooled down, we'll talk again."

She whirled around and headed for the bathroom.

Liam grabbed her arm before she could get away and glowered at her. "We're not done talking to you, Raine. Sit and listen."

Hammer didn't say a word, merely pointed to the bed, then crossed his arms over his chest—a sure sign that he wasn't going to budge.

With a sigh, she sank down. "I think you're overreacting as much as my brother did."

Hammer bent and grabbed her chin, hovering close until they were nearly nose to nose. "I'm not a judgmental, narrow-minded piece of shit. He wanted to make a deal with us for you, precious, just like Bill did."

"Indeed," Liam added, fingers tangling in her hair until she looked at him. "We've been down this road before. We'll not be going back."

Raine gasped. "He asked for money?"

"No." Hammer shook his head. "He wants you away from us 'freaks.' In fact, he demanded we hand you over today."

"He threatened us," Liam growled. "That makes him no better than your father."

Threatened? Hell no. River had gone too far with that. People lost their tempers. Sometimes they even made wild accusations. But with the Kendalls, threats usually meant retaliation. She didn't want more violence or intimidation. She certainly didn't want another Bill in her life.

"Now you want to keep assuming that River is rational or harmless?" Hammer challenged.

That had Raine shaking her head. "Maybe not."

"Of course not! He means to take you from us." Liam clenched his teeth. "I don't care what excuse he bleats on about. Give him half a chance, and we'll never see you or our baby again. I won't risk it.

You're not to talk to him."

Was the brother who hadn't troubled himself with her welfare for a dozen years really worth upsetting the tenuous peace in her new, growing family? Especially when, for all she knew, he might be Bill's clone?

"All right." She sighed, wishing she could come to some other conclusion. "I won't seek River out. For you two."

"Thank god, love." Liam pulled her into his arms. "I couldn't endure again wondering if you're alive or if some mongrel who shares your blood in his veins is going to murder you. The thought of what he could do to you and our child... I know family is important to you, and I'd hoped for your sake that River could fill some of the empty space left by your mother and sister. I'm sorry."

"Thanks." Raine nodded, then looked Hammer's way. The relief on his face filled her with a guilty satisfaction. "I'd never want to worry you."

"We appreciate you compromising. I'm simply worried we haven't seen the last of River."

"My brother. Liam's sisters..." It was a lot to take in. The day had already been exhausting and it wasn't over. "Why can't we just have some peace?"

"We will. Everything will work out." Hammer caressed her cheek. "Precious, I'm sorry about this morning."

She blinked. He almost always avoided apologizing, like it choked him as much as wearing a shirt collar that was too tight. But he'd offered up his sincere atonement without any prompting at all.

Raine wanted to say that she understood because she could grasp how guilt had been gnawing at him. If their situations were reversed, she would feel awful. But she also wouldn't have kept anything as important as another pregnancy from him.

"I needed that. There's nothing you can say that will make me love you less. You don't have to bear the pain of the past alone. But hurting me by walking out like that is inexcusable."

"You're right," Hammer agreed without hesitation.

Then she turned to Liam. Six freaking sisters she'd never heard of until today...

With that thought, she zipped a gaze back to Hammer. "Wait.

How many siblings do you have?"

He arched a brow at Liam and smothered a laugh. "None, precious. I'm an only child."

Hammer might have been guilty of a lot over the years, but at least he hadn't intentionally buried his family tree.

Raine tucked her arms over her chest and pinned Liam with an expectant stare. "Did you remember anything else I should know?"

"Watch yourself," Liam warned. "You're likely to end up with a smacked bottom."

"Promises, promises." She sent her two men a saucy stare, then threw her arms around them.

Surrounded by the two people she loved and trusted most, Raine let their warmth sink into her and tried not to think about River. But he lingered, and she hated to imagine that the last surviving Kendall male might possibly become her next nightmare.

CHAPTER FIVE

Wednesday, February 13

B Y WEDNESDAY MORNING, Raine was ready to escape her own house.

Beside her, Hammer steered his Audi down the street, toward her highly anticipated, hour-long respite. She was grateful Liam had stayed home. She didn't need another over-testosteroned protector hovering.

"I could have driven myself," Raine pointed out. "I have a standing appointment and I always manage to find my way."

"No."

She sighed. "It's just a massage."

"It's also not a negotiation. I had to pick a few things up at the grocery store anyway. So I'm driving you."

Who did he think he was fooling? "Name one time you've done your own grocery shopping in the last six years."

As Hammer breezed through a yellow light, he sent her a warning glower and gripped the wheel tighter.

"Be reasonable. River isn't going to snatch me away. If he shows up, I promised I'd have nothing to do with him. Don't you trust me?"

"It's him I don't trust."

"I get that, but you haven't let me out of your sight in four days."

"I'm letting you spend an hour away now, aren't I?" he snapped as he turned right into the parking lot.

She held in a groan, reminding herself that Hammer was simply afraid for her. "I can protect myself. Bill came out of that fight in far worse shape than I did."

He sent her a stern glower. "Don't remind me about that day."

"I don't have to. Neither you nor Liam are trying to forget. It's hard for me, too. But you've got to lighten up. Nothing is going to happen in a public place with the massage therapist the obstetrician recommended. Gloria is great."

Hammer's nostrils flared. Raine knew that look. She might as well be talking to a cement wall.

"First of all, you shouldn't have to protect yourself. That's a responsibility Liam and I take very seriously. Second, no one knows what could happen, and we're not eager to take any chances. Call me a hard-ass if you want, but either I'm driving you to and from this appointment or we're cancelling."

Do you want to watch Gloria work out the knots in my muscles, too? The sarcasm perched on the tip of her tongue, but Raine bit it back. Hammer might actually take her up on that offer.

"Seriously, River hasn't been back since last weekend. He forgot that I existed for twelve years. For all we know, he's decided I'm worthless because I'm a knocked-up slut or whatever, and he's written me off again. Fine. His loss. I don't need him."

"I told you, he's not giving up." Hammer pressed his mouth into a severe line as he pulled up to the curb in front of the spa. "That much I know."

The fit couple Raine always saw heading into the fitness studio before her late morning appointment caught her eye as they ducked in next door for their session. Their burly personal trainer greeted them with a wave.

"I have to go or I'll be late. We'll talk about this later," she promised and kissed his cheek.

He sent her a steely warning. "Yes. In an hour, when you're over my knee and you remember you're not the one giving the orders."

Hammer hadn't touched her since Saturday morning's debacle, and they hadn't had sex in weeks. He'd been particularly edgy since she'd freaked out about his ropes. She still felt terrible about that. Hammer and Liam were Doms; they might worry she no longer trusted them. Nothing could be further from the truth. Now that she knew being restrained triggered dark memories, she would mentally steel herself so she wouldn't lose her shit again—hopefully.

Raine worried this would come between them. Hammer craved having complete control, and if she couldn't give it, would he lose interest?

She opened the car door. "We both know you won't do that."

Once he would have, but now…

Hammer snagged her arm. His hazel eyes flashed a darker warning. "That's where you're wrong. Would you like me to hold you down now to make my point, precious? Either way, I'll be giving you a rosy ass before the sun goes down. Then count on Liam and me keeping that insolent mouth of yours busy all night."

Desire flipped in her chest, pulsed between her legs. Raine wanted the passion Hammer's words promised.

She knew a surefire way to get it. Hammer couldn't resist the urge to tame a brat.

She jerked from his grasp and lunged out of the car, then bent to stare at him through the open door. "Why do you need my mouth? Is your fist too busy for another workout? See you in an hour."

With a thunderous expression, Hammer jerked off his seat belt. Raine smothered a nervous laugh as she slammed the passenger door and darted into the cool spa, pungent with incense. Bamboo chimes piped softly overhead. The waiting receptionist frowned as she stared out the glass door. Raine didn't turn to look, because she knew the bear she'd baited charged her way. He should have some pent-up frustration to work off when her massage was over.

The thought made her almost giddy.

"You don't have to show me back. I know Gloria's room number. Thanks."

Raine hustled to the back of the spa before Hammer could barge in. After she used the facilities, she hurried to room number five. Inside, she breathed a sigh of relief as she set her purse on the counter. "I'm safe—at least for now. Not even Hammer would dare to follow me in here."

At least she didn't think so.

Behind her, the door shut suddenly. Raine whirled. A big body stepped from the shadows and into the dim light of the massage room. Raine knew those blue eyes.

"So I was right, you *are* afraid of him?"

She gaped in shock. "Oh, my god… River! What are you doing here? I haven't seen you in forever."

"I learned your schedule." He took her shoulders and searched her face intently. "Talk to me. Tell me what's going on."

Frowning, Raine tilted her head way up to meet his gaze. He'd grown since adolescence, now standing somewhere around six foot five. He'd filled out his once-gawky body with pure muscle. He looked hard and dangerous and immovable. She didn't want to be afraid of him, but unease twisted her stomach.

She tried to shrug free from his touch. "You need to leave. I promised Liam and Hammer I wouldn't talk to you."

"And you do everything they tell you to, don't you?" He muttered a curse. "What will they do if you disobey?"

Spank her. Maybe fuck her within an inch of her life, but she'd like that. She'd missed being with them both.

Best not to say that to her brother. He was already agitated.

She stepped away nervously. "N-nothing. I'm surprised you—"

"Don't lie to protect those fucking deviants."

Until now, River had sounded almost normal. But maybe Hammer and Liam had been right about her brother being crazy.

"You shouldn't be here. Where's Gloria?" Raine glanced hopefully toward the door. Maybe the therapist would show up to defuse this situation...or get help.

"Out with a cold. I paid the receptionist not to call you." River gripped her shoulders tighter. "I had to separate you from those two animals. Raine, I'll get you to safety."

"Safety?" She shook her head. "I'm fine. Better than fine. Where have you been all these years?"

"The army. I spent a lot of time in Afghanistan. I've only been back Stateside for a couple of months."

And he hadn't reached out to her once until he disapproved of her life. Had time and war toughened all the sanity and goodness out of the brother she remembered?

"Don't change the subject," he growled. "I won't let you be a cock slave to those two assholes anymore."

"Cock slave? Assholes?" Raine shoved at his chest. "You've got everything wrong. What we have may not look like a conventional relationship, but who the hell are you to pass judgment?"

River didn't give her any room to breathe. "The only fucking family you have left."

"You walked out twelve years ago and didn't look back. So you don't get any say in my life now."

"I left because I had to. But I'm back and I'm not a screwed-up teenager anymore."

No, he just sounded like a sanctimonious prick.

"Let go," she demanded.

"Those two have hurt you." Something bleak settled in his expression. "Storm cloud, I can't let that stand."

No one had called her that pet name in…well, since River. It softened her a bit.

"Really, you just don't know them. They're wonderful to me and—"

"Do you even know which one of them fucking got you pregnant?" He pointed at her belly, looking furious. When she didn't answer, his face hardened. "That's what I thought. Come with me. I'll get that taken care of. We'll get your life back on track. I have money."

Get that taken care of, as in…abortion?

"No!" Raine struggled to dislodge his grip. "God no! If you're not going to listen, leave me alone."

"Listen to what? All the crap they've brainwashed you to say? I won't let them force-feed you any more of their Kool-Aid. You don't have to give birth to this product of rape. I'll take care of everything. You'll have other kids someday—with the right guy."

"Rape? They've never…" Horror scalded her. "Ever. Get away. You're not touching my baby! Or me."

"The procedure won't hurt," he promised as if physical pain was her primary concern. "Come with me. We have almost an hour before Hammerman and O'Neill know you're missing. I'll have you far away from them by nightfall."

He was serious and he had a plan. Fear screeched inside her.

"If I needed protecting from anyone, it was Bill. But you weren't there to save me or Rowan." She shook her head and tugged harder against his grip. "No. I want this baby. I love Liam and Hammer. They've given me everything and made me so happy."

"Being used and abused? How have they convinced you that's happiness?" His eyes narrowed as anger filled his big body. "You just don't know any better. Do they tag team you? Does one hold you down while the other rapes you? You're such a little thing, storm cloud. Do they get their kicks overpowering you? Do you call that love?"

"What the hell are you—"

"They probably shove their dicks into you at the same time and… Fuck. Just the thought makes me angry and sick." He shuddered as if he had to shove down his rage. "That terrible part of your life is over. You're coming with me, and once you see what vile scum they really are, you'll thank me."

Raine wrenched against his hold now. She couldn't fight him off physically, and as far as she knew, no one else was in the spa except the receptionist, who had sold her out. She had to talk her way out of this.

"I'm not fucking going anywhere with you."

"Don't be afraid. It's okay. I don't think less of you. I'll have to kill those two freaks, but—"

"They're not freaks. I'm not brainwashed. I'm in love! Will you shut up and listen?"

His face filled with pity. "We've already wasted ten minutes. I'm getting you out of here."

River tugged her toward the door. Raine dug in her heels, but he was so damn big and strong.

"Stop! No, you can't do this… You're totally misunderstanding the situation."

"Let them prove it to me. Until then, my priority is your safety."

Raine didn't like the resolve on his face. She opened her mouth to scream, but he spun her around, dragged her back against his chest, and planted his hand over her mouth in one quick move. Barely a moment later, he lifted her off her feet and hauled her out of the room.

Panic iced her veins. She struggled, kicked, grunted, even tried to elbow him. His abs were hard as stone, and her blows bounced right off him.

He was definitely stronger than their father had been. If River managed to drag her off, she could only imagine how difficult he would be to escape. Granted, he wasn't plotting to rape and kill her. At least he hadn't sounded like that sort of lunatic. No matter what, she could not let him haul her away and rip her child from her womb. What that would do to Hammer and Liam was unthinkable.

Raine wrestled hard for freedom. River simply clamped his arms around her more tightly and headed down the hall, toward the exit at the back.

Someone had already propped the door open. Her brother didn't look surprised, merely put his shoulder into it and burst out into the sunlight.

Ten feet away, she spied a black truck with dark-tinted windows. He pinned her under one beefy arm and worked a hand into his pocket. A moment later, a beep and the flash of headlights told her the vehicle belonged to him.

River was planning to toss her in it.

Sheer terror flashed through her system, roared in her ears. She broke out in a sweat. Her heart chugged so hard it hurt. She couldn't breathe.

This is really happening.

No. No. No!

She redoubled her efforts, kicking his shins, pummeling his middle with one punishing elbow after another. She screamed again, cursing the fact that his hand muffled the sound. God, how was she going to stop him?

"Stop fighting me. It'll be over soon."

What the hell did that mean? Why did this shit always happen to her?

Never fucking again. She refused to be anyone's victim.

Raine bit down on his finger until she tasted blood while blasting her heel back into his knee.

He dropped her with a curse and an incredulous glare, sucking his offended finger into his mouth. "Goddamn it!"

She didn't stay long enough to discern the consequences. Instead, Raine turned and ran for the open door to the spa. If she could get through it, kick away the block of wood propping it open, then slam the portal behind her, it would lock automatically. She could be out the front again, maybe hiding somewhere River wouldn't find her until Hammer returned. Anything that would get her away from her crazy brother.

She had barely taken two steps toward freedom when River grabbed a handful of her T-shirt and hauled her back against him.

"Hey," a man to her right called. "What the hell is going on? Let her go."

Raine turned to the voice. One of the trainers who worked at the fitness studio next door. Big and bulky, the bodybuilder looked like her brother's match in size and strength.

"Help me!"

When the guy sprinted headlong toward them, River set her behind him. "She's my sister. Butt out."

"She obviously doesn't want to be in your company. Back off." The good Samaritan glanced her way. "Go inside and call the police. I'll hold him here until they arrive."

"Thank you so much." She didn't dare linger any more, so she dashed back to the spa.

"I'm not giving up on you," River called after her.

Chills shot up her spine, but Raine didn't stop, just kicked the doorstop aside and wrenched the portal shut behind her. When she heard it lock, she dragged in a relieved breath. Her hands trembled when she swiped at the tears running down her face, grabbed her purse, and dashed into the reception area. Only the bitch behind the counter who wouldn't help her sat there, acting like she didn't exist.

But outside the glass door, Raine spotted the most reassuring sight of all.

Hammer leaned against his Audi, waiting on her. When she launched herself outside, she didn't have to say a word. The moment he zeroed in on her, concern charged across his face. She ran for him as if she couldn't reach him quickly enough. He ate up the ground between them. As she fell into his arms, he caught her in a tight, protective embrace, then drank in her sobs and held her so close.

AFTERNOON SUNLIGHT BLAZED into the living room through the picture window overlooking the front lawn. Despite the surprisingly warm day and feeling Raine curled up on his lap, icy resolve filled Liam.

He tried not to think that if she hadn't kept her wits or if the trainer next door hadn't been enjoying the temperate day, River might have taken her and Liam wouldn't be holding her now.

In fact, he might never have held her again.

Liam clutched Raine tighter and nuzzled her neck, breathing her in. She trembled, curling her fingers into his shirt, as he gently stroked her hair.

"Are you all right, love?" he whispered.

"Still a little shocked, but better now that I'm home with you two."

"Are you sure you don't need a doctor?"

She shook her head. "I'm fine. He didn't hurt me, just scared me. I'm upset that I couldn't make him understand."

"From the sounds of it, he didn't give you much chance to explain. We know that feeling." Liam wanted to murder the wankstain. And he'd barely been able to let go of Raine since Hammer had rushed her home.

Since then, the police had come and gone. They had interviewed the bodybuilder in the alley, as well, who had corroborated Raine's version of events. But River had managed to fend off her burly rescuer and vanish without a trace. The LAPD was gunning for him now.

Liam was hyperaware the bastard was well trained to reappear anytime and anywhere. He could pull off nearly anything to take Raine from them without a whisper of warning.

Pacing the length of the room, Hammer looked disheveled and pissed off. He had long ago ditched his cloak of civility, having tossed his coat on a nearby chair and his tie on the armrest of the sofa. He prowled like a caged lion as he clutched his phone and barked into the device.

"What do you mean you don't know where to find him? I need to talk to Seth Cooper now."

Whatever the man's assistant said on the other end did not reassure Hammer. He glowered. If the woman could have seen him, she would no doubt have run screaming.

"I understand cases can be unpredictable. So is the one I've given him. Have him call me the moment he surfaces."

After the woman murmured some platitude, Hammer stabbed at a button on the screen and barely managed not to hurtle the phone across the room. Instead, he flung himself on the cushion beside them with a growl. Liam shot him a warning stare. Macen's agitation wasn't helping to keep Raine calm.

"You okay, precious?" He turned to her, his tone surprisingly tender.

"Don't get worked up, Macen."

"You're upset," he bit out.

"My head is racing. I'm shocked my own brother tried to abduct me. Since he grew up under Bill's roof, I'm sure he had a rough childhood, too. But I'm not violent, so I can't make excuses for him. You tried to tell me what he was like, and I didn't really believe you. I'm just sad."

Hammer sighed. "I'm sure it's hard to accept."

Raine rubbed at her forehead. "Yeah. I just need…"

"What?"

"Tell us how we can set your mind at ease," Liam bade softly.

Raine sighed. "I need to bake."

"Not alone," Hammer shot back.

Liam rolled his eyes. "What he means is, if you need a bit of space, love, we'll be just a room away."

Macen gave him a dirty—but silent—glare.

"Thanks." A little frown knit her brow. "Are all the doors locked?"

"Every last one," Liam reassured.

"We've both checked. More than once. And the alarm is set."

But Liam couldn't deny his concern that simple security wouldn't keep someone as determined as River from stealing her away for long.

With a lingering kiss, Raine pushed off his lap and stood. Instantly, he missed her in his arms. Anxiety filled him. Liam had to remind himself that she needed to be in her kitchen more than he needed to clutch her fiercely.

She dropped a similar kiss on Hammer's lips. Macen tangled his fingers in her hair and seized her mouth as if he intended to throw her down on the sofa between them, strip off her clothes, and tunnel inside her. Raine opened for him, breathless, eager.

On edge, Liam waited. Sexual healing would certainly help them all…

Suddenly, Hammer stiffened and set her on her feet, away from him.

Damn it.

"Will you check on me soon?"

Liam hated the uncertainty in Raine's voice. She shouldn't feel insecure in her own home. She'd endured too much bloody trauma in the last three months. When the hell would it stop so she could heal and they could live in peace?

"Of course," he promised.

Hammer put on a smile. "Try and stop me."

"Thanks. You shouldn't worry about me. I know you will anyway, but I'll put some music on. In an hour or two, I'll be fine. River rattled me. But I won't let him scare me from living my life."

Liam believed that. Raine was a fighter. She had her vulnerable moments, but she always forged ahead.

When she disappeared into the kitchen, Hammer shot to his feet, looking as if he was barely keeping his shit together.

"Don't go after her," Liam warned.

"We should make sure the son of a bitch isn't lying in wait."

"It's empty. I cleared out all the contractors before you two reached home. I've checked the house from top to bottom. The police were here. They searched, too. Let her find her center. We need to find yours."

As Chopin drifted in from the kitchen, Hammer started pacing again. He raked his hand through his hair. "How the fuck do I do that? He almost stole her from under my nose. He could have driven her away in that black truck and I wouldn't have known until it was too late. At least the spa owner already fired that fucking greedy receptionist."

"It could have happened to either of us. If I had driven her, I would have dropped her off, too, never imagining River would be waiting inside to steal her. Don't beat yourself up. It'll do no good. Let's talk about how we protect her going forward."

Heaving a worried sigh, Macen dropped onto the sofa, elbows braced on his knees, head in his hands. "How can I help with that when I keep fucking up?"

"Ah, Macen… Don't blame yourself. We need to stay strong and together. If we don't, we'll only compromise her safety."

"I know. I'd feel better if we had some information about this fucker, but Seth has suddenly disappeared. According to his assistant, he grabbed his 'go' bag early this morning and told her he'd check in when he could. She has no idea how long before he surfaces."

That explained why Seth hadn't answered his mobile when Liam had called earlier. "Is he working on a case?"

"I guess. She didn't know which one."

Liam hoped Seth turned up soon, but until then, they would manage. "Have you called Beck?"

At that, Hammer managed a bit of a smile. "He's taking Heavenly to lunch. Again."

"For the third time this week? It's only Wednesday." Liam had to grin, as well. "I'll bet he hasn't so much as kissed her."

"Not yet. He was bitching about the"—he cleared his throat—"lack of contact yesterday."

Liam loved that delicious irony. "Ah, there is a god."

Hammer chuckled. "So the sexually frustrated doctor will be here shortly."

"I'll enjoy that." Liam listened to the banging of bowls and the clanging of spoons, soothed by the sounds, inhaling the wafting cinnamon scent of Raine's baking. "What do we do, Macen? Hire bodyguards?"

"I don't care how qualified someone else is, they can be bought off. I don't trust a stranger with Raine's safety."

Liam agreed completely. "I doubt she would even tolerate it."

"Good point."

"She's a wee thing but her temper can be fearsome."

"You got that right, brother." Hammer sighed. "What a cluster-fuck. I think you two better start spending your days at the club. It's more secure, especially now that we know who we're looking for. River won't get in again."

"That will slow the remodeling around the house, but with the kitchen mostly done, Raine will be patient about the rest."

"She'll have to be."

It was Liam's turn to pace. "I've got to tell you, I'm beginning to feel as if the pin is out of the grenade and I'm just waiting for the next explosion."

"Don't fucking ask what else could go wrong."

"Not saying a word." Liam shook his head. "At least we've got Valentine's Day to look forward to tomorrow. Would you mind picking up Raine's gift while you're out?"

"You sure you don't want to? It was your idea, man. Your design. I'll get her some flowers and chocolate, I guess. Pregnant women like chocolate, right?"

Liam rolled his eyes. Macen might have fucked his way through half of Los Angeles, but he was clueless about romance. "I intended the gift to be from both of us, something special for our first Valentine's Day with our girl. After all, she'll be the mother of our baby come August. We have to show her how much we love her."

"You already bought her a goddamn house. Maybe I should buy her a new car or…" He tossed his hands in the air and gaped at Liam. "Jesus, man. I don't have a fucking clue."

"I hadn't noticed." Liam snorted. "I'm sure she'd appreciate the sentiment, but since she won't be driving herself anywhere—at least not while River is lurking—a new car seems pointless. But I wouldn't mind you buying me one."

"Oh, fuck off. You've got money. Buy your own damn car."

Liam flipped him off. "You can find something else to add to the gift if you like. I want you to feel as if it's from us both."

The ringing of Macen's mobile cut into their conversation. He yanked it from his pocket and frowned at the screen. "It's Dean Gorman."

"The cop?" He was a member of Shadows and had helped them through the investigation the dark morning Raine had been in Bill's clutches.

"Yeah. Maybe he's got information." Macen pressed the button to power the speakerphone. "Hi, Dean."

"Hey, Hammer. Liam there with you?"

"We're both here," Liam answered. "Got any news?"

"Raine's brother is at the precinct. The captain is interrogating the shit out of him now."

Relief deluged Liam, and he exhaled a burst of tension. Beside him, Hammer did the same, a smile slowly spreading from ear to ear. Liam followed suit as they high-fived each other.

"Where did they catch the bastard?" Hammer demanded.

"Well, they—" A chime pealed in the background, and Dean swore. "Shit. Armed robbery in progress. I'll call you back."

The line went dead, but Liam didn't care. "River is behind bars. That's bloody brilliant! Let's hope the wanker gets what's coming to him. Why don't we tell our girl?"

"That he won't be scaring the shit out of her again any time soon? Absolutely."

Hammer crossed the living room and shoved into the kitchen. Liam followed, inhaling a sweet, spiced scent. His stomach rumbled. Based on the smell, Raine had baked them something wonderful.

Suddenly, Macen halted in his tracks, a dead stop just inside the portal.

Liam barely managed to keep himself from plowing into his friend's back. "What the…"

When he glanced around Hammer's shoulder, Raine knelt near the door, holding a plate of warm snickerdoodle cookies—and not wearing a stitch. Liam nearly swallowed his tongue. She blinked up at them, her expression imploring. A sensual electronica tune, punctuated by chanting and panting, hung in the air like an unspoken seduction.

"Something sweet, gentlemen?" She batted her lashes their way.

"Oh, fuck," Hammer murmured under his breath.

"If you're offering, I'd love to. Liam, you…in?" Raine sent him a bewitching smile.

"Hell yes." He peeled off his coat and reached for his belt. He'd been waiting for this moment forever.

Their girl was smart. She had listened to every word of advice he'd given her after their unfinished breakfast the other morning. She was taking charge. Normally, the Dom in him would object. But Hammer needed the encouragement—and the orgasm with their girl. Frankly, he could use one himself.

Macen grabbed the plate of cookies from her hands and chucked it onto a nearby counter. Then he bent and wrapped his hands around her still-small waist, lifting her onto the island in the middle of the room. He shoved her legs apart, stepped between them, and grabbed her face in his hands. "What the hell are you doing?"

"Trying to get your attention. Is it working?" She bit her lip and began unbuttoning Hammer's shirt.

Liam watched his friend. One little shove and he'd tip over.

"Why?" Hammer demanded.

"Because I want you and I miss you. And when you two touch me, I feel safe. Nothing that happened to me today was your fault. Don't think it was."

He pulled away and swallowed hard. "I didn't protect you."

"You did everything except hold my hand and help me across the street like a two-year-old. Hammer, you can't plan for crazy."

"I have to! River made it clear that if I don't, you could be gone."

"Easy, mate. He's in police custody now." Liam calmed Hammer with a pat on the back, then glanced Raine's way. "That's what we came to tell you, love."

"That's good...I guess." She looked relieved but sad on her brother's behalf.

"I'm sorry it came to this," Liam offered.

"I'm not. He's getting what he deserves." Hammer held her close. "Why would you think otherwise?"

"He tried to abduct me, and I know that's how you see it. But I think he actually believed he was protecting me."

Liam gave her a skeptical glance. "Or he's as mad as Bill. But let's not talk about him now. Come here to me." Liam cupped the back of Raine's head and planted a kiss on her waiting lips, lingering to savor her sweetness before he bent to her ear. "Good girl."

When he pulled back, she gave him a conspiratorial wink.

Hammer still looked torn. "Are you really ready for this? For us?"

"Macen, our wee wench is naked, pregnant, lusciously ripe, and begging to be devoured. I say we feast." He tossed off his shirt and yanked down his zip.

Hammer still hesitated, studying Raine intently.

She thrust her hands on her hips. "Macen Daniel Hammerman, if you don't lose the pants and put your cock inside me somewhere in the next two minutes, I'm going to hurt you."

Liam couldn't hold back a belly-shaking chuckle as he stepped out of his trousers. "I think she's made herself clear, mate."

For a moment, Hammer gaped at her like he didn't know who she was. Then decision crossed his face and he snapped out of his haze.

"If that's what you want..." He tore at his shirt. "It's so fucking on, little girl."

There was the Hammer they knew and loved. The man needed to

stop thinking with his guilt and reconnect with Raine. She yearned for the reassurance of his passion and love. This would be good for them all.

Liam hung back and watched Raine skim her palms up Macen's chest and curl them around his shoulders, helping him slide the shirt to the floor. "Promise?"

He unfastened his belt, then ripped into his slacks, his zipper a seductive hiss. "That you'll be satisfied and sore before we're through with you? Oh, yeah."

"Exactly," Liam added.

With a come-hither smile, she leaned back on the island, braced her heels on the edge, and spread her legs. "I can't wait."

He turned to Hammer and stroked her thigh. "Our girl can be more than a mite persuasive when she's a mind to."

"No shit." Hammer dropped his pants and lunged between Raine's legs, naked and more than ready. He teased her opening with the tip of his hard cock. "Be careful what you wish for…"

"Whatever you dish out, I'll take and happily beg for more." Her voice had turned throaty.

Liam couldn't wait anymore. "Fuck her, Macen."

"My pleasure." Hammer enveloped her hips in his big hands.

Impatiently, he lifted her, pulling her down onto his cock in one hard stroke. She arched, her head falling back with a gasp, fingers clinging to his meaty biceps. They looked striking together—Hammer so big and dark and rough, Raine so small and fair and lovely.

Clenching his teeth and digging his fingers tighter into Raine, Hammer pivoted her around on the rectangular island to lay her flat on the granite, palming his way to her breast while he thrust deep. "You feel me?"

"Yes." Her head fell over the edge with a cry.

Restless need burned through Liam's veins, shooting straight to his cock.

Macen sent him a wolfish stare. "You want to keep that sassy mouth busy?"

"Fuck. Of course I do."

"Pull her hair. Give her something to scream about."

Liam thrust his fingers into the dark silk of her mane and tugged just the way she liked it. "Open, wench."

She eagerly parted her lips, eating him up with her hungry eyes. Liam counted his lucky stars as he guided her head toward his aching cock and slid into her mouth with a guttural groan. Her tongue curled around the crest, teasing his most sensitive spots. The girl had learned him well. Pleasure rolled around his shaft and tore its way up his spine before he shuddered in carnal bliss.

As he glanced down her body, Hammer dragged in and out of her pussy, toying with her clit. Together, they listened to her muffled gasps and whimpers while they watched her writhe and burn between them.

Liam shoved in farther, probing her throat as she worked him over. "Oh, fuck. Love…"

"It's been too long, precious. God yes. Squeeze me with that little pussy. Hmm… And every time I fuck you harder, you suck him down deeper."

Hammer slammed into her again. Raine wrapped her sleek legs around him. Liam cradled her head and thrust even farther inside. She keened out. He picked up the pace as he shuttled rhythmically over her tongue in hot, urgent strokes. How the hell was he going to last?

"Sweet jesus, Raine. I swear you suck away all my self-control."

"She's damn good at that," Hammer gritted out. "It's every bit as hard to resist this cunt. Damn… We're not going to make it to the bedroom."

Liam shook his head. "I can't let go of her that long."

"Doesn't matter. We'll fuck her again there, too."

"That we will." Liam immersed himself again in her sinful mouth, surging ever closer to ecstasy.

Then his ear began to itch. An annoying tickle at first, and he absently scratched it. But it spread to his lobe, then burst with heat that tingled and burned.

Liam knew that feeling—and precisely what it meant.

He pulled out of Raine's mouth with an incredulous jerk. "Oh, bloody fucking hell. This can't be happening."

Hammer let loose a long, low growl of pleasure. "Yeah, it can. We're goddamn amazing together."

Raine blinked at him, eyes glassy, lips swollen. "What's wrong?"

It was all Liam could do not to heed his screaming cock, but the itch in his ear flared to a blistering heat. "Get dressed, both of you. Where the fuck are my pants?"

"What? No!" Hammer protested. "Screw that. This is getting really good and—"

"My ear is on fire."

"Your ear? What the—" Hammer gaped. "Oh… Now? Are you fucking kidding me? How long have we got?"

"Not long enough." He glanced at Raine with regret. "Maybe two minutes."

Hammer swore an ugly streak and pulled free of her body.

"Hey!" Raine sat up, looking between the two of them with a scowl. "What is going on? Come back here! What does your ear have to do with your cock, Liam?"

Neither man answered. Hammer hopped into his pants and scanned the room for her sundress.

"Have you two lost your minds? Pregnant woman with needs here!"

Macen found her clothes and tossed them her way. "Put your dress on."

"Not until one of you explains." She slid off the counter and planted her hands on her hips, stark naked. "What's wrong with you guys?"

Hammer shouldered into his shirt, glaring Liam's way. "He has something to tell you."

As he scowled at Macen, Liam's fingers flew up his buttons. "Thanks for throwing me under the bus. Hell of a best mate you are."

"I told you, you should have already come clean about this shit. And we're going to have a conversation about timing. Motherfucker…" He pushed his way out of the kitchen.

"There'd better be a good explanation for this, Liam O'Neill. I was close and—"

"I'm sorry." He tugged at his burning ear.

He almost didn't want to look at Raine. She was confused and angry…and he'd run out of time to fess up. But damn it, she also stood naked and rosy pink in front of him. Liam wished like hell he had a few more minutes to lose himself in her softness.

Instead, he grabbed her dress from her fist and fumbled for the hem, thrusting it over her head and down her curves.

"Stop! I can do that myself." She batted his hands away. "If you don't tell me what's going on right now, you will absolutely be sorry."

He raked a hand through his hair and tugged on his singed lobe. "Where are your knickers?"

"I wasn't wearing any."

Normally, he would applaud that.

"Murphy's fucking law." Liam closed his eyes, pondering the distance between the kitchen and their bedroom. There was no way she'd have time to run upstairs and grab a pair now. He knew that for certain when his ear twitched and tingled painfully again.

"What are you talking about?" she insisted, then gasped. "Your ear is beet red. Did something bite it? Let me look…"

A scrap of white silk caught Liam's attention. With a curse, he shoved her bra in the nearest drawer, on top of the silverware. "You know I love you, right? Remember when I mentioned my six sisters? Well—"

The doorbell rang. He'd run out of time.

"Oh, Liam, it's for you," Hammer hollered from the family room.

Liam shoved his way out of the kitchen with a frustrated growl. His cock ached, and he doubted he'd be getting relief for that anytime soon. His wait would, no doubt, depend on how long Raine relegated him to the doghouse.

"Bastard," he snarled at Hammer.

"I'll be happy to hand you back that shit shovel, too."

"Why can't Hammer get the door? Who is it? Did you know we were having company and forget to tell me?" Raine followed, tugging on Liam's sleeve. "Oh, god. Are you saying your sisters are here?" Her eyes went wide with panic. "I need to put on makeup, change, find some damn underwear. I'm not even wearing a bra."

She finger-combed her hair, horrified, and he didn't have the heart to tell her his sisters would be the easy lot to handle.

"No, love." He sighed tiredly. "We'll talk soon. For now, come hold my hand and smile."

Liam marched to the entryway, dragging her behind. He planted his palm against the door, inhaling roughly and looking for fortitude. But he was only delaying the inevitable.

Hell, maybe he shouldn't be so gloom and doom. Maybe this was a good sign.

That hope firmly in place, he pasted on a happy face and yanked the portal open. "Hello, Mum."

"Mom?" Raine squeaked beside him, then tore her hand from his and smoothed her rumpled dress.

Behind them, he sensed Hammer's silent laughter.

His mother gazed his way with a slight tsk as she stepped in the house. "Hello, Liam, darling."

Dutifully, he hugged his mother and kissed her cheek. Yeah, he shouldn't have put off calling her to say that he'd moved, started a new relationship, and now had a baby on the way. But then again, he shouldn't have to explain.

His father strolled in with a wry smile and gave him a hearty hug. "Hello, son."

Liam slapped his back. "Da. It's good to see you." Really, it was. His father was his best hope for sanity. "I suppose I don't have to ask what brings you here." Liam reached for his wee wench's hand. "This is—"

"Raine." His mother beamed at her. "How nice to finally meet you. I've been waiting for years to have another daughter." She shot Liam a dainty glare. "Not that my son has bothered to tell me anything. But never mind that." She pulled Raine in for a hug. "So happy I am to clap eyes on the woman who's tied my boyo in knots."

"She's not the one doing the tying, Mum," Liam drawled. "As you well know."

Behind him, Hammer chuckled.

Raine's jaw dropped and she turned twenty shades of red. "Liam! Oh, my... I'm not... I mean—"

"It's all right. You love him, lass. And Liam adores you. Hammer, too. However you three choose to express that is up to you."

Raine looked somewhere between speechless and wishing the earth would swallow her whole. "How do you..."

"Know?" Mum smiled. "Don't be embarrassed. You and I will be very close. You'll see." His mother placed a hand on Raine's belly. "And the babe! Such a thrill... Would you like to know the gender? Who the father is?"

"No," he and Hammer both said in unison.

"Focus, my love," his father suggested.

"You're right." She smiled at Raine. "I'm Bryn, by the way."

"Nice to meet you. Liam didn't tell me you were coming. I would have cooked a nice dinner, been more presentable, and…"

His wee wench was embarrassed. She shot him a glare that warned he might not get any dog food in his doghouse. He likely wouldn't be getting any help with his bone.

"Oh, don't blame him. He didn't know I meant to visit until his ear started itching, I'll bet."

Raine looked completely confused. "So he didn't mention me but told you about the baby?"

"No." His mother smiled. "But he can't keep much from me."

Raine stared as if she had no idea how to interpret that comment. Something else Liam knew he'd have to explain later.

Bryn held a hand out behind her. "Duncan, come meet the girl I've been telling you about. Isn't she lovely?"

Rolling a suitcase in one hand, his father held out the other to Raine. He winked and gave her a beaming grin. "Ah, aren't you the bonniest thing I've seen in a long time. Come give me a hug, then."

Raine's expression had morphed from confused to overwhelmed.

"Mum. Da…" Liam groaned and took Raine's hand again, trying to reassure her. "This isn't a good time."

His mother scoffed. "How long did you expect me to stay away? You should have told her about the family by now."

"You're not exactly easy to explain."

"If I waited for you to ring me, this babe would be out of nappies." She huffed before bustling closer to Hammer. "And Macen. I've been looking forward to seeing you again for so long. And we'll finally be family! Come here and give me a squeeze. You get more handsome every time I see you."

"Bryn, you sweet woman." Hammer picked her up and dropped a kiss on her cheek. "How the hell have you been?"

"Quite well. I'm sorry for all you've been through. The years have been difficult, to be sure. But it was all for the best." She gave him an empathetic smile. "I did try to warn you…"

"You did." Hammer pursed his lips together, then turned to Liam's father, giving him a hearty handshake. "Duncan, it's good to see you. Your timing might have been better."

His dad smiled. "Bryn mentioned that. Sorry."

"Um, I didn't mean to be rude." Raine looked utterly rattled as she extended a hand toward the couch. "Would you like to sit down, Mr. and Mrs. O'Neill? Can I get you a drink?"

Mum shook her head. "That's not why we've come, lass. And there's no time for that now."

"Oh. All right. Well…did you have a good trip? Where did you come from?"

"Liam's told you nothing?" Mum glared. "That scamp. We came from Ireland, of course."

Raine blinked, then frowned his way. Yeah, she had a lot of questions he'd better answer soon.

"Hey! So you saw the stragglers I found at the airport," a familiar voice said as he appeared in the doorway, another massive suitcase in hand.

Liam whirled. "Seth?"

He grinned slyly. "When your mom called me to say they'd be flying through New York on their way to see you and that I should come along, I decided…what the hell. If I'm going to fall off into the ocean, this is a hell of a place to go."

"Thanks for the heads-up, mate."

Seth grinned. "Your mom said you'd know she was coming."

He had—at the worst possible time.

"You're a good boy." Bryn patted Seth's shoulder. "A tragic past, sadly. But the best is coming. You'll see."

Seth just smiled and moved in to hug Raine. "You doing okay with these two lugs?"

"Right now, I might be ready to leave them for you." She rolled her eyes.

"Nope. I knew her first. After all, the princess and I have already scened together." Beck chuckled and slanted a glance Raine's way as he stepped through the door. "Haven't we?"

"That's not what I'd call it." Raine shook her head. "And you're never touching me again."

"You should both bugger off and leave our girl alone." Liam poked at the pair. "Mum, Da, I'd like you to meet a good friend of ours, Dr. Kenneth Beckman. Beck, my parents, Bryn and Duncan."

"It's a pleasure to meet—"

"Kenneth, dear. I've been waiting to meet you," Bryn cut him off with an excited coo. "So full of secrets... But you're not nearly as scary as you want everyone to believe. Well, come on, then. Give us a kiss."

As Bryn bustled closer, Beck gaped in silence. For once, the man had no snappy comeback.

"It's all right," Hammer assured, slapping Beck on the back. "That just means she likes you."

Still looking shell-shocked, he bent and quickly pecked Bryn on the cheek.

"Lovely." Bryn wasn't smiling anymore. "Now, then... You're all here for a reason. I'm sorry I've no more time to explain, but it's important you understand you're family to one another, whether you're blood or not. You've trouble ahead, and each and every one of you has a role to play during these tough times. Seth and Kenneth, you'll be essential. And Liam, dear, follow your da's example. He taught you well."

So his mother had come for some reason other than the baby. Damn it all.

Liam rubbed at the back of his neck. "Sit down and tell us more."

"No time for that. I hated to barge in on you earlier, but I'm afraid I've waited too long as it is." To his surprise, his mother looked Hammer's way. "Macen, brace yourself."

Hammer froze. "Oh, shit."

Liam went rigid with dread. "Mum, don't. We can't take any more. We've been through too much, and we've got a baby on the way."

Bryn made a beeline for Raine, wrapping an arm around his lass's delicate shoulders. "No matter what happens next, you mustn't blame yourself. None of this is your fault."

"*Mo grá*, ease off," Duncan suggested. "You're scaring everyone, especially wee Raine."

"I'm only here to help," Bryn assured. "She'll see that soon enough."

"What trouble is coming?" Hammer sidled closer, his face grave.

"How does she know there's trouble? Would someone please tell me what's going on?" Raine demanded.

"Of course Liam didn't explain that, either." Bryn slanted another chastising stare his way. "Well, dear, I'm fey."

Raine blinked. "You're not a fairy."

"No, dear. We're psychic. It runs in the family..." She sent Liam a pointed stare. "When everyone remembers their gifts."

He shook his head. "Mum, don't..."

"Sorry, son." She turned to Hammer. "Macen, dear. Call your lawyer and do it now."

Fear gripped Liam's gut. "Lawyer?"

Hammer turned ashen. "Why?"

Suddenly, she sighed with regret. "I'm sorry. Time has run out."

Right on cue, the doorbell rang.

"ANSWER IT, MACEN," Bryn said softly. "It's for you."

The gravity in her tone made Hammer's gut tighten with dread. He darted a glance at both Liam and Raine. She still looked a bit confused, but dread racked Liam's face.

With a curse, Hammer clenched his jaw and pulled the door open.

Two uniformed officers stood on the porch. "Mr. Hammerman?"

He reared back, confusion needling his brain. What were the police doing here? He had no other family they could report as dead. Had there been a break-in at the club? Or had River somehow escaped custody?

"I'm Macen Hammerman. What can I do for you?"

"We need you to come with us to answer some questions."

He scowled. "About what?"

"We'll explain at the station."

That made him wary. "Legally, I don't have to answer questions."

"True, but you can either come with us voluntarily or we can make this official and arrest you."

Hammer's heart stuttered. "For what?"

The officer looked at him in disgust. "Kidnapping, rape, sodomy, and oral copulation with a minor, pimping, human trafficking... Do I need to go on?"

The ground beneath Macen crumbled. Shock and panic deluged him. This was *not* happening.

River. The motherfucking prick had given the cops his "proof," whatever that was. Hammer noticed the officers weren't calling Liam a rapist, so this must have something to do with the fact that he'd taken Raine in as a minor.

"No!" Raine exploded. "None of that is true. There's been a mis-understanding. A mistake!"

Hammer blessed her for wanting to save him, but he feared it wouldn't help now.

He turned a grim expression Liam's way. "Call Sterling Barnes. Have him meet me at the station."

"I'm on it, man." His friend looked pale and worried.

"River did this." Raine rushed to the door and faced the cops. "Whatever my brother is saying, it isn't true. I'm the supposed victim, but I swear I'm here of my own free will. I always have been. Don't take Hammer away when he's done nothing wrong."

"Everything will be sorted out at the station," the officer assured dispassionately. "Mr. Hammerman, if you'll come with us?"

Macen gave the cop a curt nod, then settled a tender gaze on Raine. "It'll be okay, precious. Don't worry. I'll be back home in no time."

"He will be," Bryn assured.

Raine wrapped her arms around Hammer's chest. "Let me come with you. I'll fix this. I'll tell them—"

"No." Hammer cupped her face and gazed into her eyes. "No need for you to be interrogated. I'll sort this out and see you soon."

"But—"

Hammer slanted his lips over hers and silenced her with a hard kiss. He breathed in her scent and clutched her soft, lush body while imprinting every one of her subtle nuances on his heart. "I love you."

Tears filled her eyes. "I love you."

He turned away and squared his shoulders. Whatever evidence River had presented might look damning, but Hammer was prepared to fight any allegations with his last, dying breath.

As the cops led him toward their patrol car, Raine rushed from the house with Liam by her side. "I'll find that asshole brother of mine and make him fix this."

Hammer spun; fear warred with anger. "I don't want you anywhere near that son of a bitch." He pinned Liam with a silent demand. "Do not let her even talk to that sack of shit."

"I'll take care of our girl." Liam pulled his cell phone from his pants pocket. "Ringing up your lawyer now, mate. No worries."

"Absolutely none," Hammer lied for Raine's benefit, then climbed into the back of the cruiser.

The officers locked him in the backseat. Through the grimy window, he looked back at the two people he loved most and the house they shared, wondering if anything would ever be the same again.

Concern flattened Liam's mouth into a tight line. He held Raine, who wore every worry on her pale face. As the car sped away, he couldn't take his gaze off them.

Especially when Raine's eyes slid shut and she collapsed in Liam's arms.

CHAPTER SIX

A MOUNTAIN OF anxiety suffocated Hammer as he waited in the precinct's cold, empty interview room. He struggled to tamp down his anger and project a cool veneer of indifference. This wasn't his first rodeo, so he wasn't about to let the pricks watching his every move behind the two-way glass see him sweat. But inside, he felt the earth shifting beneath his feet in a landslide of shit.

Kidnapping, rape, sodomy and oral copulation with a minor, pimping, human trafficking... If this didn't go well, Hammer knew he could go down for life.

Ignoring the authorities' prying eyes, he pulled out his cell phone, desperate for an update about Raine. After they'd watched her collapse in Liam's arms, the bastards driving the squad car had refused to stop so he could see if she was all right. Thankfully, Liam had already assured Hammer that their girl was fine. Emotional distress had merely gotten the better of her for a moment. Still, Hammer wouldn't rest easy until he was back home with her in his arms. But now, he could only wait.

For someone to stroll into the room and grill him.

For his lawyer, Sterling Barnes, to slide into the chair beside him and keep this interrogation from going south.

For some resolution to this shit storm.

Macen wished he and Liam had throttled River Kendall when they'd had the chance. Whatever the son of a bitch's circumstantial evidence was, it must be incriminating as hell.

Since even the truth would look damning, Hammer had to hope that mercy and justice would prevail.

He wanted to pace but remained seated, staring at a fixed point on the table in front of him. It tested his control, but if he gave the goons on the other side of the glass any indication he was going stir crazy, they would only isolate him longer, try to unhinge him.

When the door finally opened, two plainclothes detectives entered, one tall and thin, the other short and balding. Hammer quickly sized them up. No-nonsense types. Good, he wasn't in the mood to play games.

"Macen Daniel Hammerman?" the taller detective asked with a cordial smile.

"Yes?"

"I'm Detective Winslow. This is Detective Cameron. Thank you for coming in so promptly."

"I wasn't aware I had a choice," Hammer drawled.

The balding man, Cameron, smirked.

"As a formality, I need to read you your rights," Winslow advised. "And inform you that this interview will be recorded."

While they Mirandized him, everything suddenly became terribly real. But Hammer mentally drew up his armor, refusing to let fear claw into him.

"Do you understand these rights I have just read to you?" Winslow asked.

"I do."

"With these rights in mind, do you wish to speak with us, Mr. Hammerman?"

"Sure. Why not?" He shrugged nonchalantly.

After the detectives recorded the usual preliminary jargon on tape, Winslow pulled out a stack of notes from a satchel.

"Let's cut to the chase, gentlemen. What is it you want to know?" Hammer prompted.

"I understand you own a private sex club called Shadows. Is that correct?"

"Not precisely, Detective Winslow. It's not a sex club, but a private BDSM club. There's a big difference."

"But members do have sex at your establishment, correct?" Cameron asked with a lewd gleam in his eyes.

"If all participants are consenting and no one is at risk, it's allowed. Come by sometime and see for yourself."

"No, thanks. I don't need to beat my wife so she'll sleep with me," Cameron patronized.

"Let's move on," Winslow directed. "Do you know a woman by the name of Raine Elise Kendall?"

His gut tightened. "Yes."

"And what exactly is your relationship with her?"

"Why?"

"Because your last six years with her are pertinent to our investigation," Winslow answered. "Some rather disturbing information has been brought to our attention that could result in your arrest."

Thanks so much, River, you fucking asswipe.

"Such as?" Hammer slowly clenched his jaw.

"Don't play dumb," Cameron sneered. "The officers who brought you in already advised you of some of the possible charges. You know, those pesky kidnapping, human trafficking, statutory rape, extortion allegations… There's more if that's not ringing a bell for you."

God, even more charges than they'd first mentioned.

Hammer steeled himself. Six years ago, he'd taken Raine in from the alley behind his club, fully aware how his gesture would look to the outside world and that he could be prosecuted as a sex offender for doing nothing more than helping an abused girl find safety. But as the years had gone on, that possibility had grown distant. It certainly had been the furthest thing from his mind two hours ago when he'd been in the kitchen with Liam, balls deep inside Raine. He'd been sure of his future then, in command of his destiny, wrapped in love, believing that his biggest problems were all in his head.

In a matter of seconds, all his bliss and hope for the future had been ripped away.

Terror pulsed in his veins. Denial screamed in his head. He began to sweat. But Hammer forced himself to gird the walls concealing his fear.

Sucking in a steadying breath, he arched a brow pointedly at Winslow. "Those are some serious allegations. Obviously, someone has made erroneous assumptions about my relationship with Ms. Kendall." Hammer waved his hand dismissively. "What evidence do you have to substantiate such absurdity?"

"Plenty," Cameron sneered. "You wanted to cut to the chase, Mr. Hammerman. Let's do that. We know that when Ms. Kendall was a minor, you bought and paid for her, like some pet you had bred for your pleasure. After her shit-sack father sold her to you, you moved her in to that club with you and raped her. You like having sex with little girls?"

"I've never had any sexual contact with a minor." Hammer didn't elaborate. Anything could be twisted to incriminate him.

Winslow continued. "According to our investigation, you also kept her prisoner at Shadows, pimping her out to guests and friends. Was Mr. O'Neill one of them? You all live together now. Isn't that right?"

Cameron leaned close and pinned Hammer with a lecherous gaze. "Then again, this wouldn't be the first time you two shared pussy."

Hammer itched to reach across the table and rip the detective's head off. Instead, he gave the man a brittle smile. "Sounds like you've already made your mind up. I'm through answering questions until my lawyer arrives."

"Yeah. You should definitely lawyer up, pal," Cameron spat.

The pair left. After an interminable twenty minutes, Sterling Barnes walked through the door. The detectives were right behind him.

"Gentlemen, I'd like some time to confer with my client," Sterling announced.

After the dipshidiot duo left the room again, Hammer turned to his lawyer, dying to speak.

Sterling shook his head. "We're still being recorded."

"I know." Hammer reeled off the litany of charges LA's finest wanted to level against him. "I've never committed any of those crimes."

"If they had anything concrete, they would have already arrested, booked, and processed you. Let them finish their questioning, but don't answer unless I nod. Maybe we can skate through this shit without getting our socks dirty."

"Fine." Hammer swallowed. "Let's get this over with."

Sterling spoke at the mirror. "We're ready to begin, gentlemen."

Seconds later, Winslow and Cameron returned.

The tall one started in first. "When did you first meet Ms. Kendall?"

Sterling nodded.

Six and a half years ago. Friday, August eleventh. "I don't recall exactly."

"Where did you meet her?"

Hiding in the alley behind Shadows. "I don't recall that, either."

"How old was she?" Cameron demanded.

Sterling intervened. "You've basically answered that. Don't repeat yourself."

Hammer just smiled. "Next?"

Winslow narrowed his eyes. "How old was she the first time you took her to bed?"

His lawyer shook his head at that question, too.

Last November fourth, three short months ago. God, he'd wanted her for so long. "Can we step this up? I'd like to go home."

But that wasn't happening anytime soon. The hours ticked by like days, and it seemed as if there was no end in sight. Hammer soon realized the two officers wouldn't be satisfied until they'd nailed him to the wall.

"In a rough estimation, Mr. Hammerman, how many sex partners would you say you've had in the last…oh, I don't know…since your wife committed suicide?"

"Irrelevant to the charges, Winslow." Sterling shook his head in disgust. "Don't answer that, Macen."

"Was your late wife younger than you, Mr. Hammerman? Was she the first child you molested?" Cameron quipped.

"I already told you, I've never had sexual contact with a minor." Even when he'd been a minor himself, he'd seduced grown women left and right. But clearly these two clowns thought they were going to mindfuck him. Amateurs. "I was a year older than Juliette. She was twenty when we married. But I think it's interesting you assume I had a child bride. Do your questions stem from your own personal experience?"

Cameron sent Macen an arctic glare. "You and your late wife didn't have children? Not even a little girl for you to practice on?"

"Why would you think that?" Hammer quizzed. "Is that what you do with your daughters?"

Sterling cleared his throat. "We're all quite aware that Mr. Hammerman has no dependents."

"Well, none that have been born yet," Winslow added with a sly smile. "Rumor is, Ms. Kendall is pregnant."

"How many times did you have to force her to have sex with you before she conceived? Or did your pal, O'Neill, knock her up? I bet you're holding out hope for a little girl so you can repeat the cycle," Cameron jabbed.

"That isn't even a viable question," Barnes objected.

"What types of sexual acts do you most often engage in, Mr. Hammerman?" Winslow asked. "Strictly the ménage à trois? Or is Ms. Kendall a third to your homosexual relationship with Mr. O'Neill? Are you an equal-opportunity kind of pervert?"

When Winslow succumbed to Cameron's level of character assassination, Hammer felt as if he'd scored a victory. In fact, he couldn't help but chuckle as Sterling laid his hand on Hammer's arm and shook his head.

"I think they only brought me here to ask about my sex life because theirs are lacking," Macen drawled.

"At the moment, that's how it sounds," his lawyer agreed before turning his attention to the two detectives. "If you're quite finished wasting my client's time, we'll leave now so you can utilize this room for real criminals."

"Not yet." Winslow smiled and pulled out a stack of papers from a nearby file folder before spreading them over the table like a deck of cards.

Hammer went cold.

He recognized his own handwriting instantly. Each page represented a copy of a money order he'd written to Bill Kendall to stay the fuck away from Raine. Over six years' worth of payments stared him in the face.

He could imagine exactly how this would be construed, and he struggled to think of a plausible explanation. Even the truth could land him in prison.

Hammer's guts twisted. His heart raced.

"These money orders look familiar?" Winslow taunted, his eyes lighting up like a cat ready to devour a mouse. "All summed, it's a hundred and fifty thousand dollars. What could a man like Bill Kendall possibly possess that would entice you to pay him such a large sum of money? His daughter, perhaps?"

Macen felt as if the walls were closing in around him. The air thinned. His suit suddenly felt tight. Even his skin seemed to shrink, as if he needed to shed it like a snake. He reached up and loosened his tie.

"As your attorney, I'm advising you to ignore that question, too."

"Good, I'd rather not dignify it with an answer," Hammer countered.

"What were you paying Bill Kendall for, Mr. Hammerman?" Winslow pressed. "A nice, juicy virgin?"

"Obviously, you know the going rate. I don't have a clue since I'm not in the habit of buying sex partners." Macen ground his teeth together.

"Was he blackmailing you?" Cameron tossed out. "I'll bet Bill Kendall was holding all your immoral and unnatural proclivities over your head."

"You mean because he was such a fine, upstanding citizen himself?" Macen couldn't resist. "If you discount the fact that he raped and murdered his wife and one of his own daughters…"

"Hammer…" Barnes warned.

"No worries, Sterling. I thought I had a pretty open view of sexuality, but these two? Wow. Buying juicy virgins for the purpose of forced sex and breeding? And I'm the pervert here? Their fantasies are way more twisted than mine." Hammer leveled a flat stare at the two officers. "I guess working in Vice has given you some ideas over the years. What other non-consensual shit do you get your rocks off with, boys?"

Ignoring his volley, Winslow scowled. "Did you arrange for Bill Kendall to kidnap his own daughter so that Ms. Kendall could kill him in 'self-defense' and you wouldn't have to pay her father whatever else you owed him?"

Hammer couldn't help but blink at the absurdity of the question. "Dig out your own police reports, gentlemen. One of your peers labeled him a sexual predator and killer. I wouldn't have put a flea in his path."

"How much money did you still owe him?" Cameron pressed.

"Hammer," Sterling cautioned.

Seething, Macen breathed through his anger to keep his shit together. This fucking game was pissing him off. "I'm worth eight figures, gentlemen. If I paid him anything, I assure you two thousand dollars a month would hardly motivate me to plot such a ridiculously convoluted murder."

"Are those all the questions you have?" Sterling interceded.

"Just one more thing." Winslow smirked. "Mr. Hammerman might want to consider getting off his high horse, because we have an eyewitness who has corroborated that not only did Raine Kendall work at your club, but she spent nearly every night in your bed since you bought her as a minor."

Witness? Who the fuck could that lying sack be? Everyone who joined Shadows signed tight legal documents that ensured nothing happening inside the club's walls made its way to outsiders.

"In fact, the witness said you bragged about it and saw Ms. Kendall act as your domestic slave, cleaning up after you. Cooking for you." Winslow sneered. "You like apple spice muffins, don't you? We hear you controlled her bank account, too, so she couldn't leave you."

"Don't respond to that," Barnes snapped.

Macen couldn't—without the truth being twisted to make him look guilty as hell. Only those who had spent time with him knew he liked apple spice muffins and that Raine made them for him. That he controlled her bank accounts because he'd never wanted her to worry about money again.

Who could the damn Judas be?

Winslow went on. "According to our witness, you also arranged for Ms. Kendall to have a public beating at your establishment, followed by a sodomizing—all while you watched."

Hammer knew exactly which night the detective referred to. Only a member of Shadows could know about it. Someone had talked—and misrepresented everything about his relationship with Raine to suit their own purpose.

His heart raced, sputtered. He racked his brain to remember who had been there for that debacle. Who hated him enough to unleash this sort of vendetta?

He was in far deeper shit than he'd imagined.

Christ. This could not be happening. But even his body knew it was as his lungs froze, his mouth went dry, and his heart all but beat out of his chest.

The life he'd waited years to enjoy was slipping through his fingers. Liam would be left to care for Raine alone. And what about their child? Would he ever know the baby they'd conceived in love?

Damn it, he wasn't going down without a fight. "I suggest you bring in your *witness* and get your facts straight, because someone is feeding you a metric ton of bullshit."

"Trust me, Mr. Hammerman, our witness has an impeccable reputation," Winslow assured.

"Let's end this charade. Everyone in this room knows you're guilty. We've got the proof right here in black and white," Cameron growled, scattering the copies of the money orders all over the table. "Give us a statement. Plead guilty. Maybe the DA will reduce the charges he plans to file against you and you'll only go away for five to ten years. If you want to keep pretending you're a model citizen, I guarantee a jury will lock you up and throw away the key."

"I've done nothing wrong," Hammer growled. "You can take your evidence and shove it up your ass. If you're going to arrest me, then fucking do it. Otherwise, I'm done here."

"Easy," Sterling murmured.

Hammer was beyond that. If he didn't get out of this claustrophobic sweat box in the next ten seconds, he was going to come completely unhinged.

"Aside from yourself, who else had sexual relations with Ms. Kendall when she was a minor?" Winslow continued. A look of renewed vigor lightened his face. "That will count as a charge of prostitution, but we'll let you share that sentence with the other schmucks if you'll give us names."

"Stooping to psych warfare seems beneath even you, Winslow," Hammer sneered. "What makes it worse is that you suck at it."

"Oh, you're familiar with the tactic? Guess you've been in trouble far more than your records show." Winslow turned to Sterling. "Did you get him cleared of other crimes, too?"

Sterling branded the man with a scathing glare. "As my client has stated, if you're going to arrest him, do it. Otherwise, I'm taking Mr. Hammerman home."

Macen didn't wait for either detective to reply, he simply stood and headed toward the door with Sterling on his heels.

"Don't leave town, Mr. Hammerman," Winslow called out as Macen stormed from the room.

"Come on. I'll drive you home," Sterling offered. "We can discuss the particulars in the car."

Hammer was about to take the man up on his offer when Dean Gorman passed by and caught his eye, pulling out his cell phone. Striding closer to Hammer, Dean pressed it to his ear and pretended to speak into the device. "Don't look at me. We need to talk. Be in touch soon."

Following Dean's directive, Hammer kept his eyes pinned on the wall at the end of the corridor. He gave no hint of acknowledgment.

Inside, his ragged nerves twitched. What would happen next? How the hell would he stop it?

As he and Sterling rounded the corner, heading toward the front door, Beck and Seth jumped from their seats, both wearing identical looks of concern.

"How's Raine?" Hammer asked anxiously. "Is she all right?"

"Relax," Beck soothed. "She's fine. Pregnant women faint. It's nothing to worry about. How are you, man?"

"You free to go?" Seth asked, arching his brows.

"For now." Turning toward Sterling, he shook the man's hand. "Thanks for coming down. I'll swing by your office in the morning and fill you in on all the details."

"Please do. I don't much like trying to represent clients when I'm in the dark."

"Understood."

As Sterling walked away, Hammer exhaled, wishing he could blow out all his exhaustion and fear with it. "Come on, guys. We'll talk in the car. I want to get the hell out of here and back home to my girl."

For as long he could.

RAINE WRUNG HER hands as she sat in an ancient chair surrounded by ugly yellow walls and dirty, speckled linoleum, finding it hard to breathe. Beside her sat an attorney she'd met all of five minutes ago. Hammer was, even now, being questioned for crimes he hadn't committed. And they wanted to drag her in, too?

"Don't be nervous," the distinguished man nearing forty leaned over and whispered.

Calvin something. She was too rattled to recall what. He'd introduced himself with piercing eyes and the smile of a shark.

"Sterling filled me in on what he knows and—"

"I'm not a victim," she cut in. "Hammer did nothing wrong."

"Sterling indicated that you probably wouldn't give the police much to support their investigation."

"I won't help them send someone innocent—whom I love dearly—to prison."

Minutes after Macen had been taken away, more police officers had shown up and asked to question her and Liam. She was thankful that with one phone call, Sterling had arranged attorneys from another reputable law firm to meet them at the station. Because money talked, the lawyers had come running.

"You don't have to say a word, Ms. Kendall. They can't force you to answer questions."

"But I have to make them realize Hammer has never harmed me in any way."

"It's unlikely they'll drop their investigation simply because the 'victim' doesn't want to cooperate. For all we know, they have other evidence, and they're running with it. If you want to help Mr. Hammerman, then your job isn't to tell them everything. It's to *not* give them any information that might dig him a deeper hole."

"But he helped me, he rescued—"

"They don't care. As far as the detectives are concerned, he's a sex club owner in an alternative lifestyle who's behaved inappropriately with a minor in some form or fashion. They'd like to see him behind bars."

"No. That's not Macen at all. He's—"

"It doesn't matter what I think. Don't lose your cool and don't lie. If any question strays too deep into territory you think paints Mr. Hammerman in a criminal light, refuse to answer. And you don't have to say anything that incriminates yourself. If you're even remotely unsure about a question, look at me. I'll guide you."

Raine nodded. She hated being jittery. After all, she had the truth.

But that didn't stop her nerves from jangling.

A female detective summoned her a few minutes later. Raine's stomach tightened as she followed the woman into a small gray interview room. Calvin trailed behind, pulling out the chair for her when the cop bade her to sit.

"Raine Kendall?" the female asked.

She looked no-nonsense, maybe around thirty. Her long, dark hair bisected her back in a severe ponytail. She wore almost no makeup and a button-down shirt that looked just this side of masculine. With both a badge and gun strapped to her belt, she gave off an impatient, don't-fuck-with-me vibe.

And she intimidated the hell out of Raine.

"Yes."

"I'm Detective Perez. I'd like to ask you a few questions about your association with Macen Hammerman. Do you know him?"

"Yes."

"How did you two meet?"

Raine looked at the attorney. The answer to that could be so misconstrued and land Hammer in more trouble, but Calvin probably didn't know enough to realize that.

She shrugged. "I don't remember exactly."

"What's your relationship with him currently?"

Raine sorted through possible answers and tried to choose the safest. "We live together."

"You have sex with him, correct?"

"My client doesn't have to answer that," Calvin piped up.

"It's relevant to our investigation." Perez glared. "I need to establish how long Ms. Kendall has been a sex slave."

"What?" Raine rolled her eyes, really wishing everyone would stop assuming she was a victimized slut. "I'm *not* a sex slave. Hammer and I are in a committed relationship, and I'm with him of my own free will."

Perez raised a dark brow at her. "You're living with and committed to Mr. Hammerman, but you're also living with Mr. O'Neill? Having sex with him of your own free will, as well?"

Now Calvin looked every bit as annoyed as Raine felt. "My client has stated that she is not a sex slave. She is a legal adult, and who she chooses to have sex with is her business."

Raine tilted her head and tried to keep her cool. "Have you ever been married?"

The detective blinked. "Twice."

"Did you love both of your husbands?"

Perez looked at her as if the question was ridiculous. "At the time, of course."

"Then you should know exactly how it's possible to love more than one man in your lifetime. I just happen to love mine at the same time, and they're okay with that. Now, do you want to ask me real questions, or did you just bring me here to shame me?"

By her side, Calvin chuckled under his breath. "Moving on…"

The detective's face hardened. "When did you and Mr. Hammerman begin having sex?"

"If you're asking whether I was a minor, the answer is no. I was a very-much-consenting adult. If you're asking whether he ever mistreated, abused, raped, neglected, or in any way hurt me, the answer is also no."

"Did he pimp you out? Force you to have sex with himself and others? Did he make his living off your back?"

"Hell no! This is ridiculous. You clearly know nothing about either of us."

"I know you're pregnant." Perez shot her a superior glance. "Do you know who the father is?"

"No, and if not knowing was a crime, then most of the people who ever appeared on a daytime talk show would have been arrested. Macen Hammerman has done nothing except make me a happy woman. And I'll tell anyone who asks me the same thing."

Now Calvin laughed outright. "Any other questions?"

The detective scowled, and Raine had the impression these two had tangled over an interrogation before.

Perez leveled Calvin a really nasty stare. "Tons, actually." The woman tossed down stacks of paper on the table in front of Raine. "These are copies of money orders, written out to your father. Two thousand dollars a month over a span of six years. Did you know Hammerman was paying your father?"

Raine glanced at the pages, her entire body clenching tight. She recognized Hammer's handwriting, so she had to be careful. "I've never seen those before in my life."

That was the truth.

"The way I understand it, you worked for Mr. Hammerman, kept his books."

"Yes, but—"

"He wrote out a money order every month and you never saw or heard anything, despite the fact that you did his accounting?" Perez sent her a skeptical glare.

"I kept the club's records, not Hammer's personal ones. He's a private man, and I don't know everything he does. If these copies came from my father, I'd be very skeptical. He was an abusive alcoholic, murderer, and rapist, always out to make a quick buck. I don't know if these money orders are even legitimate. My father swiped some guy's checkbook once and wrote hot checks for a week when I was a kid. So the more likely scenario is that my father was extorting Hammer for money."

"Because he was having sex with an underage girl?"

"My client already stated that she did not have sex with Mr. Hammerman as a minor. Do you really need to keep treading the same ground?"

Now Perez slapped her palms on the table between them and zeroed in on Raine. "Doing some simple math, you were underage when you went to live with Mr. Hammerman at that skanky club of his, weren't you? Glare at me all you want, but you dropped out of high school at seventeen. The day you turned eighteen, you renewed your driver's license and listed Shadows as your place of residence. Mr. Hammerman's name is on every one of your bank accounts. Now you want to tell me you're not a sex slave being held against your will?"

"That's exactly what I'm telling you." Raine forced herself to stare down the detective. "None of what you just said proves anything except that I'm attached to one of the men I love."

"We have video evidence of him appearing to rape you."

Raine flipped an alarmed glance at Calvin, then remembered he didn't know anything. But she knew her passion for Hammer.

"You don't have to comment on that," the lawyer put in.

Oh, but Raine wanted to.

"I don't know what video you're talking about…" Probably club surveillance she had no idea how they would have gotten their hands on. "But what may appear like rape to you is bliss to me. I like rough sex, and that's not a crime. I consented every single time."

Perez sent her a quelling glance. "You're telling me that a fragile little thing like you enjoys being mauled by a man who's bigger, older, and far stronger?"

"Yes. It's called submission, sweetheart." Raine couldn't resist.

"So you admit you're a slave?"

"No. If you don't know the difference between a submissive and a slave, you'll never understand a word I say. I *choose* to give my power to him and I can take it back like that." She snapped her fingers, then she looked over at Calvin. "Get me out of here. I won't stay since she's not interested in any truth that doesn't crucify Hammer."

"I agree." Calvin rose and grabbed his briefcase. "Let's go."

Beside him, Raine leapt from her chair. She wanted to go home. She wanted to see Hammer and Liam. She wanted to put this shitty night behind them.

"Wait!" Perez called out, finally getting off her high horse. "Ms. Kendall, you don't have to protect Hammerman. We see victims like you all the time, manipulated by some experienced charmer who knows how to lure an innocent girl into the sex trade. What did he give you that you lacked at home? Money? Affection? Did he prey on your insecurities and make you feel pretty before he took you to bed? Before he shared you with his friends and associates?" The detective rounded the table and cupped Raine's shoulder. "Don't let him get away with this. Just say the word, and we can lock him up. He'll never hurt you—"

"Don't touch me." Raine jerked away. "And don't patronize me. You and your lurid fascination need to get a life. Hammer is an amazing man, and no matter how you try to put the most salacious slant on our relationship, we love each other, and I'll defend him with every breath. If you're looking for a witness to testify against him, it won't be me."

She didn't wait for either Calvin or Perez to reply. She jerked open the door and marched out without looking back.

At the end of the hall, she caught sight of Liam pacing, waiting for her. She ran to him and threw herself in his arms. "Are you all right?"

"Fine, love. Are you? What did they ask?"

"Terrible questions that made me out to be a spineless puppet. I lost my temper." She turned to Calvin, who had just caught up. Apprehension twisted her stomach. "I screwed that up for Hammer, didn't I?"

"No." Calvin looked like he was still laughing. "I think it's safe to say if this goes to trial, the prosecution won't be calling you to testify on their behalf."

Probably not. But Raine still worried there would be a trial, followed by a prosecution and a railroading of justice. She was terrified that Hammer was going down—and she could do nothing to stop it.

CHAPTER SEVEN

ON THE DRIVE home, Hammer bitterly recounted his interrogation to his grim-faced friends. Seth shook his head at the detectives' allegations.

"All I want to know is where to find River," Beck piped up. "I'd like to ignore my Hippocratic oath for a few hours and unleash a shitload of non-consensual pain on that cocksucker."

"Get in line," Hammer grumbled.

The rest of the ride seemed unusually quiet. Beck was never one to mince words, but after that quip, he exchanged a few glances with Seth that had Hammer frowning.

"Something else going on?" he asked them.

Seth pulled into the U-shaped driveway as dusk turned to night. He and Beck seemed to share another silent conversation.

Now Hammer was downright suspicious.

"Nope," Beck quipped. "Now…do you want to hang out in the car with us, connect to your inner vagina, and discuss your feelings? Or would you rather spend the night with Raine and Liam?"

No contest.

"Find your own vagina," Hammer shot back. "I'm going inside."

Garden lights illuminated their house. As he stared at the warm gray stucco structure, fear and what-ifs gnawed at him. His heart was behind that glossy black door, shining from those big picture windows. He ached to lock himself inside with the two people he loved most, find respite in Raine's body, and spend every moment giving her memories with Liam.

Someday, memories might be all he had left.

"Good man." Beck clapped him on the shoulder. "Call if you need us."

"But not too early. Now that I'm back in town, I plan to track down a certain luscious blonde and ask her out. If all goes as planned, I'll be soaring sweet little Heavenly to the heavens," Seth drawled.

Beck jerked around and pinned the big PI with a death glare, growling out a barely human sound somewhere between low and menacing.

Remembering the ugly, World War III-like battles he and Liam had once waged over Raine, Hammer shook his head. "Time can be short. You two should take your own advice and put Heavenly between you. Thanks for the ride."

Macen exited the car and charged into the house with long, urgent strides. Raine and Liam leapt up from the couch and rushed toward him. He crushed her in his arms and gripped his best friend's shoulder in a brotherly hold.

"You're home! Oh, thank god." Raine wouldn't let go of him.

That suited Macen just fine. He didn't want to let go of them, either. There would be time later to discuss the darkness. Right now, all he wanted was to lose himself in the love around him.

"She's been climbing the walls with worry," Liam whispered as he threaded his fingers through her inky mane. "We both have."

Hammer cradled Raine's face in his hands. "I saw you crumble from the back of the cruiser. Are you all right?"

"Fine," she assured. "Really."

Hammer kissed the top of her head, then glanced at Liam. "Thank god you were there to catch her."

"I'm glad, as well. As you see, she's fine physically. Emotionally, I think we're all a fucking mess," Liam admitted.

"Let's talk about that later," Hammer croaked, holding her tighter.

Liam took Raine's hand and gave it a squeeze. "Love, I think what Hammer needs now is you."

"No. What I need now is *us*."

Emotions lumped in his throat as he shoved down the fear that he might lose these two perfect-for-him people. He breathed Raine in, branding the solemn moment in the deepest recesses of his memory.

Just in case.

"Well, then…" Liam said. "Let's give the man what he needs."

Raine blinked up at them. Hammer sensed she was torn between talking about his interrogation and easing his strain. But she shelved it and reached around his nape to pull him down with a welcoming kiss. He covered her lips with his as she put her worry aside to help him. To serve him. To provide him her comfort, her touch, her love.

Liam stood beside him with a warm hand on his shoulder and his lips on her neck.

Their presence was the perfect balm.

They were his home.

Moments slid by. It might have been ten or a thousand. Macen only knew when he drew away from her kiss he felt calmer, almost centered again.

He drank in the tears welling in Raine's eyes. They were all too attuned not to sense one another's distress. Hammer hated like hell that his worry spilled onto them. He couldn't promise forever, but he could do his best to ease them tonight.

Hammer turned to Liam. "Where are Bryn and Duncan?"

"Sleeping off jet lag. Mum should know better than to interrupt us now. I put them in the guest room on the other side of the house, just in case."

Too far away to hear Raine's screams. Though with Bryn, sound wouldn't matter.

"So tonight is ours."

"I'd like that," Raine whispered.

Liam palmed her crown. "Let's go."

With a ragged breath, Hammer lifted Raine against his chest. She curled her arms around his neck and reached out for Liam. Their fingers entwined while Hammer led them upstairs to their bedroom.

Macen laid her on their bed, in the spill of the silvery light from the adjoining bathroom, and followed her down. Without a word, she opened herself to him, unconsciously unfurling her arms and legs. He covered her, braced his elbows on either side of her head, and brushed skeins of her glossy raven hair from her cheek. And he stared. Fuck, he could do that forever and not get tired of the view.

But he probably didn't have that long anymore.

Refusing to waste another moment, Hammer lowered his head and touched his lips to hers. Everything about her was soft. He pressed forward to deepen the kiss and savored the moment as if rediscovering her for the first time.

His heart tripped.

How many times over the years had he thought of stripping her bare, taking her body, hearing her scream for him? Controlling her, undoing her, drinking in her power? Far, far too many to count. At times, he'd have sworn he would burn alive because he couldn't have her. He'd kissed her hundreds—maybe thousands—of times since he'd become her lover, but he'd never paused to relish the gravity of the instant their lips first met. Now, the simple connection undid him.

"Macen?" She blinked up at him.

She wanted to know what was wrong with him. The answer was everything, but that wasn't her fault. Raine had shelved all her worry to give him succor. He had to do the same.

"Shh. I'm here right now."

Tears shimmered in the corners of her eyes. "I'm here always."

His chest buckled. Hammer swallowed, then he dipped his head to kiss her again, this time brushing his mouth over hers. Like always, her cheeks flushed. She softly exhaled. Her lips parted.

When he bent again, he couldn't stop his hunger. He clutched her silky hair in his fists and seized her mouth, plunging deep.

She blistered his control, and he saturated his senses with her. His head screamed at him to slow time down and bask in this breathtaking moment. Make it last forever. But Raine whimpered, curling her hands around his shoulders and wrapping her legs around his hips. Desperation tightened her grip.

Desire crashed through Macen like thunder, and he was lost.

He dragged in rough breaths and surged inside her mouth to lay claim. Raine tangled her tongue with his. He ate at her, starved for her taste. She imprinted her flavor on his taste buds. He pressed her into his heart.

The bed dipped as Liam joined them. Without breaking their kiss, Hammer rolled to his side, taking Raine with him. She wound her thigh over his hip and pressed her pussy against him, letting herself be swept away. He held tighter and took her lips again, diving in deeper.

Then Liam spooned her. Their hands brushed in her hair before the man dragged her shirt down one side, kissing her exposed shoulder, working his way up to her neck.

Raine shuddered, loosed an aroused breath. She reached back to grip Liam's thigh so she could touch them both before she arched in surrender.

Macen inched back. As the drugging kisses ended, fear and anxiety crept back in. He refused to scare her now or ruin the sanctity of the moment.

But she knew, and her face crumpled. Tears spilled.

"Don't." He thumbed the drops away and clutched her cheeks, comforting her with a lingering touch of their lips.

Against him, he could feel her body jerk with a silent sob, but she nodded, exhaling into him, giving him her silent trust.

Liam took her hand in his, caressing his broad thumb across her knuckles. "Love."

Yes, he should be the one to soothe her. Hammer couldn't promise her a future, and Liam might be left to pick up the pieces soon. Besides, once Macen had stopped insisting on having her all to himself, one of his greatest joys—and turn-ons—had become watching his best friend pleasure their girl.

Cupping her shoulder, Hammer pressed a kiss on her forehead and turned her to Liam.

Instantly, she reached out, latching on to the man. He took her face in his big hands and scanned her expression, silently seeking. Liam loved her. Of that, Hammer had no doubt. He could see it glowing in his friend's eyes.

A little frown worked between Liam's brows. His friend worried a lot. But Raine moved in, laying a soft, searching kiss on his mouth before skating her lips up his cheek, across his forehead, then working her way down his nose. A breath later, she surged forward and fused their mouths together. Liam met her more than halfway, clutching his fingers in her shirt and all but inhaling her. Hammer watched the love ebb and flow between them.

A bittersweet pang twisted his guts. He'd spent fucking years wallowing in the past—in worry, guilt, and other useless emotions. He'd been an idiot. A fool. For the first time, he shoved it all aside and simply marveled at the utter devotion they had forged. At the unconditional love that now melded the three of them.

Captivated, he stared as Liam and Raine poured themselves into the hungry kiss. Liam soothed her, stroked her as she writhed gently, open, accepting. Hammer felt the tremors of need rippling through her. His friend answered by drawing her closer, almost as if he intended to absorb her.

Hammer realized they needed affirmation of their love and connection every bit as badly as he did.

When Liam eased away, Raine rolled to her back, glancing between them as they shifted above her. Hammer stared at Raine's swollen mouth and her blue eyes full of turmoil. She looked close to breaking again when she reached out to them, torment in her touch. In unspoken consolation, Macen nuzzled his cheek in her hand, then turned to kiss her palm. He drank in the feel of her slender fingers, the burn of her flesh, the love in her eyes.

Beside him, Liam rose to toe off his shoes, shuck his shirt and pants. Hammer followed suit. Raine watched them with a desperate gleam. Some reckless part of him wanted to dive onto the bed again and ravish every inch of her. But if this was one of his last chances to savor their love, he wanted to take his time and surround her with the tenderness and devotion she deserved, immerse himself in them.

He and Liam shared a glance as they shed the last of their clothes. A look told Macen they were in the same place—heads and hearts. They would focus on nothing except one another.

Together, he and Liam prowled toward the bed and tugged off Raine's blouse and bra. The silky fabric whispered away to slowly reveal her soft skin—shoulder, swell, breast. His breath caught. She glowed. Every time he thought Raine couldn't get more beautiful to him, she proved him wrong.

Beside him, Liam unveiled her other breast with a soft curse of need.

She glanced between them, her lips trembling. And she held her arms out to them.

Hammer didn't waste another second.

He fell to his knees beside her, cradling her swelling flesh in his hand. Then he swooped down to suckle a berry-hued nipple between his lips. From the corner of his eye, he watched Liam bathe her other breast in reverent attention.

They drew her deep in their mouths, lavishing all their focus on her adoration and pleasure. Raine softly sighed and held their heads to her breasts, moaning, giving herself over to them completely.

As he curled his tongue around the bud and reveled in her arching and soft cries, he trailed his fingertips down her body, skimming the curve of her waist, pushing her yoga pants down, and inching to her naked folds.

Liam's hand was already there, arousing, exploring. "How does it feel with both of us touching you after so long, love?"

"Better than good. Meant to be." Her voice cracked with emotion. "I don't ever want this to end."

None of them did.

Melancholy hung in the air. If Hammer let it, that desolation would crush him, so he focused on their intimacy. He filed away every shred of love they shared and committed it to memory.

Liam tugged her pants off and curled his fingers into her opening, making room for Hammer to skim her swollen clit.

As they enveloped her cunt, she spread her legs open to them. No coy games, no barriers. Just soft moans of pleading and worship that fired his desire to insane, head-swimming heights.

Dizzy, drunk on her, Hammer lifted from her breast. God, he couldn't even glance at her without wanting to swallow her whole. His blood scorched. His cock throbbed.

Nothing could ever fulfill him the way being with Raine and Liam could.

Growling, Macen dove in and slanted his lips over Raine's. Sweeping his tongue along every crevice and recess of her mouth, he poured out his longing as one sweltering kiss rolled into the next. He drank in her flavor and tucked away every nuance so he could pluck it out when he missed her most…like every fucking day.

He stared at her pretty mouth. "Precious."

"I love you, Macen," she whispered.

Christ, how was he ever going to survive without her?

"I love you, Raine," he whispered. "I always have. I always will."

Hammer trailed his tongue toward her navel. He tasted the salt of her skin as he caught sight of Liam's glistening fingers working in and out of her core. Her feminine scent hung strong and alluring in the air. Macen had no doubt he and Liam would take her in every way until she was limp and spent and thoroughly loved.

As Macen's stare trailed down the naked flush of her skin, he zeroed in on the barely perceptible bump of her belly. It would be indistinguishable to someone who wasn't her lover. But to him, the changes were staggering.

"Wait there. Don't move." He vaulted off the bed.

"Where are you going?" She sounded worried.

"I'm not leaving," Hammer assured. "It's just… I need to see you."

He flipped on the canned lights overhead, bathing the room in brilliance, before dashing to both the nightstands. Once he'd turned on the bedside lamps, he climbed back onto the mattress, loving the way the soft glow illuminated her like a pearl.

His gaze drifted over the darkened flesh of her tightly drawn nipples before caressing its way back to where their baby grew inside her protective womb. Ever since the ER doctor shocked them with the news of her pregnancy, he'd comprehended that she carried life inside her, but seeing the evidence now made it sharply real.

Would he ever see Raine's belly grow ripe and full if he was locked away? Would he feel the child they had created roll and kick beneath her stretched skin? And when this sweet little miracle entered the world, would Liam and Raine welcome this baby alone? Macen knew he might miss the first cry of life, the feel of the wriggling bundle in his arms, and the clean scent of their child. He wouldn't rub the warm skin or peach-fuzz hair beneath his lips. He wouldn't be there to watch their little one grow, to protect, guide, and teach the million and one things he ached to bestow.

"Macen?" Her voice shook.

Even Liam froze behind her, waiting with a scrutiny he could feel.

They wanted his reaction. Words jumbled in his head.

This baby would need him someday. And he needed his son or daughter, too. Hammer closed his eyes.

With one reckless act, River might well rip him from this blissful family and all his wildest dreams. A ragged breath tore from his lungs.

While everything inside him seemed to crumble—his control, his future, his fucking soul—the silence in the room screamed through his head.

They were both still watching, waiting. It seemed crazy to him they'd actually worried he wouldn't find a pregnant Raine attractive.

Hammer shoved aside the looming ugliness for later and focused on the two people he loved. He pressed his lips against the life growing inside Raine. "You've never looked more beautiful."

Liam relaxed against her. "It's true, love."

Jaw clenched, Macen sank his fingers into Raine's belly, desperate to brand their child with a father's touch. He wanted to beg them all not to forget him. But that would be selfish.

He said nothing and began to pull his hand away.

Before he could, Liam anchored his palm over Macen's knuckles.

Understanding sheened his best friend's eyes. "Whatever happens, I've got this. You need never worry about Raine or our bairn, my brother."

"Our baby will always be safe and loved," Raine swore.

Hammer choked. He couldn't say how fucking grateful he was. Instead, he nodded and memorized the feel of Liam's hand mingled with his as they covered their woman's swelling belly.

A sob tore from her throat.

As much as Hammer struggled to regain his composure, he refused to allow dread and what might happen to destroy their remaining time together.

Positioning himself between her legs, he took her hips in his hands and brushed a kiss on the inside of her thigh. "Give everything to us, Raine."

"ALWAYS," RAINE VOWED, forcing herself to breathe.

Inside, she unraveled. She wanted to rail and scream and ask a million questions. The LAPD had upset her, but to see that they'd rattled the usually unshakable Macen Hammerman…

His interrogation must have been grueling, brutal, and painfully personal.

They obviously believed he was guilty of their terrifying array of charges. *Oh, god…* Would he go to prison for the heinous crime of helping her when she'd needed it most?

And the last thing he needed now was to hear that she and Liam had been questioned, too. Liam had been right about that. At this moment, Hammer simply needed their love. No matter how difficult it was to shut out her fear and grief and put him first, Raine vowed to do it.

"Anything you need. I belong to you two." Under him, she spread her knees wider, inviting him deeper into her.

"Raine…" He choked.

As her heart shredded, she gripped Liam's hand, silently begging him for strength. He hovered beside her, a gentle command in his eyes. She *would* surrender. She *would* set Macen at ease. Then he scooted closer to lay an affirming kiss on her lips. "I'm here."

As she nodded gratefully, Hammer dropped his head and kissed the bare pad of her pussy as if he'd never touched anything more fragile and treasured. As if he never wanted to leave.

The reverent gesture both humbled and undid her.

For years, he'd been the master of his domain, able to bend life to his will. He'd been her everything. Everyone else had left her. Not Macen. He'd been steadfast. He'd protected her against all odds. He'd earned her trust, even as he denied himself the love she'd ached to give him—love he'd needed so badly—while he waited for her to mature and bloom.

Now that they shared something so special and real, he couldn't be leaving her.

Liam caressed her cheek, offering more of his strength. Her insides twisted again. Her Irishman had always shown her such tenderness and patience. He'd listened, offering either exquisite understanding or punishment—whichever she needed—at precisely the right time. Like now.

Both men loved her, even when the personal cost had been deep and harsh and almost impossible.

How could she pack a lifetime of love into this small sliver of time? How could she do anything less than surrender her everything to them?

She nodded Liam's way. His tender smile was full of heartbreak as he dropped a kiss onto her lips and nudged her open to sweep inside at the same moment Hammer licked his way up her most sensitive spot.

Shocking pleasure slashed through her grief. It had been so long since the three of them had become one. She wanted them with every cell in her body, every beat of her heart, every thought, every breath. Every way they could take her.

With a cry, she arched up to them.

They knew precisely how to work together to dismantle her resolve and ramp up her desire. They had an unspoken communication she'd be forever grateful for but would never fully understand. It was almost as if they were halves of the same soul. Raine feared one would never be whole without the other.

She would never be complete without them both.

As if sensing she was letting sorrow distract her again, Liam grabbed her wrists and pinned them over her head. Hammer anchored her hips to the bed in his unrelenting grip. They had immobilized her—as a team—in an instant. They both knew that taking away her control was the fastest way to hijack her thoughts. They wanted her surrender.

Raine melted for them—an act of love she'd happily give over and over.

"That's it," Liam murmured over her lips. "Give me your tongue."

She opened, accepting his sweep into her mouth again with a hitched cry. Hammer traced her slick folds, then teased her clit, suckling it, nipping it, rhythmically laving it until tingles raced and thoughts drifted away. Until she thrashed between them.

"Excellent. Now arch your breast into my hand." The low, intimate demand sent another hot thrum of need through her. Raine did as Liam asked. "Perfect. Her nipples are tight."

"Her cunt is juicy." Hammer grunted before he lowered his head again.

She gripped the sheets, caught up in the hot, driving rush.

Liam pinched her nipple. "Her surrender is so heady."

"Let's make her come so hard her fucking knees shake."

"Please." Raine dissolved between them. "Yes. I'm yours. Forever."

"Precious…" Hammer swallowed tightly.

"Ah, love…" Liam released her wrists to caress her as he nibbled at her bottom lip.

She sent him a longing stare and parted to allow him anything he sought. He probably saw the tears swimming in her eyes. As always, he would understand. He would also wipe them away and replace her woe with bliss.

As he kissed her, Macen thumbed her clit before taking her into his mouth again. Raine closed her eyes and just felt.

As if her fingers had a will of their own, she combed them through Hammer's hair. He needed a trim. It was curling slightly at the ends. For a man who prided himself on ruthless control, he wouldn't appreciate the subversion of his will. But she enjoyed sinking into his soft strands and tugging gently as she lifted her hips to offer him every bit of herself.

He took her in a ravenous press of lips, a slide of his tongue. Her desire swelled, brimmed. She clutched him desperately.

His scent blended with Liam's, surrounding her, filling her head. The dual press of their bodies intoxicated her and tugged at her heart. She knew the sounds each made when they gave in to their pleasure, the way each smiled when she amused them, the words each used to praise her, and the expressions each wore when they told her they loved her.

Her heart had never been fuller.

She clung to them as if she could defy fate and hold them forever. She fell into arousal, determined to wring every memory from this night she could.

Hammer rimmed his finger around the opening of her pussy. She clamped down on air, her sex clenching with need, aching for one of them to fill the empty space. Liam added to her pleasure, bending in slow adulation of her nipples with his mouth.

"Take me. Please..." she begged with a breathless moan.

"We plan to, love. All night long." Liam nipped at her sensitive buds again.

Hammer lifted from her wet center, his lips glistening. "When we're ready, and you're so desperate you can't breathe. Not a second sooner, precious."

With a mischievous gleam in his eyes, he crawled up her body and cinched a hand in her hair, then slanted his lips over hers and claimed them. He forced the salty-tart tang of her own essence onto her tongue. Her taste buds exploded as he swept in deep.

His thick shaft lay hard against her mons, teasing her. Raine fought the urge to rock her hips and guide him through her swollen folds. But she wasn't in charge. She didn't want to be. All Raine wanted was to love her men, to hand over her entire being and feel their devotion in return.

As Hammer trailed his tongue down her throat, she lifted her heavy lids and saw Liam propped up on his side, watching with a heated stare as he stroked his engorged cock.

Greedy desire melted through her like warm chocolate. She couldn't wait to feel them rhythmically stretching and filling her together. As if reading her mind, Hammer wrapped her in his arms, then rolled to his back, setting Raine on top to straddle him and nestling his erection against her folds. He stared at her as if he couldn't fully drink her in. Raine gazed back, lost in the fierce passion burning in his eyes.

Liam grabbed her hips and pressed in close behind her, singeing her flesh. She arched, her head falling against his shoulder as he molded the damp skin of his chest to her back. He pressed hot kisses along her neck and rocked against her, grinding her wetness along Hammer's cock and dragging the man's iron shaft over her tingling clit with the kind of friction that had her gasping.

Macen let out a guttural moan. "Fuck, yes."

"He likes it, love," Liam whispered as he reached around her and cupped her heavy breasts. "How good will you feel when his fat cock is pushing deep inside you?"

Her nipples throbbed for attention. Desperate for Liam's touch, Raine arched, but he splayed his fingers wide, avoiding her needy peaks. "Please…"

"You want something, precious?" Hammer traced around her nipple, too, teasing, taunting.

She dug her nails into his shoulders. "Please!"

"Answer him first," Hammer commanded, tone gravelly.

She didn't even remember the question.

"I-I can't think. Macen…" When Hammer slid his cock between her folds again, his thick crest nudging her pouting clit, she groaned and shivered. "I want. I ache. I need."

"You'll be begging and sobbing before we're through," Hammer taunted as he finally plucked her burning nipples, igniting a ripple of fire up Raine's spine.

She let out an incoherent cry.

"Such pretty sounds you make," Liam purred against her ear. "Reach down and slide your fingers in your pussy, Raine, then bring them to my lips. I'm starving for your taste."

They were her Dominants, and she couldn't do anything but obey, especially when they made her feel coveted and adored.

Liam urged her onto her knees, and Raine reached between her legs. She dragged her fingertips over the thick veins of Hammer's cock. When he sucked in a breath, she wrapped him in her fist, savoring his hard, eager heat.

"Jesus." Hammer bucked his hips. The tendons in his neck bulged as he thrashed his head.

With a siren's smile, Raine let go and dipped her fingers into her wetness. After she coated them, she darted her gaze over her shoulder and met Liam's stare, breath held as she lifted her digits to his mouth. When his lips closed around them, she reveled in his moan of approval, her belly tightening as he licked and suckled her fingers clean.

"Like that?" she whispered as she kissed his jaw.

Liam didn't answer. He tangled his fingers in her hair and kissed her breathless. Her heart rate climbed again when Hammer skimmed his palm up her thigh, heading straight for her pussy.

"Now," he barked. "I don't think I can wait another fucking minute."

"Easy, mate." Liam rushed to the nightstand. "Let me prepare her properly."

Hammer's moan rang with frustration. "Hurry, damn it."

Before she could second his demand, he dragged her toward his chest, melting her in a searing burn of flesh, muscle, heartbeats. With her ass in the air, Liam dragged his tongue down her spine, laving every inch. As she writhed to meet him, he gripped her cheeks and bit gently at each. Sparks of delight lit her up as he spread her open to him and worked a pair of lubed fingers past the crinkled flesh of her rosebud. Gentle but insistent, he soothed her tight muscles until she relaxed and groaned.

Hammer lifted her up enough to latch on to one of her nipples. With spine-bending suction, he bathed and scraped her hard peak.

She hissed at the swelling pleasure she felt between them. Euphoria heated her blood. Her nails sank into Hammer's shoulders as they laid claim to her together and she gave them her control.

Macen turned his attention to her other nipple. "Open your ass for him, precious. Let him get you nice and slick so he can slide that thick cock deep inside you."

Raine gasped for breath as they tormented her aching body with busy hands and lingering mouths. Whimpers and moans slipped from her throat. Though neither said a word, Liam and Hammer communicated in silent understanding, working together to keep her poised between them until she shuddered and bit her lip to hold in a scream.

Finally, they began to work their cocks—inch by inch—inside her, stretching her needy flesh. A keening cry tore from her throat as they both slid home. Grunts and groans, moans and whimpers—the language of their love—echoed off the walls. Their musk swirled with the scent of lust and wrapped itself around her.

Raine was lost.

She reached for the rushing bliss, desperate for the affirmation and promise in their embrace. With each surging thrust and forceful lunge, they bestowed on her not only a physical mating but a gift. A vow that no matter what tomorrow might bring, in their hearts they would be joined together for life.

As Liam inched out from her pulsing rim, Hammer plowed his wide crest deep and long. Their driving rhythm ignited her blood, singed her skin. She melted in a silent plea for their mercy and gave them every bit of her body. The urgency of their grips, the insistence of their lovemaking, told Raine they intended to claim her soul together.

As one, they stilled, paused. She shivered, the need beyond her control.

"More... Oh, god. Please. Macen. Liam. Don't stop..."

Hammer lashed his fingers over her nipples until she moaned. "Who gives the orders here, precious?"

"Definitely not you, greedy little minx," Liam chided as he pinched the cheeks of her ass.

"Please, Sirs," Raine mewled. "Please, give me more."

Tears of frustration and need stung the backs of her eyes. She wriggled her hips, trying to escape the burn engulfing her front and back, but neither man moved an inch. Clamping down around them both, she squeezed tight, hoping to encourage the sublime rhythm that had nearly sent her over the edge—whatever would end the blistering conflagration.

Her men both hissed out choice words before Hammer pinned her with a devilish glare. "What does topping from the bottom get you?"

Raine wanted to scream. "Nothing, Sir. I just need—"

"We know exactly what you need, love," Liam assured sternly. "We need it, as well. But you don't determine when or how we let you fly, Raine. You know better."

She did. And while guilt pinpricked her, the thrumming demand pumping through her veins obliterated everything but her craving for them.

"Beg again, precious." Hammer reached between them and toyed with her clit. "Beg loud and long."

"Please end this misery. I want you both. Need you so badly," she gasped. "Help me. I'm dying to feel you deeper and give you pleasure."

"There's our submissive beauty. Take us. Take every inch," Liam muttered thick and hot in her ear.

He and Liam began to seesaw inside her while a kaleidoscope of colors flashed behind her eyes. They sank deep, retreated, then repeated the process until the friction had her clawing the sheets.

"That's it," Liam crooned. "Milk us, Raine. Squeeze tight."

Her pleading wails reverberating, Raine clamped down around them and tossed her head back at the towering ecstasy crashing toward her. Hammer's face contorted as he fought for control and busied his thumb, batting her clit ruthlessly. Her will to resist climax began to crumble. Panic mixed with urgency. The thought of failing them devastated her.

"Help me. Oh, god. Please. I-I… Macen. Liam," she cried, her voice cracking.

"Such pretty tears," Hammer grated out, his jaw clenched. "Liam?"

"Yes." He slid his fingers around her throat, his chest plastered to her back as he plunged even deeper. "Fuck, yes. Now. Before I go up in flames."

Hammer gripped Raine's chin and fused his gaze to hers, tumbling her into an infinite swirl of passion. "Come, sweet girl. Come hard and long for us."

His tender permission unlocked something in Raine's head—and heart. Hammer usually growled the command, but this time, he was—in his own way—begging her to remember him as her lover for all time.

A sob ripped from her throat as she shattered and fragmented, all the way to her soul, taking Hammer and Liam with her.

CHAPTER EIGHT

L IAM DETERMINEDLY STARED into his food, saying nothing through their quiet takeout Chinese dinner. Hammer frowned, especially when he also noticed Raine fidgeting and shooting the other man glances while she picked at her orange chicken and chow mein.

When Macen caught her flashing him a guilty stare, he threw his chopsticks down. "Okay, spill it. What's going on?"

Raine grimaced, then deferred to Liam with a questioning gaze. That made Hammer's gut knot tighter.

"We didn't want to worry you when you first came home, and we all needed the time and touch we shared together." Liam set down his chopsticks, obviously weighing his words. "After the police took you away, another cruiser showed up. They asked Raine and me to come in for questioning, too."

Hammer slammed his palms down on the table. He clenched his jaw, trying to hold his temper. None of this was their fault...but he was mightily pissed off. "You're just now telling me this?" Their silence was telling—and damning. "Sterling said nothing. Beck and Seth said nothing. You let me tell you everything about my interrogation and didn't say a word? Goddamn it."

"You had enough on your plate to worry about, mate. Spilling it all sooner would have only been another burden for you. Sterling arranged for us both to have lawyers present. My interview was short, maybe ten minutes. I wasn't in Los Angeles when Raine was a minor. I could prove I hadn't even met her until last September. They asked me if I'd ever raped Raine. Of course I denied that, and they can't prove otherwise. They wanted to know how long you and I had been friends and where we met. I told them I had nothing to say. When they asked me about my sex life with you two, I told them to piss off."

God, the police seemed intent on dragging everyone he loved

through the mud.

He zipped his gaze to Raine. "How long did they grill you?"

"Probably close to an hour. The detective seemed determined to make me into a victim, but I set the bitch straight."

Fuck. "I'm sorry you both had to go through that." Guilt railed Macen.

"It's not your fault. You didn't ask for this." She reached across the table and took his hand.

He gripped hers in return. "Tell me what they wanted to know."

She shrugged. "Probably a lot of the same stuff they wanted to know from you, like if you and I had a sex life when I was a minor and why you gave money to Bill." She paused, looked down at her hands in her lap. "They said they have a video of you appearing to rape me."

"A video?" He gave a thunderous scowl. He barely managed not to fling the table aside in rage. His entire life and the people he held dearest were being denigrated and threatened—and he was helpless to stop it. "What fucking video could the police possibly have?"

"I don't know." Raine shrugged. "They never showed me anything or gave me any information about it. Maybe they're bluffing."

Yeah. Maybe the cops were simply employing a tactic designed to encourage Raine to talk about her supposed abuse. Just like it was possible their mysterious witness was nothing more than a ruse to make him talk.

"They must be, because that never happened," Liam added.

Raine nodded. "I told them that. Just like I told them I like rough sex."

Hammer hadn't thought his fury could get hotter, but his urge for violence thickened again. She should never have had to admit anything about their private life to those prying, lecherous bastards.

"What else?" he asked.

She spoke in halting words. It didn't escape Hammer's notice that she gave the barest answers possible. But the breadcrumbs she did leave him to follow had his vision narrowing to a fiery red haze. "I'm going to dismember your brother, precious. With my bare hands. I'm going to tear his fucking head off—"

"I'm plenty furious with him, too. But Detective Perez didn't hurt me," she promised. "The worst thing that terrible woman did was intimate I'm a sad sack doormat of a whore. Not like I haven't heard that one before…"

"But you're not, goddamn it." He pounded a fist on the table. The rattling of glasses and plates didn't give him an ounce of gratification. "I'd love to have that fucking bitch's badge for judging you."

"Macen…" Raine rose from her seat and slid onto his lap, working her fingers through his hair. "I don't really care what some cynical, sexually frustrated workaholic thinks of me. In fact, no one's opinion matters a whit to me except yours and Liam's. Everyone else can go fuck themselves."

Liam smiled. "I won't even chide you for your language, love. That's perfect."

It was, but the fact she had to defend her life at all ate at Hammer.

He passed Raine onto his friend's lap and stood with an angry jerk. "I'll be back."

She tried to leap up. "Wait! Where—"

Liam clamped his arms around her middle and held her down as Hammer tore at his clothes, doffing every stitch, and tossed the garments in the nearby laundry room. "Shh. Let the man breathe."

Reminding himself to thank his brother later, Hammer wrenched the back door open, then slammed it so hard behind him the glass rattled. He headed for the pool and dove in.

He hit the water, gasping. That shit was fucking freezing. But nothing else was going to cool him down.

After some hard laps, he lifted himself out of the water and dripped all over the deck.

Raine hustled toward him with a concerned gaze. She clutched a big beach towel and wrapped it around him, along with her arms. "Feel better?"

He stepped back. "I'm getting your clothes all wet."

"I don't care."

Hammer worked free from her embrace and looked down at her beloved face. Weariness pulled at her. "Go to bed, precious."

"Liam just 'suggested' I head upstairs for a bath and bed, so I'm going. I think he wants to talk a little more. I made you two coffee."

Always thinking of him, even when she'd had a terrible day, too. Even when she should be more worried about her future and the life growing inside her.

"Did you get enough to eat?" he prodded.

"I'm fine. Don't worry about me." She kissed him softly and headed back into the house.

He watched her go. "That's like telling me not to breathe."

Liam poked his head out moments later and handed him a pair of sweat pants and a T-shirt. "Coffee's ready inside, mate."

Once he'd dressed, Hammer slid across the kitchen table from Liam, drinking his java and wondering how much longer he'd have the luxury of enjoying a brew and quiet moment like this with his best friend. So much to say…so little time to convey everything.

"What's next?" Liam's two soft words broke the silence.

"I have to see Sterling in the morning. After that, I should have a better handle on what to expect. If this goes to trial, I'm worried Raine will have to testify."

Liam's scowl said he didn't like that, either. "I know. Even if she doesn't cooperate with the prosecution, she's the 'victim.' Barnes will need her to testify on your behalf. I wish there was a way that didn't involve her reliving everything she's already been through. But she's stronger. She'll manage, Macen. I know you were angry that the police questioned her today, but don't underestimate our girl."

"I just hate seeing her dragged through this shit."

Quietly, Hammer worried what all this upheaval would do to her emotional progress, but he didn't speak the words. He simply had to believe in her and support her as best he could for as long as he was able.

A knock on the front door interrupted his musings. He and Liam frowned. Neither were expecting company, especially near midnight. His heart stopped for a moment. Were the police coming back to…what, arrest him? Already?

"I'll get it." Liam stood.

"I will." Hammer beat him out of the kitchen, knowing he had to face his own mess. "I'm sure it's for me."

With a sigh, he wrenched the front door open, braced for more uniformed officers and a pair of handcuffs not intended for play. Instead, he found Dean Gorman standing on the porch, wearing sunglasses and a baseball cap pulled low, along with a ratty leather jacket, T-shirt, and jeans. The car parked at the curb didn't belong to him.

"Hey." The cop's voice sounded grim.

Hammer understood instantly that Dean had taken a huge risk by coming here. "Can you come in?"

The officer looked over his shoulder, then nodded, peeling off his shades. "For a minute."

Stepping back to admit him, Hammer's guts twisted. Dean couldn't have good news.

"Hello," Liam welcomed. "Coffee?"

"No, thanks. I can't stay long. I also can't talk to you from my personal cell anymore, in case they subpoena your phone records. That's why I dropped by unannounced."

"I totally understand." The truth weighed heavily on Hammer. He'd become the criminal. The courts might say he was innocent until proven guilty, but in the eyes of the force, he was dirty as sin. "Seat?"

Dean shook his head. "I just came by to give you what information I can. I'm sorry about what went down today. I didn't get to finish giving you a heads-up earlier, but it wouldn't have mattered. At that point, I didn't know you'd become a suspect. I'd just seen River Kendall waltz into the station of his own free will with a briefcase and a lawyer, and I thought you'd want to know. Then I left for the armed robbery call. Sorry."

Hammer shook his head. "You went above and beyond. Thanks for trying to help."

"Raine okay?"

As okay as she could be, given the circumstances. "Fine. Getting ready for bed."

Gorman nodded, all business now. "Here's what I can tell you: Winslow and Cameron? Watch out. They're ruthless. They feed off each other and they play to win. Years in Vice have warped their minds, and they're convinced everyone remotely involved with BDSM, swinging, club sex—anything not 'normal'—is a pervert or pedophile. They will never see your side of the story with Raine, so don't try."

"My lawyer advised against me opening my mouth in general."

"Smart." From the inside pocket of his leather jacket, he withdrew a manila envelope. "These are the pictures Seth slipped me of Raine, taken after the last beating her father gave her before she ran away. Detectives Bates and Sanchez put them in Bill Kendall's file since they helped to establish that Raine acted in self-defense. Being from homicide, they weren't so interested in the fact that you had photos of a minor. But Winslow and Cameron will flip their shit if they find out. I don't know if anyone scanned these into our digital evidence system. They're months behind, so maybe not. Just in case, I thought I'd remove the physical copies from the evidence room. But you didn't get them from me. Thank goodness you had the foresight not to admit you'd taken the pictures. Saying that Raine had given you these images in case her father came after her again was perfect."

Hammer snagged the envelope from Dean. He owed the man, who'd risked both his livelihood and his freedom to help, a huge debt. "Thanks."

Dean nodded. "Get rid of them. They're a liability you can't afford."

"Absolutely. Now that Bill is dead, Raine would feel better if they were destroyed anyway."

"Do it fast. You can bet Winslow and Cameron will show up here and at Shadows in the next few days—maybe hours—with search warrants. It would be better for everyone if these copies and their originals disappeared. In fact, get rid of anything in either location that can incriminate you. Pictures or surveillance video of Raine at Shadows before she turned eighteen should be high on your list, too. If you have either saved on your phone, cloud, or computer, wipe everything clean. Delete old accounts. Start new ones. And you never heard this from me." He peeled off his cap with a sigh. "It would mean my ass."

A gong of foreboding resounded through Hammer all over again. Everything was happening so quickly, and he hadn't seen the search warrants coming. Which overwhelmed him because he should have.

"I can't thank you enough, man. I'll take care of everything from here. If anyone asks, you're not a member of Shadows, and I don't know you."

Gorman nodded grimly. "Thanks. Sorry it has to be that way."

"I completely understand. Don't think twice."

"We'll keep your tracks here clean," Liam added. "Is there anything else we should be doing to keep Hammer out of jail?"

"Listen to Sterling Barnes. He's one of the best. Don't lie more than you have to and don't lose your temper. And one last thing." Dean handed him a folded scrap of paper. "I debated about this but...in Raine's shoes, I'd want to know. Of course, I didn't give this to you, either. But here's River's current address. It's a rent-by-the-week place. He refused to list a phone number. This might not be much help, but maybe you can get some answers from him."

Hammer tucked the information in the pocket of his sweat pants. The last thing he wanted was Raine anywhere near the bastard, but he and Liam would go have a "friendly chat" with River. "So no one intends to charge him for attempted kidnapping?"

Gorman shook his head. "Somehow, he convinced them it was a 'misunderstanding.' Slippery bastard."

"Indeed." Liam looked shaken.

About like Hammer felt.

"Thanks for the heads-up."

"No problem. Best of luck. If you need more information, it'll be tricky but...get a burner phone and call me." Dean slapped him on the back. "Sorry I didn't have better news. Good night, you two. Hug Raine for me."

"We will. Night." He shook the cop's hand, then showed Dean out the door, watching him hop in the car and drive south. Macen couldn't help but feel as if his future was heading in the same direction.

Thursday, February 14

LIAM AWOKE IN darkness and sighed wearily, the silent summons heard.

What does a man have to do to get some shut-eye around here?

As his eyes adjusted to the dark, he saw that Raine lay facing him. Hammer spooned her securely in his arms as they slept. Liam was glad. No telling how many nights they had left together.

As much as he hated to face that reality, poking his head in the sand wouldn't help any of them.

Quietly, Liam left the bed and dressed, then tiptoed down to the kitchen, smelling the teapot brewing.

Sure enough, as he rounded the corner, his mother sat at the table, sipping from her cup. The lights above warmed her auburn hair. She didn't speak, merely gestured Liam to his waiting mug.

He joined her at the table. "Morning, Mum."

"Mornin', son. I'll not keep you long, but 'tis best if we talk privately."

He agreed. "I'm worried about Hammer. What do you see?"

"If you were listening to what's inside you, you'd already have a clue." She slanted him a chastening stare. "Why've you not paid attention to your gifts and developed them? They won't go away simply because you choose to ignore them. Best to make peace, son. They're a part of you."

Liam frowned. "How are they gifts, Mum? A bloody burning ear when you decide to visit? Seeing the auras of animals and plants? Weirdly knowing things that don't always make sense until after the fact? All that's bloody useless when I need it most. And since I was a wee lad, your riddles have driven me daft at times."

"Think of your abilities like a tool. You can't be much good at using them without practice. But if you hone the skill, you'll be a master craftsman one day." Bryn touched his cheek. "So don't be thinking your sight is of no value."

"Maybe I'm just stubborn."

"Maybe?" she parried back with a smile.

"I wanted to live my life my way, not with my future fixed by a fate I couldn't escape."

"Good grief, seeing doesn't mean you have no choice. In fact, a whole world of limitless possibilities opens up. You have an innate warning system, while others rely on the information at hand and their judgment. Auras can be helpful. Tell me, when were you ever bitten by a dog?"

Liam paused. "Never, that I recall."

"Animals are drawn to you. They know you sense them. Same with plants and trees. They're living entities, so their auras are a clue about the state of their being." Her smile became a fond grin. "Remember when you'd cry if someone gave me flowers? You'd tell me they were bleeding."

"Mum, I was five. Knowing the state of my garden doesn't help me with my problems now."

"If you paid attention, it might. But you've been tuned out for years. What color was Gwyneth's aura?"

"I don't know." Liam hadn't thought much about it, and he didn't want to dwell on the she-beast.

"Tune in and think."

Liam sighed. Best not to fight his mother when she was determined.

He closed his eyes, and suddenly it filled his head. "Green. And muddy brown."

The colors of his ex-wife represented anger, jealousy, petty backbiting, and lack of heart. In fact, he couldn't picture Gwyneth without the ugly air around her anymore. He frowned.

How had he bloody married the bitch?

"Exactly," his mother praised. "And Raine's aura is—"

"Blue and white. Vivid. Vivacious." He pictured her bold and glowing. "She's lovely."

Bryn smiled proudly. "Indeed. I'm sorry if I frightened her when we arrived."

"Why didn't you let me know you were coming sooner so I might have explained?"

"If you'd been paying attention, you would have known as soon as I started packing my bags. Why hadn't you told her about your family, son?"

"I didn't know what to say without sounding mental." He took a long swallow of tea. "It's so good to see you and Da. How is everyone?"

"Your sisters are well and send their love. Got any bikkies?" she asked hopefully. "I rummaged around in the pantry but couldn't find any."

"Cookies, Mum. They're called cookies here." He smiled. "For someone who seems to know everything, I'm surprised you can't find them. Raine baked some snickerdoodles. They're in the jar. Hang on." He rose again and brought the brown ceramic container decorated with fleur-de-lis back to her.

Bryn plucked one out and dipped it in her tea before taking a bite. She hummed. "I didn't know what a snickerdoodle was, but it's delicious. You're a lucky man. Raine will fatten you up in no time."

"I'm sure she will." He sensed the speech rolling through her head. "So what's on your mind? You didn't travel to California because you suddenly decided you needed to meet my wee wench or 'talk' to the baby. And you didn't wake me up in the middle of the night for something sweet."

"As Macen's problems unfold, you'll do more harm than good—both of you—if you don't stay logical and calm."

How the hell was he supposed to do that now, when everything they'd worked hard for was dissolving before them? "I know you mean well but—"

"I'll not be patronized, Liam." Her eyes glittered like green fire.

He winced, then took a cookie from the jar and dipped it in his tea. His mother could be mild and affable—until someone nipped at her temper. "That wasn't my intention. But if you simply wanted to tell me to ease up, you could have called."

"Well, we *did* come to meet Raine. The wee bairn is a powerful incentive, too. Sure you don't want to know *anything*?"

"Very sure. We've talked. We'd all like to be as surprised by the sex of the babe as we were by the fact Raine was pregnant. Nor do we care who fathered the babe." He slanted his mother a glance.

"I understand." She patted his hand. "It'll be obvious soon enough. And this one will have your lovely's eyes."

The thought made Liam smile. Since learning that Raine was expecting, he'd been hoping to see her bright blues in their next generation. "Out with the rest. Why did you wake me in the middle of the night?"

She stared at—or maybe it was through—him, as though seeing something more. "To reason with you, son. Raine has to talk to her brother. Give her your blessing and let her go."

"Mum—"

"She'll find a way, regardless. Wouldn't you rather her do it without sneaking around and feeling guilty? So you can make sure she's protected and safe?"

Macen's interrogation by the police had likely ignited his fiery lass's determination to fix everything. That meant she would want to confront River.

"It's too bloody dangerous. I'll not have that wanker anywhere near her. He tried to abduct her! Do you realize the damage he's done? I swear, if I get my hands on that son of a—"

"Of course I know. But what do you expect? Everything he's learned about Raine's life so far paints a sordid picture."

"In his mind."

Bryn reached out and laid her hand on his arm. "Most folks can't see beyond their own noses. And it's not as if either of you has convinced Raine to marry you. Are you expecting her to give birth without a husband?"

Liam had expected this prodding from his very Catholic parents. "I proposed. So did Hammer. She said no to us both."

"So you're giving up?" Bryn shook her head. "Raine is still finding her path. So is River. He's her big brother, Liam. She's all the family he has left. You know that for a warrior, there is no greater regret than failing those you love and should have protected."

He knew. It was one reason Hammer had been struggling. "River has been Stateside for months, gathering information on us and twisting it all to hell. He could have initiated a fucking conversation before going off half-cocked!"

"You're not too big for me to wash your mouth out with soap, Liam O'Neill!"

He didn't mean to be disrespectful, especially when his mother meant well. "Sorry."

"I suspect you should be. I'm sure you and Macen welcomed River with open arms," she said tartly. "And thoroughly explained your relationship with Raine when he came callin', right?"

"He'd already made up his mind. He hurled ugly accusations, jumped to conclusions—"

"Just as well it wasn't your foot in that shoe, I'm thinking. Imagine how things might have seemed to you if Caitlyn, Maeve, or any of your sisters were in Raine's situation."

Liam growled. Raine had said something eerily similar. "That's not the point, Mum. The man's a menace and not to be trusted. He wouldn't listen to a bloody word any of us said anyway, even Raine. He meant to take her from us. He threatened to abort our child."

"That's River's fear talking. Yours is barking, too," she pointed out. "Why are men so bloody hardheaded at times? Your da can be the same."

"Because we're men."

She huffed. "You listen to me. Raine has to save Macen from himself. She's the only one who can. And to do that, she needs her brother…without you two interfering."

Anxiety ripped through him. "What if you're wrong? We can't take a chance he'll hurt her or cart her away."

"Oh, Liam." She sighed. "River loves her. He believes he's doing right by his sister. He's only concerned for her well-being. His heart is in the right place, even if he is going about things a mite cockeyed."

"A mite?" Liam scoffed. "I don't like it. And neither will Hammer."

Bryn's face softened. "No matter. She'll go. Why don't you send the lads with her? Seth and Kenneth are good boys. They'll watch over her."

"Who? Oh, you mean Beck." Liam frowned. "Don't call him Kenneth. He hates it. And you know that."

Bryn just gave him an impish smile. "He needs a woman to put him in his place now and then."

"God help me." Liam gave a mock scowl. "I'll think about what you've said."

"Best do it quick."

That meant Raine already had a plan. *Damn it.*

"We appreciate you coming to visit, and I know you want to help…but I have to ask, where were you when Gwyneth tormented me last winter? Couldn't you have warned me she was full of tripe when she presented me with the boy she claimed was mine? Or when Raine's mongrel of a father kidnapped her and—" Biting back the memory, he hung his head and fought to control the burn behind his eyes.

"I tried to help with Gwyneth," she reminded gently. "Before you even married her. But you were set on the shrew. I warned you, but you wouldn't hear a word of it. Told me to keep out. I respected that, though I don't mind telling you, 'twas difficult."

Bryn had never been one to hold her tongue.

He grimaced. "No doubt. And I should have listened."

"As for your ex-wife's return and all that led up to Raine's kidnapping, you know the sight is not always clear. The future's not set in stone, like the past or present. That's why I know the sex of the babe and who fathered it. 'Tis already done." Bryn paused as though choosing her next words. "But what might be…that's fluid. A whim can change circumstances and alter the future. I am sorry for all Gwyneth put you through. But you're stronger for it."

"I felt helpless at the time, Mum, like I was chasing my own bloody tail. I made mistakes that could have cost me the people I hold dearest."

"None of that happened. I felt your pain at the time. Your worry. But you had everything you needed to choose the right path. Next time, listen more carefully to the voice inside you." Rising, Bryn retrieved the teapot and topped off both their cups.

"How do I know it's right?"

"How do you know it's wrong?" she countered.

His mother's semantics sometimes drove him mad. "Couldn't you have just whispered in my ear?"

"I wasn't meant to interfere, Liam. Sometimes, there's no way around the obstacles in our path. Can't go under or over them. The only way left is to plow straight through. It was Bill's time to die, and Raine was meant to vanquish him. One of the hardest things I've had to accept over the years is that seeing things doesn't mean I can stop them. I had to let that play out."

"But Raine's father—"

"Got what he deserved, and your young woman is a warrior, too. She fought tooth and nail for all of you and the future you could have together. If I'd dabbled in that, I could have changed everything."

"Then what makes this situation so different?" he asked wearily.

"Macen will sacrifice himself for you both if you don't stop him, and none of you will live the life you should have together. This love you three share is special. It's been a long time coming to you all. I've known you were meant for something different since you were a wee lad. Now you're where you should be, son. With the people you should hold forever. Use every tool you've got to fight for that."

"I don't know what to do, Mum. I can't fight the law."

"Think on it, as I know you will. You'll see the way. Be Raine's rock—and Macen's, too. Together, you can find what others only dream of."

He stared into his teacup. "I don't have a choice. As soon as I met Hammer, I knew he was the brother I never had. And Raine…the first time I kissed her, it was so powerful, Mum. Looking back, I see my gut was telling me she was meant to be mine. Funny, that."

Bryn smiled. "I was like that with your father. The moment his lips touched mine, I found myself thinking, 'Oh, there you are. I've been waiting for you.' You ken?"

"I do. Even when I thought I should walk away from them both, I couldn't. Since Hammer and I put Raine between us, I've been happier than ever. What we share now is…beyond. I'd do it all again in a heartbeat."

A smile played at her lips. "I did tell you before you left New York for your 'vacation' that you'd be starting a whole new adventure."

She had. And despite being vague at times, his mum always ended up being right.

THE FOLLOWING MORNING, Hammer lifted his heavy lids to find his face buried in Raine's neck and his hand wrapped around her hip. Grudgingly, he eased away from her, then stood and stared while she and Liam clung together in a cocoon of love. At least Hammer knew that if he couldn't disprove River's accusations, they would survive without him.

In fact, he'd already devised a plan to ensure that.

While showering and shaving, he steeled himself for the dark day ahead. Hammer trusted Sterling Barnes, but he wasn't a fool. He intended to follow Dean Gorman's advice and clean house. Well, clean the dungeon. Nothing at home could incriminate him, but scrubbing Shadows squeaky could mean the difference between prison and freedom.

After donning his suit and tie, Hammer forced himself to leave the bedroom and padded downstairs. Bryn was waiting for him, coffee cup in hand, by the doorway near the kitchen.

"Thank you for knowing I needed this." He forced a chuckle.

"'Tisn't all you need, to be sure. I know you think you'll better serve the ones you love by stepping back. But it's not true, Macen.

Fight for your family and find your path."

Hammer gulped his liquid caffeine. "I just hope my path doesn't lead to a jail cell."

"Nothing is set in stone, but I suggest you watch your back." She patted his cheek.

Hammer had already figured out someone had a knife poised between his shoulder blades. He had to fucking deduce who held the hilt.

"I gathered. Thanks for everything." He held up his mug before he chugged the rest. "I need to go."

Hammer pressed his lips to Bryn's temple, then handed the mug back to her, palmed his keys, and left.

On the way to Shadows, he rang Beck, who answered on the first ring. "Everything okay?"

"At the moment. Can you meet me at Shadows in an hour?"

"Yeah. I had a full day scheduled but it's looking like my surgery might be delayed."

"I'll only need ten minutes. Can you bring an empty toy bag when you come?"

"If you're cleaning out your stash and want to pass on used equipment, no thanks."

"I won't give you anything that needs to be sterilized, I promise."

"You can trust me, Macen." Gravity filled Beck's tone. He understood.

"I know. Thanks."

After the call, Hammer arrived at the club and arranged a meeting with Sterling in two hours. Then he combed through his devices, saving documents and photos onto a thumb drive. Wiping away all traces of Raine from his computer lodged a hollow void in his chest, but he refused to share their private moments with anyone. Thankfully he'd never have to erase her from his heart and soul.

After doing the same to his phone, he reset the memory on all his devices and restored them to their factory settings. Hopefully, nothing could be retrieved or recreated by any law enforcement tech.

Then he dove into his physical files, extracting any paper pertaining to Raine prior to her eighteenth birthday that might seem incriminating—receipts, medical records, the agreement he'd drawn up and forced Bill Kendall to sign once Raine had come to live at Shadows. From his safe, he extracted the receipts for the money orders he'd bribed her father with, in addition to the original photos of her beating at the shitstain's hands.

After storing it all in a box, Hammer strode down the hall and stepped into Raine's former room. Her spirit still lingered. If he closed his eyes, he could almost feel the girl she'd been before maturity and sex and the love they shared with Liam had changed her.

The scattered pictures still lay strewn across her dresser where River had left them. Furiously, Hammer gathered them up, pausing to stare at an image of Raine in the kitchen, making him her famous apple spice muffins for the first time. When he'd taken a bite, he'd teased her by gagging and grimacing as if she'd fed him poison. When horror filled her face, he'd choked with laughter. She'd stuck her tongue out at him, and he'd snapped a picture on his cell phone, capturing the moment.

A bittersweet smile floated across his lips. "She hasn't stopped sticking out her tongue at you since."

True, but he'd never trade one single day of her sassy, adoring ways. Or the joy she'd brought to his life.

As he thumbed through the rest of the photos, he stumbled onto one he'd taken a week or two after she'd first arrived at Shadows. The guarded uncertainty in her expression pained Hammer. Since then, he'd done his best to give Raine sanctuary, chase away her demons, and help her bloom. His girl had come so far. Pride swelled in his chest.

Piling the photos on the bed, he turned and hauled out a big box from her closet. Hammer was surprised to discover a stack of greeting cards. Raine had kept every birthday, graduation, get well, and holiday card he'd ever given her. Gently lifting a brittle, dried rose, he noticed a note tied to the stem by a thin string.

GET WELL SOON. WE'RE ALL THINKING OF YOU
HAMMER

Raine's first migraine had been severe and had scared him senseless. Claiming the club members were concerned, he'd bought her a dozen red roses.

He grabbed another photo, this one of him and Raine beneath the mistletoe at Shadows' annual party two Christmases ago. Eyes closed, she'd tilted her mouth under his. Hammer remembered staring at her sweet, parted lips for a thunderstruck moment, wanting and desperate. Finally, he'd brushed a kiss across her forehead. He hadn't waited to see her crestfallen face before he had walked away.

Regret hung heavy now. He'd give anything to turn back time to stand beneath that sprig of green, wrap Raine in his arms, and devour her.

Among her treasures, Hammer found a colorful key chain emblazoned with HAPPY BIRTHDAY. He'd given it to her, along with her new car. She'd given him an ear-splitting squeal and wrapped herself around him so tight sometimes he swore he could still feel it. She'd also saved the stubs from the tickets to their first concert together, the plastic cap and tassel she'd stashed off her celebratory cake after passing her GED, and a pair of his old sunglasses she'd adopted one summer.

She'd hoarded each as a silent symbol of her love. And he'd been too mired in his notion that he wasn't good for her, so he hadn't given himself permission to love her back.

He'd condemned them both to years of misery. *What a fucking fool.*

Forcing down his strangling frustration, Macen focused on the box of their past relics. A flash of silver caught his eye, and he pulled a delicate pendant free. The chainless bauble gleamed with a filigreed *R* engraved on the front. On the back, he squinted to read the inscription.

INTO EVERY HEART MY RAINE FLOWS
LOVE, MOM

A lump caught in his throat. He knew almost nothing about Robin Kendall except that she'd been the first—and one of the only people—to give his precious Raine any love as a child. Her demented father had destroyed that. Raine didn't deserve to have anyone else ripped from her life.

Fight for your family. Bryn's voice echoed in his head.

Hammer tucked the pendant in his pocket, stashed the photos he'd gathered onto the bed inside the box of mementos, and headed back to his office. After adding all of those keepsakes to his growing stash, he plucked up the thumb drive from his desk and tossed it in, as well.

One last stop.

He made his way down the hall and unlocked the door to the operations room.

A dark head swiveled in his direction. "Hey, Hammer."

"Lewis." He nodded. "You're still keeping six months of video footage for security purposes, right?" At the new guy's nod, he went on. "Good. Just checking. I need a minute to look something up. How about you take a break?"

"Um…sure." He frowned. "Back in ten."

"Perfect."

As the kid left and the door automatically locked behind him, Macen tore into the top drawer of the filing cabinet and dragged his fingers over the dates labeled on the foam-lined containers holding the backup drives. November first, November second, November fifth.

Panic burst, surged through his veins. November third and fourth were missing.

Were those the videos Detective Perez had mentioned to Raine?

He forced himself to take a deep breath and checked the dates again, searching the other drawers in the cabinet in case the footage had been misfiled. He rifled around the security desk, checked the container of this week's drives on the wall rack. Nothing.

"Fuck!"

November third held the footage of the public punishment he had orchestrated for Raine with Beck…which had become Liam offering her his training collar and claiming her virgin ass. November fourth, a handful of hours later, showed Hammer drunk and arguing with Raine in the bar—until he'd kissed her with six years of pent-up desperation, ripped off her robe, then tossed her down. Despite her saying no more than once, he'd devoured her pussy until she'd screamed and scratched out a cataclysmic orgasm. Afterward, he'd dragged her to his room and fucked her all night.

Though his grip had been rough and uncompromising, she'd been very willing…eventually. But the tape might look damning if they wanted to cry rape.

The shit had just gone from bad to really fucking terrible.

Hammer scrubbed a hand over his face and paced, his stomach pitching.

No other drives were missing, just the two most incriminating of his life. That was no accident. Bryn had been right. Someone had it in for him.

Who the hell could it be?

Swallowing down a black rage, he righted the room so no one would know what he'd sought, then looked up as Lewis walked back in.

"Everything okay?" he asked.

No.

Hammer would have suspected the guy of swiping backups, but he'd worked at Shadows for two weeks—not nearly long enough to incite the kid's hate. Besides, Lewis had probably taken the job for the porn value of watching the footage before he filed it. Macen doubted he wanted to risk that so soon.

"Great." He walked out, letting the door slam behind him.

River was the obvious choice as the thief, but how would he have gotten into the locked security room? He wouldn't have had enough time to watch all the surveillance for the past six months. It would have taken him days to find the most damning footage. Had River planted a mole deep, or had he paid someone to dig for dirt?

Hammer needed to find out—fast.

Back in his office, he found Beck waiting, empty toy bag at his feet. The doctor gestured to Hammer's cache of incriminating evidence. "You need me to store that?"

"I'm asking a lot of you."

Beck shrugged and lifted the bag onto Macen's desk. "I've got the perfect place to keep it. Don't worry. I'll help you protect Raine and keep your ass out of the pokey."

Hammer dumped it all in the empty bag. "I owe you big."

With a manly shoulder bump, Beck sent him a sly smile. "Don't worry. I'll find a way to collect. Is that everything?" When Hammer nodded, Beck took the bag in hand. "I'll drop this off, then I have to find Heavenly. Otherwise, Seth will be all over her like flypaper."

Clapping the doctor on the back, Hammer shook his head. "I'm telling you, save yourself the shit and put her between you."

"You know I don't share my toys well," Beck quipped.

So true, but Hammer suspected he'd have to learn. "If you see Seth, can you also have him investigate Lewis, that new tech I hired? I need the kid's background, habits, finances…"

Beck frowned. "Something up?"

"I don't know. Can't be too careful."

"I'm on it." Beck nodded. "Call if you need anything else."

The good doctor departed, then Hammer left the club, locking up behind him. In stark silence, he headed across town.

When he arrived at Sterling Barnes's office, the men shook hands, then Hammer forced himself into a chair, ankle resting on his knee. "Before we start discussing these bullshit charges, thanks for taking care of Raine and Liam for me yesterday. As you probably guessed, we weren't ready for what went down."

"My pleasure. From what I hear, Raine was…feisty."

"She usually is." Hammer had to smile. "I need you to take care of something else for me."

"I'll do my best."

"Draw up full powers of attorney. Incorporate Liam and Raine into my trust."

Sterling's bushy silver brows rose. "You haven't been proven guilty of anything yet. Do you really want to do that?"

"Yes. Give them access to everything. Immediately. My investment portfolio, deposit box, checking and savings, vehicles, taxes, my properties in London, San Juan, Tasmania, and anything else I left out. That includes Shadows."

"All right, Macen. It's admirable…if a bit premature."

"Winslow and Cameron—hell, the rest of that precinct—won't rest until I'm locked away. So I want Raine and Liam to have my entire estate at their disposal."

"You know, you could also put a little faith in me as your lawyer. Start at the beginning. Tell me how you got on the police's radar in the first place."

"Got a few hours?" Hammer joked darkly.

Then he detailed the events of the past six years.

"What kind of paper trail did you leave with your bank?"

"None. I bought the money orders for Kendall out of a cash withdrawal of ten grand I took every month. I kept the receipts in my safe. That's where I also stashed the contract he signed."

Sterling hesitated. "What contract?"

"It detailed our agreement. I paid him two grand a month; he stayed the fuck away."

"Did Kendall have a copy of this contract?"

"God, no. I didn't trust that cocksucker. No way would I have given him the means to blackmail me. I was reckless at times but never stupid."

"Where are the receipts and the contract now?"

"They grew legs and walked away, along with two sets of photos taken of Raine when she first came to the club, beaten and bruised. One set is the originals. The other magically appeared recently. Ironically, you may hear that a copy of these photos somehow disappeared from the police evidence room. I have no idea how."

"I'm sure you don't," Sterling drawled. "And all this stuff walked to someplace safe?"

"Absolutely." Beck was too clever to fuck it up, Hammer knew.

"I'm glad you covered your ass, because if you're arrested, they'll search your house and your club simultaneously, probably as they're dragging you out in cuffs."

"Let's hope it doesn't come to that." Dread snaked through Hammer's stomach. "One thing I'm worried about...I'm missing two days of video surveillance." He went on to describe the footage and how he discovered it was gone. "They brought it up to Raine during her questioning."

Sterling didn't look pleased. "Damn. Let's see what develops. Maybe it won't be an issue."

"I didn't think any of this would be once Raine turned eighteen. I honestly thought I was in the clear."

The lawyer sent him a grave stare. "If they'd brought these charges against you three or four years ago, you'd be going to prison for a lifetime. They probably could have sent you away for statutory rape, kidnapping, oral copulation and sodomy with a minor—and more not-so-fun felonies."

"I didn't do any of those things," Hammer protested.

"Your word against theirs." Sterling shrugged. "Their circumstantial evidence looks damning enough. But you'll be happy to know the statute of limitations on all of those charges has expired. You're one lucky son of a bitch."

Hammer's jaw fell open. He sat forward in his chair. Had he heard that right? "You're fucking kidding me. So they can't try me for any of that?"

"No. The onus is on the defense to point that out, but I'll take care of it."

"So…I'm free?" He held his breath.

"Not exactly. You were paying Kendall as little as three months ago, so that's a potential problem. They may try to pin you with something related to bribery or extortion. Human trafficking is another possibility. But without a copy of your contract with Kendall, that would be tough to prove. After all, the purpose of the money changing hands would be your word against Raine's brother. And he wasn't around, so I'm hoping you're in the clear on that, too. The DA will go for the easier case, which probably leaves us with the three P's: prostitution, pimping, and pandering. But the minute we put Raine on the stand, I suspect she'll blow the prosecution's case to hell. And they know it.

"The other thing we have to consider is, if they've truly got a witness, we don't know what that person will say under oath and how compelling their testimony will be. Or…if the witness will be more reliable than Raine."

And Hammer wished to fuck he could think of who might testify against him. "If those charges stick, what kind of time am I looking at?"

"I'd tell you not to think about it, but you'll just Google it when you get home." Sterling sighed. "If they can convince a jury of it all— especially that Raine was a minor when it began—well, your kid could be driving a car by then. You might be able to plea down, maybe be out in half the time."

"No." Macen would never admit to brutalizing Raine for profit. He couldn't live with that.

Sterling's expression said he thought Hammer was being hasty. "We need to prepare for a potential trial. The prosecution will try to assassinate your character for the jury, especially since they don't have a tight case. Do you know anyone who can corroborate your claim that you didn't have sex with Raine as a minor?"

Zak, Raine's first. *Fuck me.*

"Yeah. There was a tape," he said, teeth gritted. "She was eighteen when she lost her virginity and…she was with someone else. I grabbed the tape as soon as I became aware of the situation."

"Great! We can—"

"I destroyed it." He certainly hadn't been able to watch Raine give her innocence to another man. Hammer already knew seeing that would have wrecked him. He would have likely murdered Zak.

Sterling shook his head. "And by the look on your face, no possibility of a backup."

"No."

"Know where we can find this guy in case he has to testify?"

Hammer closed his eyes and sucked in a deep breath. The thought of asking that pile of dog shit for anything scalded Hammer's pride. Even if he somehow managed to get the prick-assed son of a bitch on the stand, would he do more harm than good?

"I'll get someone working on that if the case goes forward." Hammer bit out the words.

"Good. Because if you can't prove you weren't exploiting her as a minor, you'll have to register as a sex offender, too."

He froze. Why didn't they just cut off his dick? "I'll lose Shadows. Hell, I won't even be allowed to go near it again for the rest of my life."

"Remember, what they can charge you with and what they can prove are two different things. They're on a fishing expedition, Macen, because you run a 'sex club.' They think you're one of society's bottom-feeders." The older man chuckled softly. "Funny, I thought we lawyers held that title."

Hammer wasn't amused.

"Stop worrying. Until they file formal charges, there's nothing to do but be patient."

Hammer scoffed. "You didn't just tell me to be patient, did you?"

Sterling grinned. "Indeed, I did, my boy. Which, of course, is like telling you to become a submissive. But I'm afraid until they tip their hand, all we can do is wait."

CHAPTER NINE

AFTER A RESTLESS night, Raine woke with Liam's heated flesh pressed against her back. She rose with a soft sigh.

Last night before dinner, he and Liam had made love to her. Then Hammer had finally told them about his police interview. After holding her and reassuring her as much as he could without making promises he couldn't keep, Macen had disappeared downstairs, taking Liam with him.

Then she'd heard the knock late last night, eavesdropped on the guys' conversation with Dean. Then Liam had disappeared for a bit during the wee hours. Hammer had rolled away from her a few hours later and left the house.

Raine sucked in a breath to hold herself together. Though both men tried to soften the truth, they were worried. It was indulgent and protective, and she loved them for it. But she was part of the problem since her brother had stirred the proverbial shit pot. So she had to be part of the solution.

Hammer and Liam might feel betrayed by her decision, but Raine intended to do whatever it took to explain to her brother all the ways he was ruining her life, then make him fix it.

After the spa incident, she obviously couldn't see him alone. Hammer had enough on his plate, and Liam might kill her brother.

Those two had to stay behind.

Darting another glance Liam's way to ensure he still slept, she bent beside the bed and retrieved the sweat pants Hammer had worn last night. She stuck her hand in the pockets, relieved when her fingers wrapped around a scrap of paper. Raine yanked it out. The address and room number of River's motel.

Tiptoeing past her sleeping Irishman, she threw herself together, then grabbed her phone from the nightstand. Two phone calls, and she'd be out the door.

Raine left the bedroom and smelled something delicious. Her stomach rumbled. Thank goodness Liam's mother had made herself at home in her kitchen.

As Raine entered the breakfast nook, she found Beck and Seth, devouring golden pancakes and bacon.

She couldn't hide her surprise. "Good morning. What are you doing here?"

Seth shrugged. "Liam's mom called and said you needed us."

Zipping a gaze over to Bryn, she blinked at the woman. "You know what I have planned?"

"Of course I do, lass. And you're right to think that Liam and Hammer will only hinder you. Go see River and reason with him. Seth and Kenneth will go along, keep you safe."

Raine smiled gratefully. "My thinking, too. Thanks."

Bryn bustled her into a hug. "I want to see you all happy, and I think you're on the right track."

Beck frowned. "I don't like the idea of going behind your Doms' backs, princess. They'll be plenty pissed off at us."

"Your brother is a dangerous guy. He's shown us he can be ruthless." Seth shook his head. "I'd feel better if Liam and Hammer knew where you were going and why."

"I'm the only one who can set River straight." Raine accepted the plate Bryn handed her with a silent thanks. "My brother will find out just how stubborn I can be."

"It will be good to have your last bit of family in your life," Bryn added.

Right now, Raine didn't care about that. Though her brother had once given her piggyback rides and swiped a candy bar from the corner store to see her smile, she'd lived this long without him.

"I'm not counting on that." She addressed Seth and Beck. "If you're not comfortable going with me, I'll go alone. But I'm definitely going."

The two men were hardly besties, and she definitely sensed competition between them over a certain blond nurse volunteer, but they glanced at one another and promptly got on the same page with a nod.

"What's this?" Liam stood tall and watchful at the entrance of the kitchen, scrutinizing the scene.

Her heart dropped. She'd really wanted to get away from home without a confrontation.

"I'm going to talk to River and make him listen. Please don't try to stop me, Liam. This is the only way I can help Macen."

"We said no. You promised us that you'd not seek out your brother." Liam's expression hardened. "There's no real proof of Hammer's wrongdoing. I doubt the evidence will hold up in court. We don't want you risking yourself."

"I made that promise before the police zeroed in on Macen. The stakes are higher now. So is the price he'll pay if I don't do this."

"River tried to kidnap you. Have you forgotten? Hammer and I never will. We almost lost you again. Do you not realize the hell he nearly put us through? And now I'm supposed to let you go meet that devil?"

Liam had always been protective, and she wouldn't have him any other way...but right now she needed support, not heroics. "If I take you with me, can you be calm and talk rationally?"

"Oh, there'll be no talking. There'll be my fist in River's face."

"This is why you can't be going with her, son," Bryn chided softly. "Let Raine handle this. She must."

"River won't lay a hand on her, man," Seth assured. "You have my word."

"Mine, too. And if the two of us aren't enough incentive, there's always my friends, Smith and Wesson." Beck patted the bulge beneath his shirt. "The princess will be safe."

Raine nodded. "I won't do anything reckless."

Liam paused as if seeking fortitude. Then he glanced at his mother and sighed. "I must be mad. Fine. I won't stand in your way."

"Really? You won't?" She hadn't expected him to give his permission—ever.

"Liam and I chatted over tea earlier, lass. He knows I'm right," Bryn supplied. "He simply doesn't like it."

"I don't." Liam approached Raine and pressed his hand to her belly. "You'll *both* be careful, won't you?"

"I promise. I'm going to surprise River. This time, everything will be on my terms. Then I'll come home to you and Hammer because you're all I've ever wanted."

"Then go." Liam caressed her hair, concern pouring from his dark eyes.

"Thank you for understanding. Oh, and Macen is with his lawyer, right?" At Liam's nod, she bit her lip. "Don't tell him about this yet. He's got enough going on without stressing about me. I plan to be home before him."

"Christ, Raine. You're asking me to deceive my best mate."

"No, I'm just asking you to keep this between us until I have good news. Once I'm back here safe and sound, he won't have anything to snarl and growl about. Well, not much."

After finishing her breakfast, Raine rose with Beck and Seth in tow. As they headed for the door, Liam set his plate aside and wrapped her in his arms, holding tight before he begrudgingly released her and kissed her hard. "Hurry home. I love you, Raine."

"I'm doing this for us." She brushed a hand over the life growing inside her. "All of us. I love you, too."

Once outside, they climbed into Seth's rental and headed to River's address. As they exited the car, the California sun beat down. A strong Santa Ana wind blew, and the hot air whipped at her hair, masking the pounding of her heart in her ears.

She rapped on the hollow wooden door and waited, feeling Seth and Beck hovering protectively behind her.

After pounding footsteps, the door swung open. River stood, frozen, his expression sharp. "Raine. Who the hell are these clowns, more johns?"

Here we go… "I came to talk to you like a reasonable human being. Stop assuming I'm a whore!"

"I didn't say you were by choice." The pity in his eyes stung her.

"These are my friends. They're here to make sure you don't pull the same stupid shit you tried at the spa."

River looked downright skeptical. "So they've never seen you naked?"

They had—more than once—but not for sex. That answer would only confuse her brother. "Is that really your biggest concern? I'm here to talk to you about the mess you've made of my life. And unlike the last time you blindsided me, you're going to fucking listen."

"If Liam could hear you now, little one…" Seth murmured behind her.

Yeah, her Irishman hated when she cursed. But now wasn't the time to think about that. She flashed a glare over her shoulder at the big blond PI.

Seth shrugged. "I think he'd be proud. Go get 'em, tiger."

Shaking her head, Raine faced her brother, only to find him with his arms across his chest.

"There's not much you can say to convince me I'm wrong. You're embarrassed you've become a victim. I understand. I'll help you out of your despair."

"Oh, my god, are you, like, a brick wall?" She charged at him, poking her finger in his hard middle. "First of all, I've never been in 'despair' with Hammer or Liam. They have both loved me unconditionally, unlike my own family. Second, I don't give a shit if you feel as if I haven't justified my life to you. You left, and I owe you nothing. So don't for one second, think I'm here groveling for your approval or asking you to rescue me. Third, I will not leave until you admit you're an impulsive dumb ass who unjustly accused Macen. The police are in his face because you and that morality stick you've got shoved up your ass have decided—without hearing my side of the story—that I'm some damsel in distress you have to save. I don't need you."

"Wow," Beck whispered behind her. "She'd make a bitchin' Domme."

Seth chuckled softly.

River scowled. "If you don't need rescuing, why didn't you say that at the spa?"

"I tried. But no. You just decided I needed abducting." She tossed her hands in the air. "I didn't have a speech prepared that day. I do now, so you better be listening."

"Look, I blame myself for not coming back Stateside sooner and making sure you were all right. It fucking eats at me that I was nearly eight thousand miles away, serving Uncle Sam, when Rowan died and you left home. I wish I could have saved her life and you years of misery, prostitution, and rape. I get that Bill was no peach, and these guys are probably better in some ways—"

"In *every* way," she swore, eyes burning. "They love me in ways I never knew men could love."

He reared back. "I don't want to hear about your sex life."

"That's it! I have fucking had it with you." She stomped her foot, fuming. "Forget about sex."

"Hard to do when I'm looking at my pregnant sister."

She stared upward, grasping for patience.

Beck and Seth were about to hear her vomit out her past. The sadist knew some of it. The PI might be aware, too... But privacy had ceased to matter. Only Hammer did.

"Do you want the truth or do you just want to stand there and judge me like a prick?"

"Oh, no." River shook his head. "I want to hear this."

"Good. Can I come in and tell you my story? Without you butting in or adding your two cents?"

"Not without us." Seth set ground rules immediately.

She turned to her bodyguards for the day. "Of course not."

When Raine turned back to make sure her brother understood, River stared warily between the other two men, then shrugged and opened the door wide. "All right. Come in."

The cool, dark motel room was nothing fancy. The bottle-green carpet didn't quite match the mustard walls. A black-and-white landscape hung above the massive bed. The kitchenette looked well used. A jug of whey protein sat on the counter, next to half a dozen discarded eggshells. Apparently, he'd just finished breakfast.

He gestured her to the desk chair near the door. There was a bistro table on the far side of the room, near the fridge. But when River offered up those seats, Beck and Seth refused to stray from her side.

With a raised brow, River sat on the edge of the bed that looked too rumpled for mere sleep. "I'm listening."

Now that she had his attention, emotions pelted Raine, short-circuiting her thoughts before she could finish them.

"Start at the beginning," River encouraged. "Bill sold you to Hammer as a minor and..."

"*What?*" Where the hell had he heard that? "Not even close. This all started because our dear daddy had a nasty temper."

River nodded. "I know. I've got the scars to prove it."

"You're not alone, though mine are purely emotional now. Hammer took me to a plastic surgeon back when…" She held up her hands and shook her head. She was getting off track. "My last couple of years under Bill's roof, I slept with a knife under my pillow. I had just turned seventeen when the drunk busted down my door one night to take my virginity."

"What?" River breathed. "Jesus…"

"I resisted. He beat me. I think he meant to kill me that night, too."

River pressed his lips into a tight line. "I thought the violent bastard just hated me."

"He hated everything, especially us. I managed to slash his cheek, grab a 'go' bag I had stashed just in case, and sneak out my window. It was three in the morning. I had eight dollars to my name and nowhere to go. He made damn sure I had very few friends."

"Yeah, he was good at isolating everyone. Manipulating and making those around him feel small."

So her brother had experienced that firsthand. Maybe convincing him that Macen was the best thing that had happened to her as a kid wouldn't be a total uphill battle. "Exactly. After I left, I wandered around in a stupor for two days. Dehydrated and starving, I was in agony. Bruises, cuts, a cracked rib. I was ready to give up, throw myself in front of a car or something… I hid in the alley behind Shadows and cried."

"Storm cloud…" He looked stricken.

"That's where Hammer found me. He took me in. He…adopted me, for lack of a better description. He fed, clothed, healed, protected, educated, coddled, helped—all the things family should do. For that, the police are calling him a pervert, a child molester? They're trying to charge him for crimes he never committed."

"After what you survived with Bill, I don't blame you for whatever choices you made. You were a kid. If you'd stayed with Bill, he would have killed you. So I'm damn glad you got out. But I blame Hammer. He took advantage of you. In exchange for his care, he forced you to give him sex."

"No, he didn't! If any man ever laid a finger on me against my will, I'd do exactly to them what I did to Bill. But Hammer never tried. I worked for him as an assistant, cook, bookkeeper, and errand girl. I kept his life running smoothly. He maintained boundaries between us, even when he knew I'd fallen in love with him. Even when I threw myself at him shamelessly."

"So he waited a few weeks before taking advantage of your gratitude and molesting you? Touching."

"Are you the world's biggest asshole?" Beck gaped. "I'm a doctor. Why don't you let me cure your condition? A lobotomy ought to do it."

She shot the sadist a chastising stare. "Please... I got this." Then she turned to River. "What he said."

Seth sighed noisily. "Liam and Hammer are right. This is pointless. He's never going to hear."

"Dude..." Beck shook his head. "I was at Shadows the night Hammer brought your sister into the club. He. Didn't. Touch. Her. God knows he fucked everyone else—"

"Thanks for the reminder," she snapped.

River sat up and pointed at her belly. "Obviously, he took you to bed at some point. When?"

"That's pretty damn personal, and she doesn't owe you an answer except that she was over eighteen," Seth reminded.

She ignored the big blond hulk. "Last November fourth. That's the first time he ever laid a finger on me, more than *six years* after he took me in. Macen never touched me, pimped me out, or engaged in any sexual behavior with me until three months ago. I was almost halfway to nineteen when I lost my virginity, and it wasn't to Hammer. Everything about that was purely my choice."

And when she remembered how badly she'd hurt Macen, remorse shredded her.

"Lousy fucking choice, too," Beck grumbled. "Zak was a raving piece of shit."

Raine gestured toward Beck. She couldn't argue with facts, but his corroboration didn't hurt, either.

Her brother took a moment to digest that. "Why did Hammerman give Bill money, if not to buy you for sex? I saw the old fuck just before he died. That's what he told me."

"And you believed him?"

River had the good grace to flush. "He kept a copy of every money order Master Pervert sent. It made sense…"

"Well—big shocker—Bill lied. Hammer paid him to stay the hell away from me. He voluntarily gave that bottom-feeding asshole two thousand dollars a month for six years to keep me safe. He bought me a car. He paid for my college." She teared up when she thought of all Macen had done for her. "He is the first person in my life to ever stay. He could have left me in the alley or called CPS, who might have sent me to a home even worse. But no. He risked *everything* to help me and expected nothing in return." She slapped a hand to her chest and began to fall apart as the enormity of Macen's sacrifice hit her again. "And because your head is in the gutter, you've taken his selfless act and convinced the police it's something dirty. He may be lost to me forever because you can't fathom sticking your neck out to help a kid in need without wanting sex for it."

Raine slapped a hand over her mouth as sobs fell free. If she'd pissed River off and he refused to recant his story to the police, Hammer would spend the rest of his life behind bars. Fear sliced its sharp scalpel down her middle and gutted her.

Seth dropped a hand on her shoulder. Raine tried to collect herself and carry on, but the hell Hammer faced drowned out her words.

"Storm cloud?" River sounded concerned.

She swiped the tears from her cheeks with a watery nod. "If it wasn't for Hammer, I would have ended up like Rowan."

"Dead in the desert?" River's voice hardened.

"It was so much worse than that. So, so much." She bit back more sobs. "You left that July, and she turned thirteen in August. He started raping her on her birthday that year. He'd gotten her pregnant twice by the time she was fifteen, and he had them terminated both times."

"Oh…" River groaned, looking pale and stunned. "I had no idea. Stop."

"No. This is the truth, and you need to hear it. Rowan let Bill molest her over and over to shield me because no one else was there to stop him. When she 'went off to college,' he killed her for the great sin of wanting to leave him. Then he turned his attention on me. I had no idea what was going on prior to that, and I can't tell you how guilty I feel for being so fucking oblivious. She suffered and I did nothing…"

Raine couldn't say more. The regret and guilt undid her.

Seth rounded her chair and knelt in front of her, concern softening his green eyes. She shook her head. If she took his comfort now, she'd only fall apart more.

She had to be strong enough to make her brother see the truth.

River rose from the bed, swallowed. "I had no idea. Bill kicked me out that summer because I challenged him about Mom's 'escape.' I was suspicious and I'd gotten big enough to fight back when he hit me for it. He beat the shit out of me a lot as a boy, but he never touched me like that… Jesus. I'm so sorry I left. I was angry and I missed Mom. After that, I was just a kid with no job or social skills, trying to learn how to feed myself and survive. I ended up street fighting for money. I almost killed a guy with my bare hands, so I went to juvie. The judge told me to enlist when I turned eighteen or go to prison, so I joined the service. Once I was there, I just wanted to forget it all and be someone normal."

"We were all Bill's victims. But why didn't you listen when Hammer and Liam tried to tell you what my life was like? Or when I explained?"

He shook his head and raked a hand over his scalp. "I'm a soldier, storm cloud. Until seventy-three days ago, that's all I've ever been. I left a commanding officer, trained to look at facts and make quick decisions. I called it like I saw it."

On shaky legs, she rose. Seth and Beck were both there, offering her their hands. She took them because she'd cried out so much of her fortitude. Damn it, she'd sworn another Kendall man would never hurt her.

"You were wrong. Hammer doesn't even know I'm here. He would *never* want me begging on his behalf." Her proud, strong Dom would rather go down with his head held high. But she'd give up her soul over and over to save him. "Liam didn't want me here, either. But I insisted because I would do *anything* for the man who's done *everything* for me."

"Princess," Beck whispered. "Take a deep breath. Liam and Hammer wouldn't want you upsetting yourself this much."

Raine knew that. She felt decimated and spent and empty of everything but the gnawing fear that she wouldn't get to grow old with Macen.

"There are only two people in my life I can't do without, and you're trying to send one of them to prison. I'm in agony and I'm begging you to stop this. Please…"

Slowly, River approached her. On either side of her, Beck and Seth tensed, poised to defend her. She stared at the stranger who had her eyes, the only other person left on the planet who knew what it meant to grow up under Bill Kendall's iron fist. Raine didn't know what she expected, but her mountain of a brother wiping tears from her cheeks with the gentlest of touches wasn't it.

"It's hard to understand, my kid sister living with two men both older, previously married, and so much more experienced. They're Doms, so I have a really good idea what they demand of you. The visual is burned into my retinas, and I'm sick at the thought of you kneeling for anyone. And you're pregnant." He rubbed at his eyes with thumb and forefinger. "It's hard to accept. But I'm trying."

"I'm not asking you to love it. I'm asking you to tell the police you got your facts wrong and make these terrible charges go away. I've said all I can. If you need to see my life for yourself, follow me home. If you don't believe how happy and adored I am then, you never will."

Praying River would come along so the healing—and her future—could begin, she released Beck and Seth and left the motel.

LIAM SIGHED.

Fifteen minutes ago, Hammer had come through the front door and deduced that Raine was with River. He hadn't taken a breath since.

"I can't believe you just let her walk out the damn door. Seriously, Liam. We're supposed to protect her from that prick, and you just…what? Usher her out with a smile and a wave. 'Sure, love,'" he mimicked. "'Go have fun with your crazy brother. Hope you come back!' Are you fucking kidding?"

"She was determined to see him—with or without our permission. What would you have me do? Tie her up?"

"Maybe. Or maybe you should have chained her to the bed, like I told you to."

"Is that your solution to everything?"

Hammer surged into his face, turning three shades of red. "At least we'd know she's safe."

"We both know how she handled restraints last time we tried. Be reasonable. We can't make Raine a prisoner in her own home. I worry about her, too. But she's strong-willed, a survivor. And she's no one's fool."

"No, we're the fools for letting her walk out the door!"

"She's well within her rights to come and go as she pleases."

Macen looked as flexible as a brick wall. "River's unstable. Maybe he took too much shrapnel to the brain. Or hey, maybe he's as fucked up as their old man. Either way, we're here with our thumbs up our asses, and she's god knows where."

Liam didn't need Hammer's rant to remember what was at stake. In fact, the longer Raine was gone, the more worry began to creep in.

Doubt was a sly son of a bitch.

"I told you, she's not alone. Beck and Seth are—"

"Not you and me. What if they can't stop River and something happens to her?"

That possibility had skidded through Liam's brain more than once. "I know it's a risk, and I'd never be able to live with myself if—"

"Trust me. You wouldn't have to." Hammer speared him with an angry glare, pacing across the living room floor.

"I have to believe she'll come through that door any minute now." That gut instinct his mother had told him to home in on said so.

And if he was wrong, if Raine didn't return, he'd end River Kendall in every gory way he could conceive.

Before Macen could start the argument again, Raine slipped in the house with a jangle of her keys, Beck and Seth flanking her. Relief spread through Liam.

He clapped Macen on the back. "See, mate? She's good as gold."

Hammer wasn't listening. He scooped her up in his arms and crushed her against his body for a long heartbeat. Then he reached down and swatted the hell out of her ass.

"Ouch!" she yelped.

Liam maneuvered his way between Hammer and their girl, rescuing her backside—for now.

When Raine skittered back, they caught sight of her face. She'd gone blotchy, her eyes red and puffy. Worry choked Liam by the throat.

Hammer gripped her shoulders. "What happened? Are you hurt?"

"No, Macen." Her soft voice sounded weary. "I'm perfectly fine."

"Bullshit. You've been crying. What did that motherfucking bastard do to you?"

"Nothing. Talking to him, dredging up the past, was just very emotional."

Hammer clenched his jaw, clearly trying to rein in his temper. "But nothing else is wrong?"

"No."

"Good," he barked. "Do you have any idea how out-of-my-fucking-head I've been? You promised you'd stay away from that nutjob, yet the first time I turn my back, you run off to meet him."

Beck and Seth sidled up to Raine as if they weren't finished protecting her. She merely raised a hand to stop them and shook her head. "I'm sorry, Sir."

In a graceful swoop, Raine lowered herself to her knees at their feet, palms up over each thigh, head bowed.

Liam's heart skipped a beat. *Clever girl.* Pride swelled inside him.

A hush fell over the room.

Macen released the pent-up breath he'd been holding and dropped to one knee, cupping her chin so he could lift her gaze to his. "Why?"

"To help you." She met his stare, as if willing him to understand. "I had to convince River to tell the police he'd been wrong about you."

"Did I ask for your help?" Hammer arched a brow.

"No. You never would. But my family has brought us enough grief and pain. I felt like it was my responsibility to end that for good. I'm sorry I worried you."

Liam cast a sidelong glance at Macen, who clenched his teeth, looking ready to explode.

"Mate…" Liam tried to be the voice of reason.

"Responsibility?" Hammer's nostrils flared. "The responsibility for your mind, body, heart, and soul belongs to Liam and me. What your family does is not a reflection on you, so it's not your job to clean up their fucking messes. Assuming the role of your own protector is the equivalent of taking back your submission."

Liam couldn't argue with that. He hoped Raine didn't try.

"That's not how I meant it," she assured. "But I'll accept whatever discipline you decide to mete out."

"Damn right you will. Later. And when I'm done, you'll remember never to play one Dom against the other again."

"Yes, Sir." She bowed her head.

Her acceptance seemed to ease Hammer. He lifted her to her feet and hauled her against his chest once more. "If anything had happened to you... Jesus, Raine."

Then he claimed her mouth with brutal tenderness. Liam's heart kick-started back into a regular rhythm. He gave them a moment more before embracing them both, peppering kisses up Raine's neck.

When Macen released her lips, Liam swooped in, framing her face with both hands and kissing her soundly, savoring her softness and warmth. "We were worried about you, love."

"Are you going to punish me, too?" Confusion furrowed her brow.

"No. It's Hammer's permission you didn't have. But I'll not stand in his way. You could have waited to ask him, too, and you chose not to."

"But—" Raine pressed her lips together, shelving her argument. "I didn't."

"Be glad I'm not the one dishing out the punishment, princess. It's possible Hammer will go easier on you." Then Beck glanced at Macen's face. "Or not."

With a slap on Seth's shoulder, Liam turned to the lads. "Thank you both for watching over our girl and bringing her back safely."

Hammer leveled a cold glare at them. "I'm sure I'll thank you one day, but it won't be today."

Beck laughed. "Didn't think it would. If you want pointers on really making her ass glow—"

"We don't," Liam cut in.

Seth tried to repress a smile. "Raine did a fine job of getting her point across."

Beck scoffed. "She lit a fire under River's ass that would put an Eagle Scout to shame. I should have snapped video of that shit for you. Hammer, she made you sound like a fucking saint."

Raine bit her lip. "I really did."

Liam wasn't surprised in the least. He took their girl's hand.

"C'mon, Hammer," Seth ribbed him. "You're berating her for trying to help you, and it's Valentine's Day."

Macen glared. "Someday, I hope you love a woman who scares the shit out of you."

The smile slid off Seth's face. "I have, and you know it."

Liam wanted to smack Hammer upside the head for opening his mouth and inserting his loafer.

At least he had the good grace to wince. "I didn't mean—"

"I know," Seth cut him off. "Just remember to enjoy your someone special. Not everyone has that. Beck and I are going to raid your refrigerator, give you three a minute."

"That cool, princess?" Beck shot Raine a meaningful glance.

She looked a little nervous but smiled. "Perfect. Thanks."

The whole exchange struck Liam as odd.

Hammer frowned as he watched the guys amble into the next room. But with a shake of his head, he turned to Raine. "Before you tell me everything that happened with River—and I mean every last detail—Liam and I want to give you something." He reached into his pocket and drew out a little red box, then placed it in her palm. "Open this, precious. Happy Valentine's Day."

"There's a lot happening now, but we wanted to give you something memorable." Liam stroked her hair and pressed a kiss to her temple.

Raine lifted the lid and her eyes widened. She sucked in a happy gasp as she plucked the delicate silver bracelet from the box.

"Oh, my... It's beautiful!" Tears of joy filled her eyes as she clutched it to her heart. "The pendant my mother gave me... You found it."

"In your closet back at the club." Macen nodded.

"Mom gave me that necklace when I turned seven. She said that although I was her baby, I was grown up enough for something pretty." Raine pressed a hand to her trembling lips. "I wore it every day after she died. The chain it came with broke the night Bill..." She shook her head and refused to finish the sentence. "I put it in my pocket, then tucked it away at Shadows. Thank you so much. And more charms!"

She examined the three entwined filigree hearts—one representing each of them. She had to wipe her eyes again when she spied the tiny silver baby booties. Unconsciously, she placed a palm on her belly.

Liam turned to look at Hammer. They shared a glance of uncertainty.

"We didn't mean to make you cry, love."

"These are happy tears. It's perfect!"

He grinned in relief. "I designed the trio of hearts myself. Hammer and I found the baby booties together."

"I can't thank you enough." She wrapped her arms around them and held tight.

"It's just as beautiful as the photo you texted me when you picked it up. Her mother's pendant was the perfect addition. See, you're not all bad with the touchy-feely shit," Liam whispered in Hammer's ear.

Macen smiled. "We're glad you like it, precious."

"I love it. I couldn't have asked for anything more meaningful."

He and Hammer worked together to latch the bracelet around her wrist. She beamed as she looked at it gleaming in the light.

"I hope you like what I got you at least half this much." She hurried across the room and drew two small wrapped boxes with white satin bows from her purse. Dashing back, Raine handed one each to him and Hammer.

They unwrapped their gifts in unison. Liam smiled when he noticed Macen pluck up a key ring identical to his, attached to a thick silver medallion. He flipped it over and read the inscription. "Love has a beautiful new meaning with you in my life."

Liam bit back the emotion lodged in his throat and brushed a kiss over her lips. "Thank you, lass. You bring a beautiful new meaning to my life, too."

"I loved you yesterday. I love you still. I always have. I always will." Hammer's voice sounded thick and low as he read her gift to him. "Oh, precious. You know that's precisely how I feel."

She stroked their faces. "Good. Please keep that in mind..."

Liam pierced her with a suspicious stare. "What have you done?"

She wrung her hands—always a bad sign. "I need you to take a deep breath and keep an open mind."

"Oh, shit," Hammer groused.

"It's fine. Really." She glanced somewhere over their right shoulders. "We just have a visitor…"

Raine didn't finish the sentence. Liam whirled around to see what had distracted her. Beck and Seth strode around the corner and back into the living room—with River Kendall right behind them.

Liam lost his mind.

"What are you doing here?" He charged at Raine's brother. "Get the fuck out!"

Fists clenched, teeth bared, Hammer followed with a feral roar.

Beck and Seth blocked them. Like they were…what? Protecting Kendall? Liam scowled. *Oh, hell no.*

Pandemonium exploded. Raine tried to reason with him, but her words were lost in a din of angry wasps filling his head.

"Step aside." He set her behind him.

She tugged on his arm with all her might. He shrugged her grip off.

"You cocksucking asshole, how dare you set foot in this house!" Hammer pinned River with a stare that promised violence, snarling the warning around the doctor's shoulder. "You're a motherfucking dead man, Kendall."

"I'll be happy to help him," Liam spat.

"That's enough!" Raine screamed over the chaos. "You accused him of not listening, but you're not doing any better."

Hammer shoved against Beck again. Liam surged forward to help him push the other man aside. Seth blocked his way. The swarm of wasps in his head buzzed louder. A red haze of fury filmed his gaze.

"Take your bloody hands off me and get out of my way, Seth. I will lay your ass out."

"No, you won't." The big PI's calm tone belied the vise-like death grip he had on Liam's arm. "Give Kendall a chance to explain. If you don't like what he says, Beck and I will help you kick his ass."

Seth's offer did nothing to appease the rage surging through Liam's veins. Instead, he tried to shove past his friend again while Beck and Hammer fought their own brutal struggle. Yells and curses filled the air.

Somewhere in the back of Liam's head, his mother tugged at his thoughts, chastising, as she darted down the stairs. He cursed under his breath.

"—I mean it, damn it!" Raine stamped her foot angrily, her face a glowing red. "Will you two Neanderthals give my brother a chance to speak? I asked him to come here, and neither of you will undo in two minutes what took me two hours to accomplish!"

Hammer snarled. "That son of a bitch can't say anything that will change—"

"I'm sorry for what I've done to you, Hammer. Liam," River interrupted with a somber frown. "After seeing how concerned you were for Raine just now, I'm hoping you understand that I was out of my head with worry for my kid sister. She's all I have left. And I'm only here because she told me to come and see your relationship for myself. Now I...understand what she's been trying to get through my stubborn head," River bit out as if eating crow burned his tongue. "You both love her."

"Of course they do." Bryn suddenly appeared with a smile, Duncan by her side. "Now that we've cleared that misunderstanding up, why don't you all sit down and chat?"

Liam couldn't breathe past his anger. He clenched his fists. The last thing in the world he wanted to do was look at River Kendall across his table and pretend he didn't hate the home-wrecking bastard.

"Pull it together, son," Duncan said quietly in his ear. "It's time to listen and heal."

It took all his will and strength to swallow his fury back long enough to nod his father's way.

"Great idea, Bryn." Raine turned to Liam and Hammer. "Take a nice, deep breath. Act like adults and listen. Please?"

"Watch yourself, girl," Hammer warned.

Rage still seethed under Liam's surface. "You're on thin ice."

"Behave, boys. I'll make us some tea," Bryn offered before darting away. "Duncan?"

The pair left, and Liam wondered if they'd taken his only hope of sanity.

"You good here, princess?" Beck asked.

She hugged the sadist and sent him a dry smile. "I think we'll be okay. I don't know what the world is coming to when I'm the coolest head in the room, but we'll make do."

Seth pressed a kiss to her forehead. "Go get 'em once more, tiger. You can do it. We'll check in with you soon."

"Go take Heavenly to dinner," she suggested.

"I plan to." Seth flashed a cocky grin. "Before I have her for dessert."

Beck looked dead furious. "No, you fucking won't."

Beck and Seth argued all the way to the door. In the interest of not committing murder on Raine's pale beige carpet, Liam let them go.

He settled around the kitchen table with Hammer and Raine. River sat last. The animosity and blame still weighed heavily on Liam as Raine recounted everything that had transpired in River's hotel room.

His heart ached, knowing she'd once again had to relive the anguish she'd survived.

"I only wanted my sister safe. What I saw from the kitchen just now..." River looked stunned. "I'm sorry I didn't listen sooner."

"I know," Raine softly whispered.

River appeared contrite enough, but Liam wasn't convinced the man could possibly understand the depth of love the three of them shared in a five-minute glimpse.

"As touching as your apology is, it doesn't solve the mess you've made of our lives," Hammer hissed. "Or the fact that you upset your sister even more with this fucking stunt. They hauled her downtown yesterday for questioning. She's pregnant, you stupid ass. And she had to put up with strangers calling her a whore and grilling her about her sex life."

"I'm sorry. If I could take it all back—"

"The damage is done," Liam snapped. "Unless you can fix it, I don't think we have anything to say."

"I'll do everything possible." River met Liam's sharp gaze. "I'll visit Detectives Winslow and Cameron and explain that I should never have believed the bullshit my father fed me before he died. If Raine defends you, too, I don't see how the police have a case worth pursuing."

Liam didn't, either. Except the supposed witness and the missing security footage disconcerted him.

Trying not to borrow trouble, he stood. "Don't be letting the door hit your ass on the way out."

Raine blinked at him, mouth agape, while Hammer stared River down coldly. "Guys…"

"No, it's okay," River insisted. "In their shoes, I'd be pissed off, too. Assumptions in war can save your life. In love…apparently they're dangerous. I'll fix things. I want to keep you in my life, Raine. And I want you happy."

"Then start by apologizing to our girl," Liam demanded. "You fucking made her cry, you—"

"Liam," Raine interrupted, settling her hand over his. "Fear of losing Macen and the life we share is what made me break down. Well, that and hormones."

"You want to fix things?" Hammer challenged, obviously not quite believing River's contrition. "Start by telling us who you're working with inside Shadows. Who's your mole?"

River looked confused. "I don't have an informant."

"Really?" Hammer scoffed. "How did you know about Raine's apple spice muffins, then? And where the fuck are the missing security drives?"

"I have no clue what you're talking about," River swore.

"Bullshit." Hammer looked ready to throw punches once more.

River held up both hands. "I might be hardheaded, but I'm not a fucking liar. You wanted me to listen to you? I'm on it. But I'd like the same."

Hammer studied the man with a steely gaze, then finally gave a grim nod. Not seeing another option, Liam followed suit.

But he knew they'd be putting their heads together later in private to figure this out.

Raine sighed in relief. "Thank you."

"We like to make you smile, love." Liam could at least say that with honesty.

He didn't trust River, but if the bastard was telling the truth, that was good for Raine…and bad for them all. His dread ratcheted up.

"What are you doing tomorrow?" she asked her brother suddenly.

Liam flipped her a scowl. Did she mean to invite the meddlesome git to dinner?

"Looking for a job." He shrugged. "But I'll make time for you."

"Would you, um…" Raine bit her lip.

Liam had a suspicion he knew what his lass was reluctant to ask. "Raine, you don't have to—"

"I do," she countered softly, then regarded her brother. "I've never visited Mom's and Rowan's graves. I think I'm ready now. I'd like it if you came with me."

He and Hammer should be the ones to accompany her on such an emotional undertaking. Liam bristled. "Maybe you should wait until after the babe comes."

"The extra stress isn't good for either of you," Hammer pointed out.

"Why don't you all consider going?" Bryn bustled to the table, carrying a fresh pot of tea. "That way Raine and River can say their good-byes, and you two will be there to comfort her."

Raine darted a hopeful gaze between him and Hammer. They exchanged a silent glance.

Hammer sighed. "All right. We'll go with you, precious."

"Thank you." Raine's smile looked both wobbly and tender. "How's noon tomorrow?"

"Great," River said. "I won't say I'm looking forward to it, but it's time I paid my respects."

"Excellent." Bryn kissed Liam's cheek. "Sounds like you're all getting along. Your da and I are going to pop out for an early Valentine's Day dinner, then. We'll be back in a bit."

After Mum hugged Macen and Raine, his parents left.

Liam no longer had to be polite. He stood, hoping River would get the hint. "We'll meet you at the cemetery, then."

Raine's brother did, indeed, grasp his unspoken suggestion. "Okay. I'll…head over to the police station and clean up the mess I made. Night, all. Happy…um, Valentine's Day."

As Raine rose and enfolded her arms around the man, Hammer pinned him with an icy stare. Liam shot a warning glare of his own, promising a slow and painful death if River backstabbed them again.

He and Hammer both wrapped a protective arm around Raine as they walked River to the door and watched him drive away.

Once he was gone, Liam pulled her into his arms and held her tightly. "It seems I've been waiting half my life to have you back, love."

But he didn't stop there. Liam also claimed her mouth in a slow, sultry kiss.

She sent him a sweet smile when he lifted away. "I needed that."

"What you need is your ass spanked bright red," Hammer growled before sinking a fist in her hair and pulling her mouth to his.

Desire jolted Liam as he watched their heated kiss. And a feeling of something close to calm returned. If River followed through, maybe this nightmare would soon be over.

As Macen reluctantly eased away from her lips, Liam faced him. "So now that we're alone, what information did Sterling have?"

"Good news…and bad. And speaking of Sterling, I need to call him and let him know that River intends to recant. Let's change for dinner. Mélisse? I've got reservations. Or…" He sighed. "Mother Dough?"

That was a huge concession for Hammer. He loved good food, but Raine had been craving pizza since her pregnancy began.

Her eyes lit with excitement. "You'd do that for me?"

His expression hinted that he should check his own sanity, but he nodded. "Pizza it is. While we're eating, I'll explain everything."

CHAPTER TEN

WHEN RAINE, LIAM, and Hammer returned from a tasty Valentine's Day dinner, they found a note lying on the kitchen table.

YOUR MOTHER AND I DECIDED TO SPEND THE NIGHT AT MONTAGE BEVERLY HILLS FOR OUR OWN ROMANTIC CELEBRATION. ENJOY YOUR NIGHT.

LOVE,
DA

"Looks like we have the place to ourselves tonight," Hammer drawled.

Raine giggled at his devilish grin, feeling lighter than she had in months. Knowing that Macen couldn't be charged with most of the crimes he'd been questioned for and that her brother meant to undo the fiasco he'd caused filled her with relief. Her big, bad Dom still had some healing to do, but maybe she and her men could finally live, laugh, love. Grow old together in peace with their children surrounding them.

"I'm glad you're in a good mood. Because there's still the matter of your punishment."

Raine blinked at Hammer. "On Valentine's Day?"

"It's the perfect occasion to turn your pretty, heart-shaped ass red."

Though his hungry tenor had her aching with a pang of desire, she had something in mind. "But I had this whole plan—"

"There'll be time later." Lust gleamed in Liam's dark eyes. "After Hammer extracts his penance."

"All right." Arguing would only make it worse. "Can I have a minute to hang up my dress so it doesn't wrinkle? I'll meet you in the dungeon."

Hammer eyed her suspiciously. "Don't keep us waiting, precious. Or it will cost you."

"I won't. I promise." Raine raced up the stairs, into their bedroom. As she stripped off her dress and settled it on the hanger, she glanced regretfully at the lingerie she'd worn underneath. She should take it off. They had a standing order that forbid her any clothes in their private dungeon.

But damn it, she'd been planning tonight's sexy celebration for weeks, scouring everywhere to find just the right scrap of temptation. The thong—silky red and black secured in a tiny bow directly over her pussy—was a tad snugger than when she'd bought it. The transparent top was a frilly bit that flowed away from her body, exposing her navel and the hint of her growing baby belly.

If she didn't change, she might please the hell out of her men...or bait the bears. Either outcome meant she got to glory in their Dominance. And the looks on their faces when they caught sight of her would be well worth an extra spanking or two. Besides, they could all use a release of tension. Making love the other night had been exactly the balm they'd needed to reaffirm their commitment.

Now she could give them a much-needed opportunity to reestablish their control.

"No guts, no glory," she muttered, then headed down the hall, still half-dressed.

As she slipped into the dungeon, Raine darted a quick glance at both Liam and Hammer. Pleasure and pride spread through her at the mix of shock and lust etched across their faces.

Trying to repress a smile, she knelt before them and cast her gaze on the carpet below. "Sirs."

"Raine, what made you decide to break the rules and prance in wearing this pretty bit of fluff?" Liam asked, not sounding particularly pleased.

Damn, had she screwed up? "I bought this second gift, and I wanted to surprise you two tonight."

"So you chose to disobey us? You couldn't wait until we got to the bedroom?" Hammer's humorless chuckle sent a shiver down her spine. "Oh, little girl..."

"I didn't think we'd make it that long, Sir."

"Are you begging for more of our attention?" Liam's voice rang sharp. "Or are you merely trying to provoke us?"

Both.

"Like I told Macen earlier, I'll take whatever punishment he gives me."

"Indeed you will, precious," he assured. "Starting now. Stand."

Rising, Raine sucked in a deep breath and pressed down the anxiety bubbling in her stomach. They'd only been in this dungeon a handful of times. She knew Hammer and Liam had tried to give her time to heal after the ordeal with Bill. And while she was iffy on the bondage right now, she ached to submit to them—show them her growth, prove she was ready to surrender her control, and hope that someday soon she'd feel their collar around her neck.

When Macen placed a possessive hand at the small of her back, she drew in a steadying breath. Something shifted inside her. Jagged nerves began to smooth. They would take care of her.

He led her to the cross and pressed her against the cold, polished wood. A shiver rippled through her. Her nipples drew taut. Excitement and anticipation hummed in her veins.

"Arms above your head. Spread your legs wide," Hammer growled in her ear.

Trying to control her thoughts and her breathing, Raine braced herself to feel the fleece-lined leather cuffs clamp around her wrists. But Hammer's hand simply remained fixed at her back. She turned a quizzical glance at him over her shoulder.

"No, I'm not going to bind you to the cross. But you will remain exactly in this position throughout the duration of your punishment. Is that understood?"

It was a comforting mercy. "Thank you, Sir."

"I'm going to talk. You will remain silent. Don't speak or try to justify yourself."

"Yes, Sir."

"Good girl." In long, sweeping circles, Hammer drew his hand up her spine, over her shoulders, then down to her ass before repeating the motion again. "You broke your promise to me and scared twenty years off my life I'd rather spend enjoying you."

Because I had to help you, she screamed internally.

"Instead of coming to me and explaining your plan, you simply left. Oh, I know why you chose not to inform me. You didn't want to upset me, didn't want to cause an argument." He leaned close to her ear. "You didn't want to hear me say no."

That's part of it, but not all. Those words burned her tongue like hot coals.

"While I'm grateful you convinced River to recant his ridiculous story, your actions jeopardized the trust I have in you. You risked damaging the connection between the three of us. Keep at it, and we'll fall apart." Hammer continued trailing his hand over her flesh, but his slow, reassuring caress almost hurt now. He gave to her even when she'd disappointed and scared him. "From now on, you will ask permission from *both* of us before you run off half-cocked. Is that clear?"

"Can I speak now, Sir?"

"Only if you're going to respond with a yes or no."

She sighed in frustration. "Yes, Sir."

With a snort, Hammer slapped her ass with a stinging swat, ignoring her yelp. "I'm not convinced you meant that, precious. But you will before your punishment is through."

Raine didn't have time to question his meaning. He left her, stalking toward the toys displayed on hooks and shelves along the wall. Without hesitation, he grabbed a black leather whip.

Her eyes widened. The breath left her body. Her mouth went as dry as the desert, and her heart thundered triple time.

"What's your safeword?"

"Paris." The answer slipped out automatically.

"Keep that in mind. You may need it tonight."

Every muscle turned to stone. She looked for a place to retreat, but with Macen scrutinizing her every reaction and Liam at her back, she had nowhere to turn.

"I don't like punishing you." He uncoiled the whip. "I prefer to claim your submission by drowning in your soft body, but you've left me no choice. Hopefully, I'll leave a lasting impression on you tonight so you'll think to include me in your future decisions."

Macen closed in until they stood face-to-face. She searched his eyes for mercy. All she saw was censure. Her belly flipped.

He took possession of her lips in a savage kiss. She gasped, grateful for the sign of his affection. Then he shocked her by gliding the cool leather plait of the whip over her cheek. Fear and desire collided inside her in a tangle she didn't understand.

Then Hammer tore away from her lips and looped the whip behind her neck, releasing the popper. The snake-like implement slid across her back as he circled behind her again. She felt him breathing against her nape as he dragged the tail over her back, arms, and legs. Raine shuddered and struggled to pull herself back from the ledge of rising panic. She'd always been terrified of the whip, and icy panic raced under her skin now.

Liam paced up on her left, watching wordlessly. Raine shot him a beseeching gaze.

"Do you trust Hammer, love?" he asked, strolling to the cache of toys.

"Of course. But—"

"No buts. You do or you don't. And if you do, then don't look to me to save you from the punishment you've earned." Liam grabbed a blindfold from a small drawer and dangled it from one long finger. "You're trying to play your Doms, one against the other, sub. Again. That stops here and now. Understood?"

His biting tone caught Raine off guard. "Yes, Sir."

"Good. Count, precious." Hammer stepped far behind her.

Oh, god. He's really going to do this.

Clenching her eyes tightly shut, Raine tensed every muscle and held her breath, waiting to feel the blistering pain she knew he could inflict.

But a whisper-like caress fanned over her taut flesh instead, so soft Raine wondered if she'd imagined it. Lashes fluttering open, she turned her puzzled stare Hammer's way.

"What was that?"

His face hardened. "I told you to count, girl. I've already laid the first stroke across your ass. Face the front and do as I've said."

When she hesitated, Hammer lifted his arm and drew the serpent over his head, then flicked his wrist. A thunderous crack rent the air.

Trembling and gasping, Raine whirled back to stare at the wall, unable to catch her breath—or reconcile the whispery sensation she'd felt with the certainty that whip could cut her open.

"One." Her voice sounded breathy and uneven in the still room.

Hammer brushed her backside with another barely perceptible kiss from the whip.

She still couldn't quite understand. She'd seen Beck work subs over dozens of times, always inflicting excruciating pain and sometimes drawing forth blood. When she'd stolen glimpses of Hammer using the whip, he'd usually been subtler, less invasive, but wasn't the point of this agony?

"Two."

"Relax," he commanded.

Raine darted another glance back to see Hammer coiling up the whip. "Is that it?"

Macen stormed toward her and gripped her hair in a tight fist. Her scalp sang as prickles skittered over her skin and slid down her spine.

Yanking her head back, he locked her in a fierce gaze. "Yes. When you saw me pick the whip up, you were terrified. Right?"

She still shivered all over. "Yes, Sir."

"Yet you didn't use your safeword. You let me continue, despite worrying I meant to inflict the worst possible pain?"

Raine winced. "Yes, Sir."

"Why?" His voice dripped disapproval.

Her heart lumped in her throat. "Because it's you. Even when we've had our problems or fights, you never wanted me to bleed."

Frustration and desire clashed all over his face. Clutching her hair even tighter, Macen slammed his mouth over hers and swept in deep. She tasted his desperation.

"That's right," he growled finally. "You knew deep down I would keep you safe. But when I came home from Sterling's office to find you'd gone to see your brother, I didn't have any such assurance of your well-being. I was out of my mind with worry."

Raine felt like shit for putting him through hell. She bit back the explanation he hadn't given her permission to give.

"The panic you felt when I pulled out this whip..." Hammer dangled the leather coil in her face. "It wasn't even a tenth of what I felt when I discovered you'd gone. You fucked with my head, little girl.

So I just fucked with yours."

Quid pro quo.

"I'll apologize until I'm blue in the face because hurting you hurts me," she murmured. "But no matter how much you punish or mindfuck me, I will never lie and say I wouldn't do it again."

"Why is that?" He bit out each word.

"I know I'm supposed to be learning a lesson, but the fact remains that River wasn't going to listen to anyone but me. I had to fix this mess, Macen."

"And you wanted me to…what? Thank you for putting me through hell?"

"Trust me. Watching the police haul you off for questioning was hell for me. I get it."

"Not the same. You knew I would be back."

"I hoped and prayed you would. But I had no guarantee."

"Sterling wasn't going to let me rot in a cell."

"If he had the power to get you out, I knew he would. But he's not God or the president." She gritted her teeth. "Don't be so stubborn, Macen. You let him help you. Why won't you let me? I can't just sit here when I might have the power to save you."

"It's not the same. Me conferring with my lawyer wasn't a risk to my physical well-being. You running off to meet with your crazy-assed brother put you in horrific danger."

"You're missing the point!"

"What point is that? The one in which you think I'm helpless? From here, it looks like you willfully disobeyed me and met with a lunatic who tried to kidnap you and kill our unborn child because you thought I was incapable of using my resources or devising any sort of strategy to save myself."

"I never thought you were helpless!" The fact that would even cross his mind stunned and horrified her. "But I'd risk my life and your wrath if it meant a happy ending to any situation that threatened our lives together." She sighed heavily. "Look, I'm sorry I worried you. I'm sorry I disobeyed. But I'll always do whatever it takes to keep you alive, free, and with us. Over and over again. Because I love you. I can't imagine living my life without you, without Liam. You two and this baby we've made…you're my whole heart."

"Son of a bitch," Hammer cursed as he released her hair, then clutched her to his chest, gripping her tightly.

In less than a heartbeat, Liam was there, wrapping the two of them in his arms and kissing her lips. Raine drank in his comfort, absorbed the heat of their bodies, savored the completion of her soul.

As Liam pulled away, Hammer swooped in. "I love you more than words can say."

He claimed her mouth with a burst of passion that curled Raine's toes.

"Now that your punishment is over, lass, let's play in the dungeon. Would you be up for that?"

The mischievous glint in Liam's eyes sent a rush of excitement to thunder through her veins. "I'd love that, Sir. And don't you two owe me some Valentine's Day sex?"

"Cheeky wench." He shook his head. "We do. We also owe you a little torment for that racy scrap of silk you're wearing that's driving me mad."

"Absolutely." Hammer paused and studied her, head cocked. "Would you be willing to try something for us first?"

Raine nibbled her bottom lip, wondering what he had up his sleeve. But she'd survived that surprisingly tender whip. She could handle more.

"Anything."

Emotion rolled over Hammer's face before he crossed the dungeon and gathered a bundle of rope. Logic told her they would never hurt her, but that didn't stop a ribbon of dread from winding through her. She fought the urge to back out of the room.

Picking up on her sudden mood swing, Liam gently tugged her close to his chest.

"I won't tie you down or dredge up the past, precious," Hammer promised. "And this isn't a test of your submission."

"We want to help you enjoy again something you once loved," Liam added tenderly. "To do that, we need to learn where your breaking point lies."

"Exactly. When it becomes too much, we expect you to tell us. If you don't, I'll get the whip out and use it in earnest.

She hesitated. "You really won't be disappointed if I use my safeword?"

"We'll be sorely disappointed if you don't," Liam vowed solemnly.

"But I don't want to ruin our night. I wanted it to be special...perfect. And—"

"I can only think of one thing more special and perfect than pushing your limits." Hammer sidled in with a sexy grin.

"And we fully intend to make time for *that* soon." Liam winked.

Oh, goody. "All right. I'll try."

"You won't be lying down for this. Standing should give you a different perspective. Just lean against the cross, like before," Hammer instructed as he handed a short length of rope to Liam.

Raine's nerves were already rattled as she pressed her chest against the wood once more. Her breath sounded loud in the room. Behind her, she could hear the two men whispering, plotting. It sent her heart racing. She had to remind herself this wasn't a test of her fortitude.

Suddenly, both men stepped behind the cross, shoulder to shoulder. Their faces filled the open V in front of her.

"Keep your eyes open and on us, lass," Liam demanded.

"Yes, Sir."

Hammer gripped her shoulder and squeezed. "Be brave. We're right here and we won't leave you."

"I know." She did, but it was little comfort when the rope in their hands made Bill's face flash through her mind.

"Take a deep breath, precious."

Nodding, Raine filled her lungs while he and Liam each looped the rope loosely around her wrists.

Before she had a chance to react, her Irishman feathered his fingers down her cheek. "This rope is nothing more than scraps of silk twisted together."

"Tell us where you are." Hammer's voice sounded low and concerned in her ear.

"I-I'm good."

"Let me rephrase. Are you here with us in the dungeon or someplace else in your head?"

"I'm here with you both," she assured. And so far, she was.

"Good." Hammer brushed a kiss over her lips as they slowly cinched the ropes a bit tighter.

She focused on the smooth texture of his mouth, drowning out everything else. Then he pulled away. But Liam was there, seamlessly taking over where Macen left off.

Their soft, reassuring kisses kept her anxiety at bay. Her men were diligent and beyond patient as they showered her with reassurance and praise until the soft silk cord pressed tightly against her wrists. Victory filled her. When Liam rewarded her with a sweep of his tongue inside her mouth, tangling and dueling, she whimpered softly. He drank in her delight. Raine clutched her hands into fists, wishing she could touch her Doms.

Then tingles prickled in her fingertips. The sensation raced down to her palms. The last time her fingers had fallen asleep because she'd been restrained...

Bill's face suddenly swam in her vision.

Without any warning, Raine dropped into a vat of inky darkness. Panic and fear engulfed her.

She tore from Liam's lips. "Paris!"

As Raine tried to jerk away, Hammer and Liam dropped their ropes.

"Easy..." Macen soothed as he wrapped his arm around the cross and captured her waist. "You're here with us. You're safe."

Before he even finished his sentence, Liam circled behind her and hoisted her into his arms. "I've got you, love. And I'm not letting go."

Raine looped her arms around his neck as he carried her to their bedroom. She cast her gaze up at him, hoping to latch on to the safety net of constancy in his eyes. There it was, just as he'd promised. He never faltered or shied away. As always, her Irishman was steady and determined to give her what she needed.

Just beyond him, she caught sight of Macen, watching her with the scrutiny of a Master and the concern of a lover.

God, she'd be empty without them both.

Though she felt held and supported in every way, a fine tremor still ran through her body. She curled up tighter against Liam's chest. Everything inside her jumbled into a vulnerable sort of triumph. All in a few days, she'd confronted Macen's potential legal troubles and her brother. She'd begun to face her fear. Tomorrow, she would accept the deaths of her mother and sister. She was growing stronger, healing.

And now she wanted to take this raw devotion spilling from her heart and give to her men.

Liam set her on the bed and followed her down, enveloping her left side. Seconds later, Hammer followed, plastering himself against her right. Raine breathed in the moment—their hands warming her skin, their lips in her hair, their voices in her ear.

She was safe. She was loved.

Now she needed their touch, to feel their reassurance deep inside her. She craved their three hearts coming together to beat as one because they were her life and her breath. They were every smile, every tear.

They were her soul.

Rolling to her side, she faced Liam, curling her hand around his head and caressing down, bringing him closer until their foreheads touched. She grabbed the strands of hair growing at his nape, kissed the bridge of his nose. The urge to draw him deeper bled into Raine and filled her chest until it hurt. When Hammer sidled up behind her, wrapping his beefy arm around her waist and brushing her hair aside to kiss his way down her neck, the ache of love only spread.

She was truly blessed.

Liam took her face in his hands and searched her expression. "Raine?"

"I'm okay now. Nothing is wrong." She reached for Macen's hand and brought it against her heart while tilting her head back to him. "It's so right."

Then Raine pressed forward. Liam met her halfway. Their lips collided. He surged in. She yielded. They melted together, tongues stroking, breaths mingling, heartbeats syncing. Desire drizzled through her blood, sweet, sugary, sinful.

"Let him in deeper, precious." Hammer spoke against her ear. "I love to watch you accept the pleasure he gives you. Take it all. Yes…"

Macen's voice swirled in her head, mixing with the languid, clever skill of Liam's kiss to send her senses spinning. She shuddered, sinking into a chasm of arousal.

With another nip at the sensitive flesh of her neck, Hammer disentangled his fingers from hers and cupped her breast, leisurely flicking her nipple with his thumb. As she gave a supplicating arch toward his touch, he twisted the hard bud between his thumb and finger. Liam swallowed her gasp and gripped her hair in his fists, pulling just enough to jet the electric tingle in her scalp all the way through her body. His control over her kiss became utter command. Thoughts melted away as Raine tumbled into the endless moment.

She surged closer to Liam, seeking his body heat, relief from the ache seizing her lungs, boiling her blood. His cock grazed her belly, but it wasn't enough of him. It never would be.

A frustrated moan slipped from her chest.

Liam broke the kiss, and it was Hammer's turn to take her hair in his fist. His tug was gentle, but it left her no doubt in that moment that he'd taken charge of her. She tilted her head back toward him, giving in to his silent demand.

As if the men were on some silent wavelength, Liam took the opportunity Hammer had presented him to unclasp her top and release her breasts. Macen plucked at the little bow between her legs, exposing her pussy. Liam's lips closed around her nipple while Hammer's fingers slid against her slick furrow.

Desire converged, heavy and devastating.

She scratched at Liam's shoulders, panting hard, skin melting, blood burning. "Please…"

Raine cried out for relief. Love. Dominance. Them.

As Macen rubbed toying circles around her clit, his lips brushed her ear again. "Your surrender is heady. Your begging makes us hard. Keep burning, baby. We're going to push you to the edge of orgasm and make you hold it. When you're desperate, that's when I'll work my fat cock into your narrow backside. You can plead all you like, but you'll be forbidden to come, especially as Liam eases that thick crest of his into your little pussy one wicked inch at a time. Once you're packed full of us, then…" His breath heated her nape as he chuckled. "But if you think you're ready to beg now… Oh, you haven't even started."

Raine didn't doubt him for a moment. She whimpered, writhed, silently imploring them to start.

Liam bit at her nipple, sending a shock of pleasure-pain trilling across her senses. She was still processing the fine shiver when he urged her to face Hammer. Suddenly, she was looking into Macen's molten hazel eyes.

"Kiss him," Liam demanded thickly behind her. "And spread your legs for me. Now, Raine."

Their power converged in the air around her, swirling tighter, faster, like a whirlpool sucking her under. The gravity of it was unbeatable, so she gave herself over, drowned willingly—and obeyed.

As she layered her mouth over Hammer's, he was ready, crashing into her and taking her with a demand that stole her breath. As Raine let go of the last shred of rational thought, she bent one knee and placed her foot flat on the mattress.

Liam had plenty of space to slide his big hand between her thighs. He plunged his fingers inside her slick opening. She gasped into Hammer's mouth.

Neither man showed her mercy. Macen's kiss and Liam's digits both delved deeper, determined to take more of her. Her Irishman bucked against her, pressing every dizzying inch of his hard shaft against her backside.

"Hammer will soon be fucking this ass, love. While he's filling you, I'm going to watch your face. Every widening of your eyes, every gasp, every shiver of pleasure, I'll drink it in. While I've got my fingers in your cunt." He wriggled them—as if she needed the reminder—and added a softly brutal swipe of his thumb over her throbbing clit. "And tormenting you in every way I know how."

"Liam," she gasped.

"Once Macen has buried himself inside your wee opening, I'll be sliding your body down to mine and squeezing my way into your pussy. Such a sweet, tight fit." He groaned. "But you'll open to me and give us all of yourself, Raine. Is that clear?"

Hammer didn't release her mouth so she could answer. Desperate, she moaned, clung, squirmed in agonized need.

"Yes." Satisfaction laced Liam's voice. "You will."

Every single time you want me.

While she lost herself in Hammer's unrelenting kiss, she swooned at the feel of Liam's fingers strumming her every sensitive spot until she didn't care if she couldn't move or breathe. She only cared about the honeyed pleasure they oozed all over her, thick and seductive...and so close she could taste it.

Finally, Macen eased back, leaving her with eyes closed, lips parted, body disintegrating into a puddle of liquid desire while Liam continued toying with her screaming clit. Gaze raking down her body, Hammer stroked her hip while he watched his best friend torment her. His eyes turned a deeper shade of magnetic allure.

"She's on the edge, trying so hard not to disobey us and come," Hammer murmured. "Fuck, she's pretty."

"And so hot around my fingers. She'll burn our cocks."

"I'm looking forward to it." Macen eased off the bed. "You mind keeping Raine flushed and desperate? I want to watch while I get ready to fuck her."

"My pleasure."

No, no, no! But Raine was beyond forming words. Instead, she mewled and continued to melt under Liam's sweltering touch. Hammer gave her a bawdy smile as he shucked his clothes, revealing the big body that never failed to have her biting her lip in need. With a slow gait and a tall staff, he prowled to the nightstand and drew out a tube of lube.

Raine knew what he intended next. Her breath caught. These two always made this act the most potent thrill, had her feeling delicate, submissive, and taken.

She begged Hammer to hurry with her eyes.

He juggled the tube in his hand. "You want something, precious?"

Liam's fingers did another sweep over the terrible ache behind her clit. "Answer the man. I'd like to hear this, too."

Holding her breath to fight the climax railing at her, she tried to gather her words. Her thoughts slid around like oil. But every place they touched her burned like dry kindling under their flame.

"Silence, love?" He bit at her shoulder and heaped on more suffering.

"Fuck me," she managed to gasp. "Now. I…need…you."

"There it is." Hammer smiled again. "But it sounds like she thinks she's giving the orders."

"It does," Liam mused.

Lunging on the bed, Hammer grabbed her hair in his hand again, his face hovering right over hers. "Do you give the orders?"

"No," she blurted. "You and Liam. Please…"

He eased the grip on her hair, then stroked her cheek. "Good answer."

"You could reward her," Liam suggested slyly.

Yes, yes, yes! But she said nothing, merely blinked at Hammer, silently supplicating. His smile widened. God, they were enjoying their power. And she was relishing every second of surrendering to them.

"Or *you* could," Macen tossed back. "But you didn't have an orgasm in mind, right?"

Liam shrugged. "Of course not...yet."

"Then we're on the same page." He flipped open the cap of the lube.

Raine froze, suspended in the throes of this excruciating ache, hoping, praying...

Until Liam took his fingers from her clit. Another swipe or two and she would have been tumbling into a gasping, stunning euphoria.

And both disobeying and disappointing them.

Pressing her lips together to hold in her protest, she put her faith in them. They would eventually end their torture and give her the most sublime ecstasy.

"Her face is priceless," Hammer drawled. "You're fighting it, aren't you, precious?"

She gave a wild, shaky bob of her head, not trusting her words.

They grinned as Liam rolled her to face him, then eased onto his back, sending her sprawling on top of him. "On your hands and knees, wench. Give him that lush, wee ass he wants."

Raine scrambled to comply, poised over Liam and blinking into his eyes as Hammer stepped up behind her. She heard the squirt of the lube, felt the cool gel slick across her rosette, then imagined him slathering the liquid all over his shaft. God, she couldn't breathe. Her heart was about to beat out of her chest.

Suddenly, the tube plopped on the bed next to her knee. Macen's body heat warmed the backs of her thighs. He palmed her ass. "Arch your back."

"Down on your elbows," Liam added. "Look at me."

Instantly, she obeyed. His eyes, usually a warm sepia, had darkened to a raw umber, and she couldn't stop herself from breathlessly plummeting into their depths. She had no beginning; he had no end.

Here she found her undoing, both her enslavement and her salvation.

She whispered his name. He palmed her crown.

Then Hammer set his crest against her opening, worked past the ring of muscle, and inched inside her at a crawling pace that had her digging into Liam's shoulders with a gasp.

"You must be doing something right, mate. I've got her nails in my skin."

"Yeah." Macen sounded strained. "Her walls are clenching my cock. Oh, fuck."

"I intend to…in good time." Just as he'd promised, Liam worked his hand between them and circled her clit again.

Raine sank her fingers deeper into him with a high-pitched whimper that seemed to come from someplace in her throat she'd never used. Liam paid her no mind, just watched her face as Hammer gripped her hips, pressed forward, and slid deeper.

God, she wanted to wriggle, find more friction—anything to end this incendiary agony. But she had nowhere to go, no way to usurp the ruthless control they had over her body. Hammer filled her at his own pace, and Liam enjoyed every helpless emotion that ripped across her face.

Finally, Macen gave a guttural groan from deep in his chest. The hair on his thighs gently abraded the backs of hers. He surged forward, trying to root in even deeper, but he was in to the hilt. All she could do was gape as he dragged the swollen head of his cock over her sensitive tissue.

"Hurry the fuck up, man." Hammer rocked back, then shoved in again, pushing her closer to Liam—and the edge. "Holy shit."

"On it. Lower yourself onto me, love. Give me your cunt."

He didn't have to tell her twice.

Raine gladly sat back on his cock, standing thick and waiting between her legs. With a wriggle and a nudge, she began taking him in, her hungry pussy swallowing inch after inch. The sting of the stretch they demanded of her openings as she took them both always had her grappling to accommodate and marveling at the wondrous feeling of completeness they gave her.

Beneath her, Liam surged up the rest of the way. As he fell back, Hammer invaded. Their perfectly synchronized dance drove her up, soaring toward an intoxicating rapture that would launch her straight to the heaven only they could give her.

Liam lunged. Hammer parried. She moved with them, sinking her teeth into Liam's shoulder, moaning. Astonishing. Exhilarating.

Perfect.

They felt as if they were made for her. Yes, they'd all had struggles, but each of them had fought their way back to the others time and again. For this. Because they were meant to be.

And she couldn't hold back the wrenching, undeniable love she felt for them anymore.

Heaving for her last sane breath, she lifted her lips from Liam's skin. The purple love bite there barely registered as she howled out for them. "Please…Sirs. I'm begging."

"Fuck, I could almost beg, too," Hammer muttered.

"With you, mate. Christ…" Liam panted, a flush rushing across his skin. "Nothing turns me on more than watching you come. Do it, Raine. Shatter hard!"

She jolted, her entire system bucking and spasming as she splintered into a million pieces for them. As they crashed into her, they followed her into bliss, roaring out a chorus of curses and groans. The aftermath was a hush of whispers filled with devotion, tender kisses, and an unspoken hope that their every tomorrow could be this full of love.

Friday, February 15

AT NOON THE next day, Raine emerged from Hammer's Audi at the cemetery. Wearing a somber gray suit, Liam opened the door for her and held out his hand. By the time she gathered the flowers she'd brought, placed her fingers in his, and stood, Macen was beside him, locking the sedan with a concerned glance her way. River pulled up in his big black truck and killed the engine. He was slow to emerge.

As they left the parking lot, everything became more real. Her entire body trembled.

"You don't have to do this today, love," Liam offered.

Maybe it wasn't the best timing in the face of everything else going on but… "Yeah, I do. I know you want to protect me. But I owe my mother and sister my love and respect. I've waited too long as it is."

Raine squeezed his hand in unspoken thanks before she released him.

"We understand. We're here for you," Macen murmured.

With a grateful smile their way, she gathered herself and walked the rolling hills toward the edge of the park where Hammer and Liam had arranged for her mother and sister to be buried side by side. She needed to thank them for that, too. It had taken weeks for the investigators to find their complete remains and arrange for their transfer into her care. She'd been distraught, racked with morning sickness, nightmares, guilt, and grief. As always, they'd shouldered so much of the burden, sheltering her from the worst of the storm.

Swallowing, she trekked the last steps softly, almost afraid to read the headstones. Seeing her mom's and sister's names freshly etched in marble would make everything so much more real. But they had already been gone for years. If she'd felt abandoned by them in life—believing they'd voluntarily left her to escape the hell Bill had wrought—they must have felt she'd utterly forsaken them in death. She'd regret that forever.

Forcing herself to look at their graves, she blinked through tears. No blinking them back anymore.

Her loved ones were here…yet not. They'd never be with her again in this life except in her heart. Maybe if she was lucky she'd see something of them in her coming child. She'd cling to that hope. Somehow, she'd have to make do with that possibility, though it would never be enough.

Her body bucked with sobs that came from nowhere. All she did was cry now, it seemed. Pregnancy had sharpened her emotions, and they bled just under her skin every day. But finding River and laying the other Kendall women to rest with him while dealing with the doubt swirling over Hammer's head… She just couldn't hold her mourning in anymore.

She'd barely dragged in another ragged breath when Liam and Hammer flanked her, bracing her, lending their strength. A few feet away, River watched, looking stoic, his eyes almost too blue in his sunken sockets. No missing the guilt tightening his face.

"Precious?"

Hammer wanted to know if she was all right. Honestly, she wasn't sure. Everything inside her felt confused, brittle, lost.

But she'd come to get closure with the two women who had most impacted her youth. She'd come to give them her love and promise to carry their memories into her future.

She didn't want to worry Macen even more, so she nodded his way. Then, through her watery vision, she knelt in front of her mother's grave and placed the flowers in the holder. Liam took the other bouquet from her grip and helped her to her feet again.

As she stared at the gentle mound of earth, Raine stuttered. It wasn't lively, as her mother had been. It didn't hold her or laugh or brighten up her world. Her mother had moved on, and Raine wasn't sure what to do now. How did she say good-bye, wish a peaceful death to the woman who had given her life?

"I miss all the time we didn't have together. I hate that years separate us like a divide. Wherever you are, I love you."

A million memories she'd locked away for years rushed back. Mom had always been about doll clothes and dress-up, baking sweets to lift her spirits and pretending to leave home on great adventures. They'd act as if they were traveling to Africa or China or Fiji. Or Paris. Mom had always wanted to go there. Every once in a while, her mother would get a gleam in her eye, hand Raine a suitcase, and tell her to believe the world could take her anywhere. Looking back, those episodes usually happened after she'd heard her parents arguing. Inevitably, her mom would be wearing a lot more makeup than normal over the next few days and walking on eggshells around her dad. But never once had Robin ever pretended that she wouldn't be taking Raine with her on these faraway escapes.

The clues had been there. Her mom would never have left her kids of her own free will.

Raine fingered the bracelet Liam and Hammer had made for her with the pendant her mother had gifted to her. Despondency crashed in. And she fell apart.

"I'm so sorry I believed for so long that you'd left me. I'm sorry I yelled at you, blamed you... You tried to give me normalcy and hope. I didn't..."

Face in her hands, she cried in anger, at the futility of her mother's death, for her own youthful inability to understand, for the years afterward of poking her head in the sand because she'd been getting by and the truth had been too terrible to contemplate.

As her shoulders shook, Macen curled a hand around her waist. Liam smoothed his hand down her back. They were there in silent support—steady, stalwart. Constant.

"Storm cloud…"

She lifted her head to watch River approach. This wasn't just about her sorrow. River must have tons of it, too. The tight clench of his jaw and the rapid blinking told her that he worked hard to keep himself together. Whatever his faults, he'd loved Mom, too.

"You okay?" Her voice shook.

"Are you?" His face almost broke. He swallowed, looked away, and got it together. "Mom wouldn't want to see you cry. That's why I gave you that nickname, you know. She always said you were a sweet Raine, not a storm cloud. But when I was a punk kid, it was more fun to tease you."

The memory burst out of the dark corner she'd shoved it in, and she laughed through her tears. "You always tried to make me cry back then. Bully."

"I thought it was a big brother's job to tease his sisters." His smile fell, and he dragged in a shaky breath. "I can't believe he killed her."

"And we'll never know exactly why." Raine closed her eyes. Of everything that pained her about her mother's murder, that might hurt worst of all.

"No. But I suspect she wanted to leave him and take us kids."

"He would never have allowed it. The day I killed Bill, he told me he'd been sure she was having an affair with his brother."

River shook his head. "That must have been all in his delusional head. Even if it was true, would you blame her?"

Never. "I just wish she'd gotten out alive."

He shifted his weight from one foot to the next, his gaze darting, as if desperate for some way to focus his energy away from his emotions. "Yeah. But I try to look for the silver linings, tell myself that things happen for a reason. If Mom had really taken us from Bill, I would never have joined the army. You would have never met Hammer and

Liam."

River was right. She'd give up almost anything to still have her mother in her life today. But she would give up everything to keep the men she loved.

"I hope Mom can see us now and that she's proud."

Her brother looked Hammer and Liam's way—seeking silent permission?—before he stepped closer to her and dropped his hand to her stomach. "She'd be happy for you. I want you to be happy, too."

That might be as close as River ever came to saying that he approved of her choices. Raine didn't expect him to understand exactly. But if he accepted her, the loves of her life, and the coming baby, she'd embrace him as part of her new family with arms wide open.

Standing on her tiptoes, she hugged him. He crushed her against his massive chest and gave her a tight squeeze. It was odd, embracing a relative stranger and sharing their common grief. But they would always be tied by blood and circumstance and memories. It meant something. It was a start.

When she stepped back, Liam was beside her again, hand on her shoulder, proffering the other bouquet of flowers. She gripped the stems in sorrow, plastic crinkling, and mouthed a silent thank you.

Then she dragged in the most difficult breath all day and stepped in front of Rowan's headstone.

As she placed the flowers in the plastic holder, regret came in a landslide that nearly buried her. Had she known, on any level, what Bill had been doing? What Rowan had let him do so he'd stay away from her younger sister? No…and yes. Something hadn't been right, and she hadn't questioned the relationship between her dad and her sister too hard. She'd asked Rowan if she was all right a few times, but her quiet, studious sibling had never been forthcoming. So Raine had let it go. How much tragedy could she have avoided if she'd paid attention to that nagging in her gut that something evil lurked in the Kendall household? Or would she simply have accelerated the tragedy?

Raine would never know, and that came with its own regret.

What could she possibly say to the sister who had given so much innocence and life to save hers?

"I can never thank you for what you did for me, and I wish I could have somehow erased the hell you endured. I'm sorry I cursed you for leaving me to Bill as if you had a choice. I didn't know…" Raine felt the onslaught of more tears, seemingly more desolation than she could take. "I wish I'd seen the amazing things you could have accomplished in life. I hope that, wherever you are, you finally found something better than the best lip gloss or the perfect prom dress. I'm sorry you never got to see the last Matrix movie. If it helps, you didn't miss much." She tried to smile because her sister had never been one for tears. "I hope you and Mom found each other up there. I sincerely hope you've found peace."

"Oh, kidlet…" River bowed his head. "I would have found some way to protect you if I'd guessed Bill's plans. He never let on that he wanted me out because he wanted you."

Her brother choked as if he had more words to say but simply couldn't get them out, then he fell into a terrible sorrow-filled silence. Raine reached for his hand. He clutched it for a heartrending moment before he enveloped her against his body again. Last time, he'd been supporting her, helping her with grief. Now he clutched her like a lifeline.

They shared anguish without words, and Raine was silently grateful.

It was early days yet…but maybe she'd found that silver lining River had mentioned. Maybe she'd have her brother in her life again. And if the police dropped all these ridiculous charges against Hammer, she might finally have said good-bye to the darkest parts of her past today—and said hello to a beautiful future.

Saturday, February 16

LIAM LAY CURLED into Raine, resting his head on one elbow as he watched her sleep. She hadn't had much of it lately. He and Macen hadn't, either, but they weren't nurturing another human being within their bodies.

Her inky lashes curled against translucent skin, now bruised with dark circles. She fidgeted restlessly.

Liam's heart ached for her. "Rest easy, *mo grá.*"

He brushed aside an errant lock of her lush hair, frowning at how vulnerable she appeared in repose. His lass was under so much stress.

As if his merely thinking of Raine had roused her, she opened her eyes, the color of warm waters, clear and deep enough to drown a man in. "Why are you awake?"

He kissed her gently. "Not tired yet. Are you all right?"

"I should be sleeping like the dead now that it seems Macen's legal troubles should be more or less over, but I just can't shut off my brain." She sighed. "And our little peanut seems to be sitting on my bladder."

Her wry smile had him chuckling.

Snoring rent their silence, and they both turned to look at Hammer sleeping soundly on the other side of Raine.

"Cuddle up to him and go back to sleep, love. I'm heading downstairs for a cup of tea."

He pressed a soft kiss on her forehead and left the bed, groping for his sweat pants. In short work, he had them on and headed quietly out of the room. He'd bet his parents were up, and he could use the time with them. No telling how long before they packed up and headed back to Ireland. Now that their crisis was seemingly averted, he was a bit surprised his mother hadn't mentioned it. Maybe she felt that something uneasy giving her a nagging tug, too.

Halfway down the hall, a shuffling had him turning back to find Raine rushing to catch up to him, belting her robe as she hustled.

"I'll go with you. Tea sounds good," she whispered as she took his hand.

The big house was quiet until they approached the kitchen. Then the sound of his father's voice became louder with every step.

"Aye, lass. I will. You tell those boys that Grandda said they best knuckle down, then. If they do, I might bring them each a bag of lollies from America."

They couldn't hear the reply, but his father laughed as they entered the kitchen. Duncan gave Raine a warm smile, and Liam was grateful to his da for trying to set her at ease.

She nodded in greeting and made her way to the teapot before pouring two cups. As she slid one across the counter to him, Liam squeezed his father's shoulder and took a stool beside him at the bar, drawing the cup Raine had poured closer.

"You're in luck, then. Your brother and Raine just walked in. Do you want to say hello?"

Liam smiled and arched a brow, but his father nudged the cell into his hand instead, not saying which of his sisters was on the line.

"Hello?"

"Fancy that, then. It only takes Mum and Da going halfway 'round the world for me to hear from you. How are you, stranger?"

He'd know that voice anywhere.

"Maeve…" He grinned around the teacup and gave his da a wink. Raine stood across from them, dunking a cookie in her tea. Even with all the commotion lately, some of his parents' idiosyncrasies had still rubbed off.

"We can't wait to meet Raine. Mum has gone gaga over her. They really like this one, Liam. We're so excited for you. And by the by, I always knew there was something more between you and Macen. But it's all good," she assured. "Um…how does that work exactly?"

Liam sighed. "Yeah, it's not like that."

He saw Raine laughing behind her hand as Da concentrated far too hard on stirring his tea.

"No judgment here."

"Bloody hell, Maeve. We're in love with the same woman, not each other."

"Whatever you say… So, when are you bringing them home for a visit?"

"I doubt it will be before the baby is born, but we may try to surprise everyone. How are you and the lads?"

"Same. Nothing much changes here. How are you all holding up? Da told me about your recent drama. Your life is so fascinating. There's always something going on."

Liam snorted. "Be thankful you're not living it. But we're all good now, thanks. Every day seems to be some new bloody challenge, but we always manage to get things sorted."

"You do. I won't embarrass Raine by asking to speak to her, but tell her that she has a whole parcel of family who already love her and can't wait to meet her and the baby. Know we are thinking of you all, Liam. Love you."

He sent Raine a smile. He loved the idea of her and the children he and Macen would have with their lass in his family. "I'll tell her. I love you, too, Maeve. Give everyone our best."

"I will. Pass me back to Da to say good-bye."

Liam gave the mobile back to his father and listened while he rang off.

Duncan set the phone aside and rose to get more tea, but Raine grabbed the pot.

"I've got it. Sit." She refilled his cup.

"Thank you. Why are you both up at this hour? You especially, lass. You need your sleep." He patted her hand gently across the counter. "You have so much going on in that wee body of yours, making a brand new person. 'Tis a lot you're asking of it on so little rest."

"I'll try again after my tea," she promised. "What time is it in Ireland?"

"Hmm, there's eight hours' difference. Since it's just after one here, it's a bit after nine in the morning at home. Hence my reason for being up and on the phone."

"Da doesn't do computers," Liam teased.

"We don't get along is all," the older man blustered.

"I could show you, Da. It's not hard."

Duncan shook his head. "I'm too old for that now, lad. I do best in my garden. Happy as Larry, I am, with a bit of dirt and my plants."

"You still feeding the neighborhood?" Liam asked.

"When the weather cooperates, aye."

"I'll bet your vegetables are better than store-bought," Raine remarked.

"The best, lass." He looked adorably proud. "I grow more beefsteak tomatoes and string beans than Mum and I can eat, so she shares the extras with the family. The rest are passed on to neighbors and friends."

"I'm sure everyone appreciates it." Raine smiled. "I'd love to see your garden one day."

"And so you shall. Just have that scamp bring you home..." He nodded Liam's way.

"I'm getting to it, Da. His garden is famous, you know. That and his family are his favorite subjects. Come and sit. He'll tell you all about it." Liam rose and gave Raine his seat while he emptied the dishwasher.

As Raine eased onto the stool, he slid clandestine glances their way. She'd been a bit shy with his father. Understandable since her experience with her own had been so horrendous. Besides, with everything going on, there had been little time to talk except at meals. But Liam needn't have worried. His father was adept at encouraging her.

Before long, they chatted like old chums. She looked relaxed and engaged. His lass even laughed when Da pulled out his wallet and pictures of his grandchildren spilled out. When his father sent her a sheepish glance and said just how much he missed them all, Raine laid a gentle hand over his. Da appreciated the gesture, smiling as he gave her delicate fingers a squeeze.

Then something flashed across her face. Liam saw the happy light in her eyes dim. She eased her hand free and rose, fidgeting.

His heart caught, and Liam shot his father an apologetic stare as he started toward her. Da stopped him with a look.

Breath held, Liam hung back and watched.

"Raine?" his father prompted.

"I'm sorry. I know you're nothing like my father but..." She sighed. "I should be getting back to bed anyway. It's late, and I—"

"Sit for a bit more, lass. You've nothing to fear from me, I promise. I'd like to talk to you a minute more is all. Liam is right there, see?"

Her stare darted to where he stood just by the pantry. He gave her an encouraging nod.

She hesitated, then slowly sat once more. Everything inside him screamed that he should go to her, protect her. But his father had always been the most loving, kindest person in Liam's life. She was safe.

Deliberately, Duncan turned his stool to face Raine, took her hand, and held it gently in both of his. "My Bryn has an interesting gift. I can't pretend I understand it, but after all these years, I know better than to doubt it. She's been proven right too many times to count. So when Mum told me about five months ago—out of the blue, mind you—that our youngest had just met the woman he'd love for the rest of his life, I was thrilled. I knew you must be special."

Raine didn't say a word, just blinked back at him with her heart in her eyes.

"'Tis no secret we hated Gwyneth," Da drawled dryly.

Liam scratched at his nape. "You two weren't quiet about it."

"She made you miserable, son. That was enough for me. You deserved better than that vampire."

"Water under the bridge, Da. And you were both right."

Duncan gave him a sad smile. "Years ago, when he met Macen, Bryn told me that Liam's quest for happiness would be the most difficult of all our children. Years passed, Gwyneth came and went, and I worried my boy would remain lonely. Then not long after she mentioned you, Bryn said Liam had decided to move to Los Angeles to stay with the people he loved. She said everything was falling into place."

Curiosity got the better of her. "But Liam didn't say anything to Bryn?"

"Not a word."

"It happened so gradually," Liam remembered. "When I came to visit, I'd had no intention of moving here. Then that morning you and Hammer argued, I asked you to stay with me. Remember?"

"I'll never forget."

"I think I suspected then. A few weeks later, I told Seth I wasn't going back to New York for Thanksgiving. The following week, he came here instead, and I asked him to watch my brownstone when he returned. I'd already bought you this house. By then, I'd decided my life was with you."

"So...without you telling your mother, she saw all that?" Raine looked puzzled.

Liam nodded. "She can sense when people make decisions, especially important ones."

Da nodded. "My Bryn is an empath and a seer. She feels the emotions of others deeply and can 'see' in all directions—past, present, and future. Your man there is touched with it, too. Out of all the kids, he's most like her."

"Geez, Da. Raine doesn't need to hear this—"

"Yes, I do." She nodded earnestly.

Duncan chuckled and patted the hand he still held, shaking his head. "You hear that, lad?"

Liam rolled his eyes. "But how could Mum know the three of us would be together when none of us were even sure?"

"She didn't say. But if I had to guess, some things are simply meant to be." Da smiled Raine's way. "Bryn said there was so much darkness in your life before Hammer and Liam brought in light and love. Lately, she's been telling me the trials and tribulations the three of you were going through, trying to fit yourselves in one another's lives. I woke up one early November morn last year to find her gloating because she knew wee Raine was pregnant."

"Even before we knew, then." Liam covered his eyes and groaned. "Is nothing private, Da?"

"Contrary to your belief, Liam O'Neill, you three didn't invent sex. And that wasn't the point anyway."

Raine blushed, pointedly not looking at his father.

"Your mum mostly talked of the anguish you've all been through." He paused. "Bryn knew afterward what happened with your father, Raine. She was a mess for a week with heartache and sorrow. She knew what you had suffered at the hand of your own kin. What she told me made me rage with the want to shield you from such a monster. Knowing you sent him on to his just rewards brings little comfort."

Raine's eyes filled with more tears. Liam scooped up a box of tissues and set them within her reach, then stood at her back, gently rubbing.

"Thank you," she choked out his father's way.

"I can't pretend to understand that terrible man, Raine. I love my girls and my son fiercely. If one of them had been in your shoes that day, I would have encouraged them to do exactly what you did. Bryn and I want to thank you for making our boy happy. I think he and Macen will be outstanding fathers, and you love one another enough to last a lifetime."

Raine sobbed a laugh. "I know. I'm so lucky to be here with them now. I'll always do my best to make them happy."

"Of course you will."

Raine smiled at him through unshed tears and gave him a quick, fierce hug. "Thanks, Duncan. I needed that."

"There you all are." Bryn bustled into the kitchen and brushed

Duncan's shoulder before giving Raine a smile and Liam a hug. "I'm still getting used to the time difference, but I can't imagine why you two are up."

"We tend to keep late hours." The truth was, Liam simply felt unsettled, and he wasn't sure why.

"Well, since you're still up, Raine, I want you to know that your mum and your sister appreciated your visit yesterday. Oh, they're so proud of you for being such a fighter. And your sister—what pretty dimples she's got—she wants you to know she's with your mother and at peace now. Though she's a bit envious that you found two such strapping men who love you with their whole hearts."

"You've talked to them? Seen them?" Raine's eyes widened. How else could Bryn know about Rowan's dimples?

"They're with you always in spirit." Mum pulled Raine in for a hug. "They want you to be happy. Now..." She looked Liam's way. "Your girl is exhausted, sweetheart. Why don't you see her to bed and come back and finish your tea with us."

Liam might have missed the importance of her suggestion...but her psychic nudge felt more like a kick. It put him instantly on edge.

"Your mom is right. I'm beat now." Raine rose. "I just want you both to know we're thrilled you're here. I'm so happy I could meet you before the baby comes."

"Of course." Bryn smiled. "Our pleasure."

Liam took Raine's hand. "Come on, love."

He led her back upstairs to bed, waiting until she was settled once more. His weary lass dropped off in seconds.

With a heavy heart, Liam returned to the kitchen to find out what had his mother worried.

She didn't keep him waiting for the news, and his suspicions that it wasn't good were confirmed by the whiskey decanter and three glasses waiting.

"Let's take our drinks in the lounge and talk there." He poured a generous measure for each of them and led the way. Liam took one of the armchairs, as did his father. Mum curled up on the sofa opposite.

He raised his glass. "*Sláinte.*"

Da did the same, swallowing the dram before setting his glass down.

His mother didn't toss hers back yet. She simply stared down at the liquid rolling in her glass, looking as if she searched for words that wouldn't break his heart.

"What is it, Mum?"

"I wish I didn't have to tell you that Hammer's struggle isn't over. You best be prepared this time. They mean business. It's far more serious."

"Oh, fuck. Sorry, Mum." The fiery liquor that had settled in his belly only moments ago did nothing to fight the cold fist of fear he felt now. "How long have we got?"

"Not long. I can't tell you when exactly, but everything is in place. The decision has been made to proceed." She looked at him with anguished eyes. "I wish the news was better, son. I know this will be extremely upsetting for you all, but you'll need to keep Raine as calm as possible and—"

"Christ, she'll be beside herself with worry and grief."

"Your bigger task now will be to keep Macen's head above water."

Liam sat back. The loss of freedom—of control—would kill his best friend.

Duncan leaned in and laid a hand on his shoulder. "We're here for you, son. For all of you."

"Perhaps it might be best if you let Macen get what rest he can. You can wake him in a bit and tell him before Raine gets up," Mum suggested.

"I'm so bloody tired of not being able to do more to help my family. It's as if we're trapped in a war zone, caught in endless crossfire, regardless of which way we turn."

"I know. And things will get worse before they have any chance of getting better. But a happy outcome is still possible. Don't lose hope." Bryn came to him, resting her hand on his other shoulder to gentle his worry.

There wasn't much more Bryn could tell him, and though they talked of family and the Emerald Isle for a while longer, they eventually left him to his thoughts and sought their bed again.

Liam didn't return to his. He sat mulling over all the events of late, trying to thread together the pieces of the puzzle. If River had recanted, why had the situation become even more serious? When he focused,

Liam could feel an oppressive force closing in, condemnation and purpose like a dragon's breath firing down his neck.

When he looked up again, the clock on the mantel said it was nearly five. Wearily, he rose from the chair and went to wake Hammer.

That part was easier than he expected. To his surprise, his mate was coming out of the shower when Liam entered the master suite. With a quiet word, he told Macen to meet him downstairs and not to wake Raine. While the man dressed, Liam tossed on a T-shirt and left him to make coffee.

Hammer didn't keep him waiting long, and Liam returned the favor by not dragging it out. It took less than two minutes to worry his best friend sick. Liam hated that he had to.

Macen collapsed on to the nearest barstool and stared out the kitchen window, into the darkness beyond. "I wish I knew who wanted to destroy me," he murmured. "Do you think it has something to do with those damn missing backup drives?"

"I've wondered that, but really, what do they prove? That Raine likes kinky sex. She admitted as much to the police. She was an adult then, and nothing that happened was a crime."

"She'll never say I raped her, so I'm not sure how they can prosecute me with that video. The only other evidence they have is the money orders, which prove nothing without the contract I gave Beck for safekeeping. The photos of Raine that Dean was insistent I destroy… Winslow and Cameron may find them in the system, and they might even know I had them. But nothing about the pictures proves that I took them or that she was a minor at the time. Nothing. If she's asked, Raine would never tell them that, either."

"No. She'd tell them she brought those photos with her or something similar."

"Yeah. I hate to have her lie, but I know she'd do it without even being asked. I just don't understand how this shit is coming back to me."

Liam ran his hand back through his hair, then poured them each a cup of coffee. "Maybe it's that bloody witness they warned you about."

"Yeah. I'd like to know who that lying fucker is."

"Me, too. If we haven't heard anything in an hour or two, I'll get a burner phone and call Dean, see if he can find out."

"Good idea. The sooner we tackle this, the better." He paused, obviously gathering his words. "Just promise me that no matter what happens, you'll look after Raine and our baby."

Liam ached for his friend's pain. "Macen, nothing's final, and we have so many reasons to fight."

"Just set my mind at ease and fucking promise me."

"Of course. You know I will."

Liam came around the bar and roughly pulled Macen to his feet and into a hug. "Don't give up, brother. We'll figure this out. You'll see."

Inside, he wasn't so sure.

"It's out of my hands now." Hammer pulled back. "Bring your coffee into the study. I have some paperwork I need you to see. The first of it protects Shadows. The rest... Well, if the worst happens, Sterling will advise you."

With a heavy heart, Liam spent the next hour reviewing Hammer's files, discussing possibilities and options.

As they wrapped up, Hammer's phone rang. Sterling Barnes.

Macen answered immediately, turning on his speaker. "The police are coming, aren't they? What's the charge?"

"Forget the police. This has escalated. Now you're up against the FBI. Someone found those pictures of Raine battered as a minor. There's a bit of nudity, and coupled with the money orders..." The lawyer paused. "They're assuming the worst. Someone really wants you nailed to a wall. Get ready, Macen. The feds are on their way as we speak."

Macen looked stricken, struggled to process his lawyer's warning, but could only gape for a reply.

Liam forced his own shock down and jumped in. "Barnes, this is O'Neill. What can Raine and I do to help?"

"Let me take care of Hammer this morning. You focus on the agents with search warrants. They're coming to both your home and the club, and everyone will have to leave both premises. Anything deemed to have evidentiary value to their case will be seized. I mean anything—paper, photographs, and especially electronics. If they ask, you and Raine should be ready to give them your phones, tablets, computers, access to any safe...everything."

In other words, their entire life would be invaded, turned upside down, seized, scrutinized. Another wave of furious disbelief seized Liam, but he swallowed it back for Hammer who still stood in wordless shock.

"I'll take care of it," he promised.

"Call me when they arrive," Sterling instructed. "I'll have more instructions then. Macen, I know this is a lot. Right now, I don't know how we'll get out of this clusterfuck, but I promise I'll do my damndest."

"Thank you." Liam quaked as he took the phone from Hammer's numb fingers and ended the call.

"The motherfucking FBI?" Hammer staggered back into the living room and sank into a waiting chair.

Seconds later, the doorbell rang. He and Macen exchanged a glance. This could be the end; they both knew it.

Hammer rose, stiff and stoic, and made his way to the door. With a tight grip on the knob and a sharp intake of breath, he braced himself, looking for the courage to open it and meet his fate.

"Macen?" Raine called from behind him at the top of the stairs. "What's going on?"

He turned to Liam, jaw clenched tight. "Don't let her see this."

Liam thoroughly agreed, especially when he glimpsed a horde of cars and agents outside the window, just waiting to descend.

"I've got your back. We'll see you soon." Giving Hammer a brotherly clap, he crossed the room and took the stairs two at a time.

"What's going on?" Raine watched him ascend with a wary gaze and tried to dart past him. "No. This can't be..."

Liam grabbed her around the waist and hauled her off her feet and into his arms, grateful when his parents seemed to melt out of the woodwork to stand beside his best friend. "Let him go with dignity."

"No!" she screeched even louder. "They can't take him. Macen..."

"Stop," Liam insisted. "Barnes will have him out soon."

Hammer didn't turn to look at her again, and Liam hid her face in his shoulder. "Don't look. Don't make this any harder for him."

Raine tensed. He could feel the fight in her. She wanted to argue with every cell in her body. Instead, she clutched at him, digging her nails into his skin.

Liam grimaced. The pain of her wee scratches was nothing compared to the agony gashing his chest when Hammer opened the door.

Things got ugly fast.

"Macen Daniel Hammerman, I have a warrant for your arrest for the purchase of a minor for the purposes of sexual exploitation. Please turn around and place your hands behind your back. You have the right to remain silent—"

"Liam?"

"I've got her, mate," he assured.

"Anything you say can and will be used against you in a court of law."

Hammer wasn't listening to the feds. "Take care of her."

Liam kept Raine's face buried against his neck. "I will."

Raine's jagged sob resounded above the chaos in the room. "Macen…"

"You have the right to an attorney…" As the agent led him out the door, he clamped handcuffs around Hammer's wrists.

The click sounded ominously final.

CHAPTER ELEVEN

WITH HIS ARMS stretched uncomfortably behind him in the back of an unmarked car, Hammer's shoulders screamed. Liam and Sterling had warned him, but he hadn't truly been prepared for the terrible reality of the feds hauling him away with his hands secured behind his back. Now, he tried to force himself to relax. He'd cuffed many subs over the years. They'd survived, sure. But Macen wasn't a sub, and being bound like one pissed him off—and demeaned him—even more.

Purchasing a minor for the purpose of sexual exploitation? Bullshit!

Obviously, River hadn't done a stellar job of recanting his claims to the authorities—if he'd even tried at all. He'd bet the prick had been blowing smoke up his ass, plotting all the while to zap him from Raine's life. No doubt the motherfucker would devise a way to get rid of Liam next.

I'm sorry for what I've done to you, Hammer. Liam.

"You're not yet, you fuckfaced son of a bitch. But if you didn't keep your word, I'll make sure you will be soon," Hammer muttered to himself.

Inside the station, he tried to block out the booking process. After the humiliation of being fingerprinted, having his mug shot taken, and being divested of all the personal property in his pockets, an officer led him down the narrow, steel-cage hallway filled with cursing and shouting. The armed officer directed him inside an empty cell.

He should have been grateful he was alone, but once the door rattled shut behind him and the lock clattered like the lid of his coffin, Hammer's rage reawakened. He wanted to beat the fucking shit out of someone—preferably River.

Avoiding the dilapidated mattress and its dingy sheet, Hammer paced the eight-by-eight cell. His thoughts swirled in a furious cyclone while niggling doubt began burrowing in his brain.

River wanted Raine in his life. Even the cynic in Hammer had believed her brother intended to clean up the mess he'd made. If he'd tried—if he hadn't been the one who'd stolen the security footage from Shadows—then someone else was behind this sabotage on his life. But who? Who had he pissed off enough to warrant this vile revenge?

Yes, he'd been a snarling prick at the club for the past few months, snapping at members over the slightest provocation. But had he seriously wounded another Dominant's pride so deeply they'd resort to ruining his future with Raine and Liam? Carl lacked the balls. And no one else with a beef readily leapt to Hammer's mind.

"Shit." He scrubbed a hand over his face.

Maybe this vendetta went back further. Hell, Juliet's mother had vowed over her youngest daughter's grave that she'd see Hammer dead for his "irresponsibility and abuse." Since she'd never hired a hit man, could the old woman have found the next best opportunity?

"Face it, fucker. Your life has been bleak since Juliet killed herself." And looking back, too many of his darkest days had been self-imposed. He'd hurt the people around him too much.

It was entirely possible he was paying for it now.

Hammer heard voices and footsteps coming down the hall. Stepping toward the bars, he craned his neck. The sight of a uniformed officer escorting Sterling Barnes sent a blast of relief through him.

"Sterling," Hammer exhaled. "Thank christ."

"Don't be too happy to see me, Macen," his lawyer replied grimly. "This shit has gotten far deeper than you or I imagined."

"What?" Hammer's stomach rolled up to his throat. "River didn't recant, did he?"

Sterling darted a perturbed glance over his shoulder until the officer stepped back.

"He did, but I'm afraid it was too little, too late. As far as they're concerned, you committed a crime, and River's opinion is irrelevant. They also have the two missing surveillance videos from Shadows."

Dread gripped Hammer's gut. "I wish I knew how the hell they got their hands on those."

"Once you're arraigned and we start preparing for trial, the prosecution will have to tell us the name of their witness, as well as how they obtained the footage during discovery. I don't know if that information will help anything, but…"

Yeah, Hammer doubted it, too.

"The state is also reserving the right to file its own charges and is only deferring to the feds for now because their sentence will be longer. But if the federal charges don't stick, the state will probably try you for rape. From what I heard, November fourth is…damning."

Hammer bit back a curse. To someone only watching, it probably looked brutal. He'd been drunk and in no way gentle when he'd heaped six years of pent-up passion on Raine.

"I swear it was consensual," he argued—like it would do any good.

"The audio is fuzzy, so that's not clear…except the part where you're yelling and she says no. I'm not doubting you. But your number one problem right now is the photos they're using to corroborate this federal charge. Raine is so bloody and bruised. They think you beat her for fun, snapped pictures as trophies, and shared them with your kinky friends."

"Oh, hell no! I have never lifted a hand to her in anger. I never would."

"The beating isn't the worst part of those snapshots legally. Because a bit of pubic hair and the crest of a nipple are visible, the feds are using the photos and the money orders to substantiate their charge of purchasing a child for sexual exploitation. They'll probably admit River's original statement, too. Even though he recanted, an experienced prosecutor can plant the seed that you coerced him to retract his statement by threatening his sister."

Hammer's knees buckled. He gripped the bars and swallowed the bile rising in his throat. All the blood in his body plummeted to his feet.

"How many years if I'm convicted?" he managed to choke out.

"Thirty…in a federal prison," Sterling murmured bleakly.

Fear, stark and merciless, gnawed at Hammer. His heart smacked against his chest. "No! No fucking way. I can't go to prison for a crime I didn't commit. Someone is setting me up. I need to find whoever it is and end this goddamn charade."

"I've already talked to Liam a couple of times. He has a PI on it. They're looking into it now."

"Seth? Yeah. He's the best. Hopefully, he'll be able to dig up evidence to save me."

"Even if he can't, when Raine testifies, she should be able to shed positive light on the case."

He hated to heap more stress on her. "Will the prosecution try to discredit her?"

But he already knew the answer. The feds would do their best to chew her up and spit her out. They would slap him behind bars without an ounce of regard for the truth. The injustice made Hammer want to howl.

"You can guarantee it."

"She's fucking pregnant!"

"Calm down. They're not going to beat her, Macen. I'll do my best to protect her on the stand."

"No. If they're going to take her apart, she's not testifying. She's already under too much stress. I won't let her do anything else to risk this baby."

"One step at a time. Now that you've been indicted, come Monday, you and I, along with some of my colleagues who specialize in federal criminal cases, will go before the judge for your arraignment."

"Monday? Monday!" Hammer roared. "I can't sit in this fucking cell until then. Can't you post my bond now?"

"It's the damn weekend. The wheels of justice won't turn again until that's over. So keep it together and let me do my job. I'll have you out of here as soon as I can."

Clawing for control, he clenched his teeth. "How is Raine holding up? Do you know?"

"I'll find out for you."

Sterling would, but Hammer knew Raine. She was probably devastated. He hoped like hell she wasn't crawling inside her shell, where Liam would be hard-pressed to reach her. "Tell her not to worry about me. Tell her"—his voice cracked—"tell her I love her."

Sympathy settled onto the older man's face. "She knows, but I'll be happy to remind her for you. Look, I know things seem bleak, but I won't stop until I've turned over every pebble, rock, or boulder to clear your name."

"I appreciate that," Hammer replied, wishing he shared the same conviction. But all he could picture was Raine and Liam without him, and the ocean of tears she'd be crying if he never returned home.

They said good-bye. As he watched Sterling and the cop disappear down the hall, he felt gutted. Lost. More desolate than he'd been when Raine had run away from Shadows, abandoning him and Liam.

He supposed he should look for silver linings. This shit storm hadn't happened years ago, when Raine had still been a girl. At least Liam would be by her side to give her love and protection if Hammer could no longer be there himself.

It would just hurt like hell.

Macen stumbled to the lumpy cot and sank down, not giving two shits about the condition of the bed. Bracing his elbows on his knees, he took his face in his hands and bit back the scream trapped inside him.

Thirty years was a lifetime to lose—away from Raine and Liam, and the baby he ached to raise and watch grow. He could well be a grandfather before he tasted freedom again. And after spending three decades behind bars, what could he go back to? Liam and Raine would have forged a new life without him, sharing more children and happy years that didn't include him. When he was finally released, Macen would be an outsider looking in.

And after thirty years apart, how would Liam and Raine explain his sudden return to the family they'd raised? How would their children ever grasp the fact their parents had once been a threesome, especially if they'd never mentioned it before? His reappearance could cause unconscionable damage.

But more disheartening was the thought of Raine waiting all those years, pining for his return, and blaming herself for his fate. She would dutifully visit him while he rotted, sit across from him and share stories of her happy life with Liam. It wouldn't take long until Hammer resented his best friend for living the dream they should have shared together. How long would it be before he turned his venomous rage on Raine and sent her away for good because the sight of her ripped him in two?

The thought of never holding her in his arms again made Hammer shake. Memories of him and Liam sinking inside her soft body together and taking her to the stars would never be enough to last him through the interminable years. He'd eventually go crazy, longing to feel her wild beneath him and shattering around his cock, her screams echoing in his ears. The notion that he would never again know the pleasure and love they shared unleashed a new realm of anguish inside him.

He couldn't put Raine, Liam, or himself through that kind of torture.

Hammer lifted his head and scanned the cold, depressing cell.

He'd make bail in a few days, but if it appeared he would serve the next thirty years trapped behind bars…

"I can't."

Macen raked a hand through his hair. He refused to spend his life trapped in this hell, just as he refused to hold Raine and Liam hostage. If Sterling exhausted all options, he'd have some tough decisions to make.

A black veil of regret enveloped him. Instead of spending the last six years making memories with Raine, he'd let guilt consume him. Like a cancer, it had festered, convincing him he wasn't worthy of Raine's love. He'd spent his nights sticking his dick in women who didn't matter while ignoring the only one who did. And for what? Had years of mental self-flagellation made him a better fucking man? No.

He'd let remorse convince him he wasn't whole enough to lead Raine down her submissive path without fucking up her life. He'd insisted that his Dominant needs were too harsh for her to handle because he "required" a slave. Hammer scoffed at himself. The truth was, he'd spent years greedier for a sub's power than her heart. He'd been a manwhoring coward.

He hadn't really lived.

Until he and Liam had embraced Raine.

Prison wasn't anything new for him. He'd been so determined not to repeat the sins of his past that he'd locked himself away years ago.

Hammer stood and paced again. If he somehow made it out of this mess, he vowed to change. He'd open up and share his entire soul and make up for all the years he'd spent wallowing. He would live life to the fullest. Happy. Content. Committed.

Sending up a silent prayer, he did something he'd never done before; he dropped to his knees and begged.

For mercy.

For this fucking nightmare to end.

For the chance to live a long, happy life with Liam and Raine—and never look back at his past again.

CHAPTER TWELVE

AS LIAM WATCHED the feds lead Hammer away in cuffs, the world disintegrated under his feet. But he clutched Raine against him at the top of the stairs and hid her face. She didn't need to see the unfolding horror. He would damn sure keep his promise to Hammer and protect their girl.

Later, he'd think about the fact that life as they all knew it—wanted it—could be over.

Terrible silence fell, punctuated only by Raine's struggles and sobs. His chest opened, bleeding out from a hollow, gaping wound. Anxiety rushed in to fill the chasm.

"Let go!" She pushed at his shoulders and tried to break free. "We have to do something. Help him. Now."

Liam gripped her tighter, a hand at her nape, another at her ass, as he sat on the top step, plastering her against his torso. Though he forced her to straddle him so he could contain her, Raine still tried desperately to wriggle free.

Da stepped inside the house again and closed the door with a somber shake of his head.

So it was done. Hammer was gone.

Liam pressed Raine tighter against him. She might need him...but he would need her, too, now that he felt as if half his soul had been ripped away. And they would have to lean on one another for the next ordeal that would literally beat down their door in a handful of minutes.

"You're right, love. We're going to help Hammer. Be still while I call Barnes."

She tried to stand. "I'll go. Get dressed. I'll demand the police—"

"It's beyond the police, Raine." He didn't want to heap this on her, but he refused to withhold the truth. "This is a federal matter now."

Raine paled. "The FBI took him?"

"I'm afraid so."

If anything, she seemed more frantic. "What the... I have to talk to them. Maybe they'll listen if I tell them what really happened." She gave him another push, then a frustrated grunt when he wouldn't let her free. "Liam, I have to fix this. Everything is my fault."

He took hold of her face and forced her to look at him. "Nothing is your fault. Do you hear me?"

She shook her head, dark hair mussed and spilling around her. "I'm the one he stuck his neck out to save, so I have to make the FBI listen."

"They don't want you in the middle of this now. Neither do Hammer and I. Let me call Barnes so he can do his job."

Liam gave his mother a mental nudge, and she appeared almost instantly.

Bryn eased beside Raine and drew his girl into her arms. "Shh. Try to calm yourself. You can't think the worst."

"How do I convince these people that Macen is innocent? Tell me what to do..."

"I don't have the answers. What I know is that your wee one is taking on your stress. Neither of your men would ever want you both so dismayed." Bryn stroked Raine's hair, soothing her. "Have faith. Nothing has been decided yet."

Instantly, the fight seemed to leave his lass. She let out a ragged breath, curled protective palms around her belly, and drew her legs to her chest. "I'm sorry."

Liam didn't know whether she meant her apology for him, their child, or whomever would listen. And she didn't say anything more, just rested her chin on her knees and worked on breathing. But he felt the tension pinging off her. Anyone who didn't know his girl might think she was sedate. Inside, she was a live wire. Watching her shut down tore at Liam's heart.

Cursing, he tugged out his phone and rang Sterling Barnes, who answered immediately.

"Hammer is gone. How do we help him now?" Liam asked quietly as he paced away from Raine and his mother.

"Have the federal agents arrived to search the premises?"

Liam glanced through the living room window at the gathering throng. "They're outside."

"Nothing to do except let them in, give them access, and leave. Everything related to Hammer's lifestyle, especially his relationship with Raine, is now open for scrutiny."

"Fuck." Liam hated feeling powerless to help the ones he loved. He despised being squeezed so tight by circumstances beyond his control that he couldn't breathe. "We had so little warning. Raine's not even dressed—"

A pounding on the front door drew everyone's attention. Da looked his way for direction. Liam swallowed. He had to make a decision…but he didn't actually have a choice.

"We'll let them in." Liam sighed into the phone. "Anything else?"

"I'm en route to see Hammer now. I'll send you the numbers for some reputable federal bail bondsmen. Start arranging a substantial amount of cash, something in the six-figure range. Beyond that, you'll simply have to wait. It's time for me to earn my money. I'll call when I have news."

Thankfully, liquidity wasn't a problem. But like Raine, Liam wanted to do something to help free Hammer and end this nightmare now.

The knocking became more insistent. "FBI. Open up. We have a warrant to search the premises."

Raine froze, staring at the door, then at him with wide, terrified eyes. "There's nothing here for them to find."

"Liam?" His father pressed.

"I'll talk to you later, Barnes." He ended the call and didn't bother putting his phone away. The FBI might take it from him in moments anyway. Besides, he had to warn someone at Shadows.

"Mum, take Raine to our room. Help her get dressed. Quickly. We only have seconds."

Raine looked like she wanted to argue but turned and disappeared down the hall, Bryn in tow.

"Son?" Da asked from the living room.

"Don't open the door yet. One minute." Liam scrolled through his contacts and found Pike's number, dashing off a text to expect the FBI at the club's doors any minute.

The Dungeon Monitor sent back two words: They're here.

And he could do nothing to help them or protect Hammer's club. Bloody hell. All he could do now was shield Raine.

He called out to her and Mum. "Hurry!"

"Last warning. FBI. Open up or we'll break the door down."

"Fucking wankers," Liam muttered. "Da, open it."

Duncan nodded and reached for the latch as Raine emerged wearing a pair of yoga pants and a T-shirt, looking pale and shaken but resolved. She'd fastened her Valentine's Day gift around her wrist.

"Good girl." He took her hand in his and gave it a firm squeeze. "We'll need to leave until they've finished their search. We can't go to Shadows. They'll be combing through the club, too."

As if those words had punched her in the chest, Raine gasped just as his father opened the door. Federal agents swarmed in.

A tall blond bruiser approached Da. "Where is Raine Elise Kendall? We have a warrant to search her property, residence of Macen Daniel Hammerman."

Everyone turned to look at her, and Liam held his breath. Would she crumble?

"I'm Raine Kendall." She gathered herself and descended the stairs, her voice carrying over the collective din. "Show me your warrant."

She faced down the official, chin raised. Liam had never been prouder of her.

The big agent met Raine in the middle of the living room. Liam stood right beside her, supportive and protective.

"I'm Agent Wade Kelly." He pointed to a no-nonsense woman stepping across the portal. "This is Agent Vera Singh."

"Ms. Kendall wants to see the warrant," Liam reminded with an edge in his voice.

The fed raised a suspicious brow. "And you are…?"

"Liam O'Neill, Ms. Kendall's partner. We both live here with Mr. Hammerman. We'd like to see the damn warrant."

Agent Kelly motioned to Singh, who handed Raine the paperwork without a word.

She opened it with trembling fingers. Liam scanned the multiple pages of the document as she did, but the words swam before his eyes. SEXUAL EXPLOITATION OF A CHILD jumped out first. Then he saw

THEREFORE COMMANDED TO SEARCH THE PREMISES OF... Signatures, an official-looking seal, and references to seizing property filled the rest of the space.

God, this was so real and happening so bloody fast.

He felt Raine's stare on him. She wanted to defy this court order, but she knew that wasn't an option. A sense of violation tightened her face and burned in her eyes. Liam could almost read her mind. This was her first real home, and these investigators were going to trample all over it, defile the peace she'd found here.

Someday, somehow, he'd make it right for her again.

Until then, Liam could only take her hand. "Let's leave so the agents can do their job."

As soon as he entwined his fingers with Raine's, he felt the fight she hid just under her skin. But she managed to nod.

When he looked back, his parents stood behind them, ready and waiting.

After a quick search of Raine's purse, Agent Singh seized her phone. She endured the intrusion in stony silence, but Liam knew she wanted to scream. To his surprise, they didn't take his cell phone.

As Agent Kelly shoved them out the door, Raine took one last look through the portal, obviously wanting to imprint her sanctuary firmly in her memory before the tornado of search teams hit it.

Liam curled his arm around her waist and plucked her off the porch. After prodding her to his SUV, he ushered her to the passenger's seat and buckled her in. He didn't ask if she was all right. She looked somewhere between ready to explode and a breath from falling apart. When he caressed her face, he felt her struggle.

"I'll take care of you," he swore.

Raine looked over at him with hollow blue eyes. "You didn't sleep all night, did you? I'm sorry. You've tried so hard to comfort me... You're upset, too."

He sighed heavily. "Gutted."

"You're always giving me a shoulder to lean on. You don't have to be the strong one. I'm here for you, too."

Liam kissed the top of her head. "I have a feeling we may need each other before this day is over."

She nodded, and Liam knew she was wondering how either of

them would survive without Macen.

His parents climbed into the backseat, and Liam zipped away from the house. The gloom in the vehicle matched the mood of the overcast day. He drove north with a destination in mind. After all, they had a few hours to kill.

When he pulled up to the pier, he grabbed Raine's hand. "Let's get some breakfast."

"Aye," Da seconded his suggestion. "I'm starving."

His mother stepped from the car with a smile in her voice. "You're always hungry. It's the Irishman in you."

Liam appreciated his parents' attempt to lighten the mood, but he wasn't actually hungry. He'd bet Raine wasn't, either. She looked out the windshield, lost in worry.

"You have to feed the baby."

"You're right." She blinked, joining him in the present again. "Liam, what happens next?"

"I don't know. We can only take things one step at a time. Once Sterling calls, we'll figure out the rest." He stepped out of the car and came around to open her door, holding out his hand. "Come with me."

She nodded and laid her trembling fingers in his palm.

He led everyone to the little burger joint that opened for breakfast, allowing patrons to take advantage of the vast view of the Pacific Ocean. As they took their seats, the water seemed to disappear into the thick fog that would likely burn off by noon.

A few people strolled along the shoreline. A handful of hopeful fishermen cast their poles off the end of the pier, just a few feet from where the morning surfers caught their waves. Everyone seemed mired in their own thoughts.

The place wasn't crowded yet. They ordered quickly, but it was a solemn affair. The food arrived in minutes...then sat barely touched. Even Da, who really did eat all the time, pushed his potatoes around his plate. Raine forced herself to eat half her eggs and a piece of toast before chasing it with a few swallows of tea.

Liam felt more worry settle in his shoulders.

She'd gone too quiet and was up in her head, either doomsday scenario-ing herself into a knotted ball of nerves or plotting some daring rescue he'd completely object to. Or both.

"Raine?"

She tried to smile at him. "I'm fine."

Like hell. Pregnant, sleep-deprived, overwrought… She was bottling up before his eyes.

Liam wished they could go home so he could pull her into familiar surroundings and crawl inside her head, make her give her worries over to him. But in public, with his parents mere feet away, how the devil could he do that?

Did she think he would break if she leaned on him any more? That he lacked the spine to carry her burdens? Or did she think that only Hammer was strong enough to do that for her?

Da got up to pay the bill at the register. Mum slipped away to the toilet.

The question ate at Liam.

"Hammer's arrest will become public knowledge, won't it?" Raine asked into the silence.

"Yes."

Another worry she'd chew on, damn it. The press had been merciless after Raine's ordeal with Bill last December. They'd focused their spotlight on her being a supposed sex worker. Hammer had been at the center of the controversy, as well as being the face of it, giving all the statements until the vultures and their poison pens had left them alone to pick the flesh from someone else's bones.

"Reporters will have a field day with this." She sounded bitter.

"I don't give a damn what anyone thinks about me. Nor, I suspect, will Hammer." He took her hand. "Don't worry, Raine. I'll protect you."

"You don't have to." She shook her head and tried giving him a smile full of dry irony. "I'm capable of saying 'no comment.'"

Of course she was, but she'd let Hammer say it for her many, many times a mere two months ago. Why did she imagine he wouldn't take on that role?

Da dropped a hand on his shoulder. "Ready to go?"

"Yeah." Liam was more than ready to find someplace he could explore precisely what was in Raine's head—and right any misconceptions she might be harboring.

"Raine?" his father prompted.

She rose, looking pale and brittle as she tried to smile. "I'm ready. Thanks for breakfast, Duncan."

As they headed out, Liam held back, pretending to look around the kitschy little restaurant. Bryn played along.

"I know, son." She patted his hand. "I'll keep your father occupied. You have a talk with your girl."

Thank god his mother understood. "I'm worried."

"You've both been through a lot already today. Just make certain you're not taking on troubles that aren't real."

Was he? Liam frowned. Did Raine simply want to stand on her own two feet now…or did she think him too weak to handle her care? Or maybe she didn't want just one of them. After all, when he and Hammer had finally agreed to share her at the lodge, she'd made it perfectly plain that she would have them both—or neither. It was also the reason she'd refused their proposals. Since then, she'd done a fine job of giving them equal devotion and surrender. But now, if Hammer was gone for good, Liam had to wonder…would she still want the love they shared? Or would she leave—and take their baby with her?

Bad enough to lose Hammer. Losing everyone else would destroy Liam.

"I'll do my best, Mum." He kissed her cheek.

She shot him a quelling glance. "She's falling. Be gentle but firm."

"I love you. Now butt out."

Bryn rolled her eyes. "I'll take your da and go."

She bustled off and wound her arm through Duncan's, leading him off to explore the pier.

Liam found Raine standing at the railing, staring out at the ocean. Looking for answers? He approached and took her hand. "Walk with me."

She didn't argue, just let him lead her down toward the crashing waves.

Away from people and noise.

Away from cops and questions.

Away from everything they couldn't do for Hammer right in this moment.

Just the two of them, reaffirming—or dissolving—what they

shared.

He dragged in a deep breath of salty air, calming the turmoil inside him. He sensed it pinging from her, as well.

They walked for long minutes, not speaking, simply holding hands. Then the distance and silence between them became too much for Liam to bear. He pulled her closer and wrapped his arms around her. "Talk to me, lass."

She looked up at him, confused and lost. The devastation in her gaze bloody near crippled him. "And say what? I'm scared. And so fucking angry. I just want to hit something."

She was winding her emotions—and their baby's—into a fervor. When he placed a hand on her belly, the distress magnified. The force of it sizzled across his palm. *Damn.*

He understood the stakes. It was his responsibility to make her purge this toxic worry.

"Tell me more."

"What more can I say that you don't know? Macen needs us. I realize we had to leave the house, and the view here is pretty, but we don't have time for—"

"Centering you? It's my first priority. If Hammer were here, he would insist on it, too."

"But Hammer isn't here. He's being incarcerated as we speak. And we're standing around, worrying about me and—"

"That's Dom 101, sweetheart. We shelve our own concerns until your needs are met. Get your fear and frustration out, then we'll move on. Scream."

"Scream?" Raine stared at him as if he'd lost his mind. "What will that do except make me look like a fucking idiot? Stop trying to 'adjust my attitude' or whatever. Let's do something productive."

He tightened his grasp on her. "I will stand here all day long if I have to until you"—he palmed her stomach again—"and the baby are calm again. So scream or talk. Those are your two choices."

She cursed under her breath, staring out at the ocean again. "All right. Everything that's happened *is* my fault. And no one will listen to me when I swear I'm not a victim. I gave the police the truth, but it was inconvenient, so they tried to twist my words. They've already convicted Macen in their minds and—"

"They aren't the jury." He slipped his hand into her hair, giving the strands a tug. "Stop assuming that he's going away forever."

"How can I not worry about that? He must be pacing his cell, wondering whether he's going to rot his life away in that shitty—"

"That's enough," he said in a low, warning rumble. "Stop."

"Stop what?" Her laugh sounded halfway hysterical. "Stop worrying? Stop caring? What is it you want me to stop doing, Liam?"

"Stop blaming yourself. Stop assuming the worst before it's happened." He tugged her until he could see into her face. "Do you think this attitude helps you? Or helps our child? It certainly doesn't help me or Hammer."

"I know." She looked up at the gray clouds, her face mottled. "I need him. I can't do this without him."

Her words frustrated the hell out of Liam, and he shelved his urge to shake her. This wasn't about him. She needed his Dominance, and he'd commanded her to vent her feelings. If she whipped him with her tongue because it made her feel better… Well, he had big shoulders. He could handle anything.

Except her leaving him.

"Stop thinking I can't clear your head and give you the kind of boundaries Hammer does. Give me your problems."

"You don't need them! You need me to be a big girl and stand on my own two feet."

He glowered at her. "I understand you believe—"

"You don't understand anything," she lashed out. "How can you? I don't understand this shit. I don't understand why this happened. I don't understand what the hell I'm supposed to do. And I definitely don't understand why you're trying to be my big, bad Dom right now."

Oh, she didn't?

Liam slid into a brutally familiar headspace. Dominance filled his veins. He embraced his darker, uncompromising side. And once he uncaged it on Raine, the submission she gave him in return would be a balm vital to them both.

"You think I'm acting?" A humorless chuckle rolled from his lips. "Until now, I've only shown you my tender adoration. It's what you needed when you first accepted my collar. When Macen and I took you to the lodge. When my ex-wife returned to wreak havoc. After that monster of a father kidnapped you. All these months Hammer's been running from his ghosts. But make no mistake, I will show you just how demanding a taskmaster I can be. So either voluntarily hand me your concerns or I'll pry my way inside your head and twist you inside out until you give them over."

She'd paused, staring at the waves gathering and rushing toward them, breaking thunderously on the sandy beach. The sea foam spreading messily as it caught in the onshore breeze, while the gulls screeched as they dove and circled on high. The wind whipped at her hair. She tossed it back absently.

She sniffled. "I know you're worried about me and the baby. I worry about the little one, too. But how do I not worry about the man I love? I'm scared Macen's never coming back."

Her lashes fluttered closed as tears trickled from the corners of her eyes. Liam didn't have the heart to lie and tell her everything would be fine.

"He will. Barnes will make sure of it."

"But for how long?"

"That's out of our hands, Raine."

"I don't…" She crossed her arms tightly over her chest. "I don't know if I can live with that. I…"

Suddenly her fury churned the air. She broke away from him and started to run. Startled, he watched her for a moment.

See how she sped away like the goddamn fucking wind. Jesus. That's it, love. Get it out of your system.

Liam started after her.

Acting on pure instinct, Raine darted like a wild thing. She glanced over her shoulder, sensed she was being hunted by a bigger, stronger predator. Arms and elbows pumping madly, hair flying about her in all directions as her legs propelled her forward, she dashed, her feet kicking up sand and wash.

Fast twitch. But she's a sprinter. Won't last long.

In fact, she didn't get far before the burst of fury ran out and she nearly tripped on her own feet, collapsing on the wet sand with a sob.

Liam was a second behind her, scooping her up in his arms and dragging her against his chest.

"Put me down," she insisted even as she wrapped herself around him and held tight.

He sank to the sandy grains beneath him and dragged Raine into his lap, rocking her. He muttered soothing sounds in her ear and rubbed her belly, trying to calm her upset—and the baby's. "It's all right."

"No." Raine beat weakly at his back with her fists in between ragged cries. "It's not!"

"Is that all you've got?" he prodded, his tone deceptively mild.

"What do you mean?"

"Sir," he corrected. "You will address me as Sir until I say otherwise. Do you understand, sub?"

She stubbornly refused to answer.

"Do you?" he prodded. "C'mon, Raine. You're itching for a fight. Let me have it. Let's bleed off your fucking attitude. Or do I need to blister your ass right here and now to make my point? Because I will." Liam grabbed her by the hair and yanked until he knew her scalp tingled with a sensation just shy of pain. "Think carefully before you answer. I can be your greatest comfort or the most relentless bastard you've ever met. That's up to you."

"What the fuck do you want from me, *Sir?*" She spit out the words as more tears swam down her face. "I'm lost. I'm scared. I'm angry. And I know I have no right to throw this goddamn hissy because you're hurting every bit as much as I am and…" More sobs took over. "I'm sorry."

He stroked her hair. Now they were getting somewhere… "I know. Scream."

"What?" She stared at him incredulously.

"You heard me," he growled in soft warning. "Scream."

"How is that—"

"Do it now." He cupped her chin, forcing her face upward, and dragged her mouth open. "Scream!"

She let loose a whimper.

"Oh, come on. You're stronger than that, Raine. I expect more. Give it to me."

Her second attempt went the way of the first, swallowed up by the crash of waves and the stiff morning wind.

"Pathetic," he tsked, shaking his head. "You didn't even startle the birds. Stop being a bloody coward. Or is this you being a victim?" He pushed her off his lap and rose to his feet.

She grabbed his hand and yanked him back. "You bastard!"

"What did you call me?" He whipped around and pinned her with a dark glare, his voice cold.

Raine let go of his hand. She thought about inching away—but she wouldn't back down. "Bastard."

"That's Sir Bastard to you. Do you have a scream in there after all? If you could roar at the assholes who've taken Hammer from us, what would that sound like?"

She got to her knees, bracing herself by digging her fingers into the wet sand. Her lips pursed. Her face turned red. Her eyes burned a fiery blue. She glared at him like she hated his guts right now, and he didn't care, because he was finally getting through to her.

Raine gritted her teeth. Then she flung fistfuls of sand, threw her head back, and let loose a howl. The sound pealed across the beach, long and loud, over the surf, carried by the wind. People in all directions turned to stare. Liam didn't give a shit. Her wail was filled with such misery that it cut him to the quick. Primal, soul-deep pain. He blinked away the burn behind his eyes.

There was her heart. Fierce. Full of love. God, she would fight for Hammer. Good. It might take both of them to save him.

When she ran out of air, she looked at him again, defiant and sad and still seething with fight.

He gave her a nasty smile sure to set her off. "That was a decent start. Again."

Twice more she poured out her grief to the gulls as the wind carried her screams away. Until her throat turned raw. Until her body shuddered and the tension left her. Until she sank to the sand again, face in her hands, small and spent. Until she cried.

"That was perfect, love. I'm proud of you."

She cupped his cheek, her red-rimmed eyes full of gratitude, of worship. "I feel better. Thank you, Sir."

Heart bursting, he gathered her up and into his arms. He brushed a hand over the babe, relieved to feel calm, even a bit of tumbling into slumber. A million feelings pelted him as he carried Raine back to the pier. She'd worked off her stress. In fact, she gave out completely and slept against him, resting her head on his shoulder in a silent show of trust.

He still had no idea where he stood with her. If Hammer was gone, would she stay?

Heaving a deep breath as he reached the car, he was relieved that his parents didn't say a word when he slipped Raine's slumbering form into the front seat and they left the beach.

When they pulled into the driveway, the FBI had cleared out. Liam hoped like hell he could get Raine into bed so he could deal with whatever mess the search teams had left behind. When she woke…he'd deal with her.

He handed Da his keys. When his father opened the door, the disaster that greeted him nearly took his legs out from under him. This was just another injustice Raine didn't need now.

"Don't worry about a thing, son. We'll soon have everything set to rights," Mum insisted. "I raised seven children, remember? I've seen worse."

"True," Duncan murmured. "But I'd have pulled out the strap for this mess."

"You're all bluster. The strap…" Bryn swatted Duncan's arm. "Enough with you, man. Start tidying down here." She turned to Liam. "Why don't you take your girl upstairs?"

Since they both had sand all over them, he supposed the bath was a good place to start. "We'll take a quick rinse and I'll be down to help you directly."

His mum frowned. The expression turned into an angry scowl when she took in the disheveled state of the bedroom. "Don't be ridiculous. Raine doesn't need to clean up this mess. She needs your comfort."

Liam turned to look at his mother. Somehow, he didn't think she meant his wee wench needed a hug.

"Now you're catching on." She shooed him into the master bathroom, which looked far closer to normal than any other room in the house. "Don't make the rinse too quick."

He stood and blinked at her. Had his own mother just told him to make love to Raine?

"Of course." She shook her head as she left the room, muttering to herself. "Sometimes men can be so thick…"

Liam looked down at Raine lying in his arms, so trusting and peaceful. He hated like hell to wake her. Even without makeup, with tears staining her cheeks, she looked beautiful. Rumpled, windblown, all warm woman, precious and alive. His, by god.

Instantly, his damn cock went hard with need for her, despite everything they'd endured today, despite everything beyond the door.

"Raine, we're home. Wake up, love. Let's take a soak together."

She came awake in layers, inky lashes fluttering open, those stunning eyes coming alert as she took him and her surroundings in. Then she stretched like a cat and yawned. "Oh, my god. I just…fell asleep on you?"

A smile twitched across his mouth. "You died, at least for a couple of hours."

"Sorry. Did you carry me back across the beach?"

"I did. All hundred pounds of you," he teased. "My arms are broken now."

She huffed. "Any news on Macen?"

"I'm just as anxious as you, but we're still waiting for Sterling to call. I'll make all the arrangements for his bail, but until then, our hands are tied. So let's get you cleaned up."

"Clean…" She froze. "The house! Should I ask how bad it is out there?"

"Nothing that can't be put to rights again. Mum and Da are tidying up now. Not to worry." Liam set her on her feet. She didn't wobble…much, just watched him in the mirror as he started the bath. "Come to me now."

Raine pulled off her T-shirt as she wandered to the side of the tub where he sat and stood between his legs. He bent to kiss her bare belly, then worked his lips up to the swells of her breasts, pausing a moment to revel in the feel of her silky skin against his so rough. She stroked his hair, her slender fingers working through the strands, drawing a rumble from deep in his chest.

When she reached past him to pick one of her bath oils and added it under the running water, he smelled the musky-floral aroma in the air. He gripped her tighter. "Put your hands on my shoulders."

He waited until her fingers curled around him. Only then did he push the waistband of her yoga pants over her hips, trailing his broad palms down her pale thighs, lifting her knees one at a time to strip away the garment.

"Liam?" She cooperated absently as concern settled onto her face. "I said a lot today. Did I upset you? You helped me so much, but…are you okay? Do you need something from me?"

To tear off everything you're wearing with my teeth and fuck you until you cling to me. Until you scream my name. Until you admit you'll always belong to me.

Instead, he clenched his teeth and swallowed back the words.

"Liam?"

She wore only a simple cotton thong and a matching bra he could see through. Her breasts were swollen with hormones and flowed over the cups. Steam and some flowery-earthy fragrance swirled around the room, making him goddamn dizzy. Raine was pregnant, traumatized, and she needed his comfort now.

He swallowed back a groan. "I'm fine."

"You're not. Talk to me."

"I said I'm fine." He grabbed his own T-shirt in a fist, yanked it over his head, and tossed it free.

She thrust her hands on her hips and cocked her head, staring like she had something to say and was debating the wisdom of opening her mouth. The hint of her attitude turned him on more. He couldn't take his bloody stare off her, the flash of her blue eyes, the black curtain of her hair framing them. Just fucking beautiful. He ached to latch on to her pouting nipples already. They were darker now and more distinct through the simple white bra. Liam could almost taste them.

She leaned closer.

His control snapped.

"Come here, wench." He pulled Raine against him.

She stumbled into him, wearing a secret little smile. Was he just giving her what she'd goaded him into? He didn't know and he didn't bloody care.

Through the soft cotton, Liam licked straight across the hardened flesh of her nipple. Heard her gasp and felt her answering shudder.

"Liam…"

"I want you." He gripped her ass in his hands, spreading his thighs wider and pulling her in tighter. "Give yourself over."

With his newfound access, he wrapped his lips around the hard bud, teasing the flesh with his tongue, then suckled deep, gathering, pulling her breast in with the fabric. Every inch of her was indelibly carved in his memory. With his teeth, he abraded the tender skin, hearing her hiss of delight. As she clung, her fingers dug into his scalp.

"Shoulders," he reminded.

"Yes. Sorry, Sir."

Pulling back, he wrestled for self-control and turned toward the tub. The water had risen, so he shut off the tap and tested the temperature. "Come on. Let's get you warmed up."

"I'm not cold, Liam, just a bit dirty from the beach."

He pinned her with his stare. "Shame. I don't intend to clean you up right away."

Her cheeks flushed.

Liam brushed the thong down her thighs, hovering above her pussy to breathe deeply of her scent. "I love your smell, your taste. I can never get enough of you. It's changed a bit with your pregnancy. You're sweeter."

He left the panties puddled at her feet and glanced his way up her body, to the wet spot around one erect nipple. The other stood just as hard yet dry in its cotton cup. "Hardly seems fair, does it?"

She caught on quickly and shook her head. "Nope. You're a tease, Liam O'Neill."

"Tease, am I? I'll show you a tease." He pushed her back gently and stood, his erection straining against his jeans.

He pulled the snap and undid the zipper, inching it down carefully, aware of her gaze following his every movement. He stopped halfway, allowing only the thick stalk and head freedom from the tight confines. He sighed in relief, smeared his thumb across the swollen crown through the glossy offering leaking from the tip, and rubbed it between his fingertips.

"Whose cock is this, Raine?"

"Mine," she breathed. "All mine."

"Look at me. Take your bra off and show me those gorgeous breasts."

Slowly, she reached behind herself, unclasped her bra, and peeled it free. She stood for a moment, pushing her hair back, cupping her breasts, and looking up at him as she skimmed her thumbs down the outsides of her swells, toward her nipples that tightened and lengthened to her touch.

He groaned helplessly. She did that to him. She had no idea the power she wielded.

"Feel better now?"

Raine sent him a soft smile of gratitude. "Yes."

"Good. Get in the tub. Sit with your legs spread so I can see my pretty pussy. Do it now."

Her eyes went dark with arousal. A flush of color stained the tops of her breasts, her throat, her cheeks. He ached to sink his cock into her, feel her soft tissues gripping and squeezing him tight. Jesus, just the thought…

He lifted her around the waist. "In you go, wench."

He held her as she dipped a dainty foot in the tub. Once she'd settled into the water and splayed herself wide for him, she sighed sensually, making a great show of piling her hair into a messy knot and arching toward him. Then she leaned her head back and blinked up at him with sensual expectation. The woman knew how to make him so bloody hard…

Liam pushed his jeans down his hips. She watched his every move, eyes drawn to his shaft, thick and long and screaming with need. He fisted it slowly from root to tip.

"Your cock, is it?" The muscles in his belly flexed and rippled with the movements of his hand.

"Mmm. It is," Raine moaned. He watched as one of her hands inched between her parted thighs toward her clit while the other curved around her breast.

"None of that now," he insisted. "That's all mine to pleasure. And I do mean to please you. But I want you to see me first."

Her lips parted as she watched him stroke his cock. "I do see you, Liam. Always."

He stepped into the tub, inching closer until she could only see his hand stroking up his thick-veined shaft before he slid his fingers back down in a slow, torturous crawl.

He kept on until she looked ready to pounce on him, until he honestly couldn't last a minute longer.

Then he sat in the warm water and pulled her roughly over him, her back plastered to his chest, her legs still splayed wide. With a whisper, he bade her to guide his cock to her opening. Then he shoved up.

One thrust.

Hard.

Deep.

With a groan, he wrapped his arm beneath her breasts. With his free hand, he fisted her hair as he set his mouth against her ear and plowed her with hard, sharp strokes. "You think you'll be leaving me if Hammer goes to jail? Be taking our babe with you? You've got another think coming."

"What?" she panted, breathy, confused.

"You heard me, Raine. Never. Not happening." He plunged inside her again. "Do you understand me?"

"Liam." She melted against him. "I don't... I wouldn't... Oh, god. I can't think."

He fucked her deep again, the need rising, desperate, grabbing him by the balls. "Do you understand me?"

"No. I mean, yes. Why would you think—"

"At the lodge. You said you'd not have me without him." He shoved into her once more, finding his way even farther inside her. "He's my brother and I love him. But you're mine, too, Raine. Do you hear? Mine."

"Liam..." She flung her head back to his shoulder, eyes closed. "Yes. Yours."

Something in him relaxed at her admission, even as the primal need to claim grew. "I'd die without you, love. You're staying with me, no matter what. If you leave, I will hunt you to the ends of the earth."

"Never." She rocked with him, lost in pleasure. "Liam, love you."

"I love you, too. Did you hear me?"

He licked her throat, bit her where her pulse beat wildly. Her nails dug into his arm. Her thighs shook as she fought to rock with him as he pummeled himself into her with swift, merciless strokes like a battering ram.

"I can't hold back," she panted. "Please…"

"Promise you'll not leave and take our babe first."

"Never." She shook her head wildly. "Can't do without you."

Satisfaction burned through his veins. Tears filled his eyes, leaked from the corners. The need to fill her with his seed rushed to the fore. "Come with me, sweetheart."

She screamed his name as she fell apart for him. Liam buried his head in her neck and tried not to sob like a fucking baby as her sweet pussy clamped all around him and bliss poured through him like lava, turning him inside out. He emptied himself inside her. Finally, he felt whole again. Almost.

Sunday, February 17

THE FOLLOWING MORNING, Raine woke in their big bed to find Liam lying on her right, staring at the ceiling. The bed on her left, where Hammer should have been, was cold. Empty.

Yesterday, she'd surrendered her tears and concerns to Liam. She didn't want to start the morning doing the same. He would take them, but if they were going to save Hammer from this awful fate, she had to stop wallowing and use her damn logic. The detectives hadn't investigated anything. They'd smelled blood in the water and saw a quick conviction for a supposed sexual predator who didn't deserve his freedom to find another victim. So far, the federal investigators had done even less to discern the truth, probably for similar reasons.

Saving Hammer was up to her and Liam.

"Morning," she murmured. "Did you sleep?"

"More than I'd thought; not as much as I should."

"Ditto." Raine rolled over and cuddled up to Liam, giving him a soft kiss.

He cradled the crown of her head and savored her lips for a sweet moment before he pulled away with a sigh. "Macen is like a ghost in the room."

Here but not. "Yeah. He should have been with us last night. We'll be able to arrange bail today, right?"

Liam's face tightened, and Raine's hope plummeted to her toes.

"Sterling called me back late last night. He's working on that now, and the wheels are in motion. But…this is a serious charge, and there's no guarantee he'll be granted bail."

"What?" she screeched. "He's got a clean record. He's not violent. He's—"

"A flight risk. He has a passport and a lot of money."

Raine lay back and tried to imagine Hammer gone for the weeks or months it might take to get this trial underway. A night was already killing her. She wouldn't last. And what if the trial was a sham? What if they put him away for life?

"You have a passport and money," she said.

"I'm not a flight risk, love." He gathered her against his side again. "You should know that after yesterday."

"Maybe…you should be. Maybe if Macen makes bail, you two should skip the country and hide out someplace safe."

Thunder rolled across his face. "Didn't we cover this? Where do you think you'll be, besides between us, I mean?"

She closed her eyes. Raine didn't want to upset Liam. She'd felt his ferocity on this subject. But maybe he'd see the logic… "I'll be here. I don't have a passport. I've never needed one."

"No."

"It isn't my first option. But you two could hunker down some-place safe. I could eventually follow. Maybe after the baby is born, the heat would die down—"

"You think we should just piss off and leave you, our woman, while you're with child? So we can while away our days and…what, sip fucking mai tais on the beach, like we don't have a care in the world? We could never have contact with you or our child again because the feds would, no doubt, be watching. And of course we could never return, either. So we'd all be apart forever…" He cocked a brow at her. "Thought this through, did you?"

She winced. "Okay, so not completely. I'm just trying to come up with something helpful."

"Do you want to guess what Hammer's reaction to your suggestion would be, love?"

Liam's silky warning made her flinch. Yeah, he would swear a blue streak before he gave her a bright red ass. Liam and Macen were too protective to simply leave her here alone, especially pregnant. The submissive in her appreciated their meticulous care. The woman in her just wanted her men happy and free.

"I can guess." She sighed. "But we should consider every option, even the crappy ones."

"Next grand idea?"

Raine sighed, not surprised by his attitude, though she was both slightly miffed and relieved. "I don't have any more right now."

"Hammer's arraignment is tomorrow. If he makes bail, we'll have him home in the afternoon. We'll discuss ideas together then."

Horror spread through her. "He has to sit in jail another fucking day?"

It said a lot that Liam didn't balk at her language. "I'm afraid so."

"Can we at least see him today?"

Liam shook his head. "If he didn't want you to see him be arrested, he certainly doesn't want you to see him in a bloody jail cell. We'll get to clap eyes on him in the morning at the arraignment."

"But we can't wait that long to *do* something. We have to figure out who's behind this and why, or I'm worried the trial will be open and shut and—"

"I've thought the same thing and I'm ahead of you. I texted Seth and Beck last night. They'll be 'round shortly so we can put our heads together."

"Good." She bit her lip, wondering how Liam would take her next piece of news. "It's kind of funny. I had a similar idea. I, um…called my brother. He'll be by this morning, too."

Liam sat up and glared at her. "I don't want that wanker here."

"He wants to help," she argued.

"Oh, he's helped plenty. Don't you think?"

"River is sorry. He tried to tell the police to drop the case. He made a mistake. We've all made them. He's the only family I have left."

"You mean besides Hammer, me, and the bairn?" He shot her another cross glare.

"Family with blood in my veins who knew me as a kid." When he looked unmoved, she sat up with an angry huff. "What if I'd decided to hold a grudge against your parents for barging in on us unannounced at a really bad time?"

"They were only trying to help."

"Uh-huh."

Liam looked frustrated now. "They apologized."

"Really? Hmm…"

"It's not the same, wench. Hammer would be with us now if it weren't for your brother."

She sighed, deflated. "I know. Can you just be civil once? He wants to be a part of the solution. I know Seth is a PI, but River was a Green Beret, so he's got skills, which could really come in handy if we have to figure out who wants Hammer behind bars."

"The last time he used his skills, he added two and two and came up with Hammer in the slammer." Liam rose, tossed on his boxers, and paced. "I don't like it."

"I know." She rose to her knees and crossed the bed, grabbing him when he drew near and pressing kisses across his jaw. "But it would make me happy." She reached inside his underwear and stroked his cock, gratified to feel him harden in an instant beneath her palm. "Really happy."

He answered with a groan. "How happy?"

"Sublimely, ecstatically happy." She dragged the elastic down over his stiff cock, past his hips, and breathed over the purple crest. "You might even say orgasmic."

"Would you now?" He thrust his hands in her hair. "Tell me more, you wicked wench."

"My pleasure," she breathed, then engulfed his cock in the depths of her mouth.

Silky, hot, salty, all man…Raine absolutely loved to get her mouth on him. He was a playground for her taste buds. A high for her olfactory senses. A thrill for her submissive heart.

Neither of them wasted time. He wanted it hot and hard, and she gave it to him in fast, rhythmic strokes, punctuating each with a drag of tongue and a gentle scrape of teeth.

Liam gripped her hair in his tight fists. The sensual distress in his hiss and the prickling tug on her scalp aroused the hell out of her.

"Jesus, Raine. That's it. Suck me deep. All the way to your throat."

She did exactly as he instructed, fondling his balls with one hand, stroking his length with the other. She swallowed on the head of his cock.

"Oh, fuck. Raine," he panted as she worked his shaft faster. "Woman…"

She moaned on him, lifting away for a second to arch closer and feed his length between her breasts and up to her swollen lips before she tongued him. He staggered on his feet and gave her another sexual growl. In her mouth, she felt him harden more and swell.

"Raine!"

Yeah, she had him now—and she couldn't wait. "Give it to me."

Suddenly, he tugged on her hair and pulled her off his cock. "I will—when you're not topping from the bottom. Get on your back. And spread those pretty thighs."

Something about yesterday—or everything—had let loose the Dominant in him. Not that she was complaining…

With her heart racing, she met the dark burn of his stare and eased back on the middle of the bed, legs splayed. When he climbed between them, face first, she swallowed.

Damn it, arousing him had already turned her on. If he was going to torment her with the orgasm he wouldn't allow her to have, she was toast.

Maybe some preemptive begging was in order. "Liam…"

"Not a word until I say so."

Then he pushed her thighs wide, sucked her clit into his mouth, and speared her with a pair of fingers that knew exactly where to probe to have her gasping and tensing to hold back her orgasm in under a minute.

"You're wet." He sounded pleased.

"Always for you."

Now he sent her a dark glower. "I said not a word."

Shutting up now… But god, she wanted to whimper and plead, especially when he dragged his tongue through her folds again and settled over her clit with a nip of teeth. His damn fingers joined inside her once more, finding the perfect spot and…

She was a goner.

Suddenly, he gripped her hips, vaulted up her body, and pushed his cock through her swollen, sensitive flesh—all the way to the hilt.

She bit her lip to hold in a wail.

He grabbed her hair again and tugged, then ran his tongue up her neck before settling his lips against her ear. "You hold that scream until you're going to come. Then you shout to the rooftops. I want your cry echoing around our bedroom. Yes?"

"Yes," she panted out. "Yes…"

Apparently satisfied that she'd yielded herself to him, he pumped inside her furiously, the headboard slamming the wall, his crest scraping every tingling nerve ending, his rough breath shuddering across her skin. Raine tossed her arms around him, nails digging, hips rocking as she urged him on. Of its own volition, her back arched, her sex clenched tight on him.

"Come for me, Raine. You scream hard."

God, she didn't think she could stop it. Another thrust had her gasping. A second pushed her senses higher. The next had her wailing something high-pitched, an almost inhuman keening as pleasure broke inside her. Relief, adoration, and a heart full of love followed, eventually turning her cry of ecstasy into one of gratitude.

Liam was right there with her, seizing her mouth and smothering the last of her moan as he released inside her with a bellowing growl.

Seconds later, he rolled off her, still panting. "Jesus, woman…"

Raine would have giggled if she'd had the energy—and if her worries about Hammer hadn't all come back in a cold splash. "I love you."

As if he sensed her change in mood—or flipped the same switch himself—he rose. "I love you, too. Now up with you. We have work to do."

When he made for the bathroom, she caught him by the arm again and kissed him. "Thanks for listening."

He stroked her cheek. "I'll always listen, even if I don't like it."

Since they'd bathed last night, Raine rinsed off quickly, washing her face and brushing her teeth. She didn't bother with makeup, just drew her long hair into a messy bun, threw on some cargo pants and a loose black shirt. When she looked up, Liam was waiting for her in a pair of jeans and a T-shirt, hair freshly combed.

Together, they made their way to the kitchen, hand in hand, only to find everyone waiting for them.

"Top of the morning, all," Liam greeted and pulled her closer to kiss her forehead before he let her go.

Raine looked around the room—and froze. One glance at their faces, and she knew they'd heard everything.

Oh, god... A hot flush crawled up her face.

"You did that on purpose," she whispered.

Liam just grinned.

She wished the ground would swallow her up, but no. Duncan merely cleared his throat and pretended great interest in his placemat. Bryn wore a little smile as she dished up piping hot portions of a breakfast casserole. Beck didn't bother with anything that subtle; he just laughed outright. Seth winked at her and held up his hand to Liam for a high five. Her beautiful Irishman slapped palms with his friend. Then she made the mistake of looking at River's face.

Her brother gripped the arms of his chair with white knuckles, giving Liam a look that was locked and loaded and ready to kill.

As the others made small talk and Liam poured coffee, she rushed to River's side and hugged him, setting her mouth against his ear. "Don't do this."

He kissed her temple. To everyone else, the gesture probably looked tender, but he radiated tension. "He violated you."

"I started it. I wanted him to." She pulled back enough to look into his eyes, so much like her own. She could see the storm brewing there. "You ever been in love?"

"No."

"Then you don't understand and I don't want to hear it. I love him. I love Hammer, too. Accept it or leave."

When she released River and turned away, she found Liam watching them closely, attuned to her for any sign of distress. She flashed him the best smile she could muster and held out her arms to him. He embraced her, curling her against his body, tucking her under his arm.

"It smells good, Mum."

"I timed it just right." She handed him a plate.

As Bryn slid the steaming dishes across the island, Raine grabbed them. One by one, she set plates in front of all the other men. River took his in silence.

When Liam's mother handed her an extra-large portion, Raine

balked, but the woman wouldn't hear her protests.

"You've eaten next to nothing for days."

And she was eating for two. "Thanks, Bryn."

As they all crowded around the little kitchen table, Raine in Liam's lap, her Irishman took a hearty bite and swallowed back coffee. "We appreciate you coming this morning. As you know, things aren't looking good for Macen."

Liam filled the others in on the latest developments in the case.

"Pike and I put Shadows back together yesterday afternoon," Seth volunteered. "Donald and Vivian came to play early, so they helped, too. Dean stopped by. I could tell he felt like shit. I told him not to worry."

"It's not his fault," Liam agreed.

"Anyway, he pitched in, too. I don't think the feds found anything. Raine, you might want to put Hammer's room back together. You know how he likes things."

She nodded. Macen could be very particular. "I'll do that this afternoon."

"I'll help you, love." Liam pressed a kiss to her shoulder. "But the reason we asked you all here is to help us think of who might have volunteered to be the prosecution's witness. Obviously, this is someone who's got an ax to grind with Hammer. We're looking for a longtime member of Shadows, someone there almost from the beginning who could have witnessed Raine's supposed rape as a minor. Beck, this is where I think we'll lean on you most, since you were with Hammer before he opened the doors. Raine, you know many of the long-timers, too."

She nodded. "I only missed the first thirteen months or so. I know who was around when I went to live there."

River scowled, and he was obviously wondering whether she knew them in the Biblical sense. She blew it off. He'd either accept who and what she was or he'd go away. She wanted him in her life, but she wasn't changing to please him.

Beck took a bite of his casserole and moaned enthusiastically at Bryn, who smiled. Nearly everyone else dove in and ate with gusto, complimenting the woman. Raine took a bite and had to admit it tasted wonderful.

Bryn rubbed a maternal hand on her shoulder. "So glad to see you eating, lass. There's more in the pan if anyone wants seconds." She headed to Liam and kissed his cheek. "Da and I are going to grab some lollies for the grandkids. Back in two shakes."

"My car keys are on the hook just outside the garage," Liam called to their retreating figures.

When Raine turned back, she discovered that Beck had already devoured every bite. Wiping his mouth with his napkin, he sat back. "Longtime members… Nick is a great bartender. Been there since we opened the doors."

"He likes everyone," Liam protested. "I don't think he's got revenge on his mind."

"I agree," Raine added. "What about Master Carl?"

Beck shook his head. "Hell no. He's got short-man's disease. He's all bluster and no balls. Besides, he's only cranky now when someone delays his play with his new sub…whatever her name is."

Raine slapped a hand to her heart and gaped. "*You* don't know the name of a sub? Are you feeling well, doctor?"

"Ha! I've just been busy."

"You don't mean preoccupied, do you?" she probed. "Maybe you've got someone more…Heavenly in mind?"

Seth scowled. "Hey. Scrub her from your dirty mind."

"Fuck you. Like your mind is any cleaner." Beck rolled his eyes. "Pike would never turn on Hammer."

"Ever," Raine agreed. "Hammer helped him pay his mother's hospital bills. He has no reason… Knotty Master, too. He's, like, the happy sadist."

"Yep." Beck leaned in. "You know, princess, maybe we should go further back. What about Zak?"

She stared down the doctor, wishing she could slap the man. "Really? You had to bring him up?"

"He might be on to something," Liam mused.

"Who is he?" River asked.

Raine sure as hell didn't want to answer that question. No one else did, either. Silence hung around the table for an uncomfortable minute. She got up and grabbed a water bottle from the fridge because she couldn't sit here and wait to be humiliated.

"Raine's first," Beck finally said.

"First what?" River looked lost.

"Ugh." She rolled her eyes as she plopped down in an empty chair. "The guy who took my virginity, okay? It was a conquest for him. I didn't matter. He has no reason to care now."

"Except Hammer beat the shit out of him and banned him for life," Beck piped in. "I doubt Zak liked having his pretty face fucked with."

"It's not him." She shook her head. "I'm sure of it."

"What about Gabriel?" Beck drawled. "He liked you, princess. After you two spent the night together, he was willing to go to the mat with Hammer for you. He was too smart to get in a fistfight, but he was awfully willing to work around any obstacle to be with you."

Raine felt every eye in the room on her. She didn't know whose stare was more intense, River's or Liam's.

"Who's this, then?" her Irishman drawled, his dark eyes so focused on her that Raine squirmed.

Yeah, he hadn't expected her to still have secrets.

"You remember when we first got together, and you asked me how long it had been? I told you it had been two years... I meant Gabriel. Why do we have a sudden fascination with my sex life? It wasn't a big deal."

Beck snorted. "Before O'Neill here, Gabriel was the only time Hammer was truly worried about losing you."

And she'd let Gabriel down gently. She'd liked him well enough. The sex had been far better than with Zak. He'd been a decent guy. But she'd told him flat out that she was never going to love him.

She'd known that because he wasn't Hammer.

"He was disappointed, not angry," Raine argued. "Macen made sure my first two experiences were both one and done, so neither of them got terribly attached. Can we change the subject?"

Beck opened his mouth, but Liam held up a finger "Wait. Are you telling me that before you and I got together, you'd had sex twice in your entire life?"

Embarrassment burned her. She didn't want to look at anyone now. She crossed her arms and closed her eyes. "Yes. Can we move on?"

"Oh, god." Liam reached for her hand. "How did I not scare the hell out of you?"

His voice compelled her to look at him. She squeezed his hand back. "You did. But I wasn't going to let that stop me."

He looked stunned, and she could tell the exact moment he started thinking about the events of that weekend she'd first given herself to Liam, then Hammer. The weekend she had almost certainly gotten pregnant. Liam was realizing that she'd been so terribly innocent before he'd publicly claimed her virgin ass in the dungeon, before Hammer had thoroughly ravaged her that night, leaving nearly every inch of her body bitten, bruised, or marked.

"Oh, lass..." Liam looked ready to apologize or regret the way things happened. "Don't say it."

He sighed and dragged her plate in front of him before plucking her out of her chair and back into his lap. "If I'd known..."

"I wouldn't change a thing. Drop it. Please." She turned her attention to Beck. "Anyone else you can think of?"

She couldn't help but catch River's shocked expression. "Hammer kept men away from you? Really? He didn't—"

"Dozens," Beck broke in. "The standing edict was, you touch the princess, you lose your balls and your membership—in that order. He watched her just about every moment of every day."

"Haven't we beaten this dead horse? It wasn't Zak. It wasn't Gabriel. Besides, we also have to be thinking about who might have been around recently enough to have stolen that missing security footage. Someone who knew what had happened on those two dates. November third was public but..." Everyone in the dungeon had known about her punishment. If they hadn't been there to see for themselves, they'd soon heard. But November fourth, her forbidden hours with Hammer... Almost no one had known about that. "If the witness is also the thief, that rules both of them out."

Carrying a plastic bag of candy, Bryn bustled back in the kitchen with a frown. "She's right, and the person who nicked the video is someone else entirely."

"So we've got two people to look for?" Liam clenched his jaw. "Two needles in a bloody haystack?"

"Yes, son. Your witness is somehow obscured, hidden. But now that I'm thinking about it, I sense it's a woman."

Beck winced. "That actually narrows it down less. The number of women Hammer has pissed off over the years… I'm not sure I can count that high. Can you give us anything else?"

Bryn frowned. "She's a blonde. In her mid to late thirties."

The entire table groaned.

"The last eight years have pretty much been a parade of thirtysomething blondes." Beck turned to her. "Until Raine."

When she really thought about all the women Macen had slept with for years, it was a stab in the chest. No, they hadn't been together then, but he'd known how she felt. "An endless parade."

Seth nodded. "He did—I mean, he liked—a lot of blondes back in New York, too."

God, could this conversation get any more painful?

Liam rubbed her back and whispered in her ear. "He loves you."

Raine did her best to hang on to that.

Beck just shook his head. "Tell you what, Seth. You investigate everything north of the ten. I'll take everything south. We might track down all the blondes he nailed in the next…three to five years."

"Can we stay on task?" Liam demanded. "Focus on club members from the early days."

"The first one who pops to mind is Erika," Beck said.

"I remember her. She's the bitch who asked me if I was Hammer's sister and dropped her panties in front of me just before he came into the room."

"I'm surprised you didn't claw her eyes out." Liam cut a bite of the casserole and fed it to her.

Raine chewed and swallowed. "I wanted to. But I was only seventeen. She was just the first in a long line of women."

Beck nodded. "Erika wanted marriage, and Hammer wasn't interested. She didn't last long. Why wait years to get revenge?"

"Kenneth is on the right track," Bryn insisted. "This witness is a woman scorned. She's very angry."

"Maybe Angel," Beck suggested. "She had her hopes pinned on him for a long time."

Yeah, Raine remembered that skank, too. "Didn't she finally give up on Hammer and move to Denver with some new Dom last summer?"

"Yep. She seemed happy. Amber waited around on Hammer for years, too. But I heard she got married, if you can believe that." Beck looked stunned. "I mean, I know a lot of kinky girls, but damn... I heard she even had a baby."

The jealous witch had enjoyed gossiping about Hammer's prowess every time Raine walked into the room. "Wow, her husband must have his hands full." She was just glad it wasn't Hammer. "But she hasn't been here in...a year?"

"And if she's married, why ruin his life now?" Beck asked. "He's still friends with Tiffany and Misty. But they never clung to him, so I can't imagine they'd resent him now."

As much as Raine hated to admit it, they were decent women. "No, they respect him. Brandy?"

"That's her name!" Beck said. "The one with Carl now. Miracles never cease, because she's into him, too. I don't get that."

Raine didn't, either. But they both seemed way too happy together to want to screw up Hammer's life. "Chastity?"

Beck shook his head. "She came over to my dark side a couple of years ago. I don't think she's played with anyone else since. She doesn't seem to have any beef with Hammer. She might have one with me... I haven't paid attention to her in months."

"You might want to fix that," Seth suggested.

"I have other interests now." Beck looked serious—and pissed off.

"Guys," Raine encouraged. "Come on. Focus. Kristen?"

Suddenly, Seth rubbed at the back of his neck. "Yeah, I might have gone there. More than a few times."

"Last December?" Raine raised a brow at him. "I wondered why she wasn't trying to get Hammer's attention anymore."

"You and Kristen?" Beck looked smug. "That's very interesting news."

"Since I took Heavenly to lunch yesterday and kissed her, that's over."

"You're lying." Beck stared the man down. "Heavenly doesn't trust you."

Seth shrugged. "Ask her...but then to do that you'd be tipping your hand, wouldn't you? And for the record, I texted Kristen and told her we won't be playing again."

To prove his point, Seth opened his text messages and slid his phone across the table. Sure enough, he'd sent the faux blonde sub the Dear John equivalent via iMessage.

"Happy?" he prodded Beck.

The doctor looked ready to kill.

Seth just smiled. "I heard someone named Crystal was asking about Hammer yesterday."

"She's a redhead. Marlie?" Raine spit out the name with malice. "A.k.a. Ms. Nastysnatch?"

"That's fitting." Liam smiled her way.

Beck barked with laughter. "Absolutely. She's a good thought. She *hated* you, princess. I heard she hit you."

"She what?" River sat up straighter.

"Followed me to the alley behind the club and slapped me like a frustrated little girl."

"That she did." Liam tightened his hands on her hips. "There have been very few times I wanted to throttle a woman. That was one of them."

"I told her off. And Hammer tossed her out." She glanced River's way. "We probably got it on video if you want to see."

"But she wasn't a member when you were a minor," Beck pointed out.

"So she wouldn't have witnessed Hammer supposedly ravishing me as a 'child,' true." Raine would really have liked Marlie to be guilty of something she could go to jail for. "How about Honey? She chased Hammer for years. But she finally stopped last fall."

It was Liam's turn to squirm in his seat. Raine swiveled around on his lap. "You?"

"Well...I hadn't been in LA long, and she seemed—"

"Nice?" She sent him a warning stare. "That better not come out of your mouth."

"I was going to say...eager."

"You mean horny." She batted Liam's shoulder. "Men... The question is, could she be angry enough with Hammer to want to screw up his life?"

"If she's mad at anyone, it's me," Liam admitted. "But I don't think she is."

"Why would you waste your time?" Bryn tsked at her son. "You'd already met the love of your life."

Liam had the good grace to look sheepish. "I thought she only had eyes for Hammer. And back then, I thought he would kill me if I touched her."

"I had eyes for you, too," Raine whispered softly for his ears alone before turning back to Beck. "The only other sub I can think of is Eden. I saw her come out of Hammer's room a lot over the years."

Every man at the table, except her brother, looked more than a tad guilty. Raine glanced at their faces. "Are you kidding me? All of you?"

Beck gave her a crooked smile. "Looks like everyone has plowed the garden of Eden, princess. Hey, we're men. Not monks."

"No one would ever think otherwise. Trust me." Raine skewered Liam with another glance. "Anything else you want to tell me?"

"Nothing. Shouldn't we focus on the problem, love? Someone else we should consider?"

Raine sighed. "No one in particular, but I think we've barely scratched the surface."

The doctor stood and stretched. "She's right. I'm sure there's someone we're just not thinking of."

"I'll scour the membership database while I'm at the club, see if anyone else pops out," Raine said. "Maybe…I'll come up with something. What about the security footage disappearing? Hammer fired the last tech, Bryan, for a reason…"

"Hitting on members." Beck snorted.

Raine nodded. "Maybe he got mad and took the videos to black-mail Hammer?"

"Bryan has been gone a month," Liam pointed out. "And he hasn't sent Macen any demands. Besides, why would he have taken footage of you and me? Mum, you didn't hear that."

"Not a word. Just like I didn't hear you this morning, either. Or last night." She smiled faintly.

Raine turned four shades of red. Beck and Seth both howled with laughter.

"Your thief is still among you." Bryn soothed Raine with a pat on the shoulder. "I can feel that. Proud of the deception, too. Be looking at the faces you least suspect."

Raine couldn't go through another round of conjecture just now. She didn't want to look at any of her friends with suspicious eyes. Instead, she collected everyone's empty plates and took them to the sink.

"Who has access to the security room?" Seth asked.

"The new tech, Lewis, is in there most." Beck sat back in his chair. "He's a snot-nosed nerd Hammer hired two weeks ago. Other than him, the DMs, including me and Pike. Dean. Donald. Hammer. Liam. Raine has a key. Am I missing anyone?"

No one with any reason to hurt Macen. "Sometimes the cleaning crew goes in there off-hours. We usually try to supervise them but..." Raine shrugged. "It doesn't always work out."

Liam shook his head. "So we have another bloody puzzle to solve."

Raine put an arm around him. "We'll do it. We have to."

"I'll help however I can." River stood and smiled at Bryn. "Thank you, Mrs. O'Neill." Then he turned and extended a hand to Liam. "Sorry if I've been a douche."

They shook hands. "I'd have done everything I could to protect my sisters, too. And I've got six of them."

"You poor bastard." River smiled, then turned to Raine. "Call me if you need anything. I'll do whatever I can to help you be happy."

CHAPTER THIRTEEN

Monday, February 18

AFTER SPENDING THE weekend climbing the walls in an isolated cell, Hammer was glad to be out of confinement. But having judge Arnold Ayers stare him down in a federal courtroom during his arraignment almost had Macen wishing he were still behind those bars. He sat beside Sterling, trying to keep a level head as his lawyer entered a plea of not guilty on his behalf, then waved off a formal reading of the indictment. Todd Wellington, the Assistant United States Attorney, strutted like a damn peacock, silently gloating, as if he had a million ways to malign Macen's character. He gritted his teeth and resisted the urge to punch the asshole's annoying face.

"Your Honor," Wellington beseeched. "If you'll look at the defendant's extensive financial portfolio, you'll see he has ample liquidity to flee the country. He's a serious flight risk."

"Duly noted, though it's not a crime for anyone to be financially sound, Mr. Wellington." Ayers raised his brows.

"Of course not, Your Honor. I'm simply stating that if the defendant is granted bail, he could easily charter a private jet and leave the country."

"You've made your point." Ayers nodded, an edge of annoyance in his tone. "Continue."

"Thank you, Your Honor." Wellington shot Hammer a victorious smirk. "Fleeing the jurisdiction of the court aside, we as civil servants, cannot in good conscience, allow a suspected pedophile to roam free. It's our duty to protect innocent children."

Hammer snarled at the AUSA before turning his silent rage on Wellington's associates, seated on the opposite side of the room. The two ass-kissing minions in matching suits looked like bobbleheads, nodding at every derogatory remark.

Though his freedom was at stake, Macen found it hard as hell to focus on the proceedings. Behind him Raine and Liam sat, hands clasped. Beck, Seth, Bryn, and Duncan surrounded them.

If he were actually guilty—and single—it would be easy to leave the country and never come back. But could he really abandon Liam and Raine? He didn't know. Asking them to upend their lives didn't sound particularly fair, either. They'd be fugitives. If the law caught up to them, they'd all serve time in prison. Risking them and their child didn't seem like an option.

As tempting as the fantasy might be at first glance, the reality...not so much.

Finally, Sterling stood and cleared his throat. "Your Honor, the AUSA's claims are preposterous. My client poses no flight risk. Aside from being innocent of these ridiculous and unsubstantiated charges, Mr. Hammerman is an established business owner."

Wellington scoffed. Sterling shot him a glare. Judge Ayers pretended not to notice.

"As I was saying," Sterling continued. "Mr. Hammerman has roots in the community. If he were at all inclined to flee the country, he would have done so before his arrest. My client is here, in your courtroom, ready and willing to prove his innocence. Therefore, Your Honor, I implore you to set bond and allow Mr. Hammerman the opportunity to return to the community and his family."

"Motion to grant bail is accepted." The judge barely looked up as he shuffled papers. "Bond is set at one million dollars."

Hammer barely had time to digest the fact that he'd be going home—to sleep in his own bed beside Raine and Liam—before Ayers set the date for Barnes and Wellington to present their pretrial motions.

"The trial will commence April first." The judge slammed his gavel.

Hammer's stomach pitched. "April Fools Day? You've got to be shitting me." He turned to Sterling. "It can't get any more fucking ironic than that."

"Except you're not the fool. They are." Sterling jerked his head toward Wellington and the double-breasted dumb asses. "Their supposed witness will have to be God himself because, so far, the evidence I've seen shouldn't impress a jury."

"When do we find out who this mysterious witness is?" Hammer asked as Sterling stood and began shoving papers into his briefcase.

While the judge stood and retreated to his chamber, the trio of prosecutors filed out of the courtroom.

"Discovery starts today. I'll touch base with Wellington after we get your bail processed and you're free. As soon as he and I exchange findings, we'll meet and begin strategizing."

"Sounds good." But Hammer was already standing, turning to fix his gaze on Raine and Liam. They looked back at him with longing and love. "When the fuck can I go home?"

"I'll wait for the judge to sign the bail order, then personally deliver it to the clerk's office." Sterling gripped Hammer's shoulder, seizing his attention from Raine. "They'll take you to a holding area until all the paperwork is ironed out. Then you'll be free to go."

"Thanks." He took a ground-eating step in Raine's direction. "It won't be much longer, precious."

He wanted to wrap her in his arms and kiss her senseless when he saw the glimmer of hope and fear skitter across her face. She looked afraid, and who could blame her? It seemed as if something new happened to them every damn day that ripped away the foundation beneath their feet.

"We'll be waiting," Raine promised.

God, she looked so tired, so small and fragile. He doubted Liam had slept all weekend, either. They'd been through enough in the last few months, and Hammer felt guilty as hell to be putting more stress on them.

"Liam has arranged for a bondsman to meet me in the clerk's office," Sterling explained. "So if you're prepared, O'Neill...?"

"I brought enough to get you out, mate." Liam patted his pants pocket.

"How much?" Hammer darted a glance between the two men.

"A hundred and fifty thousand up front," Sterling advised. "But you'll also need to put up another million three in collateral to the bondsman."

"I'll sign over the condo in San Juan," Macen said. "It should be worth at least that."

Raine gasped, clearly shocked.

Yeah, there was a whole lot she didn't know about him because he'd never opened up and shared himself with her. Oh, he'd expected Raine to vomit out her all her truths, but Hammer had never reciprocated. He'd had his reasons, but that didn't make keeping her in the dark the right thing to do. Now especially, he owed her more. Everything.

If Wellington's lying-ass witness was convincing, Hammer might never get another chance to confess his past to Raine so she could understand the man he was today. The future wouldn't matter because his would be totally fucked.

"Sounds good. I'll have my secretary file the proper paperwork with the clerk's office right away. We should be able to get you home this afternoon." Sterling slapped him on the back as the bailiff came forward.

He held up his hand to the uniformed officer. "I need another minute." When the cop nodded, Hammer turned to Raine, arms open. "Precious."

She ran to him and cuddled close as he closed his eyes and clutched her soft body. He inhaled her scent. A lump of emotion lodged in his throat. Then Liam's arms banded around him and Raine, gathering them together in a tight circle. Hammer willed back the tears that stung his eyes. This was where he belonged.

"I love you both," he confessed in a hoarse murmur.

"We love you, too," Raine whispered, clutching the lapels of his suit as if she'd never let go.

"We do, brother." Liam's voice teemed with emotion.

As much as he wanted to linger with them, Hammer forced himself to pull away. "I'll be with you as soon as I can."

"We'll take you home when you're ready," Liam promised.

As the bailiff led Hammer toward the antechamber door, he turned and looked back.

Liam waved, and Raine blew him a kiss.

He needed them, maybe a whole lot more than they needed him. Hammer clenched his jaw. He'd find a way out of this fucking mess if it killed him.

Without a word, he left the courtroom.

After a shitload of paperwork and waiting that had Hammer gritting his teeth and ready to smack heads, Liam and Raine were waiting for him in the hallway just outside the processing office. He'd never been so happy to see them in his life. His heart pounded as the three of them clung to one another as if they'd been apart for months. Hammer kissed Raine senseless. Liam gave him a hearty slap on the back.

With their girl between them, they headed out the door.

Lost in the sweet relief of the moment, Hammer wasn't prepared for the throng of reporters that swarmed them and barraged them with questions.

"Liam," he barked. "Put Raine behind us."

But his friend had already moved into position, protecting her as Hammer pushed his way through the crowd.

"Mr. Hammerman, when did you start molesting children?" One reporter shoved a microphone in his face.

He clenched his teeth and shot the prick a killing glare. "No comment."

"Miss Kendall, did Mr. Hammerman rape you as a child?" a blonde bitch in a suit asked. "Is he your pimp? Why don't you ask the police for help escaping these two deviants?"

Raine buried her face in between the sleeves of their coats and refused to say a word.

"Back off, you bloody mongrels," Liam roared.

They still barked questions. Raine clutched him tighter.

Hammer wrapped an arm around her, pressing her between him and Liam. "No fucking comment, you vultures!"

With a shove, they burst from the press, then sprinted to Liam's SUV. He hoped they got some damn peace so they could enjoy their time together and figure out who the hell was persecuting him...but Hammer had his doubts.

RAINE STEPPED INTO the kitchen to find Liam and Hammer with their heads together, talking in low tones. They both stopped abruptly and stared when she entered.

Her suspicions launched. Her dread crashed. "What? Has something else happened?"

They glanced at one another in that silent communication they shared. Then they both shook their head.

"No, love." Liam gave her a gentle smile.

"I'm not buying it." She shook her head, hands on hips. "You're either up to or protecting me from something. I need to know."

Macen sighed. "It's nothing. The phone was ringing off the hook earlier. Fucking reporters. We took care of that."

A glance over at the handheld unit and its accompanying answering machine proved that someone had yanked it from the wall—literally. And taken a hunk of drywall with it.

Liam grimaced. "I might have lost my temper a wee bit. I'll fix it later."

As long as they were on the subject… She plucked her new cell phone from the pocket of her skirt. "I had to turn mine off. How did they get this number so quickly? I got four calls while I was trying to nap."

They both took theirs from pockets and set them on the counter. The screens were blank.

"We did the same, precious."

"Those bloody leeches could give stalkers lessons," Liam cursed.

"I should have expected them to be waiting for us." The fact that he clearly hadn't bothered Hammer.

"I knew but…I was too excited to have you back. I wasn't thinking." Raine caressed his arm in silent comfort. "Let's have a nice dinner in tonight and ignore the rest of the world. Any preferences? Your mom has done so much of the cooking, Liam. I'd like to prove that you won't starve when your folks go home."

"They know, love." Liam pressed a kiss to her cheek. "But you needn't worry about us. I'm going to take my parents out for a nice dinner and gossip about the brood back home."

"But…" Disappointment nipped at her. "It's Macen's first night back. We should all be together. We—"

Hammer cut her off with a kiss. When he eased back, she felt slightly dizzy. But the air of gravity around him righted her head again.

"I want to talk to you. Alone. Liam knows why."

Whatever Hammer had to say was important. Immediately, fear told her he meant to leave her. But Liam looked placid, almost happy. If Macen had any intention of packing his bags, they'd be fighting now. She had to trust that, after everything they'd been through, he wouldn't just walk away.

"All right."

"Excellent." Liam clapped Hammer on the shoulder and brushed a kiss over her lips. "We won't be quick. Enjoy."

He exited the kitchen, leaving her alone with Macen, who wore a determined expression she couldn't quite decipher. What did he want?

"So it's just us for dinner?" she whispered into the suddenly thick tension.

"Yeah. What's fast to prepare?"

He closed in, palm whispering up her arm, settling at her nape. He snared her with hazel eyes, making all kinds of demands without uttering a word. She sensed what he wanted wasn't purely sexual.

"Stir-fry." Raine swallowed, wondering why she was nervous.

"Can you have it ready in ten minutes?"

"Less."

She'd done all the prep the other night and just hadn't mustered the energy to cook. With surprisingly unsteady hands, she heated the wok, took out the chicken she'd already marinated, and started some quick rice.

Behind her, Hammer clung to her hips and watched, sprinkling kisses up her neck. She wanted him. Hell, she couldn't be in the same room without aching for the man. But the long caresses of his fingers and the reverent press of his lips tugged at her heart, too.

"Macen?" She turned to him. "What's on your mind?"

He gave her a wry smile. A few months ago, she would never have been able to decipher that expression. He could be deadly hard to read. Now…she could see he was something close to nervous.

"Besides everything?" he quipped.

She tossed chicken into the hot pan, satisfied with the sizzle. Absently stirring with one hand, she turned to him. "I'm here for you. You know that."

"And I thank God every day." He brushed a thumb across her cheek. "I need to tell you something I should have a long time ago. I just didn't want to disappoint you. Disillusion you. I didn't want you to see my weaknesses, faults, and imperfections."

A corner of her brain realized the time had come to add the vegetables. The rest of her was completely attuned to the man who'd captured half her heart years ago. "You could never disappoint me."

He took the bowl from her hands and poured the mushrooms, onions, and peppers into the meat mixture. "Stir."

Absently, she did, but she couldn't take her eyes off him. "What is it?"

The rice beeped. The stir-fry steamed. Raine didn't move. He wasn't severing his ties with her and Liam…but whatever he had to say was big.

"I should tell you about me." He pulled back and grabbed a pair of plates from the cabinet, then two forks from the nearby drawer.

Anticipation gripped her. Raine held her breath. Was he finally going to let her in?

She'd asked him endless questions about himself and his past the first couple of years at Shadows. He'd refused to give her more than vague answers. He'd grown up in New York. He hadn't been close to his parents. He'd gone to college but hadn't finished. Hammer had never been willing to divulge more than that.

Raine quickly dished food onto the plates and walked them to the breakfast nook, surprised to see he'd already set out a couple of placemats and napkins.

"You and Liam planned for us to be alone tonight?" she asked as she set the dishes down.

"Yes." He held out her chair.

She sat, unable to take her gaze off him. "I'm here. I'm listening."

"Eat. Liam says you've done a poor job of that lately. The doctor will scold you at your appointment tomorrow morning."

With everything going on, she'd completely forgotten. "Will you be there?"

"Liam and I both will. We wouldn't miss it for the world."

That filled her with a bit of relief. She mixed her food together and forked in a bite gingerly. With her stomach jumping nervously, she wasn't sure how much she'd get down, especially if Macen wouldn't end her suspense. "Thank you. Would you just tell me already?"

He smiled, relaxing a little as he swallowed a bite. "It's good."

"I'm glad," she snapped. "You're stalling."

Macen shook his head. "No, I'm going to tell you everything you've ever wanted to know and more. I love you and I owe you. But you know I find your impatience adorable."

Raine wanted to be annoyed, but part of their dynamic was this push-pull. A mutual poke. She mouthed off; he found a creative way to correct her...at least until they repeated the cycle because it was too delicious to ignore.

"You're messing with my temper, Macen."

He took another bite and shook his head. "Just hoping you still look at me the same way once you know everything. This will tell you a lot about who I am...and why."

"You mean like having a condo in San Juan? I had no clue."

Hammer waved that information away. "I haven't been there since before Juliet died. I should have sold it years ago. It's been nothing but rental property for a long time."

Raine understood that it wasn't meaningful to him, but Macen Hammerman knew everything about her—the vitamins she preferred, the fact that she got weepy on the anniversary of her mother's disappearance, her obsession with Caramel Caribou ice cream, the way she liked to nap on rainy days. He'd known every one of her cycles for six years. Her bra size was a given. He'd even bought her shoes that fit like a glove without her trying them on.

Finally, this man who'd been such a mystery to her might let her solve him. It didn't matter that she knew his favorite brand of underwear or could make all his favorite foods without looking at a recipe. She didn't know the name of his childhood pet, what he'd been like as a teenager, or why he never spoke to or about his parents.

Hammer ate every bite she'd made for him. Raine could only manage to get down half. Her stomach was in knots when she pushed her plate aside.

"Tell me. Everything."

With a sideways glance at her food, he frowned. "Will you promise to try your dinner again before bed? I'm worried about you."

She'd promise him a quickie on the moon if he'd just tell her already. "I will. Just..."

"Get on with it." He nodded and rubbed his palms together as if trying to decide where to start. "My parents were extremely wealthy. My grandfather was a physicist who worked with this brilliant guy named Noyce." He studied her face. "Not ringing a bell? Patent 2,981,877? The world's first silicone-based integrated circuit. My grandfather saw the potential and invested in the company that sold them, Intel. He also invested in the Texas Instruments version, too. Why not hedge your bets? He grew a few hundred thousand dollars into—"

"Millions." She'd guessed he came from money but… "Wow."

"Hundreds of millions," he corrected. "The money began rolling in when my dad was a teenager, and he came to adulthood spoiled and entitled, a lot like I did. His dad had money, so why work? My grandfather died a couple of years before I was born, and my father inherited half his fortune. Apparently, I have an aunt somewhere I've never met who got the other half."

Raine shook her head. "I had no idea…"

"The only other person on the planet who does is Liam." Hammer tapped his fork on the table and gave her a tight smile. "And he only knows because I got drunk enough one night early in our friendship to tell him."

"So your dad inherited a lot of money. When do we get to you?"

"After he married a woman almost exactly like him, and they partied their way across nearly every continent, spending millions and millions. But somewhere through the haze of booze, drugs, and travel, she got pregnant. They were self-absorbed, and I cramped their style. So I was basically raised by staff while my parents circled the globe."

"You grew up lonely." She reached for him.

He set his jaw as if he didn't want to acknowledge that, but he squeezed her hand, and Raine knew she was right. Her heart ached for him.

"I felt trapped in our house on Park Avenue. I couldn't go anywhere without having to be carted around by our chauffer or jockeying with a billion people for the same inch of sidewalk."

"I've only seen pictures of New York. It looks frenetic."

"I like it better now that I'm an adult. But it will never be home for me again."

Too many bad memories. She understood that. Same reason she'd never step foot into the Kendall house ever again.

"When I was thirteen, they sent me away to Phillips Exeter Academy. I thought I was escaping my hellhole of a house. Prep school was supposed to equip me for Harvard but...god, I hated that fucking place. It made me feel even more like I had no control over my own life."

So he'd chosen an adulthood and a kink that allowed him not only to control most everything but to be master of all he surveyed. "I understand."

"Not yet. I'm just scratching the surface." He blew out a breath as if trying to decide where and how to continue. "Growing up bored and resenting my parents' freedoms while I was stuck in school, I had this stupid, rebellious dream of being a rock star. I was going to be the next Kurt Cobain." He laughed. "I knew every note on every Nirvana, Pearl Jam, and Nine Inch Nails CD. I guilted my folks into buying me an electric guitar and amp one Christmas. They gave me a Fender Stratocaster—not because they believed in me, just to shut me up. I played the fuck out of that thing, full blast, whenever they were home."

Raine frowned. "Did they cuss you out? Ground you?"

Hammer shook his head. "They just soundproofed my room, shut the door, and left for Rio. It was time for Carnival, after all."

The bitter edge to his words made her angry on his behalf. What kind of parents took so little interest in their own son? She didn't ask if he and his dad ever played ball or if his mother baked him cookies. Clearly not. He'd grown up solitary, used to swallowing down his emotions.

That was only just beginning to change.

"I'm sorry. At least I had my mother until I was nine. And my grandparents before her. I knew they loved me unconditionally. Who loved you?"

"Until you and Liam? No one."

Not even Juliet? Raine wanted to ask but sensed he'd get to that part of the story when he was ready.

He swallowed, not quite meeting her gaze. "We spent summers in The Hamptons. Well, *I* spent summers there. My parents were...wherever. But I loved the beach—the breeze, the salty brine, the warm sand between my toes. Everything about that twenties Tuscan-style house just felt alive. It was sturdy, had character. At the end of every summer, I hated to leave and go back to that stuffy-ass school in New Hampshire.

"The summer I was fifteen changed everything. It certainly changed me. I don't know whether it was for the worst turn of events or simply inevitable." He shrugged. "My parents announced one night at dinner—a miracle they were there in the first place—that they were going on a philanthropic quest in Africa. That was their fancy way of saying they were going on safari and dropping a lot of cash on the locals for booze and sightseeing. I wanted to go but it wasn't 'safe.' That translated to I'd simply be in their way. Besides, I needed to brush up on my French. The A minus I'd gotten the previous semester wasn't going to cut it if I wanted to get into Harvard, and my French nanny, Linnet, was staying over the summer to tutor me. Tom, our chauffeur, would teach me archery and improve my swimming because good extracurricular activities were so important on a college application," he mocked.

"You were crushed," she said softly, hurting for him again.

"Yeah. And I was pissed off. The last thing I wanted was to spend the summer being looked after by a nanny I was way too old to need, especially one I'd had a secret crush on for years. Or hauled around by the beefy chauffeur Linnet constantly stared at like he was a fucking god. I certainly didn't want our housekeeper, Martha, who was older than Jesus and deaf as driftwood, poking around in my business. I'd spent a small fortune on contraband *Playboy* magazines at prep school and didn't want her confiscating a single issue."

She could picture him young, with a chip on his shoulder, walling himself off from everyone, taking solace with naked women who would never love him in return. "That summer set up a pattern that lasted for years."

"Damn near two decades, and you have no idea." He let out a rough breath. "I'm not going to lie. Now it gets hard."

Raine rose to sit in the chair directly beside him so she could cup his face. "I know the man you are today. I know the kind of unflinching care you've shown me since you took me in. Something that happened twenty years ago won't change anything for me."

Her words seemed to set him at ease. "Thanks, precious."

He'd needed that, and Raine was happy she could give him the love and adoration he hadn't received as a child. "Go on."

"With my tender fifteen-year-old feelings duly crushed, I tossed my napkin onto the dinner table, purposely scraped the legs of my chair across my mother's antique hardwoods, and tore out of the house. I ran down the beach until I saw a light coming from the pool house. Neither of my parents ever swam, but Linnet liked it, and I had recurring visions of her skinny-dipping for me." He snorted. "When I peered through the window where the blind was partially raised, she was in there, all right. She was naked, too. But Tom, our brawny, quiet chauffeur had her spread, tied down at her wrists and ankles with ropes attached to eyebolts along the back wall. He wore nothing but leather and held a nasty crop."

Raine's breath caught in her chest. "You watched them?"

"Fuck yeah. There was my sexy nanny playing out one of my dirtiest secret fantasies. In my inexperienced head, it was so twisted I didn't even have a name for what they were doing. But I wanted to learn."

"What did he do to her?"

"What didn't he do?" Hammer gazed out the window, over their backyard. But he was far away, as if he'd gone back to that summer. "Linnet liked pain, and Tom didn't hesitate to give it to her. When I first found them, he was raining blows on her nipples with that crop. They were purple, and he showed no sign of stopping. He fondled her pussy, bringing her to the brink over and over…" He shook his head. "My cock was throbbing so damn hard. I pulled it from my shorts, fisted it a couple of times, and lost my load faster than I ever had looking at a magazine. But the second Tom plucked her abused nipples and had to press his hand over her mouth to muffle her screams, I got hard once more. When he attached clothespins and started in with the crop again, Linnet cried such pretty tears. And god, the begging… I could hear her through the walls. I imagined she was crying out for me. I came a second time, just as hard as the first. But my damn cock still wouldn't go down."

"Macen…" Certainly, he wasn't still suffering unrequited love for this woman. And he shouldn't be ashamed that he'd liked what he'd seen. "You were fifteen and—"

"Too damn curious. Tom untied her and forced her to her knees with a fist in her hair. She sucked his cock until her cheeks went concave and he'd buried every inch down her throat. Watching them, I came so hard a third time I got dizzy." Hammer pressed his lips together tightly, still looking out at the wind rustling the palms around their pool. "Even after Tom filled her mouth and she swallowed every drop, they weren't done. Neither was I."

And didn't he sound...bitter? Self-deprecating? Something Raine didn't like.

"He tore off the clothespins, bent Linnet over the bar, and whipped her ass with the crop. Jesus, that turned me on again. I was nearly dehydrated, but I couldn't stop pumping myself. When he lubed up his fingers and shoved them inside her ass, I heard Linnet moan through the glass for more. Tom was talking to her, but I didn't know what he was saying. She just nodded and pleaded some more until he aligned the head of his cock against her little rim and inched his dick inside her. Watching them, I came so hard that time I growled."

Surprise pinged Raine. "They heard you?"

"Tom did. He snapped his head toward the window just as I finished spraying the ground. But he didn't do or say anything, just fucked her ass hard. When he came inside her, I climaxed again, but there was nothing left in my balls."

"So...that started you on the path to BDSM?" The pair had been irresponsible to play where a minor could see, but if Macen was thinking that witnessing them once had warped his head forever, she was going to set him straight.

He gave her a noncommittal shrug. "The next day, I could barely piss without screaming, but wasn't going to let what I'd seen go. So I found Tom alone in the garage and demanded to know what he'd done to Linnet in the pool house. He spent the next several hours explaining BDSM to me. He took me step by step through their dynamics. He was her Master. Linnet was his slave. Any desire he had, she fulfilled. It was an intoxicating thought, to get whatever you wanted—no questions asked—simply because you wanted it."

"To a kid who'd never had any affection, I'm sure." Raine wanted to reach for him but sensed he wasn't ready to return from his trip down memory lane yet, so she waited. "Tom mentored you?"

"You could say that. I blackmailed him. Tom agreed to teach me if I swore I'd never tell my parents about their kink. So that summer he taught me how to make my nanny kneel and be a good girl for me." He scoffed at himself. "The first time I ever had sex, I'd tied Linnet to my parents' bed. Tom buried himself in her ass and whispered in my ear exactly how to get her off, how to last. And for weeks, the three of us locked ourselves away from dusk to dawn. They made it their mission in life to teach me everything, especially how to fuck harder, faster, better, longer—in every way known to man. In return, I had Linnet's power almost completely at my disposal. It was so fucking potent, staggering. I'd never had a drop of booze, but I knew what it meant to be drunk."

Raine hurt for Macen. He wasn't the pedophile. They were. He'd been a kid, ripe for their picking. He might have been a hormonal teenager and thought he wanted all that, but had he really been ready? Mature enough to deal with the fallout? How much had their abuse cost him? "Then what happened?"

"I went back to school a changed man." His tone was harsh, disparaging. "I still made great grades because my parents expected it, but puberty had set in with a vengeance. I shot up, grew a beard, met a guy who made fake IDs. So for a couple hundred bucks, I was in business. The dance clubs in Boston were rich with women who fell easy for charm, money, and a hint of Dominance. I was going home with women ten or fifteen years older than me, tying them up, spanking their asses, and fucking them blind before I was a junior in high school. And every summer, I had Tom and Linnet and a lot more kink to look forward to."

Raine's mouth gaped open. "That continued?"

"For three years. Summers, holidays…oh, yeah. The Christmas I was sixteen, we fucked so much I thought my cock was going to fall off. I went back to school limping."

"You were a child." She blinked, stunned, weirdly wanting to hug him and soothe him and heal him all at once.

"Yeah, with more experience than most grown men." He raised a brow. "Anyway, before I knew it, I was packing up and heading to

Harvard. My parents gave Linnet a hefty bonus for putting up with their 'demanding child,' then let her go. Tom soon gave his notice, and the two of them took off. I don't even know where. They left without a single word. I thought I belonged with them, but..."

Raine's heart twisted for him. They'd crushed Macen, whether they'd meant to or not. "Were you in love with her?"

"No. But we were bound by our 'dirty little secret.' No one else understood me quite so well, and I just never saw it ending." He sighed. "I was wrong. So after licking my wounds, I conquered as many subs as I could find to give me that exhilarating power. It fed the need inside me...but I could never really sate it. Something was always missing."

And Raine could just guess what happened next. A little bit of math told her that Macen had married young. She'd always found that at odds with the confirmed bachelor and manwhore she knew. "Enter Juliet?"

"Not quite. As I was starting my second year of Harvard, my parents flew to Barcelona for La Mercè, another giant street party. Anyway, they were standing on the balcony of their hotel room, watching the festivities, when the terrace collapsed and they fell to their deaths. I had to fly to Spain and identify their bodies, then make arrangements for them to be flown back home, plan the funeral, meet with my parents' lawyers, and settle their estate. It was grueling and confusing and extremely frustrating. The first thing I did was sell that fucking prison on Park Avenue. The house in The Hamptons—with all those memories—wasn't far behind."

"Oh, Macen." She teared up for him. The loss of the people who had given him life and should have loved him must have been tough. He probably hadn't expected grief but felt it anyway and hadn't been equipped to understand. She wanted to touch him so badly, but he still had more to say. "I'm sorry. You didn't have anyone to help you through that. You deserved better."

"They were who they were. I was nineteen and financially set for life, so that was something... It wasn't like I was suddenly alone for the first time."

"You'd always been alone," she whispered.

"Pretty much. I was clueless about what I wanted to do, except quit school. I'd gone to Harvard to please them, but now I didn't have to live up to anyone's expectations. So I went back to New York, bought an obscenely expensive apartment in Tribeca, and started hanging out at BDSM clubs. I spent my days working out at the gym and my nights working subs to orgasm. But after a while I got bored, so I enrolled in some music humanities courses at Columbia. That's where I met Juliet."

Now Macen got quiet, pensive. "In retrospect, I think I was lonely and wanted family or permanence—something. So I thought I'd create that with Juliet. She was an art major but had to take some music courses to fulfill her undergrad requirements. We shared a class. Thanks to Tom's tutelage, I recognized her submissive earmarks inside two minutes. So I turned on my charm and seduced her. Within three months, we'd quit Columbia, moved in together, and gotten engaged." He gave a heavy sigh. "We fed each other's worst tendencies."

"She didn't have boundaries?"

"Not many she'd speak aloud. And she wanted constant attention, which I was only too happy to give her as long as she surrendered all her power." He laughed bitterly. "I thought that was love. A year later, we got married. Her mother despised me for being a controlling beast. The old woman didn't know the half of it. The hold I had over Linnet was nothing compared to the complete and utter control I wielded with Juliet. She did nothing without my permission, not even put on a sock."

Raine pressed a hand over her mouth. The repercussions of his words rippled through her over and over. "She was your slave."

"In every way. I was the king of her fucking world, and she obeyed me almost without hesitation or question. In the middle of all that, I lost sight of my responsibility to guide and protect Juliet's emotional welfare. The harder I pushed her, the more she surrendered. And the greedier I got."

"You hadn't been taught to be any other sort of Dominant." And he certainly hadn't known what love was.

"No, but I should have fucking figured it out somewhere along the way, you know? I didn't, though. One night we were at a club called Graffiti. Juliet was watching Liam work a sub. I could tell he intrigued her. I'd been itching for a threesome for years. It was the one kink I hadn't shared with Juliet. Suddenly, I was sure that ordering her to share my pussy with another man would prove just how much she was under my spell." He huffed in self-disgust. "So I invited him to join us for a drink, then back to our place to top Juliet. It went well. The first time we took her together, it was like being fifteen again. The rush, the thrill, the mind-bending sensations... But it was better because I felt like I'd found the missing half of myself in Liam. We bonded like brothers instantly. Everything was great at first. Then...not so much."

"He told me he wasn't exclusive with you two."

Hammer shook his head, still peering out the window. "It didn't take long before I suspected Juliet was falling in love with Liam. I knew he didn't love her. He was too noble to let himself grow attached because she was my wife. I was still trying to figure out what the fuck I was going to do about that when, out of the blue, she swallowed a bottle of pills I didn't even know she had a prescription for."

Raine took in his tense posture, the regret etched into his face, and she couldn't help herself. She smoothed his hair back and leaned over to kiss his jaw. "The morning you walked out, after I balked at the bondage last week... Liam told me Juliet was pregnant. Don't be angry with him. I wasn't coping, and he knew I needed to understand—"

"I'm glad. In fact, I'm grateful." Hammer swallowed and closed his eyes. "I didn't have the balls to tell you myself. I'm still terrified you're going to look at me like I'm a monster."

"Macen, I would never—"

"You should. I let Juliet down on every possible level as a husband and a Dom. I buried my wife and unborn child, packed up all my shit, and moved to Los Angeles within days. I didn't even say good-bye to Liam. I couldn't look him in the eye, knowing how horrifically I'd failed Juliet. His condemnation would have crushed me."

"Then you opened Shadows?" Raine hoped to direct him to happier times. He'd done so much good for so many people, and she wanted him to remember that.

"Yeah. I should have walked away from the lifestyle completely but I couldn't. Instead, I vowed never to take on another sub. Shadows would be my first priority. I wanted to make sure people had a safe place to play, where Doms would never be taught to feed off power like a parasite. When I opened, I literally had to turn people away and implement a waiting list. The club was an overnight sensation."

"It's a great place. You've done right by the members." She laid a gentle hand over his.

"Yeah. There's that. But I was a lousy human being. I would have cut Liam out of my life for good except…I never let go of my guilt. Just before the first anniversary of Juliet's death, I grew a pair and called him. I told him I planned to come back to New York to visit her grave. I hadn't realized how much I missed the man until I heard his voice. In fact, I missed him more than I did my late wife, which was another mindfuck." He shook his head. "That first visit was awkward and bittersweet as hell. But Liam, with that fucking compassionate heart of his, stood by me at the cemetery as I mourned and piled on more guilt and withheld the truth about Juliet's pregnancy. I didn't want him to suffer. Afterward, he took me out and got me shitfaced. But no amount of booze was enough to drown my remorse or wash away my sins."

"You've got to stop this. So much of what happened wasn't your fault. You've become an amazing man."

"The only thing I've ever done right is you." He blew out a breath, fought tears, and still refused to look at her. "And even that I screwed up for years."

His cutting honesty was breaking her heart. "Macen, don't… Please. That's not true."

"It is. Don't sugarcoat this. I don't deserve it. Because there's more." He nodded in challenge. "Yeah. That night I found you huddled by the dumpster, I couldn't stand to see you hurting. Somewhere in the back of my head, I thought by saving you I could atone. Except the unthinkable happened. I fell in love with you—fast. Jesus, that did a fucking number on my head. You were barely seventeen and I was almost thirty. Teenage girls had never held any appeal for me, even when I was a teenager. I called myself every kind of pervert imaginable. I mean, I knew I was bent but… Do you know how much I fucking hated myself for wanting you? When you turned eighteen, I nearly dragged you into my room, locked the door, and sank inside your body for days, weeks, years. I tried to convince myself that I could have you and not ruin you, but guilt and terror made me keep my distance."

Raine didn't even know what to say anymore. She just gave him her silent support, let him purge it all out, and wished he'd finally look at her.

"I fucked just about every single sub in the club, and I hurt you so much, precious. I have no idea why you love me—"

"Because you were always there for me, always protected me, wanted what was best for me, and challenged me. You were noble, Macen."

"Bullshit." He dragged in a jagged breath.

"Yes. Stop beating yourself up. Our choices and experiences have made us who we are, led us to right now, to the love we share." She placed a hand on her stomach. "Gave us the baby we're having, the future we could have if you'd just forgive yourself..."

"How can I? I didn't fix myself for years, just drowned in shame and pussy because it was easy and what I understood."

"You stayed away from me for so long because the people who should have cared for you had done nothing but use and abuse you." She understood utterly now. "You did everything in your power to make sure the same thing didn't happen to me."

Hammer nodded bleakly. "But I was a jealous bastard, too. I couldn't stand the thought of another man touching you. I wanted to kill Zak and Gabriel. I wanted to rip their dicks off."

She suppressed a little smile. *Gee, I would have never guessed...* "I understand. I lost count of how many bitches I wanted to slap."

He grimaced. "Yeah... But I wasn't just jealous. I drove everyone away from you because your heart was so...pure. I couldn't let them hurt you. If I'd given in to my craving for you years ago, I would have destroyed that—and you."

He would have. As much as Raine had wanted him then, she hadn't understood herself or her heart yet. She hadn't been strong enough to stand in the storm they weathered now and endure the driving pain. She would have crumbled before they reached the heartfelt intimacy they shared today.

"So you didn't lie to me after that first night we spent together. When you said you needed a slave, I thought—"

"I was full of shit. Yeah, I knew. But that was okay. It kept you away. I'd already fucked up once, given into booze and anger and a need for you that strangled me every fucking day. Being with you that night…holding you? It was the first time I'd felt peace in twenty years. I knew I was in love with you, but I didn't know how to show it or how to be the man you deserved. I knew how to take a woman's power and bend it to make me happy. You needed something else entirely. God, I fought myself… I still do sometimes. It's the reason I backed off so badly after Bill almost killed you. The thought of losing the only woman I've ever loved in my entire life, of losing that innocent child growing inside you… I—I can't. I'd never be able to survive that, precious." He swallowed and gripped her hand so tightly her fingers went numb.

"I'm here," she promised. "I'm not going anywhere."

"But I might be. I'm scared I'll be ripped from you. And you deserved to know everything I've told you because I couldn't leave without you understanding how much I love you, how much joy and happiness you've brought to my life. You taught me how to live, Raine. But more than that, you taught me how to love. You stood by me all these years when I was a cold-hearted bastard, denying everything between us. You've branded yourself into my soul. Merely saying I love you can't even scratch the surface of the profound feelings I have for you. I'm not even sure the words to describe that exist." He leaned his head on their joined hands. "You're everything. My breath, body, and soul. It would take me an entire lifetime to show you how I feel, and I don't have a fucking clue how I'm supposed to squeeze all that into the time we might have left. How do I do that, precious? Cram all the love I have for you into six fucking weeks?"

"By taking things one day at a time. By looking at me. Please…"

HAMMER GRIPPED RAINE'S hand, ignoring the fine tremor in his arms. Why was the simple act of opening his eyes and looking at her so fucking difficult? He'd done it thousands of times, over thousands of days. But facing her now was one of the most difficult things he'd ever done.

Because he'd just laid himself bare for her, and if he saw judgment or condemnation, he'd be utterly devastated.

"Macen." She kissed his knuckles. "Have faith."

In her. In them. In the belief that she could love him as completely as he loved her. God knew he didn't have faith in much else in life, but he believed in what they shared, all the way down to his core.

Hope strangled him as he slowly lifted his lids and focused on her.

Raine was waiting for him with big blue eyes, trembling tears, acceptance, and so much love he thought he'd burst. "Hi."

God, he was going to cry like a pussy. He blinked. Hot, acidic drops spilled down his cheeks, and he swore. "Fuck."

She gave him a watery giggle. "You're so poetic."

"And romantic. Yeah."

Her delicate fingers curled around his cheek. "I'd say that's why I love you…but that doesn't even scratch the surface."

"I more than love you, Raine. Thank you for listening."

Spilling his life story had been painful and cathartic. He'd hung on to the bitterness for years—anger toward his unfeeling parents, his depraved caretakers, and his stupid-ass self. If his parents had just given a shit, maybe he wouldn't have been such easy prey for two ruthless sexual freaks. If he hadn't been horny and lonely and ready to flip his parents the moral bird, he wouldn't have been so ready to toss away his innocence for a kinky fuck. At the end of the day, he couldn't blame anyone but himself—which he'd been doing for twenty years. His shit went way further back than Juliet, and he allowed himself to admit it. Wasn't it time to forgive himself, too? He'd made mistakes—some good, some bad. Either way, they'd all led him here, to this woman, to the love he'd been seeking his entire life, to this bond they shared with Liam.

To peace.

To pure, unconditional love.

"I always will." She brushed a kiss across his knuckles. "I've spent a lot of time the past few weeks wondering if maybe we would have all been better off if I had left Shadows that morning I threatened to. You know, the morning I sneaked in your bed and tried to seduce you."

"Oh, I remember." He enveloped her small hand in his broad palms. "You scared the shit out of me."

A smile tripped across her lips. "I was terrified, too. But if I'd walked out the door like I'd threatened, we could have saved ourselves so much pain."

"But—"

"But we would have missed out on everything wonderful. I know."

"I wouldn't have missed you for the world. I don't care what we've been through. This is worth it."

Her smile turned dazzling. "Last Halloween, I never fathomed we'd be here today. I'd never kissed you. I barely knew Liam. That was less than four months ago. Now we're sharing a house, having a baby..."

"And you've made me happier than I've ever been. I'd spend three lifetimes behind bars to have shared these past few months with you and Liam." Hammer placed his hand on her stomach. "I might not get to share the joy of raising this child. But I'll always be a part of you, Liam, and our baby. I might not be here physically, but I hope I'll be here."

He raised his hand to her heart and slanted his lips over hers.

"You will." Her voice cracked. "I don't want to do this without you."

"I hope you don't have to, precious."

Raine wrapped her slender hands around his cheeks and drew him to her lips. Hammer couldn't help but groan. The feather-soft kisses she pressed to the corners of his mouth were so heartfelt he nearly crumbled. Her sweet affection bled the ever-present anxiety from his veins. Soothed him. Calmed him. For the first time in his life, Macen relinquished his control and simply felt.

Hyperaware of the smoldering connection that always pulsed between them, Macen's senses sharpened. Time ceased to have meaning.

When he closed his eyes, he could almost see them, one still image after the other, as their love flared. Hammer pressed every picture into his memory, storing them away in case the feds locked him up. He'd cherish and relive each one when he was going mad with grief, loneliness, and need.

But he wasn't just seeing them together. He was completely in the moment with Raine, so attuned to her—aware of her every nuance—that even something as simple as her breathing awakened his senses.

The sensual bow of her lips fascinated him. He leaned closer and traced them with his finger. Her hypnotic feminine heat hovered in the air, intoxicating. She made him ache to feel her, taste her. To drag her beneath him and never let go.

"I want to make love to you, precious."

Her lashes fluttered down to her cheeks as her mouth curled up in a soft smile. "I'd like that."

"Listen to me, Raine. I don't mean sex or a power exchange. Tonight, I just want to be a man who loves a woman."

"Macen…" A single tear tracked down her cheek. "I've always felt your love."

Even when he hadn't meant for her to. Even when he hadn't given it freely.

He thumbed away the clear drop as he stood and wrapped his arms around her. "I don't know how, but I thank god every day you did."

He couldn't—wouldn't—waste another second. With infinite care, he lifted her, clutching her close as she wrapped her slender legs around him. She slid her arms behind his neck and sent him a searching stare.

"I want to touch you in ways I never have," he told her.

Raine buried her face in his neck as if she couldn't get close enough, couldn't inhale him enough, as Hammer carried her upstairs to their bedroom.

Just inside the door, she sank her fingers into his scalp and drew him to her lips again. Macen didn't even make it to the bed before need seized him. He pressed her to the wall, sank into her mouth, and poured his heart into the kiss. He made love to her mouth—tasting, tormenting, teasing—as he stroked her tongue with a sensual surge and retreat. She dragged in a breath, grabbed his shirt, grinding softly against him as she cried out in supplication, a plea for all the love and passion he could give her.

Raine writhed against the erection tenting his trousers. She arched, tossing her head back. Through the barrier of their clothes, he could feel her taut nipples against his chest. The graceful line of her neck beckoned him. Hammer couldn't resist. He feathered his lips up her skin, breathing her in, holding her tight as he worked his way back to her lips with a groan.

When he reached her, she was waiting. Their mouths melded. She felt so small but vital in his arms as he turned and carried her to the bed, then laid her across the middle, in the spill of silvery moonlight beaming through the window.

Braced above Raine, he looked down at her. Watched. Stared. She blinked up at him, lips swollen, eyes shimmering with devotion.

Hammer didn't flinch or dilute the importance of the moment with a wolfish smile or wry smirk. Instead, he bared himself without removing a stitch, allowing her to see inside him, all the way to the bone.

To his soul.

He could barely fathom how he'd managed six years without showing her his heart. How would he ever survive the next thirty? He'd come to need Raine, to depend on the fact she was right beside him. He'd simply believed that she always would be. The utter shock that *he* might be the one leaving was almost more than he could bear.

Macen trailed a knuckle down her cheek, brushed his thumb over her bottom lip. He gazed into her questioning eyes. She wore every emotion she felt on her sweet face. He could read her so easily. She wanted to be everything to him, wanted to give him whatever he craved.

Somehow, she didn't realize she already had.

"Tonight, I need your love far more than I want your power," Hammer whispered against her lips. "Take whatever you want. You don't need permission for anything."

Her breath hitched. Raine took hold of his face. "I want all of you."

"I'm yours. I have been for longer than I could even admit."

Without a word, Raine sat up and unfastened the buttons of his shirt, pushing it off one shoulder, then the other, kissing the skin she uncovered with a gossamer press of her lips. Then she unfastened his belt, toyed with the button of his slacks. With a beseeching stare, she tempted him, igniting tingles not just in his cock but all over his body. As his zipper fell with a hushed purr in the room, goose bumps broke out across his skin. Usually, he was in control of everything. Now he couldn't even control his breathing. He'd never felt anything like this wonder, the sense that her next touch could both soothe his need and wrench his heart.

Hammer suspected those weren't the only new and foreign sensations she'd bestow on him tonight. He was ready and oh-so-fucking willing to drink them all in.

The neon numbers on the bedside clock flashed blue in the shadowed room. He was shocked to see that hours had passed since the O'Neill family departed. How could it feel as though he and Raine were cocooned in some perfect, timeless bubble while wondering if, at any moment, it was about to burst?

Raine skimmed her fingers over his chest, dragging a nail softly around his nipples, into his navel, before pushing his pants past his hips and freeing his shaft. Macen forgot the clock. Instead, he drew in a deep breath and let it out as he followed her every worshipping caress. The beast within him didn't even rouse, as if knowing the man couldn't survive anymore without her love.

"I never get tired of touching you," Raine murmured. "The feel of your hard muscles beneath all that smooth, hot skin."

He sucked in an agonized breath as she tempted him with skimming palms and grazing lips. "I melt every time you touch me."

A tingling trail of awakening flesh spread until he swore his heart would split wide open.

"Take your pants off," she murmured, nipping her way up his shoulder, to his neck, pressing her lips to his jaw.

God, he didn't want to move, just stay and bask in her reverence and love.

Why had he never known how much pleasure a woman could give him when he wasn't commanding it?

Because he'd never let anyone ever have this sort of power over him.

For Raine, he stepped back. An involuntary groan of protest left his chest, but he kicked off his trousers and returned to the bed, hovering on his knees above her, just waiting.

She smiled as she ate him up with her gaze. She had the definite advantage since she remained fully dressed. Hammer found their role reversal ironic, but he didn't care. He simply closed his eyes and memorized the feel of her soft, smooth hands claiming every part of him.

When she tongued her way up his abs and circled his aching cock with her fingers, Hammer's hips bucked. She was undoing him—as she always did—but this experience was remarkably different. For a man who prided himself on control, she was unraveling him faster than a spool of yarn.

Surprisingly, he kind of…liked it.

"Raine, baby, I want to feel your skin. I have to kiss you all over." He didn't demand that she strip, and he didn't tell her that he intended to peel off her clothes. He simply started removing them.

He wanted it to take forever.

Hammer tugged at the hem of her bright pink T-shirt, nudging it over her belly, smoothing it up her breasts and over her head. He eased to his feet, helped her up in front of him. Wrapping his hands around her waist, he felt for the snap and zipper of her little skirt. He released them and guided the garment down her hips. Her bra fell away next under his deft fingers. With a smile, he palmed his way down to cup her baby bump.

"I've changed." She bit her lip.

"You're beautiful. You look even more like a woman now. Like *our* woman."

She was so exquisite, so petite and delicate compared to him and Liam. It was a wonder they hadn't broken her. She was far more resilient than either of them in some ways. She'd be an amazing mother. Of that, he had no doubt. The changes in her body were more evident with each passing day. Something else he would miss. Another ache he couldn't soothe away.

Because he couldn't resist another minute, he dropped a kiss on her lips. But his brush turned into more. He sank into her, drowned in her, falling deeper and deeper…

Goddamn, he'd miss her. Every sigh, every scream of ecstasy, every panted wail, every giggle and laugh, every fighting word, and every fucking tear she cried over him.

When Hammer eased back to drink her in, he saw heartbreak lining her face.

She sucked in a ragged breath. "Mac—"

He seized her lips again, stealing her words. He didn't want to talk about her future that probably wouldn't include him and refused to waste another second mired in regret. He wanted to merge his heart and soul with hers and carry those priceless pieces of Raine with him for the rest of his days.

Her lips quivered under his. Macen felt her warm, wet tears roll between them. Melancholy gripped him. Hammer blocked it out. Nothing and no one would spoil their remaining time together.

Cupping her nape, he gently slid inside her mouth. Sweeping over every valley and swell, he sighed as their tongues joined in a slick, exalting glide.

As he eased back to nuzzle her cheek and anoint her with tender kisses, tiny sobs escaped her throat.

Hammer's heart disintegrated. He'd finally confronted his ghosts, convinced himself that it was time to begin his life again...and now? He might lose everything.

Not without proving how much she means to me.

Thumbing the wetness from her cheeks, he shook his head. "No tears, precious. I'm giving you more power over me than I've ever voluntarily given anyone in my life. I want to commit every second of this night to memory. Will you do the same?"

Raine sucked in a shaky breath, then drew his palm to her lips. Pressing a kiss to the center, she placed his hand over her heart. "Tonight, tomorrow... I'll carry you here with me forever, Macen."

Her bottom lip trembled, but Raine kept herself together for him. She wrapped her hand around his neck and pulled him to her lips. Hammer went willingly, stroking the softness of her naked flesh, absorbing the feel of her as she lavished all her love on him. When she traced her tongue along the seam of his lips, he opened for her, letting Raine explore as she'd done for him.

Growing bolder, she circled her hand around his wrist and brought his palm to her breast. He obliged her desire and raised his other hand, kneading her heavy orbs, thumbs skimming her hard nipples. She gasped into his mouth and arched into his hands.

"I need you, Macen," she murmured.

"I need you, too."

Kissing her senseless, he pulled her to the mattress with him. She was shaking, and he brushed the hair from her face with the softest caress, then kissed her again, savoring the slickness of her lips and tongue. He couldn't seem to get his fill of her. Dragging his mouth over her jaw, he inched lower, nipping and laving the sensitive flesh beneath her ear.

She wrapped her arms around him and dug her fingers into his flesh, her nails little pinpricks in his back. He shivered and his cock jerked. He wanted to spread her wet folds and drive himself inside her. Instead, he swept his tongue lower still and captured a sweet, ripe nipple between his lips. On a blissful sigh, she lifted her shoulders from the mattress, offering herself to him. Hammer took his time, languidly bathing both breasts in liquid heat until Raine whimpered, writhed, and moaned.

The air around them thickened. Heat and demand grew urgent.

Still, Hammer had no intention of rushing these tender moments. Raine was too special, too rare, too important. Her mewls and pleas set him on fire, but it was a different kind of flame than he'd ever felt. Hammer wondered how he'd gone through life without ever knowing this mind-altering ebb and flow of unbridled passion. Until now, he hadn't understood that with someone he loved, he could give her his power and she'd surrender everything back to him tenfold.

When he lifted his head, he saw her face glowing with love—pure, raw, and true. His heart clutched. His body trembled. "I could stay here, lost inside your eyes until the end of time."

"Do it," she moaned. "Stay with me. Forever. Please."

He never made promises he couldn't keep. He wasn't going to start now. He loved her too much to lie.

Macen swallowed back the pain rising inside and kissed her softly. "I'll stay with you as long as our forever lasts, precious. You have my word."

"Our forever will never be long enough."

He nodded and pressed his forehead to hers. "Then we'll make every fucking second count."

Raising his head, he shifted his weight. Supporting himself above her with one hand, he reached between them and gripped his ready cock. In silent entreaty, Raine parted her legs.

Open.

Inviting.

Unprotected, she exposed her whole heart and soul to him.

As he stared down at her, she looked like every man's fantasy. She'd always been his.

Raine was the most beloved gift life had ever given him. She was perfect. From the inky hair spilling over his white pillow to her delicate pink-painted toes, and every sassy, strong-willed, tender-hearted part in-between.

Everything about her took his breath away, always had…always would.

With his gaze locked on hers, Hammer sucked in a shuddering breath. "Forever, precious."

"Forever." Two fat tears slid from her eyes.

A bittersweet smile tugged the corners of his lips as he aligned his crest and slowly pushed past her wet folds. Inching himself into her swollen core was as close to heaven as he would ever get.

Gazing into her tear-filled eyes, Hammer worked himself in, little by little, as Raine clutched him to her tightly. She clung as if she'd never let go. Hopefully, neither of them would ever have to.

Hammer seated himself inside her. Raine's breasts rose and fell as her smooth walls enclosed him in her heat, her very being. He withdrew from inside her with the same painstakingly slow rhythm, watching her lips part and sensation play across her face.

"You're so fucking beautiful." Hammer wanted to weep.

"You make me feel beautiful. Alive and loved. Oh, Macen…" Raine breathed as she wrapped her arms around him.

Hammer buried his face in her neck. With both hands, he gripped her petite curves and settled her onto his thighs, driving himself deeper inside her. He gently gripped her waist, then slowly eased her up and down his shaft. She cupped his cheeks and kissed him, melting her mouth against his.

Encased in their own self-made bubble of perfection, their whimpers and groans filled the air in a song of passion. Their tongues entwined and their bodies swayed—the physical poetry of their love. Slowly, sensually they ascended to the stars, disintegrating and fragmenting into brilliant bursts of raw, erotic beauty.

Boneless, spent, and thoroughly sated, they remained coupled together. He held her in his arms as aftershocks rippled through them. Hammer vowed that he would spend the next forty-two days loving and caring for her, mark himself indelibly inside her to keep his memory burning within her like a flame.

It wasn't enough. It would never be enough—for either of them.

Hammer stifled his anguish, closed his eyes, and pulled Raine in even closer. As he combed his fingers through her hair, she drifted off to sleep. As he listened to the rhythmic sound of her breathing, he savored the softness of her skin, the feel of her warm, lush body against his, the combined scents of their lovemaking.

When Liam slipped in the room and smiled at them entwined, dropping a kiss on Raine's still-flushed cheek, Macen shared a smile with his best friend. And for the first time in his life, he felt well and truly whole.

CHAPTER FOURTEEN

Tuesday, February 19

HAMMER HADN'T BEEN this anxious since his first day of boarding school. Sitting in the waiting room in the office of Raine's ob-gyn, surrounded by women—some who already looked forty weeks pregnant—Macen wanted to climb the walls. Raine skimmed her thumb over his knuckles, trying to soothe him. Would he be a nervous wreck when Raine was ready to deliver? Hell, would he even be there when that time came? The thought of missing out on the birth of their child sent him spiraling downward.

Don't go there, fucker.

After the evening he and Raine had spent making love, he'd succeeded in shoving down his fears—until now. He'd also held tight to the feeling of completeness he'd discovered then. From the moment he'd awakened this morning, he'd done his best to focus on appreciating every second of his freedom with the two people he loved. And now he'd be hearing their baby's heartbeat.

Later, he knew he'd have decisions to make.

But no way would he let dread or what-ifs spoil this moment.

Two chairs down, Liam leaned in to kiss Raine's cheek. Foreheads pressed together, they shared a hopeful, intimate glance. And when she turned to him in silent question, he couldn't leave her wondering whether he was excited to hear the first signs of their growing child's life. He caressed her belly and smiled.

Around the room, he could feel gaping stares, even outright hostility from other expectant mothers. He ignored them. No one was ruining this for them.

"Raine?" An older woman clutching a chart and wearing bright blue scrubs called as she held open a wide door.

Both he and Liam leapt to their feet and extended their hands to

Raine. She placed her fingers in each of their palms and stood, excitement evident in her exhalation. "It's time."

"Wow," a woman murmured as they passed.

"Maybe one is a friend and the other is the father," another woman speculated in a whisper that carried around the room.

Raine turned back to the busybodies. "No, they're both my men and the fathers of our baby, not that it's any of your business."

Hammer couldn't help but chuckle as Raine clutched his and Liam's arms proudly and sashayed toward the nurse. She didn't even look back to see the jaws dropped in shock. The stunned gasps from the two judgmental twits said it all.

"You go, girl," another expectant mother cheered her on as they passed.

A wide grin speared Liam's face.

Once they passed the nurse waiting for them at the portal, Hammer leaned in to murmur in her ear. "You're bad. I like it."

"I can't take you two anywhere," Liam teased.

"Me? What the fu—heck did I do?" Hammer amended his language in the mostly female-inhabited, baby-friendly office.

The nurse laughed and motioned Raine to step on the scales. After she slipped off her shoes, they watched the number appear on the digital display.

"Are you having trouble with morning sickness?" asked the nurse. "You've lost four pounds."

Hammer and Liam exchanged a glance. The stress and chaos in their lives right now had impacted her and their baby. He wished like fuck he could put a stop to it—for all their sakes.

"No," Raine replied. "I just don't seem to have much of an appetite."

Hammer sent her a scowl for lying.

"We'll start force-feeding her if we have to," Liam assured.

"I have no doubt." The nurse shot Raine a knowing grin. "You're lucky. Some women don't have one man, let alone two, helping through their pregnancies."

"I bet it's really quiet at their house," Raine joked with a saucy grin. "And they do less laundry."

"That comment is going to cost you... later," Hammer whispered in her ear.

The nurse pretended not to hear as she took Raine's blood pressure and temperature, then led them to an examination room. Hammer's replacement phone—the feds had seized his—vibrated in his pocket. He ignored the call and helped Raine onto the table.

Hammer had never been in an ob-gyn's office, but he knew exactly what sort of apparatus this was. Toying with one of the stirrups, he glanced at Liam. "One of these would be great for the dungeon at home, wouldn't it?"

His buddy nodded. "Think of the possibilities."

Sidling to the foot of the table, Liam extended the stirrups.

Raine swatted at his shoulder. "What are you doing? Stop. The doctor is going to walk in here any second. Retract those."

"Not so fast. Lie back, love." Liam stroked her thigh. "Prop your pretty little feet in these stirrups. Doctor Hammer and I will cure what ails you."

Raine's face turned bright red. Macen couldn't help but laugh.

"Liam Sean O'Neill, you are out of your ever-loving Irish mind if you think—"

A light tap on the door interrupted Raine's rant. Instantly, she snapped her mouth shut and sent Liam a pleading stare. He thrust the stirrups back in place just before the real doctor entered.

Raine's face was still stained a bright crimson.

Hammer gave her a few extra moments to recover and stepped forward. "Good to see you again, Dr. Parker. It's been a few years."

"And you, as well, Macen." The fifty-something woman glanced at Liam. "I'm Dr. Abigail Parker."

"Liam O'Neill," he replied as he extended his hand.

After exchanging pleasantries, the doctor focused on her patient. Parker was concerned about Raine's weight loss, as were he and Liam. But Raine assured the doctor she would put on more weight before the next visit.

The two women discussed everything related to pregnancy, or so it seemed to Hammer. Even Liam appeared eager to get on with the show. Or maybe he simply wanted the doctor to leave so he could tease Raine with the stirrups some more.

Finally, Dr. Parker set down her pen and clipboard. "Who's ready to hear a heartbeat?"

"I am. Are you two daddies prepared for all this?" Raine asked pensively.

"Without a doubt, love." Liam beamed. "Couldn't be more thrilled."

"Hell yes," Hammer agreed.

Raine lay back on the table and lifted her shirt. She tugged the waist of her yoga pants down to her hips and took a deep breath. Dr. Parker spread some gel-like lube over Raine's stomach. The room turned quiet, sharp with expectation, as the doctor pressed a small, handheld device to Raine's little bump. Instantly, a loud, crackling static filled the air.

Then suddenly, a soft, rapid *whoosh, whoosh, whoosh* filled the room. The smile on Raine's face could have lit up all of Los Angeles. Happy tears leaked from her eyes. Liam stood staring with a look of delight and awe etched on his face. Hammer's heart lurched to his throat. That sound was the beating heart of the baby they'd created together, pumping, growing, living.

All the fears and anguish he'd shoved down came roaring to the surface in a billowing pall of panic.

"Oh, my god. That's amazing." Raine sniffed. "That's our baby."

"It is, love." Liam grabbed her hand and squeezed. "It's the most remarkable sound I've ever heard. Oh, Raine. Our wee bairn sounds so strong."

Liam was right. And Hammer couldn't stop wondering what the hell he'd do if he missed all the other milestones of this child's life. Fuck, he had to block out his worries, not let them weigh down this miraculous moment.

Soon, he might have thirty years to waste on regret.

He rushed to Raine's side and gave her a slow, loving kiss.

When he lifted from her, Raine turned a worried gaze to him. "Macen?"

He wiped at his eyes as if overwhelmed. And he was. Joy brawled with grief, punching him black and blue. Hearing the heartbeat—like seeing the tiny bump of Raine's belly—blindsided him on a whole new level.

How could he stand not to be with them to welcome this life, to watch and share in their child's growth? How would he survive knowing that life would—and had—gone on without him?

Not here, fucker. Keep your shit wired. You can't fall into that hole now.

"It's more than amazing, precious," he finally choked out. "It's a miracle."

As Liam stepped away, Hammer swooped in and wrapped her in his arms. Struggling against the urge to put his fist through the wall, he gently cupped Raine's cheeks and kissed her.

"You're happy, aren't you?"

He was happy for her and Liam, not thrilled with the pile of rubble he was crumbling into. But he'd be damned if he dumped an ounce of this on her.

Slipping on a mask of calm, he sent her a wide smile. "I'm beyond happy. This baby will never question how much he or she is loved."

Raine and Liam would see to that.

"Never." She beamed.

Hammer stepped back and turned before dragging in a deep breath. While Parker talked to Raine, he worked to neutralize the bitter acid thrumming through his veins. But all he could focus on was finding the prick who'd set him up and every unholy way he'd take vengeance on that motherfucker's soul if he got the chance.

"See you next time, Macen." Dr. Parker smiled as she left the room.

Probably not. "Thanks," Hammer replied just before the door closed behind her.

"Let's get you cleaned up, shall we?" With a handful of tissues, Liam wiped the gel from Raine's stomach, tugged up her pants, then pulled her into his arms. "I can't believe that sound came from our baby."

"I know," Raine squealed. "It was…amazing."

Seize the moment. It might be your last.

Clenching his jaw, Hammer strode across the room and pressed himself against Raine's back. He wrapped his arms around the two, then closed his eyes and breathed her in. Bending, he peppered kisses beneath her ear. "Hearing that heartbeat was beyond amazing. You're going to be a phenomenal mother."

"Because I'll have two phenomenal fathers to help me." Turning, she tilted her face toward him. "I just know it."

She kissed him, and Hammer wished like hell he shared her confidence.

"Let's grab lunch. We need to put some meat on your bones, love." Liam cupped her cheek and turned her toward him, kissing her, as well.

"Yes, we have to fatten you up."

"Not too much. I'm not looking forward to waddling."

"But there will be more of you to love, precious," Hammer murmured.

Forcing himself to stay in the moment, he found that plateau of peace again. But he wasn't fooling himself. It would be all too easy to slide into despair if he didn't stay on his toes.

After lunch at Raine's favorite pizza joint—again—they arrived back at the house. Bryn grabbed Raine and insisted they shop for goodies for the nursery. Duncan, bless him, agreed to drive the women and haul their shopping bags. With a wink at his son and a pat on his wife's butt, the three walked out the door.

"What do you say we grab a couple beers and sit by the pool?" Liam suggested.

"Sure."

The breeze was a little cool, but the sun was warm, the blue sky brilliant. It was a perfect afternoon to relax outdoors.

"How are you holding up?" Liam asked.

"So far, so good." He nodded before taking a long pull of the bottle.

"Stop lying to me," Liam chided. "You weren't doing so good at the doctor's office today."

"No. But I pulled my head out of my ass."

"Have you? Or are you telling me what you think I want to hear?"

Hammer shot him a sideways glance. "Why would I do that?"

A mirthless chuckle rolled off his friend's tongue. "To save me from worrying about you. You're too late, by the way. That ship sailed. I know you're worried and depressed. Talk to me, Macen."

"Yeah, I suppose those are bubbling in the shit pot of my emotions."

"At least you're confessing you *have* emotions now. That's growth. Finally." Liam took a swig of his dark stout. "You're keeping something from us. What is it?"

"Christ, a few days with your mom and suddenly you turn into some fucking mind reader?"

"It's your aura. And yours isn't simply dull. It's lost its luster altogether. It's gone dark."

"I'll give it a new paint job and put some wax on it."

"Don't start that fucking dodge, duck, dip, dive, dodge crap with me," Liam roared. "I'm up to my eyeballs in this shite, too. So is Raine. Neither of us wants to lose you. Stop being an asshole and level with me."

Duly chastised, Hammer sighed and nodded.

"All right. All right. Knock it off."

Hammer sent him a scowl. "Knock what off? I haven't said a fucking word."

"It's my Mum. She's harping on me to be more understanding."

Hammer shook his head. "Christ, that's got to be annoying as hell. Does she peek in on us when we're...you know, with Raine?"

Liam laughed. "Bloody hell, no. Not unless it's an emergency like that day they arrived."

"I was damn thankful for your burning ear then." Hammer raised his bottle in a toast.

Liam joined him before they both swallowed down more brew.

Reaching into his pocket, Hammer pulled out his phone. "I got a call from Sterling while we were at the doctor's office. I haven't listened to it yet."

"Why not?"

"Frankly, I don't want to hear any more bad news."

Liam exhaled heavily, then leaned over and gripped Macen's shoulder. "I'm not trying to put more on your plate. I'm trying to share the load, if you'll let me."

"I know. This whole fucking mess is piling up on your shoulders. I hate that you might have to—"

"I'll gladly carry the load, brother. You know I've always got your back. I'll do everything in my power to care for Raine and our baby if it comes to that." Liam nodded at the cell phone. "Play the message."

With a trembling finger, Hammer pushed the button, then cradled the phone in a tight grip.

"Macen. Sterling here. Things are looking…bleak. I'm waiting on more information from Wellington, but there's something else I need to tell you. The state will file rape charges against you if the feds don't convict you. I just saw the November fourth video of you and Raine at the club. Jesus christ, Macen. After that, there's no way in hell I can keep her off the stand. Without Raine's testimony, you'll be crucified. I know you want to protect her, but that's not possible anymore. The jury will see that footage and dissect it frame by frame. We'll be lucky if it's not leaked to the tabloids." He paused. "Call me as soon as you can. We'll discuss this in depth. I'm sorry I don't have better news."

Hammer stared at the phone, dazed and numb.

"Bloody hell," Liam barked. "You told Barnes not to let Raine testify? Damn, man, an army couldn't keep her from the witness stand. You just try and stop her. She'd march right up to the judge, stomp her dainty foot, and demand to tell her side of the story."

"And then what?" Hammer spit. "Let the prosecution burn the scarlet letter *A* into the middle of her forehead? Raine… you… me… We'll all be on the cover of every fucking rag from here to New York. They'll label you a pervert and me a pedophile. Raine will get the distinguished honor of being known as a sex slave for the rest of her life. And what about our baby? It won't matter what his last name is— Hammerman, O'Neill, or Kendall—our child will carry the humiliation of this whole fucking mess the rest of his or her life. Do you want that?"

Liam's eyes grew wide as he bolted up from his chair. "No. Oh, hell no, Macen. You can't."

"Can't what?" he spat.

"Can't go through with what you're thinking about. Bloody hell, man. Have you lost your fucking mind?"

Hammer's mouth gaped open. "How do you… Bryn!"

"It's not my mother, mate." Fury flashed in Liam's eyes as he inched in close to Hammer's face. "You don't get it. I can fucking see you. Your thoughts are like a goddamn sign, all lit up and flashing neon in my fucking face. So don't tell me you're fine, Macen. I'm gut sick with worry. Don't you dare think to leave me here alone."

Hammer slammed his bottle on the table, curled his fingers into fists, and punched him in the jaw. "Get out of my head. I didn't invite you to dissect me before, and I'm sure as hell not letting you read my goddamn thoughts."

Liam raised a hand to his face and rubbed it. "So we're back to this now, are we? Bring it on, mate. I'll toss your fucking ass in the pool and piss myself laughing."

Without a word, Hammer drew his hand back again, but Liam was faster. He shoved a fist in Macen's gut, knocking the wind out of him.

"Do you want to keep going or are you ready to sit down and talk, you big, stupid bastard?" Liam spat.

"Fuck you."

"Yeah, yeah. Fuck yourself." Liam shook his head. "We can spend the afternoon knockin' each other's blocks off, which will have Raine packing her bags. At least one of your problems will be solved then, right? Or you can stop eating your testoster-oats and use your head."

"Testoster-oats?" Hammer couldn't help but laugh.

Liam grinned. "Got your attention, didn't it?"

"Goddamn you." Hammer sighed as his face crumpled and all his tension piled up. "What am I going to do?"

Before he even tried to pull himself together, Liam wrapped him in a hug. "You're not going to do a bloody damn thing except ride this out with the rest of us. Do you hear me?"

Hammer sucked in a deep breath. He could only promise to try.

"This shit storm will pass. I have to believe the three of us will survive, and when it's over, we'll still be intact. According to Seth, our life's a fucking soap opera, and these bloody dramas always get resolved somehow."

Hammer nodded, but he wondered if their luck had just run out.

"I need you, brother. And you need me. You may not think you do, but—"

"I've needed you for years." Hammer sighed. "I was just too fucking stubborn to admit it."

"It's never too late to figure things out, mate. I'm glad you did."

"Yeah, well… some of us are slower to grasp the importance of shit than others." Hammer slapped Liam on the back. "I want you and Raine to sign the powers of attorney I showed you the other night."

"Did you not hear my fucking words?" Liam pulled back with a scowl.

"I did. But I want to be prepared, just in case."

"I understand you needing to get your affairs in order, but… hell. We'll talk this over with Raine tonight. She has just as much right to help make decisions. We're a family."

"I know. Just…it would ease my mind if you'd both sign."

"I'll consider it. And I'll be bringing the shit shovel to that talk. You can explain that you refused to let her testify."

Hammer let out a long-suffering groan.

Liam looked out over the pool, a wry smile tugging the corners of his mouth. "Maybe she'll just march you down here and make you go for another icy swim."

Hammer threw his head back and laughed. "Fuck you."

LYING IN BED, Hammer stared at the ceiling while Sterling's message played over in his head on an endless loop. After he'd seen the footage of Macen and Raine's encounter in the bar at Shadows, the lawyer had sounded horrified. While everything with her had been consensual, the video obviously didn't depict that. No matter which way he turned, the only one who could save his sorry ass was Raine.

Macen clenched his jaw at the thought of throwing her under the bus. He wasn't going to humiliate his pregnant, stressed-out girl by having her explain the pictures of her beaten and bruised for a federal jury. If the state took over, she'd have to defend each frame of that damn video footage to a dozen strangers who would decide his fate. In either case, the prosecution would destroy every shred of self-confidence she possessed. The press had already painted her as a sex worker and whore. The suits who wanted him locked up would, no doubt, brand her a trashy unwed mother, too. The news and tabloids would print every lurid detail they could get their hands on. She wouldn't have a normal life anymore, and what would that do to her? Liam? Their baby?

Fuck!

Macen refused to sit by while the two people he loved more than life were destroyed in such a thoroughly callous, public way.

A strangled scream of frustration burned in his lungs.

Closing his eyes, he sucked in a deep breath. Memories of sitting in a fucking cell for two and a half days came rushing back. He'd done nothing but crawl inside his own head, letting his fears and insecurities drag him down to the darkest recesses of his soul. *You can protect them…* A voice whispered between Hammer's ears. He could also save himself from the slow, thirty-year slide to insanity if he were imprisoned.

But the cost was priceless in all the wrong ways.

Still, he'd made a vow that if Sterling couldn't prove Macen's innocence and the outcome of the trial seemed bleak, he would take his future into his own hands. He intended to keep that promise. He'd be damned before he let twelve clueless jurors decide his destiny.

But Sterling's message only served to drive home the fact that things were already bleak. Hammer's future was going up in flames and the fucking trial hadn't even started.

Never in his worst nightmare had Hammer imagined he'd be pushed into a position like this. But he had—and he only had two ways out. That realization made his heart skip and every muscle tremble.

Panic swamped him. A wave of nausea crested. Cold sweat followed. Unable to breathe, he tossed back the covers and leapt out of bed.

Yeah, he'd heard Liam's encouraging words about their future around the pool earlier and told himself his friend was right. He could still logically have hope.

Macen huffed. God, he sounded stupid, idealistic. Liam was a true friend, trying to prop him up, but Sterling had basically laid the truth out for him: thirty years. And if the feds didn't get him, the state would. There was no escape.

Pacing, he dragged in deep breaths. It didn't help. The walls were closing in all around him.

Grabbing the clothes he'd draped over the chair earlier, Hammer tried to quell his rising anxiety. His fingers shook as he buttoned his shirt.

Striding to the bed, he gazed down at the sleeping couple. Liam lay with his chest pressed to Raine's back, one arm slung over her hip, his hand splayed open, shielding their unborn child. That was Liam's way, a loving protector. Macen couldn't have asked for a better friend.

Friend, nothing. The damn Irishman had instantly been more like a brother. Liam was laughter. Honesty. Compassion. Understanding. He was the benevolent pieces of humanity Macen lacked. The amazing bastard had still given him love and devotion even when Hammer hadn't deserved it.

Emotions running high, he gazed at Raine. She looked peaceful, angelic. The lines of worry and fear that had been etched between her brows these past hellacious days had smoothed away. That's exactly how Hammer wanted to remember her, too. God knew she deserved some blessed tranquility. She'd had to endure so much pain and trauma. The last thing she needed was to atone for his sins, to be weighed down by his humiliation and shame. He'd move heaven and earth to keep her from having to testify. He would fix the problem so she and Liam could live a normal life.

They deserved that and so much more.

Macen skimmed his stare over her lips. He'd waited and wasted years, aching to kiss the erotic bow of her mouth. When he finally had, she'd tasted like pure paradise, far sweeter and more potent than he'd imagined all that time.

Regret for the way things would end pierced his heart. He hadn't even left the room and he already mourned the loss of her love.

Oh, god, how am I going to go through with this?

But he couldn't wait any longer. If he was found guilty, they would lock him up and throw away the key. There would be no eleventh-hour pardons, just ten thousand nine hundred fifty days locked in a cage like a fucking animal. His life with Liam and Raine would be over.

What good was living when all he'd ever longed for was gone?

With an aching heart and a cyclone of emotions, Hammer plucked up the powers of attorney Liam and Raine had grudgingly signed earlier in the evening. Folding the pages that guaranteed their future, Hammer set them on his nightstand. Returning to the dresser, he removed his passport from the top drawer, then palmed his keys to keep them from jingling.

He stared at Liam and Raine one last time as his throat constricted and tears stung the backs of his eyes. Hammer branded the image of them both into his brain, then clenched his jaw. He walked out of the room and down the stairs.

Passing the kitchen, he paused. Visions of Raine, naked and splayed over the granite-topped island, split him in two. Closing his eyes, the scent of cinnamon melding with Raine's feminine musk all but obliterated him.

Blood burning with the bittersweet memory, Hammer disengaged the alarm system and opened the door to the garage. Flipping on the light, he stepped through the portal and closed the door, severing the dreams of love and happiness he'd finally achieved.

Because now he had to throw it all away.

A foreboding chill slid up his spine as he stared at Liam's SUV. Placing his hands on the hood, he closed his eyes. "I'm sorry. I know you'll never understand and I'm asking the world of you. But you're the only person I trust to care for Raine and our baby. I know you'll love, protect, and provide a stable home for them. I love you, man. I'm going to miss you like hell."

Forcing himself to inch deeper into the garage, he stroked Raine's sports car. His guts twisted. Anguish, thick and black, layered over him, squeezing the air from his lungs.

As he closed his eyes once again, Raine's face filled his head. Her blue eyes shimmering with love, understanding, and compassion nearly took him out at the knees. She'd unknowingly been his lifeline for years. She'd given him the willpower to tuck away his guilt and regret so he could attempt to live again. Not for himself but for her. He'd tried to do right by her and give her a safe haven. For the most part, he'd succeeded. But now that act of kindness had come back to destroy him and their dreams.

"I'm sorry to leave you like this, precious," Hammer murmured softly. "But I love you too much to make you suffer. God knows I'm guilty of a lot of things, and maybe this is simply Karma coming back around to take its due. Don't ever doubt how much I love you. And while this has to be the end, you'll be with me forever—in this life and the next."

A single tear dropped to the hood of her car, the last piece of his physical being he would ever give her.

Hammer raised his head and wiped his cheek, then stared at the items in his hands.

The time had come to decide his own fate, to end this fucking nightmare on his own terms. His passport lay in his left hand, his car keys in his right.

Gazing at the passport, he figured he could fly to Indonesia or Nepal. Neither had extradition treaties with the U.S. He'd change his name and hair color, get lost in a chaotic city like Jakarta or Kathmandu. Neither Wellington nor any other federal asswipe would ever find him. Neither would Liam or Raine.

He would never see them again.

Never hear their greetings, laughter, or moans of ecstasy.

Never smell Liam's woodsy cologne or Raine's citrus shampoo and how they mingled together when he held them in his arms.

Never see their smiling faces, the twinkle in their eyes, or watch ecstasy flutter over their faces, wildly loving one another, fiercely and free.

Never see the beautiful child they'd all conceived together.

Hammer would be exiling himself to prison. Though one without bars, it would be a solitary confinement of pure hell just the same.

He swallowed tightly and gazed at his keys. Lifting his head, he stared at his Audi. He could imagine the shimmering chrome and sleek hood crumpled and mangled beyond recognition. Slamming into a bridge abutment at a hundred eighty-five miles an hour guaranteed total destruction, not only of his car but his body as well.

While that death might not be easy, it would be quick. Raine and Liam would at least have a sense of closure since they'd have something to bury.

If he simply disappeared without a trace, they would be left to wonder where he'd gone and if he might someday return.

Either way, Macen knew there was no coming back.

A fact that fucking ripped his heart out.

He told himself they'd grieve, but they would survive. Raine was resilient, and Liam was headstrong. They would lean on each other until time healed the wounds Hammer had gouged into their souls.

Rationally, he knew he had to sacrifice himself to save them. It was the only way he could stop the trial before it began and protect them and their child from a legacy of disgrace.

But the thought of leaving the only two people he'd ever loved crushed him like a wrecking ball. He felt his will start to crumble.

Please, God, give me strength to do this.

He sucked in a ragged breath.

"Passport or keys, fucker?" he whispered to himself. "Which one will be your final declaration of love to them?"

Prying his hands from Raine's car, Hammer stepped to his Audi. He opened the trunk, and a sad chuckle rolled off his lips. There lay a pair of Raine's sexy shoes she'd left in his car after dinner one night.

Scooping them up, he clutched them to his chest, then set them on her hood. Loving memories annihilated him, followed closely by an avalanche of guilt.

How could he simply throw away their unconditional love? Was he actually going to tuck tail and leave them like a coward? How would they ever forgive him? He, of all people, knew the devastation left in the wake of suicide.

Panic clutched his chest. Sweat streaked down his face.

What choice did he fucking have?

"Goddamn it!" Hammer roared as he wound up his entire body and heaved his keys with all his might—and fury—across the room.

They landed with a clatter somewhere in the corner, behind several boxes yet unpacked. His entire body shook with volcanic anger and fear. He felt as if he were being ripped in a million pieces. Six months ago, he wouldn't have thought twice about this decision. He probably could have managed it without too much second-guessing even a few weeks ago. But now? Now he couldn't find the courage to open the car door, let alone crawl inside and end this fucking torture.

Because you're not the same man you were then.

No. The man standing in this garage had finally learned how to love. Freely. Fully. Without the need to control or hold so much of himself back. He'd dismantled his walls, opened his heart, and spilled all his secrets. Then he invited Raine to climb inside him, where he'd suffused her with the truest devotion from the very depths of his soul.

And now you're going to walk out on her and never come back? You'll not only kill yourself but her and Liam, as well.

"Son of a bitch!" Hammer thundered.

A potent, white-hot blaze detonated inside him, blurring his vision. His composure disintegrated. His temper exploded.

Snatching the tire iron from the trunk, he stalked around his car. Fury rolled as Macen drew the weapon back with both hands and swung it full force into the driver's-side window. The safety glass fractured but held together. The shimmering, cracked web mirrored his disintegrating life.

Might as well get on with destroying it…

With a blistering curse, he belted it again, obliterating bits of hope and peace in shards all around the car.

Then Hammer turned his acid rage on the hood of the glossy vehicle. Over and over, he swung the tool, gouged the top, then the panels, before swerving onto the next pristine spot until he'd dented every visible surface. Still, he continued to grunt and curse as he unleashed a storm of resentment and panic.

Why couldn't he just do what he had to in order to save their futures?

Suddenly, the door to the garage burst open. He jerked his head to the sound. Liam thundered toward him, wearing nothing but a raging scowl.

Without a word, he yanked the tire iron out of Macen's hands and tossed it down before pulling him in for a crushing hug. "What the fuck do you think you're doing, you stupid son of a bitch? You don't get to fucking check out on us! I told you that."

Before he could reply, Liam slammed his fist into Macen's jaw with a jarring punch. The pain didn't register, only the anguish rolling off his friend in palpable waves.

Then he jerked Hammer back into his arms with a feral cry and gripped tight. "You bloody fool! Raine loves you. I love you, too. Christ, Macen. More than that, we need you. How the fuck is killing yourself or running away going to do us any good?"

"It's the only way to save you two, the baby…myself. Don't you get it?" he spit out, his voice raspy. "Our lives—all of them—will be ripped open for the whole world to judge. Raine… Oh, god. She'll either have to relive all the abuse her father heaped on her or admit she liked all the rough and dirty things I did to her for a room full of fucking strangers. I won't let her lower herself to save my sorry ass. I love her too much. You, too. I can't—"

"You stupid wanker! Do you honestly think Raine and I are so self-absorbed or weak that we wouldn't endure anything to have you with us? We don't give a shit about other people's opinions. Christ, man."

"Those cocksuckers have left us powerless." He pointed to the whole fucking world. "They've stripped away our control. I won't last thirty years in a goddamn cell. I'll go insane if I can't ever hold you both again. Or our child! Let me end this mess on my own terms. It's the only way to make things better for you and—"

The door to the garage opened again. Bryn stepped out, a pair of trousers dangling from her fingers.

"I thought your knackers might be getting a bit cold out here, son."

"I'm fine," Liam bit out but reached for the trousers.

She rolled her eyes. "You woke me from a sound sleep with your angry lightning bolts crashing all around the room. So I came out here to bring you some britches and bang your stubborn heads together until I've knocked sense into the pair of you."

Turning, Bryn pinned Hammer with a fierce stare. "Just what the devil do you think you're trying to prove, mister? You think breaking the hearts of your loved ones is going to make it all right, do you? Ha!"

Suddenly, Liam zipped his stare just above Hammer's shoulder. "What the... Mum?"

Bryn's mouth twitched as she gave him a knowing nod. "See her now, too, do you?"

"See who?" *Raine?* Hammer zipped his stare all over the garage but couldn't find her. He sure as hell didn't want her to see him coming apart like this. "What's going on?"

Liam ignored him. "No, but I can bloody well feel her."

"Who?" Hammer darted a glance over his shoulder to the spot where Liam and Bryn had fixed their gazes. He didn't see a damn thing.

"Juliet," Liam murmured.

Suddenly, Hammer couldn't breathe. "What?"

"She's standing right next to you, Macen," Bryn added softly. "And she's bloody well furious. The woman is yelling her head off at you."

His shoulders slumped. "I'm sure. No doubt she's been pissed at me for years."

"No." Bryn shook her head. "You've convinced yourself you failed her and stayed neck deep in guilt. She doesn't blame you. She's spitting the dummy because you're thinking about throwing away your life. She's screaming at you to stop."

Hammer scrubbed a hand over his face, trying to wrap his head around the fact that Bryn was supposedly seeing his dead wife in the damn garage at three in the morning. Jesus, he hadn't foreseen this at all when he'd come downstairs.

Of course, Bryn was a crafty woman. Maybe she'd invented Juliet's "visit" to help him release his guilt and persuade him to stay.

"You don't have to fabricate a reason to make me reconsider." Hammer sighed heavily.

"Ye of so little faith." Bryn clucked. "Remember your wedding night? You were in such a rush to get into bed with her that you broke your little toe on the bedframe?"

"How—" He blinked. Bryn had no way of knowing that. He'd never even told Liam that story.

"Juliet told me," Bryn explained. "She wants you to know she's here."

Hammer stood stock-still, stunned. His late wife really had come from the other side with some fucking message for him?

"Yes. She's insisting that you'll not make the same mistake she did." Bryn crossed her arms stubbornly.

"It wasn't her mistake. I drove her to suicide," Hammer argued. "This is different."

Bryn poked him in the chest. "Dead is dead." She paused as if letting her words soak into Hammer's brain. "She wants me to tell you she's sorry for hurting you deeply and never telling you the truth."

"About what? The baby?"

"All the secrets she hid from you." Bryn shook her head. "So many of them. Juliet has refused to move on all these years because she wants to set things right with you."

"I'm the one who pushed her past her limits. Kept driving her to the edge over and over, until she finally fell."

"No." Bryn cupped his hands in hers. "Let her go, Macen. You've both feasted on each other's misery long enough. Her death was never your fault. Juliet had her own problems. She suffered from depression and schizophrenia before she met you. She never told you or confessed that she'd tried to kill herself twice as a teenager. She was ashamed and didn't want to drive you away."

Hammer's heart stopped. "She'd attempted suicide before?"

"Yes. She kept that to herself, along with the prescriptions she took to regulate the chemicals in her brain. But when she found out she was pregnant, she stopped taking everything because of the risk to the baby."

"What?" Hammer tried to wrap his head around that. "Why didn't she ever tell me?"

"Oh, because she was sick. Without the medicine, she struggled to discern real from imaginary." Bryn's expression begged him to understand.

"She could have told me about the baby. Or did she think that was imaginary, as well?" Hammer railed.

"She's crying." Bryn frowned.

"I feel her, mate," Liam added. "She's devastated she hurt you so much."

"I carried all this fucking guilt for nine goddamn years. Shut out my best friend so I wouldn't have to..." Hammer paused and grabbed the tire iron off the floor.

Liam wrenched it out of his hand again and pinned him with a narrow-eyed stare. "I know why you shied away from me, Macen. But we've not had too much trouble making up for lost time, now, have we? Isn't the best life we've ever imagined right in front of us?"

Hammer turned Liam's words over in his head. Sorrow, regret, so much fucking sadness—they all strangled him, choking away his veneer.

He wrapped Liam in a hug. "Christ, I'm so fucking sorry."

"I know. We're fine, you and I." He slapped Macen's back. "Does Juliet have anything else to say, Mum?"

"She has a message for you, as well, son." Bryn's eyes softened. "She's also apologizing to you. None of this was your fault. She lied to you, too. The baby was Hammer's, love."

Liam zipped a stare at Macen.

Hammer took the news in stony silence, but shock reverberated through his whole body. Still, somewhere in his head, he knew he couldn't keep berating himself for what she'd chosen not to share. And he couldn't be angry because she hadn't comprehended what was real. And being furious with fate did no good. It just was.

For once, Macen did nothing but wish they all could have been happier.

"Macen, there was nothing you could have done to change Juliet's choice," Bryn promised. "She regrets it now and wants you to stop thinking about ending your life, whether figuratively or literally. She doesn't regret a moment of the time you spent together or the way you two spent it. She loved you as best she could and wants you happy. That's why she steered Raine to your alley all those years ago."

"She...what?" Hammer blinked.

The wife he'd spent years believing he'd destroyed had given him the greatest gift of his life?

"Aye. Juliet knew you'd save Raine. And you did," Bryn murmured. "She's proud of you for protecting and encouraging your girl. Especially for falling in love with her. Though your wife has spent more than a year or two spitting mad at you because you were supposed to focus on Raine and stop blaming yourself for her death. She's begging you to throw away that excess baggage now and be happy. Give Raine and Liam all the love in your heart and start accepting theirs in return."

Tears stung his eyes. He blinked them back.

"She says she expects you to succeed because you're too stubborn to fail." Bryn looked up at Hammer, who couldn't help but laugh. "She's just kissed your cheek and whispered her thanks."

Something shifted inside him. Understanding? Gratitude? He wasn't sure, but the weight he'd felt strapped across his back for nearly a decade suddenly lifted. He felt...liberated.

Then both Liam and Bryn lifted their eyes toward the heavens and smiled.

"She's leaving now," Liam whispered.

Bryn nodded. "Honor her and do as she asked. She's free. You need to be, as well."

Hammer reached out and dragged both Bryn and Liam into his

arms. With his head buried between their shoulders, Hammer inhaled a shaky breath. "Thank you both for saving my life."

"That's what friends are for." Liam slapped Hammer on the back.

"Thank christ," he murmured.

When they pulled away, Liam arched his brows as he took in the state of Hammer's car. "I think you'll need a bit more than wax to fix that, mate."

Hammer turned and gaped at the mangled metal that had once been his Audi. "Fuck. Guess I need a new car."

"I'd surely haul that one out of here before Raine gets a peek at it."

Every muscle in his body tensed. "What the hell am I going to tell her?"

Liam's expression turned serious. "I know we've sworn an oath of honesty with our girl, and I'd tell her most anything else, but…"

Hammer shook his head. "If she ever finds out what I nearly did tonight, it would do more than crush her. She would never under-stand."

"Ever."

"It would change everything between us."

"You're right. We should take this episode to our graves, brother. Mum?" Liam gave a sideways glance at his mother.

"I wasn't even here when Hammer decided to take out his frustra-tions on his poor, helpless car." Bryn smiled. "In fact, I've been in bed all this time. But I'm warning you both, no more antics till morning. I need my beauty sleep."

Bryn kissed both their cheeks and left. As they watched her retreat into the house, Liam slung his arm around Hammer's shoulders.

"I'm sorry," Macen choked out. "I damn near fucked everything up again. Forever."

"And you were sober, too," he joked. "Come on, let's head to the pool, tip back a few, and talk. I'll fill your head with common sense—one more time—and I'll use the bloody tire iron if I have to."

"Fuck, I need a drink or two."

"More like a bottle." Liam glanced back over his shoulder. "And I think I'll install a punching bag so we don't have to keep buying new cars."

Hammer sighed. "I lost my shit."

"It's okay. You've been wired too tight for years. I'm sure that did you a world of good."

Macen rubbed his chin sheepishly. "I think it might have."

"I'll grab some bottles and meet you on the back patio. All right?"

"That sounds more than all right."

Suddenly, Liam bent and started patting Hammer's pockets.

He jumped back and scowled. "What the fuck are you doing?"

"Making sure you've not got any bricks shoved in your pants, in case you were thinking about diving into the pool and settling on the bottom."

"No, man. You and your mom already hauled me out of the deep end. I won't ever go back there again."

CHAPTER FIFTEEN

Wednesday, February 20

"ALL RIGHT. ALL right. Hold your water..."

Liam strode to the door and peeked through the hole to ensure a reporter hadn't rung the bell. When he saw a somber Sterling Barnes on the porch, he felt his heart lurch.

Bloody hell. What now?

He opened the door. The late-afternoon sun slanted through as he shook the man's offered hand in greeting, stepped back, and ushered him inside. "Barnes. Come in. Though by the looks of it, man, you've come with more bad news." Dread rolled through Liam. "If that's the case, you're best off telling me. Hammer can't take more now."

"Actually, I do have some rather disturbing news, but I'm afraid it's for you."

Liam stopped in his tracks. If someone had decided to charge him for a crime because he'd touched Raine, why hadn't his mother warned him? Hell, why hadn't he felt trouble coming himself? "I'd best get a drink, then."

Sterling appeared even more somber. "Actually, I'd like to speak with you and Macen together. Is he here?"

"Out here, Sterling," Hammer called.

"Where?"

Liam led the way. "By the pool. We're tipping back a few. Are you done for the day? Would you like something to drink?"

Sterling considered the question for all of two seconds, then dropped the heavy briefcase and loosened the knot of his tie. "I don't mind if I do. Whiskey?"

Liam cocked a brow. "Irish or Scotch?"

Barnes gave him a rare smile. "Irish, of course. Thanks, Liam. No ice. I know the way."

By the time Liam joined the two men out on the patio, they were comfortably seated, making small talk while awaiting his return. He passed Sterling his drink, then returned to the seat opposite Hammer. Both men faced the graying lawyer expectantly.

"To good health." Barnes raised his glass and saluted them before taking an appreciative sip. "Oh, that is good. Thank you. Where's Raine?"

"Out shopping with my parents. We have the place to ourselves."

Sterling nodded. "Then let's get down to business, shall we?"

"Tell us what's going on." Hammer gave him an anxious glance. "Any news about the witness?"

Barnes gave them a pensive frown. "Nothing. I'd really like to know who this omnipotent someone is myself."

Hammer and Liam glanced at one another, suspicion ripe. They were on the same page, as usual. Together, they leaned forward in their chairs.

Hammer frowned. "What the…"

"Hell? That's what I'd like to know." Barnes held up a hand. "But nothing about this case or the way the AUSA has gone about it makes any sense."

"How is the prosecution withholding the identity of their star witness legal? I thought that was the whole purpose of discovery."

Barnes paused to sip of his whiskey. "Technically, they have time to disclose all the details. As long as I get everything before the trial itself…"

Liam looked at him incredulously. "You're joking, surely."

"No. But as a matter of expediency, they usually send over one file with all the information we need. Of course, if they gather more after discovery starts, they send that on as it becomes known, so some things are more last-minute. But feds are notorious for investigating thoroughly so that by the time they charge someone, they've got all their evidence in order. They certainly know the name of their damn witness and have for some time."

"Then why hide their identity? Unless, of course, it's someone with a grudge against Macen." Liam rested his elbows between his spread legs, dangling his drink.

Hammer snorted. "Isn't that a good question? Let me guess.

Because then we'd know who the fucker is."

"At this point, that's my assumption," the lawyer agreed.

"Whoever it is has really screwed me well," Macen quipped. "They aren't leaving anything to chance. No, sir. This fucker has an axe to grind."

"I haven't heard any fat lady singing, mate." Liam put a bracing hand on his shoulder. "Don't give up yet."

Sterling rolled his glass thoughtfully before speaking. "It's particularly important that I know what this witness intends to say in their testimony because the FBI found nothing during the search they conducted of your home or your business, Macen."

"I didn't expect them to."

"As far as potential state charges go, I'm actually looking forward to learning precisely who found—or rather, stole—that video footage. If my motion to have it marked as inadmissible flies, then they'll have absolutely nothing," Sterling reassured.

"As it damn well should be," Hammer growled. "It was a private moment between two consenting adults in love."

Sterling shrugged like he didn't understand their expression of affection, but it was none of his business. "I'm here for a different reason altogether. This is where you come in, Liam."

Hammer exchanged another glance with his friend before looking back at Barnes.

"The AUSA decided it might be a good idea to interview your ex-wife because of her association with William Kendall. At this point, I'm assuming their intention was to glean more information from Gwyneth in the hopes she could help them support the charges against Macen."

"And?" Hammer drawled, looking tense. "What did the nasty bitch have to say about me this time?"

"Nothing. Liam, I'm sorry to inform you that your ex-wife apparently got into an altercation with another prisoner in the cafeteria— over pudding, of all things—and was shanked. She's dead."

Liam peered at the lawyer. He couldn't possibly have heard that right. "Did you say—"

"Halle-fucking-lu-jah! There is a God after all!" Hammer jumped to his feet with a whoop.

"She's dead?" Liam blinked again.

"Yes," Sterling confirmed.

"Shanked over pudding. That's priceless. It couldn't have happened to someone more deserving."

Liam leapt to his feet, grabbing Hammer in a fierce hug. "Really? Oh, that's the best news I've had in ages."

With a startled frown, Barnes sat back abruptly, glancing between the two men. "Gentlemen, is this really cause for celebration?"

Hammer grabbed the lawyer's shoulder. "Since Gwyneth, that spiteful, self-centered, pretentious, conniving bitch, all but handed Raine to her raping, murdering father, absolutely."

"I can't fucking believe it! Ding dong, the witch is dead!" Liam cheered. "Wait until we tell Raine."

Sterling stood with a wry grin. "Don't trouble yourselves seeing me out. I know the way. Enjoy your…celebration. Good night, gentlemen."

Relief poured through Liam. Rather than Gwyneth potentially returning with a vengeance in the next five years to give them hell, he'd never have to worry about her again. Why hadn't he known already? Why hadn't his mother picked up on Gwyneth's death? Because she wasn't meaningful enough? Had she ever been?

Liam shook his head. He tried to think of one time—just one—when he'd been truly happy with Gwyneth. He couldn't do it. All he saw was Raine, Hammer, and the life they were building together. That's all that mattered to him. That's what he would fight for.

Mentally, he committed Gwyneth to ash—where she belonged.

RAINE SIGHED AS she looked at Seth and River across Hammer's desk at Shadows. Dusk was approaching. They'd been looking for needles in the membership haystack for hours. Time was running out.

"This is the third time we've been through this database. Seriously, I can't think of anyone who fits the description. A thirtysomething blonde who joined the club when it first opened and then—years later—suddenly decided she hates Hammer. There's just…no one. Who the hell could this witness be?"

"And why doesn't Sterling have a name from the prosecution yet?" Seth mused.

"Hang on. How do we know Liam's mom isn't full of shit?" River asked. "No offense, but how would she know anything about this witness if no one else has any idea?"

If Liam had told her about his family before they arrived, she would have been skeptical, too. But she'd seen Bryn in action now. Raine glanced over at Seth.

The big PI nodded. "She just does."

She patted her brother's big shoulder. "Trust us. But that leaves us nowhere."

Seth tapped on his computer, which they'd hooked up to the club's cloud to dive through the database. "Well, we could try again."

"Ugh, my eyes would cross." She jumped out of Hammer's massive desk chair and paced his office. "Maybe we're being too literal."

River frowned. "What do you mean? You just said that Liam's mom thinks our witness is a blonde and that she has to be right."

"Yeah." Raine nodded. "I think she is, and we should go with that. Bryn also said that whoever wants to ruin Macen is a woman scorned. Everything else...maybe we toss that out and think a little more broadly. I know it's supposed to be someone who supposedly saw Hammer 'rape' me as a child, but does it have to be?"

Both men opened their mouths to rebut her.

Her brother frowned. "Storm cloud—"

"Just hear me out. A man would look at this logically. It's black or white. It's up or down. She saw the crime or she didn't. But a woman who feels scorned might be more flexible with the truth, especially if she wasn't well hinged in the first place."

Seth and River both looked at one another. She saw their light bulbs go off.

"You're saying bitch be crazy?" Seth asked. "Yeah. I've trailed absolutely psycho-ass chicks for cases back in New York. Some of these women made that home-wrecker in *Fatal Attraction* look sane. Go on."

River turned to him. "Seriously?"

"How do you not know this?"

"Go spend ten years in Afghanistan. Every female out there is either wearing a military uniform or a burka. Not a lot of interaction, if you get my meaning."

Seth shook his head. "Oh, you need an education about the fairer sex."

River scowled. "I know my way around a woman."

"Can we focus?" Raine chewed on a ragged nail. "If we're looking for a blonde member in her thirties who felt scorned and is mental, only one person comes to mind. She's been sticking in the back of my head since we talked on Sunday. We even dismissed her...but I'm starting to think we're being too hasty."

"The bitch who hit you?" River asked.

"That one." Raine nodded. "Marlie."

"I never met her." Seth sent her a measuring glance. "Still have that footage? I'd like to see it."

Raine smiled grimly. "Looking to gage her crazy?"

"Something like that." Seth nodded. "I usually have a good sense about people."

River sat back. "Yeah, I want to see that shit, too. But are you thinking this chick just...made up whatever Hammer supposedly did to you as a minor?"

"Maybe. I don't know," she said honestly. "But the copies of the money orders, together with whatever she said, convinced the feds there was smoke at least. They found the photos of teenage me following Bill's beating after..."

"You sliced the mean son of a bitch in two?" River rubbed at her back, both giving her comfort and expressing his pride. "If you're right, the feds started putting a case together then. But if Marlie didn't actually see anything, how does she think she's going to get on the witness stand and give testimony convincing enough to put Hammer away?"

"You mean besides perjure herself?" Raine shot back. "It's her word against his."

"But she wasn't a member then," River pointed out.

"Raine is right. It doesn't matter." Seth shrugged. "The feds never said this witness actually *saw* the event take place. A witness can testify that the defendant *told* them something incriminating. Maybe Marlie was going to claim that Hammer confessed to her that he'd had sex with you as a minor or had taken those pictures of your abuse."

"But wouldn't she have to prove it?" River frowned.

Raine paced again. "Not really. The circumstantial evidence looks bad. No jury in the world is going to listen to testimony like that and just dismiss her, especially since her parents are pillars of the community or some shit."

Seth shot her a glare. "You know—"

"Liam hates language. Got it. C'mon. We have to focus. If I'm a juror, and someone tells me the owner of a sex club had a minor living there and he'd been paying her dad a lot of money for years and just happened to have pictures of her that depicted nudity…not sure I'd believe he's a good guy, either."

"Exactly. Especially since you're pretty, young, and pregnant."

"Hey, that's my sister," River piped up.

Seth shrugged. "I've already seen her naked. If I were going to jump her bones, I would have done it by now."

"What the fuck?" Her brother leapt to his feet, then shot her an accusing glance. "So I was right."

Raine sighed. "It doesn't matter. We didn't have sex, and I don't have any new and different girl parts he's never seen. Get over your thing about my nudity already."

"Hey, how are those affirmations coming?" Seth teased.

Raine rolled her eyes. "I can even recite them with a smile. Number one: 'I will open myself up and share, not only my needs but my emotions.' Number two: 'I will be totally honest at all times without fear of embarrassment or reprisal. Nor will I hold back for fear of hurting someone's feelings.' Number three: 'I deserve happiness and love.' There."

"I'm impressed," Seth admitted.

River just looked confused. "You didn't know all that?"

Raine grimaced. "Back then? Not really."

"Not at all," Seth corrected.

She glared at him. "Hammer and Liam insisted I learn. Seth was my mentor. Seriously, can we focus?"

"Your tone is bossy, little one."

Sometimes she thought of Seth as her buddy…and she forgot he was a Dom. "Sorry. I'm anxious."

He nodded and let it go. "Actually, I think you're on to something.

Let's watch the video."

With a nod, she led them both down the hall to the security room and unlocked the door. Seth and River stood just outside since the little booth was too small for everyone. Lewis, the tech, looked up at her, startled. Frankly, she was surprised to see him, too.

"You're here really early," she observed.

He blanked the humiliation scene on the monitor he'd been watching. "Yeah. Um…things to do."

More like he had his weenie to whack.

Raine tried not to gag. Lewis gave her the creeps. He always stared, not just at her but at most of the women around Shadows.

"You want something?" His stare walked all over her.

She acted as if she had no idea he was thinking perverted things about her right now. "I just need to see a security video. I know where to find it. Don't mind me."

"You sure? I'll help you."

"I'm good." She pulled open the drawer behind the desk, acutely aware that in order to see the labels, she had to bend over and practically put her butt in his face. Not a good idea. She twisted to the side, ass facing the door, and tuned him out.

"What are you looking for, Raine?"

Damn, he was nosy. "I've just about found it. As you were."

Beside her, his chair squeaked as he rolled closer. She tried not to shudder. Was he really staring at her boobs?

The drives holding November third and fourth were gone; she knew that. Thankfully, the fifth was exactly where it should be. She was just about to pluck it up when Lewis stood.

"Found what?" he murmured, inching closer, then behind her. "That video of Liam plowing your fine ass?"

Raine stiffened. He had not just said that. She stood, turned, and saw the proposition on his face. Yeah, he had.

"That's one of my favorites. I'm glad it's still on the cloud." His whisper got lower as he tried to get closer. "I watch that one a lot."

"Don't." She shook her head.

He dared to lean in and give her what he supposed was a come-on grin. "What? You know, if you like anal, I'll give it to you, sweet thing. I'd fuck you better than those dudes in their thirties. You and I are the same age, and I can go all night. Now that Hammer is going to jail, if you need someone to keep you packed tight, I'd love the chance"—he curled his palm around her hip—"to get all up in you."

Raine blinked at him, her temper spiraling up, swirling faster, until she felt like it might blow off the top of her head. She shoved his hand away and kneed him in the balls, then stomped on his instep with her little kitten heels.

When he bent over, clutching his gonads and moaning like he couldn't breathe, she grabbed his hair and tugged his eyes up to her. "Are you fucking kidding me? First, that's the most disgusting come-on ever, and you've got to be the most annoying twit to ever proposition me. Second, I'm pregnant and in a committed relationship with two men I love—one of whom is your boss. Third…" She smiled. "You're fired."

"You can't do that," he challenged, apparently finding his guts—and his balls. "You don't have that power."

She plucked her disposable phone from her pocket. "You know what? Maybe you're right and I should just call Hammer now to come down to fire you himself. He's in a great mood after spending last weekend in jail. And he's not at all possessive of me…"

The little shit finally got smart enough to blanch. "Wait. You came in here wearing that little skirt and stuck your ass in my face. What was I supposed to think besides that you were hot for me?"

Slimy bastard. "That I'm your boss's girlfriend, who was simply looking for a video in a small room I didn't even expect you to be in. That I'm a woman—not a piece of ass—and I should be treated with respect. That Shadows isn't a porn hub or a hook-up spot." She raised a brow at him. "That I'll let Hammer and Liam make you learn to respect the fairer sex."

Lewis looked ready to piss himself. "Don't—"

"Or you can grab your shit and get out of here right now."

He cursed but he started gathering his stuff. "Bitch."

"Make sure you say that again on your way out. There are two guys right outside the door who would be deeply interested in your opinion. You know Seth. He used to be a cop. The big one who's six foot five and spent ten years in combat? He's my brother."

The tech nerd paled even more and shoved his belongings in his pockets faster. "I'm leaving now."

"Good decision. Don't come back." Raine crossed her arms over her chest as he ran out of the room. She followed, watching him give Seth and River a wide berth as he hurried down the hall. A moment later, the front door shut with a resounding slam behind him.

She smiled and grabbed the drive from the drawer. Someone else would have to man the booth tonight—maybe she could sweet-talk Seth into it—but it was a relief to have Lewis the slimebag gone. Absently, she wondered if he'd had something to do with the disappearance of two days of surveillance recordings.

"What the hell happened to him?" Seth stared.

"I fired him."

"For watching the footage? He's been doing that since I arrived. I think he jacks off a bunch in there."

The image made Raine shudder. "Not anymore. I might have suggested that his anal sex proposition would not be well received by Hammer and Liam. He might have then intimated that I'm a female dog in heat. I told him to repeat that in front of you guys…but yeah, he seemed really disinclined."

River shook his head. "He's lucky he left. I would have ripped his head from his body and spit down his throat."

"Which is why I didn't tell you sooner. I don't want to clean up blood, and we really need to focus." She turned to Seth. "Before you ask, yes, I'll tell Hammer and Liam as soon as we're done here. Can you fill in for Lewis tonight? Pretty please."

Seth just laughed. "Look at you, batting those lashes over your big blue eyes. God, I'm a sucker. All right."

She stood on her tiptoes and kissed his cheek. "Thanks. Maybe I'll stop by the hospital and find Heavenly, tell her what a great guy you are."

He looked at her as if that possibility had never occurred to him and he liked his chances with the nurse volunteer if Raine talked him up. "Would you?"

She led them back to Hammer's office with a laugh, then inserted the drive into the USB port of Seth's computer, fast-forwarding to the footage in the alley. Once she found Marlie following her out, cursing her existence, and slapping her, she stopped the video.

"What a cunt," Seth spit out.

"Pretty but…a fucking bitch." River sighed. "I see what you mean about hating you."

Seth nodded. "Absolutely. And not having the firmest grasp on reality."

"She's pretty damn entitled," her brother added.

"Because she's the sort of woman who's had every man she's ever wanted her whole life. Why should Hammer be different?" She gasped and pressed her hand to her chest, imitating Marlie. "How could a perfect Barbie lose him to mere white trash?"

River cracked up.

Raine joined in the laughter. "Unfortunately, this footage only proves that she hit me once. Liam blessed her out. Ugly. I've hardly ever seen him so angry. Hammer took her aside. I'm sure he had choice words before he had her permanently removed. And everyone clapped."

"I like her as a suspect, Raine," Seth said. "I just don't know how we figure out whether she's guilty or not. We can't go to the police with a hunch."

Yeah, because everyone investigating this case had already made up their minds.

An idea rolled around in her head. Raine glanced between Seth and River. They'd object, but she was right, damn it. "Let me talk to her."

"What?" They both turned to her in unison.

"No." Seth shook his head.

"Hell no," River put in. "She could be dangerous. If she's got a gun—"

"She doesn't," Raine assured. "I'll see her in public, surrounded by people. If I lead her into a conversation, provoke her a little…"

"No matter how you incite her, I doubt she'll confess anything to you." Seth sounded like the voice of reason.

"You're right, and that's okay. See, you only understand how to get women into bed. You don't understand how they really operate."

"Do tell," he drawled.

"Yeah, I want to hear this." River leaned forward like he was hanging on every word.

"Women like her aren't that different from the playground bullies you grew up with. They're all tough and full of themselves—until you call their bluff. I won't challenge her. If I actually got her to confess, she might do something drastic—try to hurt me or go into hiding or...I don't know. But if I poke her temper and dance around the subject, I'll bet she's so proud of what she's done. Something will show on her face. I'll see it."

They were both quiet for a long moment. Their expressions said they weren't thrilled.

Raine went in for the kill. "You got a better idea?"

Seth looked at River with a grimace. Her brother sighed.

The answer neither of them wanted to admit was no.

"We'll have to talk to Liam and Hammer first. I won't put you in her path—"

"We can't tell them." Raine grabbed his shoulder and willed him to understand.

"I'm not your Dom, and risking you without their knowledge or consent is damn irresponsible."

Okay. Good point. "It's all right. I'll go alone."

"Over my dead body." Seth didn't even blink at her.

"I'm with him on that," River said. "No."

"This is my family and my future. I'll do whatever I have to." Raine wanted to stamp her foot. "I just can't ask their permission. I don't want to get their hopes up unless I know I'm on to something. Macen is... Something is really wrong. He came home on Monday and—" Raine wasn't even sure how to explain without saying too much. "He opened up to me in a way he never has. It was amazing but...he hasn't been himself since. He's frustrated, angry, withdrawn. I'm not supposed to see that but I can't help it. I'm scared. And Liam has had to shoulder so much since this nightmare began. He's constantly worried about me and the baby while trying to figure out how to keep Hammer out of prison, juggle his parents... I can't lay more on him."

"They would want you to," Seth pushed back.

"And I love them for it...but I won't do it."

"If you're not comfortable with this idea, man, it's cool." River shrugged. "I'll go with your hunch, storm cloud. It's our only lead and our best shot right now. I'll take you to find Marlie. What the hell?

Liam and Hammer aren't fond of me anyway."

Raine turned to her brother. "Really? I mean, I could go alone, but I would feel better if I didn't have to face the crazy cunt without backup."

River pulled her into his lap and hugged her. "I wouldn't want you to."

"Thanks, big brother."

"Oh, all right." Seth sighed and shot her an irritated glance. "I'll go."

She smiled his way. "If this doesn't work, then the secret is safe with me."

He glared. "What's your plan?"

Raine gave it some thought. "Can you track her down, find out what skank bar she's likely to be in tonight? I'm going to go put myself together."

"You look fine." River frowned.

"But do I look pregnant?"

Neither said anything for a moment as they scanned her figure. Finally, Seth answered, "A little. You've got a tiny bump that didn't use to be there."

"A little isn't going to cut it. I'll be back."

Raine helped herself to the bathroom in her old room. Thankfully, Hammer had left the place intact, despite remodeling so many of the others. She was also grateful that she had left behind a few cosmetics and hair implements to freshen up after working…or playing. Bryn taking her shopping and insisting on buying her a maternity dress earlier today had been serendipitous—or her own brand of thinking ahead.

Thirty minutes later, she stepped back into Hammer's office. River and Seth both dropped their jaws.

"Do I look pregnant now?" she asked, gazing down at the high-waisted red dress as she smoothed a hand over her belly.

"Yeah," they both answered.

She tossed her freshly curled hair and lifted her red-painted lips. "Did you find her?"

Seth hesitated, like he'd decided this was a bad idea after all. "What if I said no?"

"I'd look for her myself."

He groaned. "Why can't you be less persistent?"

"Because that's not going to get the job done." She grabbed his arm. "Let's go."

It only took fifteen minutes to reach the happy hour of Marlie's choice.

Just outside the door, Seth and River planted themselves, looking inside through picture windows. The place didn't look crowded yet; it was early. People were just getting off work. But she spotted the leggy blonde in a green hooker dress she would probably say matched her eyes, sipping a glass of wine.

"You can keep an eye on things from here, right?" Raine asked.

Seth hedged. "We should go in with you."

"No. You two would distract her. She'd flirt with you and ignore me. Stay here."

"I don't love this." Seth looked pissed. "But I get your point."

"If you need an exit strategy, there's a back door through that employee entrance to the kitchen at the far end of the room," River pointed out.

Marlie was a skank, not a terrorist. But Raine found the guys amusing. "Got it. I'll be in and out in five minutes."

Raine headed for the door, but River pulled her back. "Do you know what you're going to say?"

"Not exactly, but I have a plan."

"That's scary," Seth muttered.

"I heard that." She laughed as she walked inside.

"Be careful," they both murmured.

She nodded. But the minute the door closed behind her, shit got real. Raine dragged in a breath. She had to play this smart and cool. She wasn't nervous about seeing Marlie. But the stakes were high. This one conversation might determine whether or not her new and growing family stayed together.

Stop psyching yourself out.

Marlie might have more experience with men and life, but under it all, she was motivated by vanity. She was a terrible liar and she was even worse at controlling her emotions. And she'd never see this blindside coming. Raine had no problem exploiting any of that.

Lifting her chin, she headed to the bar with a toss of her hair and a sway of her hips. When she reached the long marble surface, a bartender leaned over as Raine stood on her tiptoes to sit on the stool. Being five feet tall sucked.

"Can I get you something?"

She felt Marlie's eyes on her and pretended she'd taken no notice of the woman. "Just a club soda with a twist." She dropped her hand to her belly. "I can't drink for two, right?"

"Sure thing." The bartender scurried away.

Then Raine turned and acknowledged Marlie with a roll of her eyes. "Oh, of all people…"

"Why are you here?" The Barbie looked at her as if she were a lower life form, then stared in horror at her belly.

"I'm waiting on some people."

Marlie tried to frown around her Botox. "You don't have any friends."

"Where are yours?" Raine looked around the dim, industrial-chic environment in question.

No one stood near Marlie.

The woman bristled. "I just stopped in for a drink."

"Alone. Still haven't found a man who can stand you, huh?"

The bartender set down her soda, and Raine paid the guy, smiling. She tried to ignore her shaking hands.

"I date plenty," Marlie defended.

Raine cocked her head. "Funny how nobody wants to stay."

Marlie scowled. "Why am I even talking to you? Go away."

"I have just as much right to sit here as you do. If you don't want to deal with me, you go somewhere else."

"I got here first."

Raine took a drink and tried not to laugh. "That's the best you've got? Are you five?"

Marlie's eyes narrowed meanly. "Did that Irishman knock you up and leave you?"

"Liam…" Raine shrugged. "Or Hammer. We don't know. We don't care. I'm with them both. We live together now." She leaned in. "We're really happy. In fact, Hammer hasn't touched anyone else since our first time together. He's very committed and he loves me."

The Barbie looked as if Raine had slapped her across the face. "That's impossible."

"It's not." She stroked her belly again. "He proposed to me. I can already tell he'll be a great husband." She stared into the distance with a dreamy expression. "Protective, passionate, indulgent, kind, passionate... Oh, I said that. Oops."

Marlie hopped off her stool. "You're lying. Your life isn't perfect, and I know it."

And there it was, the malicious glee on the crazy whore's face. She knew exactly what was happening in Macen's life, and she seethed with righteous anger because she couldn't stand the idea that he'd thrown her over for someone she saw as inferior. She was calling Raine's bluff.

Raine couldn't afford to put her cards on the table...yet. But oh, really soon.

"No, not perfect," she admitted. "So I'm leaving to work on that. Enjoy your night alone."

Standing again, Raine smiled. She strolled out of the bar and right into Seth's and River's waiting stares.

"Well?" her brother asked.

"She's guilty as fuck. Let's take this bitch down."

CHAPTER SIXTEEN

Thursday, February 21

"SO YOU'VE SET up the audio and video feeds, right?" River asked Seth.

The big blond PI simply stared off into space, wearing a crooked smile. River snapped his fingers. "Earth to Seth. Are you in there, man?"

Seth blinked. "Huh? Yeah, I'm good."

"I didn't ask if you were good. I asked if everything was set up."

"Sorry. I was thinking."

"About Heavenly. Again?"

"Yeah." Seth sounded like a love-sick schoolgirl.

"You toss away your man card every time you see her." River shook his head. "Thankfully, we're going to get you laid tonight."

Seth blanched. "About that… I can't be your wingman."

River gaped at him. "We're supposed to tag team this bimbo, remember? I was looking forward to finding out what the big deal is about two-on-one action."

"Eh. I tried it. With Liam. Years ago." Seth shrugged. "It's intense but not my thing. Too much swinging junk."

River had always thought he was open-minded, but these guys seemed to have done nearly everything at least once. "Don't bullshit me. You changed your mind because you're in knots over some girl you've never even kissed."

Seth glared but didn't refute him. So he'd lied to Beck about that. Apparently their competition had moved beyond the "friendly" stage.

"I gave up on Heavenly too quickly before I went back to New York. There's something between us."

"If you start singing "Endless Love," I'm going to throat punch you. I can't believe you're turning down a sure thing on the off-chance

Miss Keeping-My-Legs-Crossed might cure your blue balls."

"First, it *will* happen. Second, you don't get it because you've never met her."

"Even if I had, I'd still take the easy pussy." River shrugged.

"You say that now, but when you meet someone you're interested in spending time with *after* the orgasm, it's different. I gave up playtime with a sub I kind of liked for Heavenly. Why would I risk what I could have with a woman I see a future with for a piece of ass with a she-dragon who's probably fucked up a friend's life?"

Whatever. River was a fighter, not a lover. "Yeah, well… I've spent too many nights in Afghanistan being romantic with my fist, so I'm going to make up for years of self-pleasure and fuck this bitch's lights out."

"Go for it, soldier. I'll stay safely behind enemy lines, recording every grunt and thrust. I'll even make you a copy of the tape for your spank bank. I'm sure it's large and distinguished."

"Just like my cock." River grinned.

Seth placed a palm on his stomach. "Spare me. I don't want to puke on your boots."

River rolled his eyes.

"When you bring her to the room, get her on the bed as fast as you can," Seth instructed. "The ropes are already attached to the frame, so all you have to do is pull them up, slip her wrists and ankles through the loops, then cinch them. Not too tight—you don't want to cut off the circulation—but not so loose that she can slap you if she figures out why you're really hooking up with her."

"You made your Doms for Dummies tutorial really clear. I got it."

"Good man. I hope you brought more than one condom."

River arched his brows. "Of course. Who knows how many times I'll have to get between her thighs to make her talk?"

"Don't know. Just be prepared. She seemed like a looker, but I hear she's been plowed more than a wheat field in Nebraska. You might want to glove up twice, just in case she's carrying some dick-dissolving disease."

"Thanks. I'll double bag."

"Good. If you're going to take one for the team, you don't want to be regifting anything nasty to your next conquest, like a bad fruitcake at Christmas."

"You're sure she'll be in the bar downstairs, right?"

"Yep." Seth nodded "According to her social media, this hotel bar is her Thursday evening watering hole. A little Google mapping tells me it's close to the financial district, which is an environment rich in both men and money. Supposedly, she's meeting people later, so she's arriving early to stalk her prey—I mean, grab a table. You'll have to work fast and get 'er done before then."

"Got it." River nodded. "Walk me through all these high-tech gadgets. I don't want to fuck anything up. This may be the only chance I get to make things right with my sister and her, um…"

"Doms or lovers," Seth supplied. "I'm sure either is cool with them. But they've both asked to be her husband."

"Seriously?" That surprised River. "Then why isn't she getting married? Did Raine turn them down?"

"Yep."

"She has the power to say no?"

Seth reared back. "Absolutely. Normally I'd tell you to butt out of their business, but I get being worried about family. Your sister isn't a slave, and she doesn't give them her control because she's weak. Raine may look delicate. Emotionally, I've seen her fragile. But she has a damn strong will."

"Then why is she into the whole submission thing?"

"Hang around for a while and you might understand. But I promise you, your sister has tons of power over those two. The first time I met her?" Seth laughed. "She'd left them both without a word because they were former best friends bickering over her like idiots. For two days, they searched for her—together. While she was hanging at Beck's place, cozying up to a bottle of Cuervo—and oh—beating the shit out of your dad, Hammer and Liam were finally having the first civil conversation they'd managed since allowing her to come between them. When she came back, Raine handed them their balls. They got their shit together fast after that. Otherwise, she'd made it clear they were both going to lose her. You look shocked."

"Yeah. I watched them chastise her for coming to visit her own damn brother. She knelt at their feet and…" River shuddered. "Ugh."

"Yeah, I guess you'd see that, but let me give you the Dominant interpretation of that day. Their pregnant submissive put herself in potential danger without their protection or permission. It's their job to keep her safe, and she agreed to their boundaries. But to see you, she risked everything. If you still don't think that's a big deal, they were both ready to kill you after that stunt you pulled at the spa. So, yeah, she knelt. She loves and respects them, so that was the very least she owed them. Frankly, if my sub had done what Raine did…" Seth shook his head. "Displeased doesn't even begin to cover it."

River tried to wrap his head around that. "She'll kneel for them, have a baby with them, but refuse to marry one of them?"

"Well, the baby part wasn't planned," Seth explained. "But think of it this way: if a relationship with two is hard, it's a downright fucking challenge with three. After their jealousy issues, Raine has to be fair and equal to maintain balance. It can't be easy."

"Yeah." He still didn't like the idea of his sister shacked up with two guys both older than him…but he couldn't deny they loved her. And she loved them. "I just want Raine happy. Shut up and show me what to do."

He paid close attention as Seth pointed out where he'd stashed the recording devices in the room earlier that day, making mental notes about where he should stand or lay so Seth could capture optimal audio and video.

"Let's do a quick sound check, then you'll be good to go."

Several adjustments later, Seth gave him the thumbs-up.

"You're ready." He clapped River on the back. "Now go be a hero."

Once the guy had disappeared into the adjoining room, River took a long, hot shower, shaved, and sprayed on the pheromone cologne Raine had shoved in his hands designed to drive women wild with lust.

Carefully laying his Class A's out across the bed, River skimmed his fingers over the rows of ribbons, medals, and patches—milestones of his multiple tours in Afghanistan. Closing his eyes, he sent up a mental salute to his brothers who hadn't made it home from that godforsaken fuckhole.

After meticulously donning his dress blues, he slanted the beret on his head and slapped a hand to his bicep. Paying silent homage, he pressed his fingers against the Unit Insignia, the Special Forces,

Ranger, and Airborne rockers at the top of his sleeve. Adjusting his tie once more, he waved to Seth in one of the hidden cameras, then strutted out the door.

When River arrived at the swanky bar, he strolled in nonchalantly, scanning the crowd for the blonde. He spotted her sitting, swirling a straw in some fruity girly drink.

Tamping down animosity, River bellied up to the bar a few feet from her and ordered a beer. Almost instantly he could feel her eyes on him. He counted to ten before he raised his head to meet her stare. Definitely pretty—at least from a distance. She blushed.

After flashing him a smile, she lowered her gaze to her drink. Absently, she slid her glossy red nail suggestively up and down the straw. He'd bet she'd practiced the move on dozens of horny saps. But he didn't care who'd come before him. He was on a mission.

She wrapped her lips around the end of the straw, and her little pink tongue peeked out before she took a long pull of her drink. Her cheeks concaved with the suction. He envisioned her on her knees, sucking him down. He wasn't proud of it, but his cock leapt to life.

She set her drink down, then looked his way again in coy flirtation. He manufactured an inviting smile for her before he tipped back his beer and guzzled it in a few long swallows. Once done, he set the bottle down and strolled her way, moving in for the kill.

Up close, she didn't look quite real. Her lips and forehead didn't move naturally when she smiled. She wore her makeup thick. The swells of her breasts above the neckline of her little black dress looked way too symmetrical and perky.

River glanced down at her empty glass. "I'd like to buy you another drink."

Marlie looked him up and down, her stare lingering on his chest full of medals pinned to his dress blues and his wide shoulders. A slow smile curled the corners of her mouth. "Would you, sailor?"

"Green Beret, actually. And I'll buy you drinks until I look good to you."

Marlie threw back her head and laughed. "Well, that's one line I've never heard before, Corporal Green Beret."

"Captain," he corrected her.

"Pardon me, Captain. But I don't need another drink."

He leaned closer. "You afraid I'll try to take advantage of you?"

"No." Marlie looked away, then met his gaze once more—another practiced move. "I'm not afraid at all. I just don't need more alcohol to think you look good. In fact, I can better appreciate every inch of you when I'm sober."

"Every inch, huh? Just how many inches do you want to see, baby?"

The woman batted her lashes, managing to look breathlessly surprised by her attraction to him. Yeah, she'd been around the block a few times, and she was a hell of a practiced flirt.

"All of them," she whispered.

Score.

"Hmm." He leaned in close, face skimming her neck, and inhaled deeply. He nearly choked. Hair products and some overpowering scent. "Christ, you smell...edible. What's the name of the perfume you're wearing?"

"Guilty Seduction." She sank her pearly-white teeth into her bottom lip.

Fitting.

"Hopefully, you'll only be feeling satisfied when we're through." River trailed a finger over her collarbone, flirting with her hard silicone swells below.

Her lashes fluttered shut as she sighed in seeming arousal—a sign that he should proceed to the next phase.

River slid a knee between Marlie's thighs, nudging them apart. Then he wrapped an arm around her waist and drew her close, until her breasts all but spilled from the vee in her skintight dress.

"You're awfully sure of yourself, Captain."

"I'm a man who knows what he wants." River leaned in until his lips touched her ear. "You, naked and tied to my bed, while I explore your luscious body with my mouth until you're all screamed out."

He heard a soft gasp catch in her throat. "T-Tied?"

"Unless you're not into that." He shrugged.

"Oh, no. I've never tried but that sounds...exciting."

Liar. At least it was good to know that giving her a reaming with her fucking was going to be easy.

"I do enjoy an open-minded woman. What's your name, baby?"

"Marlie Natelnash."

"Rick Storm." He lifted her slender fingers and pressed a kiss to the sensitive inside of her wrist.

Marlie swallowed hard. "Please tell me you have a hotel room upstairs, Captain."

Was she always this easy? "I do. You want to come up?"

She glanced down at his straining erection. "Do I get to lock my lips around that fat cock about to bust through your zipper?"

Shit, she might be a plastic bitch, but his dick thought that sounded damn good.

"What are we waiting for?" River extended his hand to her.

Marlie took it and slid off the barstool. Her knees weren't quite steady, and she latched on to his arm. "You feel very strong."

"Yes, ma'am. And capable, too. I won't let you down."

"Is that a promise?"

"You bet, baby."

With her hand in his, he led her to the elevator. They stepped inside. Before the doors even closed, Marlie locked her lips on his.

Don't give her the upper hand. You're the Dom. Take control.

With Seth's words resonating in his ears, River sank a fist into Marlie's...hair extensions? What the hell?

Was there any place on her body that hadn't been Botoxed, spray tanned, or otherwise enhanced? Hell, maybe he needed to keep her away from any open flames in case she melted into a puddle of silicone and plastic.

Ignoring the hard clips beneath his fingers, he thrust out his chest and pushed her into the corner of the elevator. Marlie moaned, wrapping her tongue around his. Plastic or not, this whore possessed some mad skills with that wicked tongue. River looked forward to feeling her talented mouth dance down south.

Rocking his hips, he drove between her legs, giving her a feel for just how seriously he could violate her.

Marlie tore away from his mouth and gasped. "Good lord. All that?"

"Yeah. I'll give you every thick, hard inch, send you to ecstasy over and over."

The elevator came to a stop. River lifted Marlie into his arms. She squealed, a seeming protest that sounded more like delight as he carried her down the hall. He unlocked the door to his room, making as much noise as possible to alert Seth so he'd turn on the recording devices.

The door snicked shut. Before River could get Marlie onto the bed, she dropped to her knees, lifted his coat, and began tearing at his belt.

River clasped his hands around hers, stilling them. "Hold on, baby. Let's get on the bed…and take it from there."

"All right." With an eager little moan, she jumped to her feet, stripped off her dress, and posed herself on the mattress. "I don't usually do this, Rick. Meet a man in a bar and go to his room."

Bullshit. "That thought never crossed my mind. There's some connection between us. I'm glad you feel it, too."

"I'm sizzling all over."

"Not yet, baby, but you will. Trust me."

River stripped off his tie, coat, and shirt. He'd had a few women since returning Stateside, but none as brazen—or artificial—as this one.

Before he unzipped his pants, he paused and stared down at her. "Oh, baby, you're so sexy…"

Marlie seemed to melt at his compliment.

"How is someone as beautiful as you still single? Why hasn't some man snapped you up?"

Hurt, then anger flashed in her eyes. She quickly banked it. "I recently came out of a relationship. He left me for some trailer trash whore."

"I can't believe that." River forced a look of sympathy. "Why? Who is this idiot? I mean, his loss is my gain, but…"

"I needed to hear that." She sniffled delicately. "He broke my heart so cruelly."

She really should stick to flirting. She was decent at kick-starting desire, terrible at inspiring sympathy.

Hands on his hips, River flexed his biceps. "Where does he live? I'll go teach him a lesson for you. No man should get away with crushing someone as perfect as you."

"See, you get it. I just don't understand how he could possibly leave me for that desperate bitch in heat. She all but humped his leg until he knocked her up."

You're calling my sister desperate? Look in the mirror.

River arched his brows in mock surprise. "Did he marry her?"

"No," Marlie huffed. "So maybe he hasn't completely lost his mind. He's just too worldly and sophisticated for someone so...unpolished. For the life of me, I can't figure out what he sees in her. She's completely unremarkable. She's definitely no match for him intellectually. I grant you, she looks at him like he's a god. He owns a kink club, which isn't really my thing but...he's the type to like obedience, so this whore probably sinks to her knees the instant he points at the ground. I realize she's got a huge rack, but then...I do, too."

She thrust out her chest, breasts artfully lifted with something lacy and expensive. He wouldn't hate getting his mouth on those, but no matter how impatient his cock was, Marlie was on a roll. He couldn't stop her now.

"These have got to be the prettiest tits I've ever seen. Hmm." River scrubbed at his chin and stared. "But make me proud. Tell me you didn't take his bullshit lying down."

A terrible grin curled her mouth. For the first time, River glimpsed the viper within the pretty package. "I did at first, but I found a way to get him back."

"Good for you," River cheered. "How did you do it, turn the mousy girl against him?"

"Oh, no. I did something—" Marlie suddenly covered her mouth with her hand. "I shouldn't be telling anyone this. I could get into serious trouble."

River scoffed. "Not from me. I'm shipping back to the desert soon. C'mon. You can't leave me in agony. Whatever you hatched in that pretty little head of yours must be epic."

"It is," she gushed.

"I won't breathe a word to anyone." He dragged his knuckles over her collarbones, down, down over the swell of one breast and its hard tip. "I'll keep all your secrets safe, right here." He patted his heart and sent her a reassuring smile.

"Promise?"

"Cross my heart, baby."

She bounced slightly on the mattress with glee. "I've been dying to tell someone, and well, since you're shipping out, or whatever you call it, I'll share my secret with you. You seem like someone I can trust."

That's your second mistake. Your first was hitting my sister. But please tell me how you're framing her lover and ruining their lives.

"You can." River smiled, acting as if he hung on her every word.

"I might have told a teeny white lie to a new…friend who works in the federal court system. I persuaded him to prosecute my ex. This friend's wife just had a baby, and you know men have needs. It was bad of me, but I help him…and he's helping this case along for me."

"Very smart. Did your ex do something illegal?"

"Since actually being attracted to that white trash bitch isn't a crime, no."

River wanted to shake Marlie until her extensions fell out. For Raine's sake, he forced a wider smile. As long as this piece of ass kept vomiting up the evidence they needed to toss her fake tits in jail, he'd do whatever he had to so she'd keep talking.

Then she'd learn not to fuck with him—or his sister.

"But in case my lie wasn't enough, I did…an oral favor or two for the tech guy who works for my ex. In exchange, the nerd gave me some incriminating video of him damn near raping this tramp."

"Rape? Holy shit." What the hell was she talking about? "Did he do it? I don't want you anywhere near him if he did."

"Of course not. He didn't have to. He's that good." She nearly moaned the words. "Too good for her. He's rich, too. What a waste… This hussy can't even wear designer. I look so much better in Vuitton. But did he pick me? No." She sighed in disgust. "Maybe I should consider myself lucky. After all, his best friend has now moved in with the two of them so they can 'share' her. What a stupid slut."

"I can see where you'd think that," River forced himself to say.

"Well, she can have him now. I'd never go back to that bastard. I just want to make him suffer. He thinks he's some big, bad Dom." She smiled archly. "And I'm about to nail him for thirty years."

Translation: Macen had been a great fuck, and Marlie was pissed that he'd dumped her because she was an egotistical whore who didn't care if she ruined an innocent man's life.

"Ah." He rubbed his hands together to keep himself from strangling her. "I love a woman with a sharp mind. You're brilliant, baby."

"Thank you. I feel like a genius, bringing the 'hammer' down on him and separating him from that wretched whore all in one move. He'll be labeled a pedophile, too!" she squealed happily. "Win-win-win."

"'Atta girl. Don't ever let a man treat you any different than you deserve."

And right now, this cunt deserved to be behind bars.

"Never. He'll be going down soon now. I can't wait."

"So how friendly did you have to get with the federal prosecutor?"

"Well, he's the AUSA in this case, and there's not much evidence, so I had to be particularly persuasive. Every Monday and Friday at noon." She rolled her eyes. "He's a dull fish, and he's terrible in bed. But it's for a good cause, right?"

"Absolutely."

River darted a glance at the hidden camera on the headboard, praying that Seth was picking up every incriminating word rolling off Marlie's tongue.

Suddenly, she sobered and pinned him with a frown.

Fuck. Had she spotted the surveillance equipment?

"What's wrong, baby? Why so serious?"

"You won't tell anyone, right? I mean, I'm really not a vengeful person, but…honestly, how could I let him leave me for some unworthy bitch?"

River smiled and unzipped his fly. He either had to get this show on the road or she'd get suspicious. And he was already so pissed he wasn't sure he could find the stomach to fuck her.

"He's obviously crazy, baby." Reaching inside his pants, he pulled out his cock. "How about you let me put my hammer down in you—deep and hard?"

"Oh, my god," she whispered, staring at his cock with wide eyes. "Come here, Captain. Let me wrap my lips around that big gun of yours."

"Not yet, baby. I want to be inside you, make you scream for me."

"And you're going to tie me up, right?"

River kicked off his pants, then rushed to the bed, pulling the rope from all four corners. "You know I am. Strip out of your bra and panties. Let me rock your world."

"I can't wait." She giggled.

In seconds flat, she was naked and lying in the center of the bed. River blocked out what a vile bitch she was and focused on her centerfold body. Thankfully, his cock had no conscience.

Remembering Seth's comment about how often her fields were plowed, River turned and double wrapped his dick in latex.

"Hurry, Captain."

Gritting his teeth, he flashed her a smile as he bound her wrists and ankles. He couldn't force himself to engage in any foreplay. He'd be doing well to fuck her. It was a damn good thing that as soon as he slid inside her, his swollen head took over.

River pumped her furiously. As Marlie geared up for her third orgasm, River wished Seth would crash this party. The double condoms were strangling him, and she definitely wasn't flipping his switch. But he'd fuck her all night if he had to. He'd done worse for his country.

He might want an orgasm tonight, but he refused to have one with her.

As she bucked and writhed and screamed beneath him, he flashed a WTF scowl at the camera mounted on the headboard.

Finally, River's cell phone rang.

About fucking time, Seth. You son of a bitch.

Rolling off her still-panting body, River plucked the device from his pants.

"Hello?"

"Where are you, man? They're about to start the awards ceremony. You missed the dinner. What's keeping you?" Seth asked, per their arranged script.

"Son of a… What time is it?"

"Time for you to pull your cock out of whoever you've got it in, throw on your Class A's, and get your ass to the banquet. I'll stall. Hurry."

"Wh-what's wrong?" Marlie asked, half dazed.

"I've got to go. I'm sorry, baby." He tugged off the condoms and slipped into his pants. "But I'm being awarded the Medal of Honor tonight. I'm late."

She didn't bat a lash. "Oh, how exciting."

Clearly, the woman didn't have a goddamn clue that such awards were often given posthumously and only at the White House, never in LA.

River tried not to roll his eyes as he untied her from the bed. "A thrill."

She launched out of bed and tossed on her clothes. "I'll be in the bar until late tonight. When you get back, come find me. I'd really like to see you again."

I'd rather hang myself with barbed wire over a pit of hungry gators.

"You know I will." River gave her a broad smile.

He kissed her cheek, smacked her ass, and shoved her out the door. Waiting to the count of ten, he peered through the peephole to make sure she'd left the hall.

The coast was clear.

Seconds later, the lock clicked, and Seth sauntered into the room wearing a big-ass grin and holding a DVD. "You got her. We're so close to nailing Marlie, that slimy tech nerd Hammer hired, and that asshole AUSA to the wall."

"Fuck yeah," River cheered.

"A little more legwork, and I think I can shore this up. Hammer should be as good as free." Seth was grinning from ear to ear. "I told you your sister is a tough girl."

He had to give Raine credit. "She called it."

"By the way, how did you work Marlie so fast? You had her up here before I even finished the cheeseburger I ordered from room service."

"Hell, I was doing well to get her in the room before she raped me." River shook his head. "In the elevator, she had her tongue so far down my throat I thought it was going to come out my ass."

Seth roared with laughter.

River shuddered. "It's not funny, shithead. Please tell me you have bleach in your room."

"Why the hell do you need that?"

"To soak the germs off my dick."

CHAPTER SEVENTEEN

Friday, February 22

WEARING A CROOKED smile, Liam watched from the doorway as Raine paced the living room, peering out the bay window every few seconds. She only paused to glance at the clock.

He strolled closer and wrapped his arms around her from behind. "They're not going to get here any faster because you're wearing a hole in the rug waiting for them, love."

"I know, but it's past two. Seth and River were supposed to be here five minutes ago."

Her normal bluish-white aura had been streaked with sharp purple before she'd gone to Shadows. Now that she'd returned, it pulsed violet, which told him Raine was up to something—and determined to keep it to herself. He didn't like it.

"You're keeping secrets from me, love," Liam challenged in low tones.

She whipped around to face him, eyes wide. "Not exactly. I'm waiting for Seth and River to…"

"To what?"

"Okay, so I had a hunch. Call it woman's intuition. I didn't put myself in harm's way, just asked them to investigate something for me. River called this morning and told me they have news to share."

"And you didn't mention any of this to me or Hammer?"

"Because I didn't want to get anyone's hopes up if I was wrong. I'll explain everything shortly. Just give me a few more minutes, okay?"

"Very well. But if they don't have answers to your woman's intuition, you and I are going to have a long talk."

"We will." She nodded and turned her attention toward the window once more.

He shook his head and smirked. "You're bloody marvelous at a lot of things, but being patient isn't one of them."

"I can't help it. Waiting drives me crazy."

He nibbled the sensitive spot beneath her ear. "Hammer and I will gladly take you upstairs to occupy your mind—and your luscious body. That would make going crazy a lot more fun."

"Did someone say my name?" Hammer strode into the room, merging himself in their hug.

"I thought you were out." Raine blinked up at him. "I went to the garage to get some apple juice and your car was gone. I was hoping you'd bring me back some chocolate donuts."

Macen blanched slightly. "No, but I'll pick some up for you to-morrow morning."

The two men had sat at the pool the other night, polishing off a half bottle of scotch and tequila, respectively. They'd shared curses and even a few tears while Liam delved into his friend's psyche. Knowing the man had been so near the edge scared the bloody hell out of Liam. But by five that morning, he was confident he'd reached his pal and even more secure the fuckwit wouldn't pull a stunt like that again—ever.

Then Hammer had called for a tow truck, which arrived as the sun rose. Liam had watched gratefully as the demolished Audi was hauled to the graveyard, instead of his mate. Still, Liam couldn't help but feel they'd somehow buried a body. Maybe it was Hammer's fears. Either way, all evidence of the man's breakdown was gone.

"That would be nice but where's your car?" she asked suspiciously.

"Well…" Hammer looked his way. "My frustration got the best of me. I sort of…beat it up with a tire iron."

That was as much explanation as Raine needed.

"You what?" she gasped.

"It's all right, precious. I needed to vent, and it was time I got a new car anyway."

"That's an awfully expensive way to take out your frustrations." She scowled, then turned toward Liam. "So you yank the phone out of the wall and Hammer beats up his car. Do you two need anger management classes or something?"

"No. We plan to expend all our energies on you from now on," Hammer assured.

She cupped his chin, concern written all over her face. "Do you feel better?"

He bent and kissed her tenderly. "I feel alive, precious. The only way I could feel better is if we resolved this fucking mess."

A secret smile tugged the corners of Raine's lips. Liam hoped whatever she was hiding might make their most profound wish come true.

As Bryn and Duncan descended the stairs, the doorbell rang.

"Would you like me to get that?" Duncan asked.

"I've got it." Raine peeled herself from their arms and ran to the door.

She yanked it open. Beck and Sterling stood on the porch, wearing expectant expressions.

Liam wondered why those two were dropping by since Raine had said she was waiting for Seth and her brother. So she hadn't told him everything. Liam planned to remind her about her vow of honesty with several well-placed slaps on her milky ass soon. His palm began to itch.

"Come on in," Raine invited.

As the two men stepped into the foyer, she poked her head out the door and looked both ways, as if scanning the street. With a heavy sigh, she shut it again, then followed Beck and Sterling into the family room. The guys all shook hands before taking a seat on the couch.

"What brings you two here?" Liam asked curiously.

"I'll get us all some tea," Bryn announced, blatantly preventing the other men from answering his question.

What are you up to, Mum? he asked with a mental nudge.

She simply smiled.

"Do you have a beer?" Beck asked.

"It's two o'clock in the afternoon, Kenneth," Bryn pointed out.

He flashed her a mischievous grin. "It's five o'clock somewhere."

"You've melted your share of hearts with that smile, but it's going to take more than that to snare a heavenly heart."

Beck scowled. "I'd rather have a beer than predictions."

Liam snorted. "Good luck with that."

"I'll get you a pint, mate." Duncan slapped Bryn on the ass. "Come on, wench. You're scaring the kids with your riddles again."

Sterling looked confused but shrugged.

"Exactly why are we here, princess?" Beck peered at Raine.

She nibbled her bottom lip, then cast a hopeful glance at the door. "Well, um… Seth and River will be here any second. We'll explain then."

Hammer frowned and turned to his lawyer. "So you don't know what's up?"

"Haven't a clue." Sterling shook his head. "Raine called and said it was urgent, so I cleared my afternoon."

"I'm sorry you had to rearrange your schedule," she apologized. "They should—"

The doorbell rang again. She raced across the room, yanked the door open, then ushered Seth and River in.

Bryn and Duncan appeared, setting a variety of drinks on the coffee table.

"Well?" Raine looked at her brother, barely able to contain her excitement.

Liam watched. What the devil was she up to?

Wearing a broad smile, River grabbed her, lifted her off the ground, and kissed her cheek.

Hammer tensed. Liam gripped his friend's shoulder to calm him. Both River and Seth had the same violet aura pulsing around them, so they were in on Raine's plot. Liam watched curiously as River set Raine down before reaching inside his jacket. He pulled out a DVD and handed it to her.

"Go ahead, storm cloud. You were right. This is your show. You did good. Finish saving your man."

Wariness stamped Macen's face. "Raine, what is he talking about?"

Liam couldn't miss the hum of anticipation singing in the air. Something big was on the horizon. Huge. He fastened his stare on Raine.

"After we tried to determine which blonde had a vendetta against you, I couldn't shake the feeling that a certain person was involved," she explained. "Something in the back of my head kept telling me to check her out."

"Who?" Hammer asked impatiently.

"I'm getting there." Raine sent him a pleading stare. "I asked River and Seth to set a trap. She never saw River coming, and that's a good thing, because I think they caught her. Everything should be on this disc." She eased in next to Hammer and sent him a stare full of love. "Watch this. Especially you, Sterling. I think you'll find it…educational. And from the look Seth is giving me, maybe even alarming." Then she placed the DVD in Hammer's hand and kissed him softly. "I love you."

He stared at the flat plastic, turning it over and over in his hand. "Does this have something to do with my case?"

"It should keep you out of prison, Macen," she softly whispered.

"Seriously?" Hammer blinked in total disbelief.

"One hundred and ten percent," Seth promised.

"Let's not get ahead of ourselves just yet," Sterling warned. "What exactly is on that disc?"

"Well, River took a big one for the team." Seth chuckled.

Bryn's eyes grew wide. "Oh. Oh, my. Raine? Dear, I think it best if you and I went upstairs for a wee bit."

His girl cringed. "Yeah, I'm pretty sure I know what's on it. I'd rather wash my eyes out with battery acid than see that."

Bryn put her arm around Raine's shoulder. "Your brother's dedication to you is admirable but disturbing."

She sent River a broad smile. "Thank you, big brother."

"Anything for you, storm cloud." River smiled lovingly.

Seth darted toward the front door, returning seconds later with an enormous bag of popcorn and a wide grin.

Liam felt as if Raine had passed her impatience on to him. If whatever they were about to view could solve Hammer's case, he didn't want to piss around talking.

"Gentlemen, let's get this show on the road and adjourn to the media room, shall we?" he suggested.

"Did you know anything about this?" Hammer murmured as they paraded down the hall, the other men following, hope stirring.

"I suspected she'd been up to something, but no. I'm as anxious as you to find out."

"What the fuck is on that DVD?" Beck asked from behind him.

"I can't even begin to describe it," Seth said wryly. "You'll just have to see for yourself. Bear in mind, this is the uncut 'director's' version. And tonight will be the only screening. You'll see why."

After they'd all settled back in the plush recliners with their legs stretched out, popcorn in their laps and beers by their sides, Hammer popped the DVD into the player.

The big screen came to life with the image of River and *Marlie* coming through the hotel door.

"What the fuck?" Hammer whispered, totally stunned.

That bloody, miserable bitch. He should have known. Why hadn't he guessed—and decked Marlie when he'd had the chance? Liam was gobsmacked by the lengths that whore had gone to in order to carry out her obsessive vendetta.

I told you she was a woman scorned. His mother's voice pierced his brain.

Liam watched as Hammer stumbled back into his seat. Shock etched on his face as he stared at the screen, slack-jawed.

"Holy shit," Beck barked. "*That* fucking skank. You've got to be kidding me."

"Marlie?" Hammer choked. "She's not smart enough to pull off something this complex."

"She might not be smart, but she's cunning," Seth argued. "And she's very guilty."

"I've never been able to stand that bitch." Liam cursed, watching the drama unfold on screen.

"Aw, look. River found himself a wild skank-muffin," Beck drawled.

"Motherfucker," Hammer murmured, eyes glued to the TV. "I can't believe she's behind all this."

"I can't believe you ever fucked her," Liam chided.

"I can't believe you fucked her more than once." River shuddered.

When she dropped to her knees and began to claw at the man's pants, Sterling sat up and leaned forward in his chair. "What the hell am I watching? Who is she?"

"The first vacu-whore off the line." Beck snorted. "I thought of hitting that once, but I wanted a newer model. You know, one that hasn't sucked the foreskin off every dick in a thousand-mile radius."

"What the devil is she trying to do to you, River?" Liam asked with a laugh.

"She's hunting the elusive trouser snake, son," Duncan drawled in a singsong Irish lilt. "Be fast now, lassie. Catch it with your lips before it escapes."

"That's not a snake!" River protested with feigned indignation. "It's a goddamn anaconda."

"Watch out," Seth yelled. "The teeth of the venomous skank-muffin can shred a man's cock to ribbons."

"If her brick-hard tits don't knock you unconscious first," River groused. "Jesus, I've thrown medicine balls that were softer than those things."

Hammer simply groaned and covered his face, peering out between splayed fingers.

Like watching a train wreck, no one could look away.

When Marlie jumped to her feet and peeled off her dress, Liam howled with laughter. "Oh, look. The cankerous cock cobra has just shed her skin. Quick! Someone call *National Geographic*."

"I'm going to be sick," Hammer moaned.

Seth stood and paused the feed.

The men groaned in unison. Beck threw popcorn at him.

"Shut up, your fucking pervs," he scolded. "Sterling, you need to listen to everything she says now that River has her on the bed. When he releases his 'anaconda' and double bags it with condoms, you can tune out again."

"Double bags?" Hammer snorted. "What, did she have open sores or something?"

"None I could see on camera," Seth replied. "But I might have suggested she had critters all up in that shit. I knew Raine wouldn't be happy if River took one for the team and ended up with a case of crotch crickets."

"Just another reason I kept my mouth off her shit," River added.

"Okay, everyone quiet down," Seth instructed. "Listen."

The room went deathly quiet as he started the video once again. As Marlie confessed to sleeping with the AUSA and bribing Lewis with blow jobs to get her hands on the security drives at Shadows, Liam's temper skyrocketed.

He was sickened by the visible glee she took in lying and planting the seeds that would destroy not only Hammer but their family. And the more she maligned Raine, the angrier Liam grew. He clenched his jaw and fists. Blood thundered in his ears as he restrained the urge to snap her fucking neck.

"I want to kill that cunt." Clearly, Hammer was as livid as Liam. "Why such hatred? I never promised her a fucking thing, and she certainly didn't mean shit to me."

Liam gripped Hammer's arm. "There's the problem, mate. She's a narcissistic slut who expected you to put her on a pedestal. Instead, you tossed her aside for our girl. Marlie couldn't handle the rejection."

Hammer shook his head in disgust. "So she thought she'd put me in prison instead? What a squack-dripping, sociopathic cuntsicle. I want to fucking kill her."

When River reached inside his pants on the video, Seth stopped the DVD again.

"Aw, come on, fucker," Beck grumbled. "We want to watch the rest."

"Keep your panties on," Seth chided, then turned to Sterling. "Is Hammer free? Is there enough on this tape to clear his name?"

All eyes turned toward the lawyer. Liam held his breath as Hammer tensed beside him.

"Christ knows I'd love to say yes, but she didn't name names. If I presented this to the judge, my defense would be as circumstantial as their prosecution." Sterling looked frustrated and saddened.

"I thought you might say that, so…" Seth pulled a stack of papers from his briefcase as he stood in front of the men. "I did a little more digging. That's why I'm late. As of two weeks ago, the illustrious AUSA, Todd Wellington, acquired a mistress."

Seth handed Sterling a sheet of paper.

"From these credit card receipts, you can see that Wellington began booking rooms at The Ritz every Monday and Friday for a little nooner. So I trekked down to the hotel a few hours ago and flirted my ass off with the front desk clerk. I showed her a photo of Marlie and Wellington, and she whispered that the couple had already checked in. They were up on the tenth floor. She wouldn't tell me the room number, but I didn't really need it."

"You sly fucker." Liam grinned.

"I paced the hall for about thirty minutes with my phone in hand. When suddenly, two doors down, they walked out of one of the rooms. I turned and clicked off a couple of photos. They didn't even look my way. Wellington just shoved her up against the wall and grabbed her ass while Marlie swallowed his tongue."

"Oh, god. I know exactly how that feels," River grumbled.

"I was able to capture these…" Seth announced as he held up eight-by-ten photos of the couple groping and tonsil-swabbing.

"Holy shit," Hammer barked.

Lunging from his seat, he spun and pinned Sterling with an anxious stare. Hope radiated from Hammer, instantly washing over Liam and bathing him in a warm wave of optimism and confidence. The double whammy damn near bowled him over.

A slow smile spread over the lawyer's face. Without a word, Barnes stood and pulled his phone from his breast pocket. "I just received an email from the AUSA's office with the name of the prosecution's witness." A knowing smirk played on his lips. "Is the star of your video a…lady—I use that term loosely—named Marlie Natelnash?"

"You mean Marlie Nastysnatch?" Hammer snarled. "Yeah."

With a nod, Sterling pressed a button, then held the device to his ear.

"Hey, Arnie, it's Sterling. Yes. Yes, our tee time is still on for tomorrow. I'm calling to see if I can come by your chambers this afternoon. I've got some unbelievable information regarding the Hammerman case you need to see. This shit is going to blow you away. Oh, and you might want to issue arrest warrants for Marlie Natelnash, the prosecution's witness, as well as our AUSA friend, Todd Wellington." He paused as a grin speared his lips. "Yes, you heard me right. The pompous prick won't be strutting around your courtroom—or anyone else's. That won't be possible after he's been disbarred. Yes. I'll be bringing you more proof than you can imagine. All right. Thanks, Arnie. I'll see you soon."

"Wait! You can't take the video," Beck objected. "We haven't seen the rest yet."

Liam and Hammer ignored the horny bastard. Both stepped toward Barnes, holding their breath.

"So it's over?" Hammer asked, his voice cracking slightly.

When Liam gripped Macen's shoulder, he could feel his friend trembling beneath his palm.

Barnes patted Hammer's arm in fatherly reassurance. "I can't say definitively, but after I show all this to Judge Ayers, I believe that will end your problems." Sterling glanced over both their shoulders and nodded toward Seth.

"I have the PG-friendly version for you to take to the judge. All the confession and none of the sex."

"Perfect." Sterling smiled. "I know none of you boys would ever tape a sex act without your partner's consent and get your asses in trouble, right?"

"I'm a decorated war hero who would never do such a thing." River grinned.

"I plead the fifth." Seth winked, passing out DVDs like playing cards. "I made copies with spice for your spank banks, gentlemen."

"Burn mine. I don't fucking want it," Hammer growled.

"Mine, too. Christ, man. What the bloody hell were you thinking?" Liam groused.

"Sweet," Beck cheered as he jumped up and grabbed one.

"I'll make sure to tell Heavenly how eager you were to add to your personal porn collection," Seth jeered.

Beck flipped him off. "I'll tell her you recorded it."

After Seth handed Sterling a DVD with the confession only, along with the other incriminating evidence, the lawyer promised to call as soon as he had news, then left.

Hammer stepped over to River and extended his hand. When Raine's brother took it, Macen blinked back tears. "I don't even know how to fucking thank you."

"You don't have to, especially since I started all this. I'm just glad your taste in women has improved."

Hammer snorted and gestured Seth toward him for a manly hug. As the three stood there smiling and discussing how the sting went down, Liam's heart soared.

With the bromance blossoming, Beck eased from his chair and started the video up once again.

"Oh, look," Duncan called, pointing at the screen. "River's tying the beast down. Just like King Kong."

"You mean King Cunt." Beck snorted.

"And now he's getting ready to lay the bagpipes," Duncan laughed.

"Christ, your cock's as big as the Alaskan Pipeline. Tell me, does it have its own heart and lungs?"

River grinned, pulled away from Hammer, then took a seat next to Liam's dad. "No, but I think it scared her a little."

"That's not a big dick." Beck grabbed his crotch. "This is a big dick."

"I got so pissed off at Marlie when I was recording this shit, I wanted to march into the room with River and give her a fifty-yard cunt punt," Seth railed. "I didn't because I was afraid I'd lose my shoe."

Liam and Hammer groaned in unison.

"Oh, she's spreading her legs," Duncan bellowed. "Saints have mercy! She's got a vagina the size of a hallway. Someone toss the lad a rope."

"Trust me, Duncan," River drawled. "It would have been more appealing to fuck a hallway. I've touched mannequins whose bodies had more give than hers."

"Come on." Hammer nodded toward Liam. "Let's go find Raine."

"I'm with you. I've seen enough. Any more, and I'm likely to throw up."

As he and Hammer raced up the stairs, they met Bryn on her way down.

"Don't go near the media room, Mum," Liam warned.

"I had no intention, my boy. I'm not daft," she scolded. "Go to your girl. She's antsy to see you both."

Needing no further encouragement, they sprinted to their bedroom.

Raine turned and flashed them a glowing smile. "Well?"

They rushed to her and enveloped her between them, smothering her with kisses as she giggled like a schoolgirl. Excited. Happy. Free.

"Oh, precious." Hammer exhaled. "How the hell am I ever going to be able to thank you for what you've done?"

"Just tell me it's really over."

"Sterling is on his way to meet with the judge as we speak," Hammer explained. "He'll call soon. Then, hopefully, we'll have something to celebrate."

"We will," Liam assured. "Trust me. At least while Mum's here.

After she's gone, I might lose my Spidey senses, but for now…"

The three of them simply laughed.

It felt good.

The possibility of freedom tasted sweet. They were all anxious to start their long and happy life together. The dark cloud that had been hanging over their heads for so damn long began to dissipate.

CHAPTER EIGHTEEN

HAMMER DIDN'T KNOW how much time had passed since he and Liam had joined Raine in their bedroom. He didn't care. All he wanted was to stay close to them, keep Raine wrapped in his arms, and sink deep into her mouth.

If there were two people who embodied love for him, it was Liam and Raine. Only they'd stood by him in his darkest hours. Liam had saved him from making an irrevocable mistake. Raine was staving off his certain insanity by trying to bring an end to his legal threat. Hammer didn't even know how to express the depth of his gratitude.

A tap on the door drew his attention. Beck stood at the portal, wearing an early congratulatory smile and holding a copy of the infamous DVD.

"Seth and I are taking off. River is downstairs with Bryn and Duncan." Beck looked pointedly at Liam. "Your old man is a fucking riot, but your mom? That woman scares the shit out of me."

The trio couldn't help but chuckle. Now if Sterling would just call with some good news, his life would be complete.

Beck sobered. "I'm pulling for you guys. I hope you can put this crap behind you for good."

"Thanks." Hammer nodded as the man waved and ducked out.

He glanced at the clock on the nightstand. What the hell was taking so long? Anxiety crawled through his guts. What if Judge Ayers wanted *more* proof?

Suddenly his cell phone rang. Hammer yanked it from his pocket and sucked in a bracing breath when Sterling's name and number appear on the screen. He sank to the edge of the mattress, his heart slamming against his ribs in triple time. "Looks like it's time for the fat lady to shut up or sing."

"We're beside you, brother. No matter what," Liam pledged.

"Forever and always," Raine seconded as she knelt in front of him.

Liam stood behind her, hands on her shoulders. Their nearness engulfed Hammer in a cloak of reassurance as he pressed the button to engage the speakerphone. "Sterling?"

"Good news, Macen. It's all over. You're free. Judge Ayers ripped the local cops and the feds new assholes. They've dropped all charges against you. The LAPD has issued arrest warrants for Marlie and Todd. They should be in custody tonight."

The two-ton weight on his chest evaporated. A lump of emotion formed in Macen's throat instead, preventing him from talking. His vision blurred but not before he saw tears of joy welling in Liam's eyes and streaking down Raine's cheeks.

"Macen? Are you there?" Sterling asked. "Did you hear me?"

Liam cleared his throat. "He is and he did, Barnes. We're all a mite choked up at the moment, but thank you for all you've done to help us."

"You're welcome. I couldn't be happier with this outcome myself."

Hammer quickly wiped his eyes and tried to find his voice, but it came out rough and choppy. "Thank you, man."

"I'd usually say anytime, but after this circus, I'm going to say…hopefully never again." Sterling chuckled. "You kids have a nice night celebrating. I'll be in touch. Good-bye."

Hammer ended the call as Raine launched herself in his arms once more and Liam enfolded them in his embrace. "It's finally over."

"Indeed," Liam sighed. "Now we can start living—really living."

"It's going to be better than amazing," Raine whispered softly.

"Is there some news you might be wanting to share with the rest of us?" Bryn called from downstairs.

Liam looked at the ceiling as if searching for patience. "They'll be going home soon. I promise."

"Maybe. But then again, maybe not." Bryn laughed.

Hammer shook his head, and Raine giggled. The exhilaration of his sudden freedom merged with colossal relief. After endless, wrenching worry, it was almost surreal.

Liam rolled his eyes. "We'll have some bloody privacy soon."

"If you wanted privacy, you two should have thought of that before you knocked up your wee lass," Bryn hollered. "You'll have none once that babe comes."

"Love you, Mum," Liam called as he wrenched open the door. "We'll be there in a minute."

"I know we should go down, but I'm so happy. I just want to stay in your arms all night. I guess I should thank my brother for taking that plastic whore to bed to help us." Raine grimaced. "It was above and beyond the call of duty."

Hammer kissed her. "Way beyond. Focus on his sacrifice, precious."

"It's in the past now, where it belongs." Liam's voice was full of hope for the future.

"I couldn't have said it better myself." Hammer grinned.

He and Liam wrapped an arm around Raine's waist, then headed down the stairs.

Bryn ran toward them and kissed each of them on the cheek with tears in her eyes. "I'm so happy for you. It was touch and go there for a little bit, but you all stuck it out and fought for your family. You succeeded."

"Congratulations, storm cloud!" River scooped her up in a big hug.

"We did it. *You* did it." She wrinkled her nose. "I hope you don't have to do it again."

"You mean Marlie? Yeah, you and me both."

"Make sure you see a doctor before you use that thing on anyone else," Raine recommended.

"Trust me. I will." River made his way to Hammer, offering his hand in congratulations.

"Fuck that." Hammer embraced him. "Thank you. Believe me, I know what you did was a hardship."

Beside him, Liam laughed and brought him in for a hug, too. "Welcome to the family."

Bliss brightened the air. Joviality ensued. Within minutes, champagne corks were popping and glasses were filled.

Hammer lifted his flute. "Thank you all for the help you've given and the sacrifices you've made. To freedom, life, love, family, and happily ever after."

"I'll drink to that," Liam cheered.

"I wish I could," Raine groused until Bryn handed her a glass of apple juice. She held it up with a smile. "To us!"

Macen was thrilled to see their girl freed from all the stress and looking so happy.

As they clinked their glasses together and drank, Hammer's phone rang yet again. He tugged it from his pocket as Liam shot him a quizzical glance.

Macen checked the screen. "It's Dean."

"Maybe they've already arrested Marlie and the AUSA." Raine bounced with excitement.

"We can only hope." Liam arched a brow.

Forcing down his trepidation, Hammer pressed the speaker button. "Hey, Dean. What's going on?"

"A shit load. I assume you've heard that your neck is no longer on the chopping block."

"Yes. Sterling called a few minutes ago."

"Great. I'm so fucking happy for you, man. For all of you. I wanted to call and let you know that Internal Affairs at the Justice Department has Wellington locked in an interrogation room across town as we speak. I doubt highly he's going to see the light of day anytime soon."

"Thank god." Hammer shuddered with relief.

"That's not the best part." Dean chuckled. "Guess what I get to do tonight? I'm leaving the station in about an hour to arrest the fucking cunt who almost put you behind bars. Want to join me?"

Raine gasped and nodded.

"Where?" Hammer grinned. This night just kept getting better.

"After what I went through to get her confession, I want to see it, too."

"You must be River," Dean said. "Hell of a video, man. Outstanding job. Thank god you don't suffer from performance issues."

Raine's brother laughed. "I just couldn't think about who I was doing too much."

"Anyway," Dean continued, "if you all want to watch me haul that coldhearted bitch to jail, come to the M Grill on Wilshire."

"I know where it is," Hammer assured.

"Good. Rumor has it Internal Affairs confiscated Wellington's phone. After he put his kids to bed, he planned to hook up with Marlie there. I've checked out the restaurant's blueprints. There's a banquet room in the back. I'll call ahead and tell the maître d' that I'm meeting you there on police business so he'll give us that space and some privacy. I'll escort little Miss Plastic Twat straight to your table and arrest her there. You'll all have dinner *and* a show."

Hammer didn't hesitate. "We'll be there. But you might tell the maître d' to hide the knives. I think we're all ready to stab Marlie right now."

"Oh, yeah." Raine nodded. "I want to cut the bitch."

After Hammer ended the call, everyone found something more suitable to wear for the upscale restaurant. River headed back to his place to change and meet them there. Duncan and Bryn opted to stay home.

When the trio arrived at the eatery, River was waiting in the lot. Once inside, the maître d' seated them in the empty room in the back of the building, just as Dean promised.

"Is anyone hungry?" Hammer asked.

Raine shook her head. "Maybe after Dean arrests her, but I'm nervous right now. What if something goes wrong?"

"My stomach is as clenched as my fists," Liam agreed in a clipped tone that told Hammer the man was ready to snap.

"After is fine for me, too." River nodded soberly.

The minutes ticked by like hours. No one said much, just stared at the door, waiting.

Suddenly, Marlie and Dean entered the room. With one hand, he gripped her elbow. The other he'd wrapped around her waist.

When she caught sight of them, Marlie tried to dig in her heels, but Dean shoved her forward. Her ankles wobbled in her designer shoes.

"What the...?" Her eyes grew wide as she stared, slack-jawed, at the four of them. She pinned Dean with a hate-filled glare. "Why are they here?"

"After the shit you pulled, I figured they deserved to watch you go down." Dean gave her a brittle smile.

Hammer stood, along with the rest of his family. "We weren't going to miss this."

She reared back, blinked, then seemed to notice River for the first time. "Rick?"

"River," he corrected.

"What are you... Oh, my god. You're a cop."

The big guy laughed as he clutched Raine to his side and sauntered around the table to Marlie. Hammer and Liam followed.

"Nope." River shook his head. "But I was horribly offended by the things you said about my *sister*."

Raine looked up at her brother and smiled.

"Sister? She's your...your fucking sister!" Marlie screeched, her stare darting manically between their faces.

Hammer enjoyed seeing the moment the bitch realized Raine and River had the same eyes. Obviously, she'd never noticed. And why would she? Marlie had treated his girl like dirt under her Prada stilettos.

Marlie's face turned bright crimson. "You played me. You set me up! That's entrapment."

"Oh, no, baby," River crooned in the same whiskey-smooth voice he'd used to seduce her. "You willingly confessed to everything. Thanks for a lousy time."

"You...used me, too?" Marlie huffed.

"Yeah. Like a cheap roll of paper towels. You were the worst lay I ever had."

"Bastard!" Indignant tears welled in her eyes and spilled down her cheeks as she struggled against Dean's steely grip.

The cop simply grabbed her wrists, jerked them behind her back, slapped the cuffs on, and read the woman her rights. "You can't safeword out of this."

Marlie spat. "Let me go! This is a travesty. My parents are wealthy. I'm...I'm beautiful."

Hammer had known the pretentious bitch was shallow, but her reckless stupidity floored him. How had he ever found her remotely attractive?

Raine gave Marlie a glacial laugh as she lurched forward.

"Wait a moment, love. I just need a word or two," Liam whispered before inching closer to Marlie.

The slut's eyes grew wide. She trembled in abject fear, just as she had the night she'd slapped Raine and Liam had unleashed his verbal fury on Marlie. Time hadn't lessened her fear of the man—or his hatred for her.

Hammer watched panic play across Marlie's face as Liam leaned in closer and closer.

"You can't touch me." She sent Dean a pleading stare. "Don't let him touch me. He's going to hurt me."

Dean pretended not to hear as Liam settled his mouth in close to Marlie's ear.

"The only thing that's saving your life right now is this cop and those cuffs. You've done the unthinkable, twisted truth into lies to harm me and mine. I hope you meet with the same welcome my ex-wife did in prison." Smile cold, Liam thrust his shoulders back and returned to Raine's side.

"W-what happened to her?" Marlie paled, shaking uncontrollably.

"She got shanked in prison," Dean replied. "She was a self-centered, pretentious bitch like you. She didn't last long behind bars. Your chances don't look good, either."

"Oh, god! You can't do this to me. I can't go to prison." Marlie shook her head wildly.

"You can," Raine replied as she marched toward the evil snake, then drew back her hand. With all her might, she slapped Marlie across the face. "I'm looking forward to watching it."

The woman reared back and gasped. "You bitch! That's assault!"

Raine sent her a cold glare. "And you can't do a thing about it."

"Arrest her!" Marlie demanded.

"For what?" Dean asked.

"She hit me!"

"I didn't see anything." He shrugged.

"You liar. She assaulted me. You saw it—all of you."

"Shut up before I tase you," Dean warned.

Raine moved in with fire in her eyes and something on her mind. Hammer leaned in to hear because this ought to be good…

"How dare you try to send Macen to prison and tear our lives apart? Did you really think he could actually love you? Or did you just assume he'd be yours because you wanted him and you've never heard no your whole pampered, entitled life?" Raine shook her head. "Let me tell you, Nastysnatch, you were never special to him, just a convenient, easily forgettable sperm-whore. Hammer's devotion, love, and desire? All mine. No man, especially one with such an amazing, loving heart, could feel a damn thing for a skanky piece of trash like you."

"She's right." Despite his fury, Hammer controlled his voice carefully as he slid his arm around Raine's soft body and pulled her close. He kept his stare locked on Marlie's as he lifted Raine's chin and pressed a reverent kiss to her lips. Never once had he shown Marlie any real affection; he'd merely fucked her.

"You bastard!" Marlie hissed. "How can you put your mouth on that—"

"Be very careful," Hammer warned.

"Or what?" she challenged. "Some fearsome Dom you are, dropping to your knees to clean up her broken china and soggy fucking muffins. You're pathetic and stupid. Obviously you and that dumpy piece of trailer trash deserve each other!"

River growled.

Hammer had to hold Raine back from attacking Marlie again.

Liam stepped in and tucked their girl under his arm. "She's not worth it, love. Let Hammer say his piece."

As Liam inched Raine away, Hammer faced his nemesis. "Let's get one thing straight. To me, you were a plastic whore, no better than a blow-up doll."

"That's why she was 'obscured' for Mum. She's more artificial than real," Liam mused behind him as if he'd just figured that out.

Probably so, and they'd discuss that later. For now, Macen kept lighting into Marlie. "You're a parody of a real woman, both inside and out. No heart. No soul. Not one redeeming quality to entice any man to do more than sink his cock inside you and achieve a few minutes of empty gratification. You're a shallow, selfish, narcissistic, calculating bitch. You tried to rip me away from my best friend and our woman, and I would love to tear you apart with my bare hands."

Marlie blanched and swallowed tightly, shrinking back in fear. "Don't. Please."

"Who sounds pathetic now?" He narrowed a vicious stare her way. "I've been given something you'll never have: a second chance and unconditional love. You don't have the capacity for either. And you don't deserve them. These two people I love more than anything will always stand by me. Nothing you say or do could ever take me away from them. Think about that while you're rotting alone in prison."

Fury bubbled in his veins and throbbed in his temples. The urge to rain down his unholy wrath on the whore trembling before him thrummed through him. But her inability to let go when she should have had started this fucking disaster. He refused to make the same choice or give her another ounce of his energy.

Dismissing Marlie altogether, he pinned Dean with a forbidding glance. "Get her the fuck out of my sight."

"With pleasure." Dean grinned.

As he dragged Marlie toward the door, she spun and spat at them. "This isn't over."

"Yeah, it is," Hammer vowed.

Raine laughed, raised her hand, and waved. "Hey, bitch. Buh-bye."

CHAPTER NINETEEN

Saturday, February 23

B Y SIX THIRTY Saturday evening, Macen looked a little distracted.
Holding back an amused smile, Liam watched his friend
fidget. "What's got under your nettle?"

Not that he didn't have an idea or two why, but it would be interesting to hear Hammer's answer.

"I tried to call a few people, see if they wanted to come over for a drink tonight since your parents are leaving tomorrow. I thought it would be a nice send-off. Beck, Seth, River, Pike… They all have plans." He shrugged. "No idea what the fuck they're doing. I guess I'm a little disappointed."

Trying not to laugh, Liam turned away and pretended to pour himself a drink. Keeping Macen in the study while everyone else put the finishing touches on his surprise birthday party had been a challenge.

All day, he and Raine had been forced to get creative to keep Macen out of the house and away from all the preparation. Pike had called Macen back to the club for an "emergency" that might have involved a teeny bit of preplanned vandalism and destruction. Liam had rushed over to help, then hustled his best friend off to a guys-only lunch after the incident had been resolved, giving Hammer the argument that his mother wanted to spend more girl time with Raine.

They'd stayed for a while at the club, and Liam had noticed Hammer texting her, wanting to come home because he'd missed her. On the pretext of running errands, she'd dropped by, left them both with a gigantic smile, then driven off with a wave.

Afterward, he and Macen had decided to pay Lewis a visit. The little tech worm had tried to slam the door in their faces, but neither Hammer nor Liam had been willing to leave without making clear their opinions, as well as laying down a few threats to his pecker if the twerp ever came near Raine or Shadows again.

Satisfied they'd made their point, they'd grabbed a beer at a nearby pub before Macen had returned to Shadows to finish some long overdue paperwork. Liam had sneaked home to help with the last of the decorating and preparation. And the minute Hammer had pulled his SUV into the garage for the evening, Liam had dragged him directly into the study to stall for more time.

Thankfully, he had something important on his mind.

"My parents will be perfectly pleased without a boisterous good-bye. Hell, Mum bought half the city. It's no wonder she's still packing."

"As furious as I was the moment they rang our doorbell, they came at the perfect time."

Liam smiled fondly. "Mum has that knack."

"I'll say. All right. I'll drop the party idea. I guess I was just looking for some way to publicly thank them for all they've done to help us."

Grabbing his drink and one for Macen, Liam crossed the room and handed his friend a glass. "They know, mate. They're just glad we're together and happy."

"You're right." Hammer shot back his drink. "Still, they saved my ass."

"So did Raine."

"Yeah. Did you have any idea she'd tracked Marlie down and talked to the bitch?"

"No. Part of me wants to give her a red ass for going behind our backs—again. The other part is in awe of the size of her balls. She poked and goaded that plastic whore into all but admitting she knew you were in legal trouble."

Hammer just nodded. "If I'd walked into that bar to confront her, I'd have ended up strangling her. No way I could have simply left once she'd made that guilty comment. But Raine just plucked up and walked out. I'm still trying to decide if we should knock River's and Seth's heads together...or shake their damn hands."

"I think, for the sake of family peace, shaking hands is the better option," Liam mused. "But that wasn't what I meant about Raine saving you. I meant years ago. Think about who you'd be now without her. I suspect I'd still be a bleak bastard in denial about all my anger. My point is, we've got a house and a baby on the way. But I'd like to make it impossible for her to refuse us if we propose something like marriage again. What we need is a foolproof way to get her to accept the idea—and us—and I might just have a plan that'll work…"

Liam filled him in on the details, including some of the other joinings he'd seen online and been imagining in his head.

"I haven't allowed myself to think about that since all this legal shit exploded. I didn't dare to hope. But now that it's behind us, you're right. We should be thinking of the future. We need to make our commitment more concrete."

"Permanent." Liam nodded.

"Yeah." Hammer knocked back more of his drink. "Real for her and in the eyes of others."

They batted around a few more ideas, narrowing the possibilities into a concept that felt like them. The plan appealed, and from Macen's grin, it was obvious he felt the same.

"Tomorrow?" Hammer confirmed.

"Can you think of a better time? My parents will be gone. It will be our first day alone, happy and ready for the future. And oh, I guess it's your birthday, too," Liam teased. "Old man."

"Fuck off. I can still beat your ass."

"I don't know." Liam shook his head. "Thirty-five. Are you sure gout hasn't set in? Need some arthritis pills?"

Hammer jumped to his feet, glaring and trying to hold back a laugh.

Duncan pushed the double doors open with a disapproving stare. "What's this, then? Less than twenty-four hours after vanquishing the wild skank-muffin, you two knuckleheads are back to fighting one another?"

"No, Da. We're just teasing." Still, Liam threw a mock punch to Hammer's shoulder.

"The women are out in the backyard, enjoying the evening. Come toss back a couple with us."

Hammer picked up his drink and gave Duncan a warm smile as he headed out. Behind Macen's back, Liam gave his father a questioning stare, which Da answered with a proud little nod.

So they were ready.

Liam jogged his way up to Hammer and reached the back door first, blocking the portal. "So everyone was busy tonight, right?"

He flung open the door and shoved Macen out to a rousing chorus of "surprise!"

Their guests mingled all over the backyard. The bifold doors on the main level had been folded back to extend the indoor living out onto the patio and beyond. Floating candles with rice-paper shades in pastel colors filled the pool. Fairy lights had been strung through the trees and shrubs. An open space had been cleared for a band and dance floor at one end. At the other, a huge banquet table overflowed with delicious morsels. More tables and chairs had been set up. The fire pits had been lit to provide light and warmth. Inside, their kitchen had been transformed into a wet bar, and seating had been subtly rearranged all around in conversational clusters.

Macen looked stunned.

Camera phones flashed. The gathering laughed at his expression. Raine jumped toward him, clapping and smiling.

"Are you surprised?" She hung around his neck and kissed his jaw.

"Shocked." He glared between her and Liam. "You two cooked this up?"

"Guilty, mate. My parents helped, along with Heavenly. But our wee wench was the true instigator. She's been working nonstop since yesterday morning. What do you think?" Liam asked as he moved in beside Raine.

Hammer didn't answer him, just paused to send Raine a mock glower. "Precious…"

"Oh, have fun." She pouted. "Everyone is here to celebrate you."

Not just his birthday but the fact that he was free. It dovetailed nicely with a send-off for Duncan and Bryn, too. Just one of those shimmering pearls of an evening where everyone gathered, happy, raising their glasses and celebrating life together.

"I'm not mad," Hammer confessed. "It's perfect."

"Good." Liam slapped his back. "Oh, Pike even helped. You can thank him in a bit."

Hammer turned to him with a raised brow. "So that fire at Shadows?"

The Dungeon Monitor stepped forward with a hearty laugh. "I liked playing with matches as a kid. It came in handy."

"River, Beck, Seth… They all helped, too." Liam grinned.

"Because they love you, just like we do. So be the center of attention for one evening and smile," Raine pleaded. "We have something else for you…"

Macen peeked down the front of her dress. "Under that sexy red halter number I wish you weren't wearing?"

She rolled her eyes and skipped away. "No, perv. Over there."

Liam followed her finger. Macen did, too. The group stepped aside. A new sporty Audi sedan in a sexy, sophisticated gray came into view. Raine raced down the steps to the yard and dragged a huge red bow she'd made onto the hood.

"Happy birthday!" she yelled.

Macen gaped for a long moment, then broke out in a huge smile as he caught Liam in a headlock and shook him while everyone clapped. "What the hell did you two do?"

"Well, there was an empty spot in the garage that needed filling. Some asshole took a crowbar to the last vehicle parked there, so we've removed all those from the house, brother. This car seemed to have your name on it so…" He shrugged. "And Raine thought you'd like it."

"I love it." He kissed her. "I love you both. Thank you."

A pile of presents grew in one corner of the living room that made Hammer scowl and Liam grin. The music and food were a hit, and everywhere Liam looked, people were enjoying themselves.

For once, dread wasn't breathing down their necks…

While Hammer and Raine danced, Liam made the rounds, visiting and checking their guests.

"Hello, Master Liam—"

"Good evening, Vivian. It's just Liam here. Are you enjoying yourself?"

The older woman smiled. "I'm sorry, Sir. I mean Liam. Yes. Donald and I are having a great time."

"Thank you for coming. It means the world to Hammer." Liam hugged her warmly.

He liked these two. They were totally committed to one another and beautiful to watch together.

Moving on, Liam joined Beck, Seth, Heavenly, Dean, River, and Pike. Heavenly held all their attention, which clearly didn't thrill Beck and Seth. Liam grinned. It was a rare sight to see those two actually united on anything, even if it was simply scowling.

A few single submissives sat on the outskirts, watching the byplay, hoping for a glance—mostly from River, by the looks of it. *Like bees to honey...* Liam wondered how long before River realized it. If it took him more than two shakes, no doubt Pike would be content to pick up the slack.

"Well, I'm not really sure..." Heavenly said nervously. "I'm just a volunteer. I made the mistake of asking about his scar—"

"Well, shit. Who hasn't got scars?" Pike grinned at her, twitching the metal stud in his brow.

Beck gave him a glare that ordered him to zip it. Seth looked ready to punch him.

Liam chuckled, beyond glad that he didn't have to swim through the kinky singles scene anymore.

"I got shot once." Dean lifted up his shirt to expose his corrugated abs with a little circular scar between his ribs.

"Put that shit away." Beck rolled his eyes.

"That's nothing." River tugged up his shirt to reveal a whole collection of scars—and muscles. "I've been tagged and have so many holes and repairs from back-to-back tours—"

"Oh." Heavenly leaned in to peer closer.

"Stand down, soldier boy," Beck growled.

"She doesn't need to see your"—Seth waved in the general direction of his abs—"stuff. Put it away, man."

River and Dean shared a glance, then cracked up.

"Just making conversation." River winked.

"How about you fuck off, too?" Beck suggested.

Heavenly blinked at him, looking like she'd never heard that word in her life.

Suppressing a smile, Liam grabbed a couple of drinks from a passing waiter and handed Heavenly a fresh one. "You all right?"

"Um, yes. Fine. Thank you. Your home is really lovely. I appreciate you inviting me."

Liam cocked his head at her. While the Emily Post answer was deeply polite, he'd bet her actual thoughts weren't anything close to that. Beck and Seth were going to have a devil of a time figuring out what was going on in that lovely head of hers. He sensed it was dark—and getting darker. He made a mental note to warn them both.

For now, he simply nodded at her. "It's our pleasure. We're glad you could join us."

Beck sidled over to Heavenly and took her hand, guiding her back to his side. Funny but Liam had never imagined the good sadist could hold anyone so tenderly. "Thanks, man," he said to Liam. Then he turned his attention back to her. "Stay close to me. Lots of riffraff here tonight." He glared at Seth.

The smile she gave them had the group of men circled around her hooked. Shaking his head, Liam moved on.

Barnes was sitting in a quiet corner having an in-depth conversation with Knotty Master about…the law?

"Gentlemen, anything I can get you?"

They paused and looked at him.

"No, we're good. Thanks, Liam."

"Good piece of legal work, Sterling. Thank you for presenting our evidence to Judge Ayers."

"He hated Wellington anyway, so he grinned from ear to ear when I showed him everything. He was also damn amused by Marlie's aggressive blow job technique. He got divorced last year, you know. He asked me why he couldn't find a woman half so comfortable on her knees."

Liam laughed. "Send him over to Shadows. I'm sure we could find him one."

The other men chuckled as Liam drifted toward the dance floor. He watched his parents sway to the music. It brought a lump to his throat. He'd grown accustomed to having them here and would miss them terribly when they left for Ireland in the morning. But his mum had already assured him she would be back when Raine gave birth. Knowing he'd see her again in a few months made him less wistful.

A sentimental ballad played. As Liam circled the dance floor, Hammer and Raine came into view, all smiles, clinging to each other like two people in love. He decided to join them, crowding in behind

Raine and latching on to her hips.

"This looks like an excellent party to crash," he murmured.

"I can't remember ever being this happy. Tonight is like a dream come true." Raine clutched Hammer as she leaned back, putting her head on Liam's shoulder.

"It's perfect. I can't thank you two enough for everything, especially my new car." Macen looked up at Liam. "I'd been eyeing that one. It's extravagant."

"But well deserved."

"And to think, when you hit me up to buy you a new car, I told you to fuck off." Hammer laughed.

Raine wriggled between them. "If anyone needs a new car, it's me. I don't think schlepping the baby around in a two-seater is a good idea."

"Good point. I'll take care of that, precious." He nuzzled her neck. "Did I mention how beautiful you look tonight? Hmm. Completely fuckable and good enough to eat."

"I saw you coming down the stairs earlier. You broke my heart with your loveliness." Liam sighed in her ear, drinking in the moment. "I wish I could make time stop, hold on to tonight for a bit longer than a heartbeat. I'd like to remember you just as you are now with the light catching your hair, your eyes alive with love and laughter, and the life in your womb making you glow."

"Aww, Liam…" she breathed, craning her head to smile up at him.

"Show-off." Hammer laughed as he pressed a tender kiss to her lips.

She turned back to Macen and cocked a brow expectantly.

"What?" He shrugged in mock helplessness. "I said you look completely fuckable and good enough to eat. That's romantic, isn't it?"

She rolled her eyes. "Coming from you, I suppose it is."

"Wait," he commanded softly. "Let me try again."

Raine waited with a placid patience she almost never had.

He cupped her cheek. "You take my breath away, precious. You always have. I love you and I intend to spend the rest of my life proving it every day. How's that?"

She gave Hammer a radiant smile and drew him down for a kiss.

"Now who's showing off?" Liam smirked.

They all laughed. Both men kissed her soundly, then each offered her an arm. They got cozy in a shadowy corner of the living room, away from the guests, noise, and revelry.

Raine plopped down on the sofa. "I'm so excited. Our first real party in our new house, surrounded by family and friends. And finally, all our troubles are behind us. I have the two best guys in the world. I'm lucky."

"We have the most amazing woman." Hammer belted his arm around her waist and leaned her back against his chest. "You put up with me when I was a womanizing ass." He looked Liam's way. "You stood by me when I wasn't anyone's definition of a good friend. You both hung around, even when I was an uncommunicative prick. If anyone is lucky, it's me. You two have always done your best to be loyal, genuine, and honest. From now on, I'll do the same. Yes..." He nodded, his teasing expression saying he must be insane. "Even if it kills me."

"With that attitude, it probably will." She slapped at his thigh playfully.

Liam watched their byplay with a big smile and a grateful heart. They weren't perfect people, but they were perfect for him. "You never have to worry about me, lovely. I'm a saint."

Raine rolled her eyes. "Not even close. The very first time you got me alone behind closed doors? You had me naked in two minutes with your lips all over me and your hand up my hoo-ha."

"After that terrible public punishment I gave you with Beck?" Hammer winced. "That's something else I should apologize for. He really was supposed to just scare the shit out of you, along with giving you a mild paddling."

"I know," she assured. "But that's not what I mean. I'm talking about the morning I threw that huge tantrum." She buried her face in her hands. "Sorry. That was terrible of me."

"Waking up to a blow job was fantastic. Only time I'm going to object, by the way." Macen glanced over at Liam. "You fooled around with her right after that?"

"I did. Couldn't keep my hands off her, mate."

God, that morning seemed like a lifetime ago. So much had happened since then, yet he clearly remembered luring Raine to his bedroom, knowing he needed to keep her at Shadows to make Hammer happy…then realizing as he kissed her and felt her shatter for him that he wanted her for himself.

Liam stared at Raine, sat back. Blinked. Couldn't breathe.

Dear god, she didn't know any of that.

She bounded off Hammer's lap instantly. Liam tried to wipe the guilt off his face, but Raine had already seen that something troubled him.

"Liam?" She dropped a hand to his shoulder, bent to peer into his eyes. "What…?"

What was wrong? Something he should have confessed long ago. He frowned, cut a stare to Hammer. His friend had obviously followed the conversation and seemed to have grasped Liam's dilemma. If he confessed now, would Raine feel totally betrayed? Would it even matter that everything in his heart had changed?

Macen sent him a nod. Keeping her in the dark about the man's suicidal thoughts was for Raine's own good. Hiding this truth from her now would mostly save his own skin.

Liam rubbed at the back of his neck. "Well…I've got something to confess, love. I should have come clean about this a long time ago, and I've no excuse."

"What?" she demanded, the joy draining from her face. Wariness took its place.

"I offered to train you because I wanted to help Hammer. My best friend was lost, and I thought the only way to help him at the time would be to give him a wee nudge toward the woman he loved. Trouble was, I didn't see the danger until it was too late. One taste of you, and I was hooked. Hammer knew it, too."

She inched back from him, a furrow of confusion settling between her brows. It soon turned to anger. Her lips pursed. Hurt flared in her eyes. "You…" She shook her head. "You only wanted me so Hammer would be jealous enough to do something?"

"For the first…thirty seconds. Then I kissed you. In the kitchen. That's when it started."

"I remember."

But she didn't look inclined to accept his words or forgive him just now. Liam looked over at Hammer, who winced like maybe they'd screwed the pooch after all. *Bloody fine time to have second thoughts, mate…*

"I told you that morning where my heart was." She nodded slowly, then peered at him, eyes going wide. "I said it would always be with Hammer."

"I tried not to let it bother me. Hell, I remember telling you that I needed your trust, not your love. I've never before wished I could take something I said back so badly. God, I tried not to want you, did my best not to feel anything…but when I claimed you in the dungeon, I fell hard. Before I knew what hit me, I was in love. In my eyes, you were mine as much you were his, and I was ready to fight for you. I still am."

She blinked at him, her eyes swimming with pooling tears. "I don't know why. I fought you. I slept with your best friend the night we got together. I didn't give you everything I promised when you collared me. I wouldn't tell you I was pregnant. I ran away." She winced. "I almost chose a woman over you two. I haven't always been easy or trusting. And through it all, you've stayed." Raine lowered her head, shook it. "I'll bet you had no idea what you were getting yourself into that morning you sauntered into the kitchen, determined to make Hammer see me."

"None."

Suddenly, her entire body shook. Liam put his arms around his wee wench, slightly panicked. He didn't want her sobbing. "It's water under the bridge, love. It doesn't matter how or why we got here, just that we made it. Don't be angry—"

She tossed her head back. Tears streamed down her face—and she was laughing hysterically. "You poor man… Try to do a favor for a friend, and you wind up roped for life." She leaned in and hooked a hand behind his head. "I guess you need to spend the next fifty years making it up to me. And I need to spend the next fifty years making you glad you did."

She laid her lips over his, and he sank into her mouth, so fucking glad—and relieved—that she felt secure enough in their love to understand.

"What am I supposed to do for the next fifty years?" Hammer groused. "Watch?"

"Prove you love us just as much." She beamed at him. "Get in here and kiss me."

CHAPTER TWENTY

L IAM HAD LEFT thirty minutes ago to take his parents to the airport. The house seemed quiet, and surprisingly, Hammer missed the scent of Bryn's steeping tea. But their absence gave them back some much-needed privacy. He couldn't wait to exercise it.

As afternoon sun slanted through the windows, he leaned against the counter, admiring Raine's fluid movements as she finished the remaining dishes from last night's party and started a few sandwiches for their lunch. Pushing away from the surface, he turned her into his arms, gripping her supple hip and feeling her flesh give and mold around his fingers.

"Macen?"

He sent her a lazy grin with a hint of mock apology. "I just can't seem to resist."

And he didn't want to. He'd taken Raine in that hot August night so many years ago to save her, but Liam was right. She'd been the one to save him. With her help, Hammer had laid his ghosts to rest. They hadn't been the spirits of those he'd wronged, like Juliet, but simply a strangling guilt, thick with self-loathing and fear. They'd held him hostage for so many wasted years because he'd allowed it. He'd denied himself Raine's comfort and touch, steering clear of her because she tested his self-control in ways that terrified him. Never again. Now that he'd shed the specters of his past, Hammer committed himself completely to forging a deeper bond with the two people who owned his heart. Now that he had Raine and Liam at his side, he'd found peace, contentment, and an unconditional love he'd never known existed.

Macen felt like a new man because he was one.

Caressing her baby bump, he slid her shirt up and teased her breast through her delicate bra with a swipe of his thumb over her nipple.

When it drew up hard beneath his touch, Hammer smiled and lifted her flesh from its lacy cup, dipping his head to close his mouth around the erect bud and draw her deep. When Raine's little gasp, followed by her throaty, feminine moan, filled the air, his pride wasn't the only thing that swelled.

"Mmm…" Raine fell limp in his arms as the butter knife she'd been holding clattered to the floor. "I can't think when you do that to me."

"That's why I do it, precious." He claimed her mouth, feasting on her sweet softness, falling under her spell.

"Bloody hell, I can't leave you two alone for five minutes," Liam mockingly chided as he sauntered in from the garage.

"I tried to start lunch," Raine protested breathlessly as Hammer tugged at her lobe with his teeth and teased her nipple with his thumb again.

To his relief, Liam joined in, pressing his mouth against Raine's neck. "Who cares about bloody food? Watching you two eat at each other is far more tempting."

Raine wriggled and gently nudged at them, managing a bit of distance. "You'll care very much about 'bloody food' when your stomach is rumbling in an hour or two. Your parents at the airport all right?"

Liam gave a long-suffering sigh that Hammer related to. "Of course. They're fine."

"Let me finish making you two sandwiches. And, oh, let's figure out where we're taking the birthday boy for dinner. Then…anything goes," she promised with a smile.

"That sounds promising. Any particular restaurant you've had a yen for?" Liam asked.

Hammer arched a brow. "First, you two threw me an amazing surprise party last night. That's plenty." Then he turned to Raine with a warning. "Second, did I give you permission to end our kiss?"

He pinched her nipples with just enough force to remind her who was in charge. Hammer felt his Dominance expand as Raine sucked in a sharp gasp.

"Maybe we should forego dinner and spend some time in the dungeon." He slid Liam a questioning glance. "What do you think?"

"I'm always in favor of that, but it's not every day you turn thirty-five, Macen. And after the upheaval we've been through, I think a private celebration—just the three of us—would be perfect. We can always torment her afterward."

"Please?" Raine sent him an imploring gaze.

How could he say no? They'd been through the wringer because he'd chosen to waste his years with meaningless whores like Marlie instead of giving into his need for Raine. For that, Karma had come back around, chewing him up and nearly spitting him out.

"All right." Making them happy made him happy, too. "How about The Penthouse?"

"In Santa Monica? Love it." Raine grinned, visibly excited. "Great view!"

"It's almost as beautiful as you are."

"Flattery will get you everywhere," she promised with batting lashes.

Liam laughed. "I'll ring for a reservation. After dinner, we'll come home and remind our girl who's boss."

After sandwiches and a lazy afternoon, they piled into Macen's new car and headed down Coast Highway. He caressed the sleek steering wheel, loving the power of the ride, and smiled. They'd chosen well.

The sun dipped toward the horizon as they arrived. High above the city, their private dining alcove overlooked the glorious view of the indigo mountains and sapphire waters. Raine sat between him and Liam on a padded sectional. Hammer felt as if they'd shifted into a sublime world all their own.

After sipping sparkling cider from a delicate crystal flute, Raine set the glass down and stared at the endless ocean with a contented smile. Hammer couldn't keep his eyes—or his hands—off her, but then neither could Liam.

As their appetizers arrived, she slid a palm to her belly and gently caressed their little bump.

"You all right?" Liam pressed his hand over hers.

Macen settled his on top of them both.

"Yeah. Just thinking. We'll be welcoming a new life into this world soon."

The weight of her words lumped emotion in Hammer's throat. He was actually going to be with them—and not in some fucking jail—when their child came. He'd be there through the years to guide and raise their son or daughter. Unlike his own sire, he'd be a real father.

"If someone had told me six months ago we'd be in a committed relationship with Raine and preparing to become parents, I would have pissed myself laughing." He looked at Liam. "You?"

It seemed almost impossible. Last Thanksgiving, he and Liam had been surrounded by broken dishes, accusations, and anger in Raine's kitchen. Not long after, they'd had a debacle of a fistfight in the bitter snow at the lodge. The discord they'd provoked all faded away when he remembered the sublime perfection of the night they'd first held Raine between them.

Liam patted Hammer on the shoulder. "That would have bowled me over with a feather, mate."

Now the possibility of all their sparkling tomorrows spread out endlessly in front of them. All they needed to do was ask her one little question...

Hammer cleared his throat. "Raine, if you didn't have to choose one of us over the other, would you say yes to marriage?"

"Of course, but that's not possible." She sounded dejected by that fact.

"What if it was, in a sense?" Liam took her hand. "What would you say then?"

Tears filled her eyes and her chin quivered. "I'd be thrilled. But—"

"No buts. Just... You'd say yes," Hammer grilled her. "Right?"

Confusion furrowed her brows but she nodded. "If there was any way to marry you both without leaving either out, then of course I would."

"All fucking right," Hammer growled.

"Finally," Liam laughed as they high-fived over her head.

"What just happened?" She raised her brows, shooting both of them insistent glances. "What did I agree to?"

Liam and Hammer explained their plan.

Her smile took his breath away. "Then...yes. Yes! But not until after the baby is born. I want a real wedding dress, not something that could pass for a maternity special."

Hammer hated to wait that long. A glance over at Liam said he felt the same. But her pleading expression melted them. She'd said yes. After that, everything was a mere detail. "All right. Let's at least set a date." He pulled out his phone and launched the calendar. "August seventeenth?"

Raine's eyes flashed open wide. "That's ten days after the baby is due."

"Yeah. What's wrong with that?"

Liam shook his head. "Wanker. She'll have been pregnant for nine months. It'll take more than five minutes for her to reclaim her body."

"How was I supposed to know?" Hammer threw his hands in the air. "And why the fuck do you?"

"I've got a bloody brood of sisters, remember? They pop out babies like a muffin factory."

"Oh, my god," Raine groaned. "Don't ever refer to me as a muffin factory, Liam O'Neill, or you won't be getting near my muffin for a long, long time."

Liam scowled. Hammer threw back his head and laughed. God, it felt so good to actually find life laughable again.

"Okay, so what date would you like to get married, precious?" He handed her the phone.

Before she could answer, Liam slid his hand into her hair and tugged her to face him. "Don't ever threaten to take my muffin away again, sub."

He almost spoke the threat without cracking up…but not quite.

Raine giggled, then leaned in and kissed him. "My muffin is always available for either of you, as long as—"

Hammer slid his hand between her legs. She tensed.

"Macen," she hissed. "Don't do that here or I'll—"

"Who gives the ultimatums, precious?"

When his fingers danced over her cunt, she shuddered out a breath. "Like I said, muffin for you both."

"That's what I thought. Now pick a date, before I lift your dress and Liam spanks your muffin in front of God and everyone in this restaurant," Hammer threatened with a wink.

Raine let out a tiny squeak as Macen rubbed her slowly. "Um, I don't know. Let me think." She turned to him. "If you want me to come up with a date, you really have to stop that."

He sighed noisily but withdrew his fingers. "Hurry."

"You're so bloody romantic," Liam teased.

She couldn't help but laugh. "So if the baby is due on August seventh…"

"I have a feeling our wee one will make an early appearance," Liam murmured.

She sent him a glance that asked if he was turning into his mother. When he shrugged, her eyes lit up and a broad smile spread across her lips.

"Uh-oh, Macen. She's got that mischievous look on her face. What?" Liam demanded.

"How about September seventh?"

Liam cocked his head. "Why in bloody hell would you actually remember that date, love?"

"What? Why is that date important?" Hammer felt totally lost.

"See? He's really not good at the touchy-feely shit," Liam teased. "Enlighten him."

"Well…" She looked adorably nervous. "That's the day Liam arrived in LA. That was the beginning of us."

Macen remembered now. "That's fitting as hell. September seventh it is. Will all your…um, will you be able to fit into…oh, fuck. I'm not asking, just going with it."

As they discussed the details of their big day, the food arrived. Between scrumptious bites, they continued to talk about the day they would "officially" become one.

When the meal was through, they were stuffed, but Raine insisted they share a dessert. Soon, the waiter reappeared with a slice of mascarpone cheesecake, complete with a lit candle in the center. The other wait staff in the restaurant all gathered around their table to sing a loud and slightly off-key rendition of "Happy Birthday."

After blowing out the candle, he leaned in close to Raine's ear. "When we get home, you'll take all thirty-five of my birthday spankings."

She sent him an eager grin. "I almost wish you were older now."

"Greedy minx." Liam chuckled.

As night fell, the men sipped a glass of brandy, and Raine took a cup of tea while they drew in the city lights glistening below them.

Macen had a feeling she was fantasizing about the ceremony of their dreams.

He'd already skipped ahead to their wedding night.

Blood boiling, heart racing, he threw down the napkin and tossed back the last of his brandy. "It's time to go home."

"And share a private celebration in that big bed of ours, mate?"

A wicked smile tugged at Hammer's lips. "I thought your Spidey senses were going to disappear once your mom left."

"I don't need them for what you were thinking. It's written all over your face. In fact, I'm entertaining the very same thoughts."

"So pay the bill and let's get out of here." Raine's voice held an edge of impatience.

Sinking his fingers in Raine's hair, he held her still and nibbled at her ear while Liam devoured her lips.

"You two are killing me." She breathed hard.

"We're just warming you up, precious."

"We'll have you at a slow, rolling boil by the time we reach home, lovely," Liam promised.

Hammer eagerly thrust his hand in the air. "Waiter."

The three burst out laughing.

After the valet delivered his car, Hammer opened the back door on the passenger side for Raine but wrapped an arm around her waist, pressing his erection against her ass. "Lose the panties, precious."

She whipped around, meeting him with wide eyes. "Here?"

He nodded. "And now." When Raine darted a nervous glance at the valet, he stepped in and blocked her body. "Do it."

Hastily reaching beneath her dress, she tugged at her thong and dragged it to her knees.

"Stop," Hammer commanded. "Lean in. I'll take them from here."

As Raine bent into the backseat, Hammer tugged the scrap of silk down her calves and over her heels. He settled her onto the leather and shut the door before jogging around to the driver's seat. As he sat and put the vehicle in drive, he drew her panties to his nose and inhaled deeply. His cock sprang to life, already attuned to her scent.

Liam settled into the passenger's seat with a grin and held out his hand. Hammer obliged by dropping Raine's thong into the man's palm, watching as he inhaled their girl's tangy scent with a sigh.

"Reminds me of our trip to the lodge."

"It does." Hammer glanced at Raine in the rearview mirror. "As I remember, you were particularly needy that day, precious."

"No. I was desperate," Raine confessed. "You two teased and tormented me relentlessly."

"We were giving you your first lesson in control, proving how thoroughly we could make you ache for us."

"I still do," she whispered. "More than ever. Can you drive faster?"

He could relate to the impatience in her tone. His cock throbbed, hard to the point of pain. He'd enjoy lifting her snug, wet pussy onto him and riding her fast and hard all the way home. But tonight, he wanted to spread her out on their bed so the three of them could share every spine-bending sensation together.

He spent the drive home imagining all the dirty, wonderful ways they could make her scream. By the time he pulled into the garage, Macen's balls were churning. He was ready to shove open his door, haul Raine upstairs, strip her naked, and drag her soft body beneath him. Instead, he controlled his carnal urges, helped her from the car, and waited for Liam. Then they half led, half carried her upstairs to their room.

They'd barely cleared the doorway when he and Liam began doffing every stitch they wore, then set about stripping Raine. Anticipation zinged through the air as they explored her lush curves with their mouths, hands, fingers, and tongues. They exchanged dominant control over her body in effortless, fluid movements. With each clutch of her hair, pinch of her clit, or tug of her nipple, he and Liam moved in perfect harmony.

The beast within him stretched and yawned, slow to awaken and even slower yet to engage. Oddly, he felt as if purging his anguish and making love to Raine had tamed his inner savage. Macen wanted her like that again because he could savor her in ways he never had.

"Your skin is so soft, lovely." Liam trailed ardent kisses over her collarbones, easing lower to one breast.

Hammer slid his fingers through her hair, gently tugging her head back to capture her lips. Skimming his other hand down Raine's body, he cupped her other breast. She writhed, every move she made rocking him to the core. Her kitten-like moan hung in the air between them.

It was as if they connected on a sharper, more potent level than anytime he and Liam had taken her before. Macen wanted to harness this sensation and hold it in his heart for all time.

Easing from her lips with a smile, he found Liam tonguing her beaded nipple. "Does that feel good, precious?"

"Mmm," she barely managed to sigh.

"How wet is she?" he asked Liam.

His friend slid a pair of fingers between her plump folds, then gave a heated grin. "Very. She's more than ready."

"Liam. Hammer," she panted. "I want you both but…"

They paused and exchanged a glance.

"But?" Macen prompted.

A hesitance settled into her tone, broke across her face. "Would you… Can we try again? The ropes, I mean. I think I'm ready."

Hammer studied her intently. He wasn't sure that was a stellar idea. Not that he was afraid she'd fail. If it didn't work out tonight, they would have a next time…and a next—until she succeeded. But they'd been on one hell of a roller coaster ride the past couple of weeks. Each one had struggled to cope with the notion that their dreams might be ending. Since that morning he'd awakened hungover and feeling left out, he hadn't given much thought to pushing Raine's submissive limits. And while the three of them had grown stronger during the ordeal, Hammer wasn't in any hurry to set them up for failure again.

On the other hand, if Raine was determined to try, could he deny her?

Liam's expression reflected his own concerns. This time, they'd watch her like a fucking hawk. They were prepared and knew the signs to watch for.

"Are you sure, love?" he prodded, delving deeply into her eyes.

"Completely."

Her conviction strengthened Macen. She was willing to risk falling back into terrible dark memories for them. Yes, she loved bondage…but they did, too. She knew that.

"You don't have to do this," he murmured.

"I do. I need to try but I'm hesitant because…" She sighed. "I don't even know how to say this. I want to be with you two the way we were the other night, Macen."

Hammer understood. But the puzzled expression on Liam's face said he didn't have a clue.

"The night you went to dinner with your parents, I made love to Raine not like a Dom…just a man," Macen confessed. "That's what you mean, Raine, right?"

She nodded. "Is that even possible if you tie me up?"

Liam looked relieved to comprehend. "Anything is possible with trust, love."

"I never stopped trusting you." She looked almost horrified that either of them would think she had. "I just…in trying so hard not to think about what happened with Bill, I ignored signs. I know what to look for now. I won't say I'll never panic again. But we'll all be more aware. And I know you'll catch me."

Macen wasn't sure being aware was enough. He'd worn her trust in him thin these past few months. He ached to grant her desire, chafed to prove they were stronger together than ever, but he feared she wasn't really ready. For the first time, he was unsure whether to proceed.

It was time they negotiated with their girl.

"Precious, I would love nothing more than to tie you to our bed and make love to you again. But I need you to be honest. If the trust between us isn't strong enough right now—"

Raine looked up at him as if he'd landed on a spaceship in the front yard. "After that night you opened up about your past, I've never been more sure of you in my life."

"But I left you to Liam these past few months, ran away from you both. It's totally understandable for you to doubt—"

"Macen, stop assuming you know how I feel, especially when you're wrong." Raine eased out from between them. "First of all, I now understand why you put distance between us. My god, your wife killed not only herself but your unborn child. I can't even let myself dwell on the fact that I came close to being another woman with a child in her womb to die on you. I wish you'd told me sooner. But if you think for one minute that I'm angry or blame you for trying to deal with your demons, maybe you're the one who lacks faith in me."

Hammer stood, dumbfounded. When had she gotten this fucking strong? "Christ, I'm so proud of you, Raine. You amaze me over and over." Macen gripped her shoulders and yanked her in tight against his chest, bending close to her ear. "And yes, we're going to tie you up and make sweet love to you all night long."

"I'll get the rope, mate." Liam grinned as he pulled open the nightstand drawer and tossed three bundles to Hammer.

"On your knees." Macen turned to Raine.

She sucked in a stuttered gasp, then lowered herself to the carpet, stunningly submissive.

As Hammer admired her, pride exploded in his chest. "Wait there."

Silently, he and Liam braided the three strands of silk into a symbolic, unbreakable bond.

When they were done, Liam smiled down at their girl. "Fucking gorgeous."

"She always has been... always will be in our eyes, brother," Hammer whispered.

Raine's cheeks blossomed. She smiled at their words.

Peace settled into his chest. Not only had they all saved one another, they'd managed to help each other grow, become better lovers and people. Raine was no longer the insecure, impulsive girl who expressed her anger with tantrums and petulance. In an unbelievably short time, she'd matured into a resilient, strong, self-assured woman who would fight not only for herself but those she loved.

He was a fucking lucky man.

"Rise and lie on your back in the center of the bed, precious," Hammer instructed.

She followed his command without a word. He and Liam shared a smile, then crawled onto the mattress—each an anchor at her sides. Macen laid the rope on his pillow as he and Liam glided their hands up and down her body, preparing her for pleasure. They infused her with the heat of their touch and branded the feel of their hands onto her heart and mind.

When her milky white flesh had turned rosy and her breathing was rough, Hammer worked with Liam to thread the rope through the frame of the headboard, binding her wrists in the soft coil. They watched her intently, looking for any sign of panic or distress.

"Talk to us, lovely," Liam instructed.

"I'm good, Sir." She swallowed but nodded decisively. "I'm better than good."

The confidence in her voice filled Hammer with reassurance. A look of silent understanding passed between him and Liam. For now, they would take turns suffusing her with love while the other watched for signs of panic. It was the only safe, sane, and consensual way to help her scale her unpredictable trigger.

As if sensing their concern, Raine stared up at them. "I'm fine, Sirs. I'm safe. I'm loved. I'm protected. Don't stop."

"We have no intention of stopping," Hammer promised.

Unless you need us to.

He kept the thought to himself. She'd proven she was strong and capable. And now she was choosing to give over the power of her will in helpless surrender. He intended to bask in it and fill his primal needs, giving ecstasy back to her.

"You're going to do just fine, lovely." As Liam bent to kiss her lips, he flashed a knowing nod Hammer's way—a silent guarantee that Raine would find comfort in the ropes now.

Trusting his friend's sixth sense, Hammer paused to watch their heated kiss. His heart skipped as the palpable love ebbed and flowed between them.

His mouth watered. He wanted a taste of her, as well—everywhere. Macen eased down her lush body, leaving a trail of feather-soft kisses as he positioned himself between her legs and gripped her soft thighs. Before he could spread her open, Raine willingly parted her legs, offering herself fully.

Lifting her calf, Macen kissed her ankle, pressing his mouth to her all the way to her inner thigh, imprinting a promise to cherish her with each touch of his lips and gentle flick of his tongue. He would show her every day with his words and actions that he was worthy of her unfaltering love. Hammer wasn't letting this second chance slip through his fingers.

He knelt back in awe as he drank in the sight of her. The years he'd spent fantasizing about her—exactly this way—rolled though him in a quaking rush. He remembered the first time he'd tasted her, on the bar at Shadows. He'd been drunk, accusing, angry—a mean son of a bitch. Yet she'd never stopped longing for him, loving him with her whole heart. She wasn't a conquest, an itch to scratch, or a possession to add to his collection. This remarkable woman who lay spread out before him was his tormented past, his satisfying present, and his extraordinary future.

"Macen?" Raine's soft whisper drew him from his musings.

Jerking to attention, he found her staring, tension settling on her face.

Liam wore a matching quizzical expression. "Are you all right, mate?"

Over the past two weeks, his whole world had been nearly severed in half. But these two devoted people had helped him put it back together and smoothed out every jagged edge with their unconditional love. Hammer was better than all right. His life and this love were his every fucking dream come true.

"I couldn't imagine being better," he answered softly. "Tell us about the ropes, precious."

A broad, happy smile parted Raine's lips. God, he could spend from now until eternity drinking in that blinding glow on her face, savoring the way her inky mane spilled over their white sheets, basking in the inviting pink hue of her aroused body.

"I feel safe. Protected. Bound to you both." She wiggled her fingers and curled her hands into fists. A dreamy look of bliss danced in her shimmering blue eyes. "I'm really all right now, Macen."

"We all are, precious." He turned and arched a brow to his friend. "Liam?"

"Yes, brother?"

"Our wee wench is naked, pregnant, lusciously ripe, and begging to be devoured. I say we feast," Hammer said in a horrifically bad Irish accent.

Raine giggled. Liam laughed, but within seconds those happy sounds had been replaced with hungry whimpers and moans.

Tied beneath the driving pleasure of his and Liam's mouths and fingers, Raine writhed. Macen scored her cries and pleas into his soul as they stretched her to the edge of ecstasy, only to softly cradle her back down with soothing caresses and tender words. Over and over, they bathed her mouth and succulent pussy in sweet misery. Raine basked in their blissful torture, giving back every ounce of herself to them in enchanting surrender until their cocks were nearly bursting and spilling in need.

When they untied her hands and filled her smooth passages, stretching her full of their throbbing demand, she tossed back her head and screamed. Macen stared, stunned by her unequivocal beauty, as he and Liam followed her over in their own sublime surrender.

EPILOGUE

Saturday, September 7

"YOU READY FOR this? You're trembling."

River cupped her elbow, steadying her. Raine looked up and met his stare, so grateful to have him by her side, especially today.

"Fine. Nervous." She sucked in a shaky breath.

"Second thoughts?" River asked.

"No. Worried I'm going to trip." Raine sent him a watery laugh. "And excited. Is everyone ready? I want to do this before I ruin my makeup."

Her brother sent her an indulgent smile. "Yeah. All you have to do is climb the last step to the top of the roof and push the door open. Your two very eager grooms are waiting."

"I'm ready," she assured him with a nod.

"You are. And you look beautiful." He pressed a kiss to her forehead. "They're very lucky."

"I am, too. I thank God for them every day."

"You've all earned this happiness. Enjoy it. With my blessing."

For the past seven months, River had been the perfect big brother. God knew he'd been instrumental in Marlie's ten-year federal felony sentence for filing a false report and obstruction of justice. But Raine and River had learned to tease each other like a normal brother and sister. They'd both leaned on the other when the anniversary of their mother's death rolled around. She'd tossed him a big-ass party in May when he'd turned thirty. He'd gotten together with Liam and Hammer to return the favor when she'd celebrated her birthday at the end of June. He'd helped prop her feet up and kept her entertained as July had sweltered on and her pregnancy had forced her to suffer weeks of boring bed rest. He'd held her hand and cried tears of joy with her the day she'd become a mother. They'd grown so close in a few short

370

months.

Raine wished Mom and Rowan could be here with them. Bryn insisted they always would be in spirit, and that gave Raine comfort.

She curled her hand around his wide forearm. "I hope you find something this wonderful someday. You deserve it."

He shrugged. "Let's focus on getting you married off, storm cloud."

Raine smiled his way. "Thank you for being here, for walking me down the aisle."

They were both aware that was usually a father's duty. River had nearly as many terrible memories of the man as she did. Eager to shuttle all thoughts of Bill Kendall today, her brother stood in his place. Neither of them would give the violent sociopath who had torn their childhood apart another ounce of their energy.

River gave her a smile and patted the fingers she'd wrapped around his forearm. "I wouldn't have missed it."

"Let's do this." Raine pushed open the door that led to the rooftop access above Shadows.

Evening approached, just beginning to color the perfect blue sky with shades of yellow and orange. A gentle breeze kicked up, brushing her dark curls over her bare shoulders. The flowing silk of her white dress swished around her ankles with each ruffle of the wind, exposing her thigh through the dress's slit. The warm air caressed her torso through the transparent lace of her corset-style bodice.

She couldn't marry Macen and Liam both legally. But they weren't a conventional family, so they'd chosen to commit themselves to one another in front of the people who meant most to them in the way that made their hearts glad. Not quite a traditional wedding, something beyond a collaring ceremony, everything about this permanent handfasting had been planned as an expression of their unique love.

Raine had worn her Valentine's Day gift from Hammer and Liam—with her mother's heart pendant attached—as her something old. The something new was her dress, which she'd chosen because it paired traditional elements with very sexy details she hoped would keep her grooms squarely focused on her. The something borrowed was a beautiful pair of dangling pearl earrings Bryn had lent her for the ceremony, since she'd married Duncan wearing the same jewelry.

Something blue… The strings holding her corset together were a beautiful peacock color that held her post-pregnancy body in tight while flowing all the way to her bare feet.

The music started, simple guitar strands. Everyone rose.

As she looked toward the altar, her breath caught. Liam and Hammer waited for her with wide smiles and eyes filled with naked love, standing shoulder to shoulder under a towering arch of white, blush, pink, and pale yellow hydrangeas and baby roses. All the flowers had been tied together with flowing white, gray, and peacock ribbons.

A pair of gauzy pale drapes had been swept back from the center of the altar, framing her men. They looked so masculine and beloved, each in gray tuxedos. Hammer wore a peacock-hued vest and a black tie. The colors suited his warm skin and rugged face. Liam wore the inverse, and she loved how spectacularly handsome he looked with that rich blue tie setting off his dark eyes.

Despite her shaking legs and teary eyes, Raine managed to put one foot in front of the other and walk down a trail of peacock silk trimmed in shimmering gray, floating on a cloud of white petals.

The venue was beautiful, everything she had dreamed. Heavenly— bless her—had helped Raine create this magical vision. But it was even more perfect to her because the two men waiting for her at the end of this momentous walk filled her entire heart, owned every single day of her future, and worked together to securely cradle her soul.

Their wedding song played on. The singer's heartfelt voice vowed that he belonged to her from this moment on, before he invited her to take his hand and share forever. He promised to give her his love completely. The sentiments swelled and resonated inside her. She gave it back to them with every expression and heartbeat, every touch and kiss she couldn't wait to bestow on them.

Damn, she was going to start crying in earnest.

As River escorted her to them, Macen and Liam parted to make room for her between them, where she belonged. She caught sight of a framed chalkboard that had been propped on an easel in the center of the parted curtains.

A CORD OF THREE STRANDS IS NOT EASILY BROKEN.

Raine hadn't expected that, and her heart melted all over. She glanced at her men, pressing a hand to her trembling lips. They both beamed proudly. She'd arranged the ceremony, and reception in the club below, as a labor of love. But Liam and Macen had added this meaningful detail all on their own.

It utterly described their relationship.

She gripped her bouquet, her smile watery and full of joy.

River handed her off, each holding one of her hands in theirs. Then he kissed her cheek. "I love you, storm cloud."

"I love you, too, big brother," she managed to choke out.

He clapped Macen on the shoulder, gave Liam a brotherly nod of approval, then took his seat in the front row of silk-draped chairs, dwarfing the pink bow across the back.

Raine turned to face the future with her men.

As one, they all stood before the altar. Raine swallowed, so much less nervous now that they both held her hands and flanked her, the pillars of her life.

As she'd planned this day, Seth had helped her search Los Angeles for someone who performed poly-commitment ceremonies. Raine had interviewed several candidates but never quite felt the connection to any. None of those people had any meaning in her life, hadn't played any part in bringing her, Macen, and Liam together.

Beck had discovered he could be ordained online to perform handfastings, so he'd volunteered. Seeing him in a crisp suit standing in front of them was a bit surreal—but very sweet. When he winked at her, she gave him a teary giggle.

"Not too late to change your mind, princess," he teased.

Liam glared. Hammer growled.

Raine just shook her head and tried to swallow the lump in her throat. "It was too late a long time ago."

He gave her one of his rare, real smiles. "Then let's get you married."

Suddenly, the doctor and sadist stood taller, taking on an almost stately air. Beck never ceased to amaze her.

"We're here today to witness the joining of three people we all know and admire. They've elected to share their lives together because they're filled with love for one another. They've asked us to watch them because they'd like us to share their joy. They've chosen to celebrate their commitment on this day because exactly one year ago they all stood together for the very first time and began to fall in love."

Raine glanced over at Liam with tears falling, glad she'd remembered to wear waterproof mascara. But what she really thanked God for was the man who'd left his adopted home in New York a year ago today to unwittingly start a new future. He might have intended to come for a temporary visit, but he'd stayed and become a permanent part of their forever.

"Some of their bonds are older than others," Beck continued.

Liam glanced over her head to meet Hammer's stare. They smiled, shared a nod that said they were beyond friends, even closer than brothers. She turned to Hammer as he looked down at her. She remembered Macen the night he'd taken her in, the day he'd celebrated her college graduation, the moment he'd first touched her, the time he'd finally admitted he loved her. So many years, so many memories. Yet in some ways, they'd only begun a year ago on this date—when Liam had finally completed them.

"But they all commit with their free will and their whole hearts. Today, three officially become one interwoven, unbreakable cord of love."

From behind him, Beck produced a braid of silk that she, Macen, and Liam had previously braided together in solemn silence and abiding devotion. White, gray, and peacock strands blended perfectly, shining in the falling sunlight as he draped it across his palm. Together, they leaned in to kiss the length of silk.

"Join."

At Beck's soft command, they all held up their hands, fingers curling around the wrist to the right. Liam held her. She caressed Macen. He gripped Liam. An endless flow of love.

"This bride and her grooms have chosen a three-stranded cord as a symbol of the lives they have chosen to lead together," Beck told the bystanders.

Then he wrapped their braided cord around their joined flesh, beginning with her wrist, all the way across Hammer's hand, and ending with Liam's fingers on her.

"Liam, Raine, Macen, if you let them, these are the hands that will passionately love you, utterly cherish you, and wrap you in comfort through your lifetime. These are the hands that will hold you when fear or grief fills you. These are the hands that will wipe away every tear, whether they be from sorrow or joy. These are the hands that will tenderly hold your children and join your family as one. These are the hands that will give you strength when you need it, support and encourage you to pursue your dreams, and comfort you through difficult times. Do you commit to holding your partners with that care from now until death parts you?"

"I do," Liam promised, squeezing her hand.

"I do," Raine managed to choke out between her happy tears.

"I do," Macen vowed, looking like he wanted them to know he meant every word.

"Up until this moment, you have been separate in thought, word, and action. As your hands have been bound together by this cord, so, too, shall your lives be bound as one. May you forever be united, sharing in love and loyalty, joy and devotion."

Beck unwound the ribbons from their wrists and nodded their way. "Exchange the symbols of your new life together."

Raine set her flowers on a little pedestal to the side and untied the rings she'd secured with a tiny bow to the stem of her bouquet. She turned to Liam first with three interwoven bands of polished titanium he'd chosen. Sophisticated with a bit of masculine shine. It fit him perfectly. With Hammer's support at her wrist, she pushed the ring on Liam's finger. His warm eyes caressed her with tender adoration as he silently promised her the rest of his days.

"I love you," she whispered.

Then she loosened Macen's ring from its ribbon. Liam supported her hand as she slid the triple bands of tungsten onto his finger. The black metal looked sleek and mysterious and masculine on his hand. It was a perfect reflection of the man. When their stares met, the hazel eyes she'd seen stern or closed or unreadable for so many years were now wide open with love.

"I love you," she murmured to him, too.

Then he pulled a ring from his pocket, something the two of them had designed especially to celebrate their love for her. Raine hadn't seen it yet, but like the others, it had three bands intertwined. As she clapped eyes on it, she gasped. A ring of titanium, a ring of tungsten, and a ring of sparkling pave diamonds wrapped around one another. Together, he and Liam slid the beautiful symbol onto her finger.

"You're our life," Liam said.

"And our heart," Hammer added. "Precious."

"We love you," they said together.

Raine teared up again. The weight of the ring was more than mere metal. The gravity of their commitment wrapped around her finger, around her heart. She knew it would never dissolve or fade—and that filled her with a euphoric bliss she'd never even imagined.

"What these three have worked so hard to put together, let no asshole put asunder. And now—as far as I'm concerned—you're married!"

Raine and her men laughed, along with the rest of the small gathering.

She glanced at Macen and Liam, committing this golden instant to memory. They smiled back at her, obviously as in the moment and as gloriously happy to be here as she was.

It felt so good to be committed, joined in the eyes of their friends and community.

As she basked and looked forward to the party to follow—as well as all their tomorrows—Liam suddenly curled a hand under her chin and brought her gaze up to his. He wasn't smiling now.

"Kneel."

Raine gasped. She flipped a stare to Hammer and saw the same Dominant steel on his face.

They were collaring her, too?

Her heart fluttered in her chest. She'd wondered if they would want to express their commitment this way someday. She'd hoped but...

Instead of asking questions they would surely answer later, she gave them a grateful nod and bowed her head, exposing the unprotected length of her nape to them, as she dropped to her knees.

"Look at us," Macen commanded.

She obeyed and watched Liam lift something from his pocket and dangle it in her face. A strand of titanium combined with a strand of tungsten to support a heart-shaped lock trimmed in diamonds. The front had been engraved with their initials and the date.

Raine had never seen something more beautiful—more heartfelt—than this expression of their devotion. The fact they'd surprised her only made it more special.

He gave Macen one end of the chain as he hung on to the other. Together, they fastened it around her neck. The weight felt blessedly welcome. It had been nearly ten months since Liam had first fastened his collar against her skin, only to remove it twenty-two excruciating days later. And Hammer… Raine had never dared to hope that he would collar her, especially now that she knew he'd vowed never to take a permanent submissive and why.

Raine couldn't stop herself from reaching up to feel her exquisite new collar dangling just above her beating heart.

Liam reached in his pocket again and withdrew two little keys for the lock. He palmed one and handed Macen the other.

"You're ours always," Hammer said.

"Forever," Liam seconded. "Because we want to tie you to us in every way we can."

"Yours, Sirs." Raine thought her heart would burst as she bowed her head again and felt their stares of approval caressing her.

When they both braced a palm under her elbow, she rose to her feet.

She really was the luckiest woman in the world.

"Kiss already," Beck demanded. "Put an exclamation point on this marriage/collaring/handfasting shit so we can celebrate."

Raine laughed, feeling lighter and more in love than she ever had as she turned to Liam on her left and lifted her lips to his for a kiss.

He looked into her eyes as if he wanted to reach into her heart and hold it in his hands. He gave her a tender press of his lips and nudged inside to deepen the kiss. He lingered, imprinting himself on her heart—just as he had with their very first kiss—before he eased away. "You look more lovely than ever now that you're ours."

"You're mine now, too, buster," she teased.

"I'll not be forgetting that, I promise."

Raine blew him a kiss, then turned to Macen in silence. He took her face in his hands and swooped close, staring into her eyes for a breathless moment.

"Precious…"

He didn't have to say more than that. She knew what he felt. "It means everything to me, too."

The smile he gave her in return told Raine that she'd perfectly read him. Then he captured her lips with his, seizing her, filling her mouth for a hot spark of a moment before he eased away.

It was done. They were one.

Together, they turned to the rest of the gathering and raised their clasped hands. Their guests stood and cheered as the happy trio bounded back down the silken path to the stairwell.

Halfway there, Hammer hoisted her into his arms. She squealed in surprise, then laughter. Liam put a fist in her hair and tipped her head back before stealing a kiss. They didn't give her much of a breath all the way down to the party in the dungeon.

Most of the equipment had been pushed against the wall, moved out, or artfully hidden behind a drape so everyone could party now…and play later.

"I'll be right back, precious." Hammer kissed her cheek.

Before she could ask where he was going and if everything was all right, Liam distracted her with a soft kiss. "Are you feeling thirsty? It was a bit warm up there."

He was always kind and thinking of others. It was one of the things she admired most about Liam. "Please."

As they stepped away, guests began joining them downstairs, Beck first. He wore a wide grin and helped Heavenly, who held the other two pieces of Raine's heart, which had expanded to accommodate her little twin miracles five weeks ago.

"Hi, my baby girls. Come see Mommy." Raine held out her arms.

Heavenly smiled softly. "They're such angels. Slept through most of the ceremony. Well, Ciara did. Catronia looked around at all the colors when she was awake."

"Because she's so curious." Raine took one child, then the other, still marveling that she had two perfect bundles of girl with blue eyes, little bowed mouths and—no doubt about it—the O'Neill chin.

All their worrying that Macen had gotten her pregnant that torrid night Liam had first collared her had been for nothing. According to Bryn, her Irishman had actually done the job during their getaway at the lodge, right after Raine had figured out she was in love with him. Her pregnancy had been a shock, and she had come down some long, hard roads with her men to find this happy pinnacle in her life. But she wouldn't trade a moment. Their daughters were perfect, and Hammer doted on them like mad. The twins would have both her big, bad men wrapped around their perfect, tiny fingers.

Seth joined them next, sidling up on the other side of Heavenly. She gave the doctor and the former cop both a sideways glance. Raine tried not to smile too wide. Now that Seth had moved here from New York and hung out his PI shingle, they both chased Heavenly without mercy. There was another interesting romance brewing, and Raine couldn't wait to see how it all unfolded. First, the guys would have to figure out that their bigger battle wasn't against one another but Heavenly's reticence.

And her wide-eyed shock at the bit of dungeon equipment she could see.

"What is that?" She pointed to a spanking bench.

Not just any spanking bench—*the* infamous one on which Liam had first claimed her. The one on which Hammer had flogged her and proclaimed that she belonged to him and Liam. Raine probably should have tucked it away, but she couldn't bring herself to...and she'd been curious about Heavenly's reaction.

Seth and Beck both jockeyed to be the one to give her a tour of any equipment she'd like to explore.

Raine grinned. Yes, the sidelines would be an amusing place to watch this drama just waiting to happen.

Caitlyn, Meg, and Aisling, three of Liam's sisters, had flown out to see the nuptials. Rosaleen and Shauna had come with Bryn when Raine had given birth to the twins—and they'd been immensely helpful to her as a new mother. The last, Maeve, promised to come when her youngest got a few months older.

Raine had bonded right away with all of Liam's family. Now she felt immensely blessed. She'd started her life outside the Kendall house completely alone yet wound up blessed with so much love.

Her sisters-in-law scurried up, gooing and cooing at the twins. Clearly, they missed their own children. But they loved their new nieces, too.

After pressing a kiss to each tiny forehead, Raine relinquished her daughters to their aunts with a smile and a wave. They went happily with bright eyes.

River approached with a hug. "Committed, collared. Happy and settled. It's not exactly what I pictured for you all these years. But it's better. It makes you happy."

She nodded. "You going to stay and maybe play? Lots of interesting people coming tonight…"

In fact, Dean Gorman sauntered down the stairs in a sharp navy suit. A few eager subs followed, all looking pretty in their summery dresses. Pike trailed them, coming down the stairs in typical leather and eyeing their asses. His one concession to the event was a white dress shirt and a loose black tie. With spikes around his wrists and a wicked grin on his face, no one would accuse him of being conventional. Donald escorted his wife and sub, Vivian, who looked teary-eyed, to the bar lining the back wall. They waved, and she raised a hand in return.

"I don't know. I'd hang with Dean. He's a good guy," her brother said. "But he'll pair off quickly, I'm sure."

River had no more opened his mouth when the cop began chatting up a pretty, blushing redhead Raine had noticed recently around the club.

"The only other person I know who will stay beyond the dinner and dancing is Pike, and he's an asshole."

"Aww, you're just being kind." Pike clapped her brother on the shoulder. "Didn't you say I was a massive, bleeding douche canoe last week?"

"I actually said worse." River refused to look at the DM.

"Just because I told you to get your shit together."

"I don't need you in my fucking ear."

"If you're going to play here, you have to play right."

Oh, so River had been hanging around and checking out the scene? She sent her brother a speculative stare.

He turned a dull shade of red. "I'll leave. Besides, if you three are going to scene here tonight, I'd rather not watch."

"No." Hammer approached Raine from behind and slipped an arm around her waist. "We're leaving."

She whirled to face him. "We are?"

"Indeed," Liam said as he brought her a glass of water. "Hammer and I have decided we're going to have a proper honeymoon. River, Pike, bugger off. We'd like to talk to our bride."

Their faces were priceless. Each dutifully hugged her and shook her men's hands before turning away, bickering the moment they took a step.

"What are they arguing about?" Raine asked.

"Not what, who. They haven't found her...yet," Liam drawled. "I have a feeling she's coming."

Raine couldn't picture that, but she was learning—fast—not to discount her Irishman when he had a feeling about something. Even though his mother was a continent away, he continued to tap into whatever gift she'd passed down to him with some really interesting results.

Hammer laughed as he watched River and Pike make their way across the dungeon, toward the bar. "After the shit your brother gave us, that would be poetic justice."

"But once the children came, they'd be dumb and dumber. I don't know which one is more clueless about babies," she drawled.

That had Macen and Liam laughing even harder.

"'It's a baby-sized baby,'" Hammer chortled. "That was so damn funny."

"Not when I thought Gwyneth had really brought me a son. But now? Fucking hysterical."

Raine had heard this story and she just shook her head. "Maybe I should make that dumber and dumbest."

"Undoubtedly." Liam shook his head. "And you want to know where we're taking you for a honeymoon, don't you, love?"

She grinned. "Now that you mention it, I do. But what about the girls? Are we bringing them?"

"Nope." Hammer shook his head and withdrew some plane tickets from his coat. "We're whisking you to where you say you've always wanted to go: Paris. And after this trip, you'll need a new safeword."

She clapped a hand over her mouth as a thousand feelings all barraged her—shock, thrill, gratitude. Love. "Really?"

"We leave tomorrow."

"But who will stay with the twins? I'm breastfeeding and—"

"Shh." Liam pressed a finger to her lips. "My sisters are staying. And, of course, Vivian can't wait to sit with the girls for a spell. The rest we'll work out. We'll only go for a few days this time, but we deserve a wee break to enjoy one another after everything we've done to reach this point."

Raine couldn't argue with his logic, so she didn't try. She would miss her daughters terribly. Her men would, too. But they had to remember to invest time in their relationship to keep it healthy and flourishing. And what better time to start than their honeymoon?

"I'm excited!" She clapped.

"Next time we'll take a family trip and visit Ireland. But for now… My sisters have packed for you. Don't expect many clothes in your suitcase, love," Liam drawled.

"That suits me, precious." Hammer's eyes darkened.

Yeah, that suited her, too. She laughed, so happy she thought she might burst. "Darn…"

Just one thing would make her happier.

She looked at Liam in question. He gave her an indulgent smile and a nod.

With an excited little hop, Raine bounced over to him and peppered kisses all over his face.

"What the hell?" Hammer groused. "Where's mine?"

When she turned to him, she wore a grin so bright it almost hurt her cheeks. "Right here." She kissed him softly before she took his hand and led it to her belly. "And right here."

Macen didn't say anything for a long moment, just sent her a puzzled frown. "I don't…"

Raine bit her lip and looked at Liam. His expression told her to be patient, that all would be well.

Suddenly, Hammer's hazel eyes went wide. He jerked his stare from her abdomen back up to her face. "You're pregnant again?"

"Yeah. I wanted to give you a child, too. It's the only thing I can give you that you can't give yourself. Liam and I have been talking about it for a few weeks and started cooking up an idea…"

Macen whirled on Liam. "You didn't have a 'dire work emergency' last week."

"No, mate. Our girl ovulated and…" He shrugged. "I thought you'd make an excellent father again. I gave you a couple of nights together to enjoy, so we could be sure it worked."

Macen looked speechless and overjoyed. "A baby?"

Liam leaned in. "A son. Congratulations. My mum sends her best, too. She called me the minute it happened—literally. But I already knew."

With a whoop, Macen picked her up and twirled her around, pressing an insistent kiss to her lips. The instant her feet hit the floor, Liam wrapped her between them with a laugh.

"That's it," Hammer declared. "If we're going to have three children by next summer, you need to legally marry one of us."

Something hopeful and wanting tugged at her heart. God, she'd love that—just one more way to entwine their lives. But she'd made a vow. "I won't choose between you two, Macen. We've been over this."

He acknowledged her with a thoughtful nod of his head, then turned to Liam. "What do you think?"

"I agree, mate. It will make things far easier legally, especially whenever there are hospitals involved again."

They all remembered that terrible morning Bill had nearly killed her. Raine had called and cried for her two men, only to learn later that because they weren't family legally, they hadn't been allowed in the emergency room with her. Traditional marriage would make all the practical things like wills and deeds and titles a bit simpler. But it could complicate every other facet of their lives, especially the balance of their relationship.

"I know. But I won't choose. Let's be happy with the way things stand now."

"What if Liam and I chose for you?" Hammer drawled.

She had never considered that. But Raine was secure in the fact that she loved them equally. "You'd both be happy with that?"

"Thrilled," Hammer promised.

"Beyond." Liam nodded.

"Wait. You've already decided which one of you…"

They both shook their heads.

"We'll choose right here." Her Irishman pointed to the ground.

"Yep." Macen reached into his pocket. "Right now."

He pulled out a quarter.

Raine gaped at them. "Seriously? You're going to flip for it?"

"Got a better idea?" he challenged.

Liam raised a brow at her.

She paused, thought, tried a few ideas on for size…then shook her head and laughed. "No. It's equal and fair."

"Precisely." Liam nodded.

"Okay, man. You call it," Hammer said to him.

"Heads."

"I'll take tails." Macen winked at her. "I certainly like yours."

With a laugh, she rolled her eyes. "Do it already."

"And once it's decided, we're flying to Vegas and getting the deed done before leaving for Paris."

Raine opened her mouth to object. She wanted a wedding night in her bed, a little more time with her daughters…

Liam shook his head at her in warning and tugged gently on her new collar. "That's non-negotiable, love. Say yes."

She wasn't going to win this battle, and she could foresee a lot of occasions in the future when the testosterone would outweigh her estrogen. But they loved her and always wanted what was best for all of them. Besides, she had plenty of will of her own.

"I'm probably crazy but…yes."

A wide smile broke across Macen's face.

Liam looked pretty damn happy, too. "Do it, mate."

"My pleasure." He settled his thumb under the coin and, with a little jerk of his wrist, sent it hurtling into the air.

It sparkled in the light, spinning, twirling, nearly reaching the tall ceilings. As she looked up, they both reeled her in, planting their lips wherever they could—cheeks, forehead, lips, neck. Raine giggled.

The little clink of the coin hitting the hard floor sounded right beside her. When she tried to look, they both brought her face back to them.

She let out a frustrated huff. "Don't you want to know?"

"I already do." Liam laughed.

"It doesn't matter to me," Macen vowed. "Whatever the outcome, you belong to us both."

Raine smiled at the men who had forever enriched her life with strength, fortitude, commitment, and love. "I do."

Read on for excerpts from Shayla Black and Jenna Jacob!

ONE DOM TO LOVE
DOMS OF HER LIFE: Raine Falling (Book 1)
Now Available!

Raine Kendall has been in love with her boss, Macen Hammerman, for years. Determined to make the man notice that she's a grown woman with desires and needs, she pours out her heart and offers her body to him—only to be crushingly rejected. But when his friend, very single, very sexy Liam O'Neill watches the other Dom refuse to act on his obvious feelings for Raine, he resolves to step in and do whatever it takes to help Hammer find happiness again, even rousing his friend's possessive instincts by making the girl a proposition too tempting to refuse. But he never imagines that he'll end up falling for her himself.

Hammer has buried his lust for Raine for years. After rescuing the budding runaway from an alley behind his exclusive BDSM Dungeon, he has come to covet the pretty submissive. But tragedy has taught him that he can never be what she needs. So he watches over her while struggling to keep his distance. Liam's crafty plan blindsides Hammer, especially when he sees how determined his friend is to possess Raine for his own. Hammer isn't ready to give the lovely submissive over to any other Dom, but can he heal from his past and fight for her? Or will he lose Raine if she truly gives herself—heart, body, and soul—to Liam?

As LIAM CREPT further down the hall, he heard Raine bustling in the kitchen. Slowing his step as he reached the door, he watched her bowed head and shaking shoulders. A shuddering sob later, the girl reached for a stainless steel bowl, grabbed a few cups of sugar, some eggs, and butter.

A fond little smile curved his lips. Raine was rarely predictable—

except in this. The short-fused firecracker often flew off in ways he'd never seen in a submissive, and Liam was never sure when or how she'd explode. Obviously, she'd had no formal training, and no one took her to task. But when she started thundering like a summer storm, Raine always came to the kitchen as if being one with the dough soothed her.

Seeing her tears and defeated posture, Liam itched to rattle Hammer into next week for closing himself off from the very woman who could save him.

Raine cracked an egg over the bowl and sniffled to hold in her tears. He drew in a bracing breath. What to say to the distraught girl? If he barged in, she'd bristle and give him a cold shoulder. He had to tread carefully since he didn't know exactly what ran through her wee head. And that meant he couldn't let her in on his plan. Raine needed to feel valued, not like she was simply bait. Nor would she truly learn to submit if she believed what lay between them was only an act for Hammer's benefit. It had to come from her soul or Macen would see straight through it. His friend's jealousy must spur him to act. Most of all, he didn't want Raine hurt. If he made her his conspirator and the ploy failed, the defeat would crush her delicate heart.

"Maybe I should just quit." She grabbed a wooden spoon and attacked the dough, adding in brown sugar. "Leave. There's nothing holding me here, that's for damn sure."

His gut clenched at the finality in her miserable words. He refused to let her go without doing everything in his power to persuade her to stay. He had to act now.

Raine yanked a fresh dishtowel from the drawer, pressed it to her face, and took a few deep breaths to calm herself. A long moment later, she threw the towel down, flipped on the faucet, and shoved her hands under the stream of water. She hissed in a breath, and he frowned. How badly had she cut herself?

"Except...this is home. Where would I go?" she muttered as she cut off the water. "But how can I stay here?"

That was his cue.

Liam raised his fist and knocked on the door. Raine whipped her head around, hope brimming in her eyes. It visibly died when she realized he wasn't Hammer.

She surprised him when she cast her gaze to the floor submissively.

"Hi, Liam. Sir. Um, if you're here because you're worried or something, I'll be fine. I'll bake a batch of chocolate chip cookies and be as good as new."

So sweet. And lying. Eventually, he'd both soothe and paddle her until she learned to be honest, but for now he simply tried to set her at ease. "While I've little doubt about your culinary skills, since your baked goods are most excellent, I doubt they'll mend your woes, lass. Show me your hands."

Obediently, Raine held them out. Liam stepped closer, taking her wrists in his grip and examining her fingers. "You've a few wee cuts, but nothing serious." He gave her a smile and gently kissed her palm. "I think you'll live."

She stiffened. "I told you I'm fine."

"Your hands, yes. What about your heart?" He watched her shoulders slump. "I've come with a proposition. Would you hear me out?"

THE YOUNG AND THE SUBMISSIVE
DOMS OF HER LIFE: Raine Falling (Book 2)
Now Available!

Raine Kendall has everything a woman could want…almost. Sexy, tender Dom Liam O'Neill is her knight in shining armor, but Raine keeps pinching herself. Is he too good to be true or is this growing connection one that could last a lifetime? She's constantly torn by her abiding feelings for her commanding boss, Macen "Hammer" Hammerman, especially in the wake of the mind-blowing night he cast aside the barriers between them and ravaged every inch of her body.

Hammer, Liam's former best friend, can't stop coveting Raine. But Liam is determined to hold and guide the woman he loves and see if she can be the submissive of his dreams. However, he's finding that her trust is hard won and he needs a bloody crowbar to pry open her scarred soul. So he risks everything to win her once and for all. But once he's put his daring plan in motion, will it cost Liam his heart if he loses Raine to Hammer for good?

MACEN "HAMMER" HAMMERMAN stifled the mundane conversation with his assistant, Raine Kendall, and stood, bracing his hands on the desk between them. Though his office door stood open—he wasn't "allowed" to talk to her otherwise—they were as alone as they'd been in weeks. It was now or never. He had an important question to ask.

"Tell me something, Raine. Your period is what, five days late?"

Blood leached from her face. "Wha—I… How would you even know that?"

Because it was his business. After six years of being her mentor, caretaker, and employer, he'd recently given in to his gnawing hunger and fucked her in every way known to man. And recklessly, he'd done it without a condom. Since admitting how much he wanted her, he couldn't seem to stop. But the elaborate collar that now dangled from her neck strangled him with one indisputable fact: She was owned. Taken. Completely off limits. Property of another.

That son of a bitch, Liam O'Neill. His former best friend.

"Kind of blows your theory that I've always looked through you, doesn't it?" He smirked. "Since you came to Shadows, I've kept tabs on your cycle every single month. You promised you'd let me know if you were so much as a minute late. I've been waiting."

THE BOLD AND THE DOMINANT
DOMS OF HER LIFE: Raine Falling (Book 3)
Now Available!

After spending weeks trying to reach Raine Kendall, Dominants Liam O'Neill and Macen Hammerman have finally broken past the walls to their submissive's wounded heart. Before they can enjoy their newfound closeness, Liam's past comes back to haunt him when his ex-wife drops in—with a secret that could tear his world apart. Forced to leave Raine in Hammer's care, Liam is stuck on the outside, stewing in frustration and insecurity…and wondering if Raine no longer needs him or if Hammer alone completes her.

Always the pillar of strength, Hammer tries to help Liam while sheltering their woman. But Raine soon discovers the truth that threatens the trio's chance of a happily-ever-after. Determined to hold them together, the two men cook up a scheme to uncover the ex's secret. When an old nemesis returns and targets Raine, can Liam and Hammer come together to slay the danger and save the woman they both love?

"HAMMER. WAKE UP," a familiar voice whispered in his ear. "There's a problem."

Macen "Hammer" Hammerman jackknifed up, the fog of sleep dissipating. Liam O'Neill stood above him, over the bed.

Why the hell was his best friend waking him up in the middle of the night?

With a frown, Hammer rose on one elbow. "What?"

Liam's stare fell on Raine Kendall in the rumpled bed they'd all shared last night. Hammer glanced at the woman they both loved. Images of her moaning, melting, and writhing between them flashed through Hammer's brain like a sensual strobe. Thankfully, she was still asleep, her inky lashes fanning over her rosy cheeks.

But Liam's face tightened, the man's tense expression giving him pause. "Tell me."

"She's exhausted. Let's not wake her." He jerked his head at the open door. "Bathroom."

Hammer scowled. Had something happened after he'd crashed? Had Liam and Raine fought? No, he wouldn't have slept through that. Whether she was upset or in the throes of passion, she never held back.

What if Liam had reconsidered their arrangement and refused to share her anymore? That idea whacked Macen with fury. After years of denying himself her touch, he couldn't wait to have her again. If his Irish pal thought she still belonged exclusively to him simply because she'd once worn his collar, he'd lost his fucking mind. Hammer had rescued the scared runaway from an alley and taken care of her for six years. That damn well counted for something.

Besides, Raine needed them both. She'd only begun to lower those towering walls around her heart in the past two days, when they'd finally started working together. Sharing her might be a new arrangement, but he and Liam had been down this path before, though not with her…and not with success. Still, Raine made them better men—and partners. Hammer knew Liam had sensed the same perfection when they'd held her. Would he really want to mess with that?

Before Hammer could say a word, Liam grabbed his trousers, donned them, and stomped to the bathroom.

Hammer brushed his lips over Raine's forehead. "I won't let anything or anyone come between us, precious. I promise."

Feeling a twinge of pain in his jaw where Liam had punched him the night before, Hammer stood and worked it from side to side. Their fight had been inevitable. Jealousy and resentment had brewed for the past month, ever since Liam had taken an interest in Raine. Hopefully, the brawl had finally cleared the air between them.

Sighing, Hammer yanked his pants up and joined Liam, shutting the door behind them. In the light, Macen noticed his friend's nose was slightly swollen, but neither of them looked too worse for wear.

"I'm listening. What's the problem?"

Liam sighed. "Gwyneth just called me."

What did Liam's ex-wife want?

FALLING IN DEEPER
Wicked Lovers, Book 11
By Shayla Black
Now Available!

After a violent tragedy nearly destroyed her, Lily Taylor ran away, changed her name, and started over. When her deadly nemesis resurfaces to eliminate his loose end, she turns to the last man she should trust—a stranger with a history of violence and an intoxicating sexuality she can't refuse...

Though strong-armed into locating Lily to help put away a drug lord, ex-con Stone Sutter isn't anyone's snitch. When he finds the terrified beauty, he vows to keep her safe—but he isn't sure he has the strength to shield her from his own desires.

As an unquenchable fire sparks between them, Lily's tormentor stalks ever closer and she must overcome her darkest fear to survive. Can she trust the bond she and Stone have formed as they're falling in deeper?

"OH, FUCK. YOU'RE so beautiful. You need this now, don't you? Yeah," he agreed when she nodded frantically. "Let it take you under. Let me hear you scream."

Lily couldn't think of anything she wanted more. As she circled her hyperaware nerve endings again, her body jerked. Desire surged. When Stone bent to take her nipple in his mouth, she clasped the back of his head and anchored him to her. Not that he'd do anything except help her drown. But this time nothing would be sweeter.

He dragged a hand up to her other nipple and tangled his fingers with her own. Together, they manipulated the tip of that breast while he sucked the other hard and scraped the very tip with his teeth.

Sensations mounted again. She felt like a vessel filling up with blood, with need, with an imminent explosion. It was right there . . .

Her legs shook. Her hips jerked. She whimpered, strained for it. She tasted need.

But she couldn't seem to fall over the sweetly sharp edge.

Lily pressed harder against her clit, narrowing her circles, focusing on just how good this was going to be. The seconds ticked off in her head, slowly becoming minutes. The exquisite need was its own form of hell, and she couldn't seem to escape.

The torture dragged on, and she saw no way out. She squeezed her eyes shut, feeling defeat begin to creep in.

Stone sprang into action, popping her nipple from between his lips and grazing her ear with his lips. "You got this, baby. Focus on my voice and close your eyes. Yeah, I know that's hard, but I've got you."

Oddly, she already believed that.

"Picture yourself naked and me standing over you, stroking my cock. You know I'm going to tell you how sexy you are and how much I want you. Imagine that I'd fall to my knees between those pretty thighs. When you hold your arms open to me, I'll go right into them. Then I'm going to kiss you, touch every lush, tingling curve of your body, and when you're begging, that's when I'll slide inside you. Deep. That's when I'll stroke you slowly and thoroughly and make you claw my back as you come."

As he spoke, her desire and racing blood clashed, merged. Everything inside her roared to a screaming crescendo. The wall she'd been slamming into, preventing her from falling over, disintegrated. She envisioned exactly what Stone told her to picture. She saw herself being not just perfectly able but eager to lie back and welcome him inside her as he gave her mind-blowing pleasure and she surrendered herself completely.

ABOUT SHAYLA BLACK

Shayla Black is the *New York Times* and *USA Today* bestselling author of more than fifty novels. For over fifteen years, she's written contemporary, erotic, paranormal, and historical romances via traditional, independent, foreign, and audio publishers. Her books have sold well over a million copies and been published in a dozen languages.

Raised an only child, Shayla occupied herself with lots of daydreaming, much to the chagrin of her teachers. In college, she found her love for reading and realized that she could have a career publishing the stories spinning in her imagination. Though she graduated with a degree in Marketing/Advertising and embarked on a stint in corporate America to pay the bills, her heart has always been with her characters. She's thrilled that she's been living her dream as a full-time author for the past seven years.

Shayla currently lives in North Texas with her wonderfully supportive husband, her teenage daughter, and a very spoiled cat. In her "free" time, she enjoys reality TV, reading, and listening to an eclectic blend of music.

Connect with me online:
Facebook: facebook.com/ShaylaBlackAuthor
Twitter: http://twitter.com/Shayla_Black
Instagram: https://instagram.com/ShaylaBlack/
Website: http://shaylablack.com
Newsletter: http://shayla.link/nwsltr
Goodreads: http://shayla.link/goodreads
Google+: http://shayla.link/googleplus
YouTube: http://shayla.link/youtube

If you enjoyed this book, I would appreciate your help so others can enjoy it, too.

Recommend it. Please help other readers find this book by recommending it to friends, readers' groups and discussion boards.

Review it. Please tell other readers why you liked this book by reviewing. If you do write a review, please send me an email at interact@shaylablack.com so I can thank you with a personal email.

OTHER BOOKS BY SHAYLA BLACK

CONTEMPORARY ROMANCE
THE WICKED LOVERS

Wicked Ties

Decadent

Delicious

Surrender to Me

Belong to Me

"Wicked to Love" (novella)

Mine to Hold

"Wicked All the Way" (novella)

Ours to Love

"Wicked All Night" (Wicked And Dangerous Anthology)

"Forever Wicked" (novella)

Theirs to Cherish

His to Take

Pure Wicked

Wicked for You

Falling in Deeper

Coming Soon:

Dirty Wicked (novella) (November 8, 2016)

Holding on Tighter (February 7, 2017)

MASTERS OF MÉNAGE
(by Shayla Black and Lexi Blake)

Their Virgin Captive

Their Virgin's Secret

Their Virgin Concubine

Their Virgin Princess

Their Virgin Hostage

Their Virgin Secretary

Their Virgin Mistress

THE PERFECT GENTLEMEN
(by Shayla Black and Lexi Blake)
Scandal Never Sleeps
Seduction in Session
Big Easy Temptation

DOMS OF HER LIFE: RAINE FALLING
(by Shayla Black, Jenna Jacob, and Isabella LaPearl)
One Dom To Love (Book 1)
The Young And The Submissive (Book 2)
The Bold and The Dominant (Book 3)
The Edge of Dominance (Book 4)

SEXY CAPERS
Bound And Determined
Strip Search
"Arresting Desire" (Hot In Handcuffs Anthology)

STAND ALONE TITLES
Naughty Little Secret (Shayla Black writing as Shelley Bradley)
Watch Me
Dangerous Boys And Their Toy
"Her Fantasy Men" (Four Play Anthology)

HISTORICAL ROMANCE
(Shayla Black writing as Shelley Bradley)
The Lady And The Dragon
One Wicked Night
Strictly Seduction
Strictly Forbidden

BROTHERS IN ARMS
MEDIEVAL TRILOGY
His Lady Bride
His Stolen Bride
His Rebel Bride

CONTEMPORARY ROMANCE
(as Shelley Bradley)
A Perfect Match

PARANORMAL ROMANCE
THE DOOMSDAY BRETHREN
Tempt Me With Darkness
"Fated" (e-novella)
Seduce Me In Shadow
Possess Me At Midnight
"Mated" – Haunted By Your Touch Anthology
Entice Me At Twilight
Embrace Me At Dawn

BOUND TO SURRENDER
The Doms of Genesis, Book 7
By Jenna Jacob
Coming October 11, 2016!

After suffering a brutal hate crime, submissive Trevor Hammond's outward appearance projects the usual carefree demeanor his friends know and love. But inside, the remnants of his battered psyche and the ghosts of his assailants keep him bound in chains of anxiety.

While his Master, Moses Abrams, aka Daddy Drake, is aware of the devastation consuming his precious sub, he finds himself powerless to neutralize his lover's demons. Embarking on an unconventional journey, Drake is determined to find a way to heal and bring back the man who owns his heart.

Will his love be enough to draw Trevor back from the darkness?

LYING IN BED, Moses Abram—better known as Daddy Drake to his friends in the kink community—stared at Trevor Hammond, his sleeping lover and submissive. After having rescued his sub from yet another chronic and panic-inducing nightmare, Drake rubbed his tired eyes, searching for a thread of comfort in Trevor's soft snores. Yet no relief was in sight. The clinical diagnosis of PTSD—by friend, psychologist, and fellow Dominant Tony Delvaggio—plagued Drake. He worried that Trevor would be held captive to those inner demons forever.

Lord knew it wasn't for a lack of trying. He'd attempted to coax Trevor out of the darkness in every conceivable way. But so far, nothing had worked. Still, Drake refused to give up, even as the claws of impotence and frustration ripped his control and shredded his heart.

Swallowing the lump of anguish lodged in his throat, Drake blinked back the tears blurring his vision. Dammit, what would it take to bring his lover back? He didn't know, and it made him want to pound his fist into something hard and unforgiving.

Trevor jerked and thrashed, then whimpered softly. With an inward curse, Drake sat up and gently stroked his lover's soft blond hair.

"Shhh, it's all right, precious boy," he murmured. "Daddy's here. You're safe."

As Trevor settled once again, Drake issued a soft sigh of relief. While his lover's night terrors had lessened, they hadn't disappeared completely. He remembered the times he'd find Trevor huddled in a ball in the shower, crying uncontrollably. Thankfully those times had also tapered off. The young man only allowed a handful of trusted friends to know the depths of his traumatization. The other members of Club Genesis, the local BDSM club owned by longtime friend Mika LaBrache, hadn't a clue what Trevor and Drake were actually going through. And of course, the few times he and his sub had made an appearance at the club, Trevor painted on a happy smile, pretending all was perfectly fine.

But it wasn't. Dammit.

Spying the bottle of sleeping pills on the nightstand, Drake bit back a curse. Once *he* had been the one responsible for exhausting Trevor's mind and body with his Dominant demands and sexual needs, not some fucking pharmaceuticals. And in the wee hours of the night, like this, the yearning to claim Trevor again in achingly tender or brutally rough ways all but drove Drake to the point of madness.

He missed the compelling, mystical connection they shared exploring and fulfilling each other's dark desires. Yes, he mourned the loss of his slave, but most of all, Drake grieved for the potent love they'd once shared.

He couldn't fault Trevor for the destruction of their relationship. The poor boy had been an innocent victim. Drake owned all the blame and carried that weight on his shoulders as if it were the entire universe. From the minute he opened his eyes in the morning until blessed sleep stole his thoughts, Drake lived in the same mire of guilt day in and day out…for the past six fucking months.

If only he'd gone to the convenience store with Trevor that night instead of staying with Mika and Julianna, those prick-assed fucking homophobic frat boys wouldn't have savagely attacked and beaten his precious lover half to death.

Ice. All this fucking aftermath over a worthless bag of ice, Drake inwardly railed.

He'd exacted his revenge, in a sense. Yet, arranging for Frank—a longtime friend, sadist, and skilled tattoo artist—to befriend the frat boys, roofie their beers, then tattoo gay slurs over their faces paled in comparison to the retaliation still smoldering inside Drake's soul. One day, he planned to hunt the five down. He wanted to savor their tortured screams and pitiful pleas while he unleashed a sanity-breaking brutality and a level of pain they couldn't imagine. The agony they'd inflicted on his boy had awakened a pulsing, living demon inside Drake.

Sucking in a ragged breath, he gently lifted Trevor into his beefy, tattooed arms. There would be time later for Drake to quench his bloodthirsty vengeance. First he needed to find a way to heal his lover. Feathering a soft kiss over Trevor's cheek, Drake tasted the subtle saltiness of his skin and breathed in his familiar scent.

"Tell me how to fix this for you, love. I can't stand this distance between us. Come back to me, precious boy. Please. Daddy needs you," Drake whispered, allowing several tears to leak from his eyes.

FLOATING IN THE peaceful darkness, Trevor finally found the respite he'd sought. All too soon, he heard the screen door slam and the loud, slurred voices of monsters behind him. Fear seized him. Somehow they'd found him again. Frantically looking around for an escape, Trevor saw tall brick towers surrounding him. No doors. No windows. Not even a light to lead him out of the black, foreboding alley.

"Look at all that pretty blond hair," one of the monsters stated.

Trevor knew what was coming next and wanted to yank the long tresses from his scalp. Prove he wasn't a girl before the monsters discovered that for themselves.

"Hey, sweet thang. Wait up. We jus' wanna talk," another demon slurred. "Come on, baby."

Panic thundered through Trevor's veins.

"We're talking to you, you stupid bitch. Don't ignore us like we're not here," snarled the one with the black eyes. The one Trevor knew was going to hurt him the worst. "Come here, you stuck-up slut. You're not deaf as well as stupid, are you?"

Then, like he remembered, a hand reached out and snatched his arm, holding him in place with a vice-like grip, and spun him around.

Face-to-face with Satan's spawn, Trevor watched as the look of disbelief widened all five men's eyes.

"Oh, that's fucking priceless." A beefy, linebacker-looking guy with short-cropped hair and crooked teeth laughed. "Way to go, Everetts. You're hitting on a fucking fairy."

"I was not. I thought this faggot was a girl," the shorter man with bloodshot eyes spat with a hateful snarl. "Where do you get off making us think you're a girl, you little sperm-burper?"

"I-I was just walking to the store. I wasn't doing anything," Trevor stammered.

"Pull out your cock, Everetts. Shove it down the faggot's throat until he gags," Black Eyes urged before inching in close to Trevor's face. "You like sucking dick. So do it."

"N-No. I was...was just getting ice," Trevor tried to explain. Panic inched up his body like leeches sucking life from his veins.

"On your knees. You know the drill," Black Eyes ordered. Gripping Trevor's hair, he kicked the back of his legs and dropped him to the pavement.

Trevor jolted against the concrete, and pain screamed through his joints as a howl tore from his lips.

"Fuck you, Robinson. I ain't letting no queer's lips near my dick," the man named Everetts argued.

"Then how about we just beat the fuck out of him instead," Robinson, the black-eyed man, suggested with glee.

Trevor didn't even have time to try and cover himself or fend off the brutal blows rocking his face, ribs, and kidneys. A kaleidoscope of agony tore through him. In the distance, he heard Drake calling out to him. Trevor tried to yell for help, but one of the monsters pressed their lips to his. Wildly swinging his fists, Trevor screamed with revulsion.

Viciously biting down on the lips pressed to his, he sank his teeth in deep. The taste of copper filled his mouth as he continued to punch the oppressive weight pinning him to the soft ground.

Soft ground? What the… It's the dream again. It's only the dream, his subconscious assured. Clawing his way out of the darkness, he surfaced, blinking at the light from the nightstand that filled the room. Drake lay on top of him, blood dripping from his lip.

"Son of a bitch," Drake roared.

While Trevor was relieved that he was free from the recurring and debilitating nightmare, knowing that he'd inflicted such savage damage to his Master's lip filled him with an overwhelming blast of guilt.

Sucking in a gasp of shame, he grabbed the sheet and gently dabbed the fabric against Drake's mouth. "Oh, god. No. No. I'm sorry, Master. I didn't mean to… I was having another—"

"Another bad dream," Drake sighed grimly as he pushed Trevor's hands away. "I know."

A rolling wave of remorse drowned him in misery. Why couldn't he stop reliving the events of that horrible night and put the past behind him? He yearned to have the relationship with Drake they used to. When would these fucking night terrors ever end? Would Drake finally lose every ounce of patience and simply throw in the towel over Trevor's unpredictable mood swings and his sullen, isolated behavior?

He needed to find a way to fix things between them, but most of all, Trevor needed to fix himself. All the coping tools Tony Delvaggio gave him during their weekly sessions weren't working, leaving Trevor at a loss.

"Let me up, Daddy, and I'll get an ice pack for you," Trevor murmured, contritely.

"It's all right, boy," Drake exhaled on a heavy sigh.

With a soft caress, he pushed the hair from Trevor's face. "I tried to wake you gently, like Tony suggested. I guess I wasn't quite tender enough. It's my own fault, baby."

Trevor felt the tension and fury slowly bleed from the big man's body. As Drake stared at him with a weary gaze, he noticed the dark circles under Daddy's eyes. The sight increased Trevor's guilt even more. He swallowed the tightness in his throat.

"You haven't slept yet, have you?" he asked, already knowing the answer.

Drake shook his head as a wan smile tugged his lips.

Tears welled in Trevor's eyes. He tried to blink them back, but they spilled over his lashes. "I'm so sorry, Daddy. I'll go sleep in the guest room for the rest of the night."

"You'll do no such thing," Drake commanded before dipping his head to scrape his teeth over Trevor's flat brown nipple.

A ripple of delight danced through his system as he sniffed softly and gripped his fingers into Drake's rock-hard shoulders.

"Please...Daddy," Trevor whispered. "Please..." *Don't give up on me.*

ABOUT JENNA JACOB

Bestselling author Jenna Jacob paints a canvas of passion, romance, and humor as her Alpha men and the feisty women who love them unravel their souls, heal their scars, and find a happy-ever-after kind of love. Heart-tugging, captivating, and steamy, Jenna's books will surely leave you breathless and craving more.

A mom of four grown children, Jenna and her Alpha-hunk husband live in Kansas. She loves books, Harleys, music, and camping. Her zany sense of humor and lack of filter exemplify her motto: Live. Laugh. Love.

Meet her wild and wicked family in her sultry series: **The Doms of Genesis**. Or become spellbound by the searing love connection between Raine, Hammer, and Liam in her continuing saga: **The Doms of Her Life** (co-written with the amazing Shayla Black and Isabella La Pearl). Journey with couples struggling to resolve their pasts and heal their scars to discover unbridled love and devotion in Jenna's contemporary series: **Passionate Hearts**.

Connect with me online:
Website: http://www.jennajacob.com
E Mail: jenna@jennajacob.com
Facebook Fan Page: facebook.com/authorjennajacob
Twitter: @jennajacob3
Newsletter: http://bit.ly/1Cj4ZyY

OTHER BOOKS BY JENNA JACOB

THE DOMS OF GENESIS

Embracing My Submission: (Book One)

"I have read my share of BDSM but this book was unlike the others as in I get an even CLOSER look inside the relationships."

Twinsie Talk Book Reviews

Masters of My Desire: (Book Two)

"THANK YOU for pulling me in to this world. This world full of love, lust, and intrigue. THANK YOU for creating such a powerful connection with these characters and their lives."

Shayna Renee's Spicy Reads

Master of My Mind: (Book Three)

"From the very first pages of Master of My Mind, Jenna Jacob had me emotionally riveted, pulled into a story so intriguing, so enthralling, so spellbinding, that I tuned out the rest of the universe in order to fully immerse myself in Leagh and Tony's story."

Sizzling Hot Books

Saving My Submission: (Book Four)

"Simply beautifully written as I have come to appreciate and expect for Jenna Jacob!"

The Book Fairy

Seduced By My Doms: (Book Five)

"I loved everything about this story. It had suspense, sizzling romance, and decadent scenes that will have you BEGGING for more."

Marie's Tempting Reads

Sin City Submission: (A Doms of Genesis Novella)

"You think when a story ends its all happily ever after, but even stories can take a turn you where not expecting. I want to read more from Jenna Jacob.

Kimmie Sue's Book Review

Coming October 11, 2016

Bound To Surrender: (A Doms of Genesis Novella)

PASSIONATE HEARTS

Sky of Dreams: (Book One)

"Jenna takes all the colors of life and paints them into a true masterpiece."

Nikki's Book Addiction

DOMS OF HER LIFE: Raine Falling
(by Shayla Black, Jenna Jacob, and Isabella LaPearl)

One Dom To Love: (Book One)

"Buckle your seatbelts for the start of a yummy new BDSM series, The Doms of Her Life, in One Dom to Love."

Two Lips Reviews

The Young And The Submissive: (Book Two)

"I found myself lost in the story ignoring everything that was happening around me."

Sizzling Hot Books

The Bold and The Dominant: (Book Three)

"These three authors continue to blow me away with what they bring to these characters and the storyline. They bring out a reader's emotions so gently, so vividly, you feel like you are on the same level as one of their characters."

Shayna Renee's Spicy Reads

The Edge of Dominance: (Book Four)

ABOUT ISABELLA LAPEARL

Hello Friends! My name is Isabella and I write sexy, erotic romance. I'm a wife, mother, writer, reader and I love to ride my motorcyle.

To say it's been an extraordinary journey thus far would be an understatement…what a rush! What a thrill to realize dreams and see them go from a seed to fruition. So for all you aspiring Authors who like me, have a fire inside that burns brightly and demands to be sated by writing… Never give up.

Connect with me online:
Facebook: facebook.com/isabellalapearlpage
Twitter: twitter.com/IsabellaLaPearl

Made in the USA
Middletown, DE
02 October 2016